Mistress of Men

Mistress of Men

A Novel

Flora Annie Steel

GYAN

Published by

GYAN

Gyan Publishing House
5, Ansari Road
Daryaganj, New Delhi-110002
Phone: 011-47034999, 9811692060
E-mail: books@gyanbooks.com

Distribution Network
gyanbooks.com
India, USA, Canada, UK, Australia, France

ISBN : 978-81-212-9494-2 (PB)
First Published, 1917

2nd Impression 2023

Printed at: Gyan Press, Delhi.

Mistress of Men
Author: Flora Annie Steel

Mistress of Men

Mistress of Men

A Novel

By

Flora Annie Steel

AUTHOR OF "ON THE FACE OF THE WATERS," "MARMADUKE," ETC.

1917

To

THE MEMORY OF A GREAT WOMAN

WHO IN TURNS WAS

QUEEN O' WOMEN, LIGHT OF THE HOME,

LIGHT OF THE WORLD

PREFACE

It is impossible that the life of Nurjahân the Beautiful should remain unwritten.

Of reliable historical incident much is available, of equally reliable tradition still more; the whole going to make up a life marvellous in its romance, touching in its humanity.

In this sketch of it I have adhered in all matters of importance to the evidence of contemporaneous witnesses. That I have given a different complexion to them in many cases, I admit; but no careful student of character and motive could avoid doing so.

Briefly, Nurjahân's extraordinary personality and power—which even in these days would raise criticism in a woman—exposed her in the seventeenth century to inevitable traducing. Sinister motives were found for her every action; above all, personal ambition was held to be her ruling motive. This assertion is, to my mind, pulverized by the undenied fact that, after her husband, the Emperor Jahângir's, death, she voluntarily retired from all public life and lived a widow indeed.

In like manner she is credited with much plotting and planning, of which—beyond the statement of her enemies—no trace is to be found either in her character or her actions.

Thus, her sudden abandonment of Shahjahân is set down to personal pique and greed; but it is curiously coincident with his brother Khushrau's sudden death when in the former's custody; a death suspicious of poison to many, *even in those days*.

I have endeavoured, therefore, to make Nurjahân's character speak for itself; but in no case have I twisted actual events to suit my own estimate of it.

So much for the historical part of my task. As to the fictional part, I have done nothing save fill up with trifling incidents the gaps which history and tradition have left between the major occurrences; and, of course, supply the motives which to me, the student, have appeared most likely. All the characters, with the exception of the Strangler, once lived and died, as they are said in this book to have lived and died. For the rest, it has been indeed a labour of love to set down, from personal biography and almost without additions, a record of the most perfect passion ever shown by man for woman.

A man of many faults, Jahângir shows himself "the Compleat Lover." And Nurjahân was worthy of his love.

Nothing more need be said, except that Jahângir's ruby cup is still famous on the lips of the people. It is said to have had a name engraved around the lip, whether Jahângir's or Nurjahân's, who can say? It was last heard of in the beginning of the eighteenth century.

FLORA ANNIE STEEL.

COURT O' HILL,
TENBURY.

MISTRESS OF MEN

BOOK I

CHAPTER I

"A motley crowd, hidden within a grave—
Such is a seed; for in it crowd and crave
A million claims to life! Ah! who decides
If it grow fig or thistle? Fool or knave?"

THE sobbing cry of a new-born child rose suddenly on the still night. Far away over the grey, undulating sandhills of the desert a lighter streak on the horizon showed that the dawn was nigh; but here, beside the rude screen formed of a woman's veil that was drawn between a woman's travail and man's sleep all was dark, save for the faint glimmer of an oil cresset that filtered weakly through the stretched muslin.

The man, dozing beside the dying embers of a watch-fire, with a sleeping child in his arms, stirred and yawned. Then came his voice eagerly:

"What is't, Dilarâm—boy or girl?"

"The Prophet's wisdom be thine," was the quick masterful retort. "Will the man not let a body have time to look around?" And after a second's pause the verdict was given.

"A girl, master, only a girl."

The echo of that fiat may have roused the listening worlds to rejoice in yet another life; but in this particular one of stress and starvation it only brought dull, acquiescent silence.

Only a girl! There was no more to be said. The new-made father looked up into the fading stars above his head, then at the dim glow here and there on the wide plain which told where the watch-fires of night were turning to dust and ashes, and sighed faintly.

After a pause, the stretched muslin of the screen parted, and by the light of the cresset behind, the figure of a stalwart, full-breasted woman showed, carrying something huddled in her veil.

"A lusty child, master," she remarked approvingly. "Never did I handle a better; but of no use in God's world, when the coffers hold not one farthing for a marriage portion."

She held out her burdened veil for him to see; but he did not look. His eyes fixed themselves hungrily on the little cheek that cuddled closely to his breast. It was his son's. That mattered; the other did not.

"And the mother?" he asked after a pause. "How goes the Bibi? Is all well?"

Dilarâm squatted down beside the embers and became garrulous.

"Well?" she echoed, "what else would she be with this slave as midwife to stand between her and unnecessary anguish? Lo! as I told my lord at the beginning, a full dose of the Dream-compeller hath done no harm, but contrariwise good. Bibi Azîzan sleeps knowing not she is accursed with a girl—yet 'tis a lusty one—that will I swear."

Despite her praise, even she did not look at what lay in her veil, so none can say if the child's eyes were wide awake, open, ready to take in the light of its new life, or whether they were closed as they had been in the darkness of the old.

Either way it made no sound. And those two by the ashes of the fire were silent also. The slow light of dawn was coming faster now, and suddenly the man sighed. The woman rose on the instant and stood beside him, almost menacing, masterful.

"The die is cast, *meeân jee*," she said, "and 'tis kindest in the end. Lo! a pellet of the Dream-Compeller concealed in sugar on the tongue, and this transitory world remains not; the bud blossoms in Paradise." She paused and her tone became harder. "Sure, at best a woman's life is but poor fare! How we stomach it God knows! For my own part I had as lief that my parents had stepped in between me and it at the beginning. And, see you, master, 'tis not as if Bibi Azîzan were a cow, as we folk are, to give milk on parched grain! She hath not enough food for herself when the two strapping sons have done yelling for it, let alone for a useless girl—though by my faith she is a lusty one—and a pretty too——"

"Peace, fool!" interrupted the man hastily; perhaps he did not care to hear more of the doomed infant. "Sure, wisdom and plain figures need not to be made plainer by an ass's bray. The die, I tell you, hath been cast; another useless mouth would be unfair to these my sons"—he glanced down with almost passionate tenderness at the cuddling cheek upon his breast, and the swathed outline of another sleeping child at his feet. "And cruel to the babe herself—what hath life to offer to such as she?"

There was no answer to his question; it carried decision with it.

And now the grey horizon line beyond the sand-waves was changing to primrose, and with the coming of another day the world was beginning to stir. A flight of desert birds winged wedge-shaped into the primrose. Then a yawning man unhapped himself from his blanket, still half asleep, and stumbled to the wide circle of squatting camels which centred the camp. Another and another followed suit, and thereinafter rose strange bubblings and groanings that awakened even the most dreamful of sleepers. All but Bibi Azîzan. Behind the veil-screen she slept in a sort of low litter, and by-and-by, when the two boys had been tucked away, as ever, at her feet, and the last camels of the great caravan from Kâbul to Hindustân had swayed noiselessly adown the trackless, sandy, eastward desert, Ghiyâss-ud-din, the new-made father, and Dilarâm, the stalwart nurse, each shouldered one end of the cross pole and began to sway as noiselessly after them. But not before the latter had made her arrangements. Slipping behind some sparse caper bushes, she scraped a shallow hole with her hand in the sand, that was already warming under the first rays of the rising sun, laid something down in the hollow, and partially covered it with sand as with a blanket, since it might as well be comfortable till the end.

Was it something, or was it nothing, that useless, drugged girl baby who might in the years to come have given pleasure to some godly man, but who was now, in this time of stress, better out of the way?

Dilarâm scarcely asked herself the question, and yet there was something in the tiny puckered face appearing like a mask out of the soft sand which made her pause for a second and mutter under her breath:

"A lusty one indeed! Had the good God but given the soul-bit a male body-bit, it might have been a fine fighting man."

So she returned to her task of helping the sick mother, the very possibility of anything feminine growing up to be anything fine not occurring to her.

Small wonder, indeed, when even now, after four centuries of wisdom and progress, few thoughts of future fame or of a future career come to the parents of a female child. In that first glance a father gives his infant son, what wonders does he not see hidden in the cradle! Field Marshal's batons, titles, distinctions, riches—all these. But the face of a little daughter shows only the lines of beauty—the beauty which shall give pleasure to a man!

Ghiyâss-ud-din, however, had carefully not looked in his daughter's face; perhaps he feared the sight of it might turn him from what he conceived to be his duty; for his heart was not so hard as that of Bibi Azîzan, his wife, who at the moment was comfortably slipping out of the noose of parental responsibility with the aid of opium. But it had all been settled beforehand with infinite and painstaking thought, as everything that Ghiyâss-ud-din did invariably was; for precision was with him almost an obsession. Well born, well educated, he had been what nowadays would be called a mathematical professor in Kâbul; but he had fallen upon evil times, and had finally decided on trying his fortune in Hindustân, the land of untold riches. So, almost starving, he had accepted the post of assistant invoice-writer to this caravan, and was going through the experience methodically; for he had added up all advantages, subtracted the disadvantages, and divided out all his duties conscientiously. Even in this problem of life and death, though he regretted the conclusion to which the factors forced him, he did not dream of disputing its validity, but, tall, gaunt, burdened with a great load of responsibility, plodded on his way after the fast disappearing caravan, leaving the new life to death.

Since that first birth-cry the child had not uttered a sound. The pinch of sugar on its tongue, hiding the bitterness of opium, had brought content until the drug had brought unconsciousness.

So, in truth, the babe had scarce lived at all, and yet, as with puckered-up little face upturned to the sky it lay placid, it still held the possibility of taking to itself everything in the Great Storehouse of Fate.

The sun climbed into the brazen sky, the hills shimmered and grew opalescent in the noonday glare; and still the child slept on. But had Nurse Dilarâm been there to watch the rise and fall of the sand above its breast, she would have marvelled; for the pellet of the Dream-compeller she had given should ere this have stilled the breath for ever. Instead, it came quicker, less evenly.

A wild honey-bee rifling the coral buds of the caper thorns—whose fine fret of shadow tempered the full fierceness of the sun—hovered over the wet open mouth as if doubtful if it were not a new kind of flower, then hummed away tunefully to more familiar blossoms. A pair of desert birds hopped round the little upturned face, decided it was not fit to eat, and fluttered away.

Finally, when the fretwork of the caper shadows began to blur themselves, a great black cobra crept out of its hole hard by, and finding the sand above the child's breast warmer than the rest, coiled itself there to sleep.

And still the child slept on, though the Dream-compeller was losing its hold on the little life, which must wake to face Death.

Quaint, indeed, to think of the little soul-bit, in its little woman-body-bit, alone in the desert with all things hanging in the Balance of Fate. Crowns, Kingdoms, Power almost unlimited, Influence unrivalled!

The moon at its full rose at last, turning the lingering Indian day to night rapidly, and the sand-waves passed from opalescence to pearl once more; so faded sombrely to shadow.

Hark! what was that? Scarcely a sound. More an air-rhythm; the faintest fall of softest foot upon soft sand.

So over the darkening distance a monstrous swaying figure showed ghostly; it was the figure of a swift riding camel. And it was ridden by a man in a hurry; for Zamân Shâh, Chief Constable and Convoyer of Caravans, who had remained behind at the last camping-place in order to negotiate the transport dues payable to insure safe conduct from the tribesmen, was anxious to overtake his charge. For his was a responsible task, though none was more fitted for it than he, Yusufzai Pathân by birth, who knew all the ins and outs of frontier life. A medium-sized, merry man who could quote Hafiz by the yard, and was the best swordsman that side Delhi.

What was it that made him suddenly draw rein, slip from his high-peaked saddle, and stand peering down at his very feet? Possibly it was the big black cobra which had slidden from his camel's tread. Anyhow, he stood staring astonished at an age-long, puckered little face, that stared back at him with large purblind eyes; for the useless girl had slipped the Noose of Death and taken the Path of Life.

Yet still there was no sound, and Zamân Shâh—whose knowledge of babies, if superficial, was wide, seeing that he had a wife and family at most of the big halting-places along the route—realized that he had seldom seen a silent baby before; except once when a never-to-be-forgotten youthful romance had ended for ever as he stood looking down on a dead mother with his dead son on her breast.

But this one—he paused mechanically to lift it from its sand cradle—looked alive enough to scream like the devil if it chose——

It did. He nearly dropped the babe in surprise, so sudden, so forceful, was its howl of hunger.

For there was no mistaking it; loud, full, prolonged, the protest was for food, immediate, imperative. But how to compass satisfaction, here in the wilderness? Parched grain, the staple provant of the Eastern traveller, was distinctly unsuitable. There was the she-camel he was riding—her calf, which had gone on ahead, was almost weaned, but she might have something to appease the yell.

It was worth a trial, anyhow; so, holding the child conveniently, he attempted to milk into its open mouth. This, however, only made it yell the louder, and he was at his wits' end when by chance the teat touched the clamouring lips. In an instant they had closed on it like a vice, and remained glued to it, sucking contentedly.

He chuckled to himself as he stood laboriously holding the child, whose little arms struggled and beat aimlessly at the animal, as they would have at a human mother.

A strange group, indeed, in the rising moonlight, that sent a hard yet blurred shadow of mingled man and beast on to the soft shifting sand.

"By Allah!" murmured Zamân Shâh, when at long last the satisfied lips loosed hold. "She is better than most of her sex! She knows what she wants, and gives no trouble when she gets it. I will call her Queen 'o' Women."

It was the first intimation he had given to himself that he meant to take the gift the gods had sent him, but it was final. He was used, in his profession of Convoyer of Caravans, to the rapid making of plans, to decisive decisions and sudden actions. Then family ties sat light upon him, and some one of the many women dependent on him would surely mother the foundling; if not, he could easily find someone who would; for Zamân Shâh was a good-looking fellow in the prime of life.

So lightly, almost without thought, he tucked the now sleeping baby away in the capacious wadded coat girt about the waist with a twined girdle which to the Afghan is general hold-all, remounted, and rode on at full speed.

Within five minutes he had forgotten all about his burden and was back in some rather troublous thoughts which needed sifting; for his post of Chief Convoyer of Caravans was not without responsibilities. To begin with, the slow, undulating file of camels which, tied nose to tail, looked sideways like some monstrous caterpillar crawling on its lengthy way, often carried untold wealth. True, the major part of the packs contained nothing more valuable than dried apricots and plums, pistachio nuts, white grapes packed in little round boxes, and such like, with here and there a tiny packet of asafœtida to give flavour to the whole and bestow on the caravan an atmosphere to carry along with it.

But others held carpets and rich stuffs, while a few had precious stones—turquoise, lapis lazuli, and jade. Still more valuable things were to be found, but these were generally concealed on the persons of the travellers who availed themselves of armed escort, so that the Convoyer did not himself know what treasures he was guarding.

But whenever he found unusual difficulty in settling transport dues with the tribesmen, he had a shrewd guess that they had wind of something out of the common. And never had he met with more extortion than on the present trip. His face clouded, remembering the rupees extracted from him that very morning after vain protest and waste of time. But, praise be to Allah! the tyranny was about overpast. Two more marches would see them over the border, and the very next day he would be quit of that naked, drunken pig of a Hindu saint, who, he verily believed, was at the bottom of the whole trouble. Bad cess to the banker at Kâbul who had persuaded him to convoy the idolatrous anatomy—as if the fact that you owed a man a few paltry hundreds was any excuse for his foisting a verminous savage on good company! Zamân Shâh spat over his thoughts, then laughed sardonically at the reflection that *jogi-jee* could not have much about him, since his only clothing was a bit of twine and a rag round his waist. But perhaps he had swallowed something? Not very large, anyhow, as you could see every bone and sinew in his skeleton! Yes, it would be God's peace when he was safely handed over to the shrine!

So from that Zamân Shâh's errant thoughts flew to other things, while the swift *rewâri* camel, with its long swinging trot that had a bump in the middle, forged over the sandhills at fifteen miles an hour; a very different pace from that of the baggage beasts, its brothers.

It did not take more than an hour and a half to reach the outskirts of the little oasis, preluding a more rapid and rocky descent, where the caravan was encamped for the night, and where Zamân Shâh expected to find all asleep and snoring after the dreary, weary, slow march of the day. He was, however, disappointed. From afar he could see watch-fires blazing and hear drums beating, while as he passed on a couple of timid guards, armed with pikes, challenged him fearfully.

With an oath he gave the password, and, galloping furiously to his tent, flung himself from his camel and demanded imperiously what was the matter.

"The Hindu saint, my lord, hath had a dream. He swears if any sleep he will be robbed and murdered," bleated a head accountant, hovering between importance and fear. "And, seeing that he is a holy man——"

Zamân Shâh nearly burst with rage. "Go to Gehennum! Hindu thyself, fool!" he stormed. "Is peace for ever to be disturbed by a drunkard's dreams? Bring the foul beast hither, slaves, and I will cook his pulse for him."

A minute later the two men stood glaring at each other, absolutely different and apart, yet each instinct with overweening pride and arrogance. Of the two, the *jogi* had the better share, for one look at the dull blaze of his eyes showed that he was heavily drugged with *bhang;* and of all known substances in the world, Indian hemp is the one that makes a man feel most supreme, most god-like. So, a miserable, ash-smeared anatomy, his wild sun-bleached hair matted into a sort of crown upon his head, he stood grey and ghostlike in the mingled glare of torch and moon, giving back with interest the Mahomedan's purely physical contempt by a spiritual disdain beyond words. And yet there were traces of a furtive fear, perhaps more of a furtive watchfulness, in his dull, restless eyes and in the quickness with which he followed every movement of the crowd that pressed behind him. A fear, a watchfulness of something that was not, but might be.

"So! Saint!" jeered Zamân, "thou hast been dreaming again. I will have no drunken dreams—ay, or dreamers either—in my camp. So tell these split-eared folk something more peaceful, or, by the Prophet, saint or sinner, out you go!"

The saint gave a scornful laugh.

"Thou darest not, cow-killer! Thou art bound by thine office to shelter me till I reach the shrine."

Zamân Shâh's face grew black with passion; in an instant

his resolve was taken, heedless of his own comfort or discomfort, heedless of all save immediate reprisal.

"So be it, Saint-*jee*," he snarled; "then I see thee safe there—if God wills—this very night. 'Tis a matter of fifteen miles, not more, twelve by the gorge path. That ends it. Dost hear?"

For an instant the man looked startled, apprehensive; then with curious dignity he salaamed.

"So hath the Mighty ordained," he said. "His disciple is ready."

Zamân gave a scornful laugh. "Ay! Ready enough, seeing thine only baggage is a bag of bones and some vermin. Thus we can start without delay. Quick! my other camel, and five troopers—thou shalt have decent escort, saint!—And bring me a drink of sherbet—I sup not till I be quit, with a thankful heart, of all idolaters."

There was ever haste in Zamân Shâh's dispositions; but this one was more than usually rapid, and the listening crowd had hardly realized its sequence before the little cavalcade, with the saint perched up behind the last trooper, had started. The moon, shining bright, showed him like a skeleton against the latter's burly form, as, coalescing into a serried group, the party disappeared at full speed adown the rocky decline.

The watching crowd began to disperse, yawning sleepily.

"By Allah!" murmured one. "The Convoyer said truth. The saint had bewitched the camp. Now he is gone, I feel that I can sleep in peace."

"And I also," yawned another.

But one man looked at another man, and both were alert to the uttermost. They were both slim, small, dark-featured, and after an instant's colloquy they slipped past the camp fires and were no more seen.

CHAPTER II

"Ring round with scent the circle where thy lips
Shall touch the Bowl of Life! If the wine drips
Untouched into the Cup of Death—what then?
Since Life dies not, it matters not who sips."

ZAMÂN SHÂH rode at the head of the escort fuming with rage, and yet exultant.

By his quick decision to take a short cut, and thus, within the limits of a short, swift, but difficult camel ride, deposit the verminous idolater at the shrine which would otherwise have been reached in two days' tedious marching, he had put an end, so he told himself, to an intolerable state of affairs. Never had he had so troublesome a caravan to convoy. And it was not all dreams on the *jogi's* part; twice, at least, an attempt had been made on the camp at night; and, from his long experience of travellers, he suspicioned more than one of the Hindus of his party as being in disguise.

However, the whole affair was ended now, with no worse result than keeping him four hours without his supper; for it would not take more than that to deposit Saint-*jee* and get back. If he had had horses instead of camels, not so long; for the hill-ponies could easily have tackled a further short cut at the beginning, which was impassable for the latter's soft pads.

So he led the way in the moonlight for some three miles down the rocky ravine, till they came upon a few sparse pine-trees, and finally entered the densely wooded valley leading to the lower levels. Here a tinkle of water made itself heard below them, as, fearful of a slip among the thick carpeting of pine-needles, they went slowly along the verge of precipitous rocks. A warm aromatic air rose from the camels' footsteps, and the burly trooper bade Saint-*jee* hold fast if he did not want to save further trouble by gaining Swarga and not the shrine by being precipitated to the rocks below.

"Jest not with holy things, outcast!" replied the *jogi*. "Mai Durga stays not her hand at the *m'lechchas*."

"Halt!" came an imperious voice from ahead. It was darker here, in the shadow of the pines; but it was light enough for Zamân Shâh to see that something lay ahead which caused him to fling himself from his saddle with an oath of vexation. The path had passed from the left to the right bank of the stream by a bridge purposely placed at the narrowest part of the gorge; or rather, it should have passed, for the centre of the three tree-trunks of which the rough roadway had been made was no longer there. Peering over the edge, Zamân Shâh could see it lying askew, wedged into the rocks half-way down. Doubtless, having grown rotten, it had fallen; such things did happen, especially on little used pathways. Still it was a check, and that to Zamân Shâh's temper was intolerable. There was, however, but one thing to be done. A halt must be called, half the troopers must swarm across the remaining trunks, cut down a suitable pine to fell as near to place as possible, while the remaining men guided it by ropes. It was an operation which had constantly to be done on hill roads, and it need only take half an hour; but it was half an hour lost.

"Leave the camels, my brothers, in charge of Saint-*jee*," he ordered sharply; "his holiness is sufficient for that, I warrant. There is room round the rock yonder for the beasts to squat, so the six of us can set to work." As he spoke he began to throw off his coat. "God and His Prophet!" he continued, aghast, "I had forgot the child!"

The troopers, aghast, also, stared helplessly at the little naked new-born baby.

So for an instant there was silence; then the cool night air began to assail the little limbs so lately warm happed in fur. They stretched, curled, the mouth opened——

"Wrap it up, master!" cried one trooper hastily; "it is going to cry, and the devil himself can't stop them if they once begin! Only a woman can do it."

But it was too late. Through the still, aromatic night rose pitiful howling.

"I have milk in my bottle," said a bearded man fearfully; "belike it is hungry!"

Zamân Shâh smiled a grim smile. "And if it be so, brother," he remarked, "naught else but food will content it—'tis the veriest *shaitan* for wilfulness." Then he turned restive. Further delay meant longer supperless time for himself, and that was not to be tolerated. "Here!" he cried, thrusting the child, fur coat and all, into the unwilling *jogi's* arms—for the saint, astounded like the others, had crowded round to look—"there is that to occupy thy charity! Give him thy milk-bottle, Ahmed, and let him do nurse while better men work."

Five minutes afterwards the sound of an axe was ringing through the rocks, while leaning against one of the squatting camels, *jogi-jee* was attempting to still the infant's cries.

"He hath not the knack of the job," gravely commented the bearded trooper who had shown second-hand knowledge of nursing lore, as hideous howls still rose upon the night air; "you should jigger the babe up and down till its head whirls——"

"Be not too hard on him, friend," jeered a younger one. "Being celibate, what knows he of family matters?"

The sally brought a roar of laughter; for the lax morality of the wandering ascetic is a byword in India.

In truth, his saintship had a difficult task. The lip of the leathern milk-bottle was wide, the infant's mouth was small; the *jogi's* hand was unsteady, owing to *bhang*. So his attempt at feeding it ended in renewed roars as the cold fluid dashed over eyes and nose.

For a time he continued his effort mechanically; then interest appeared to wake in him. He laid the child down for a second and stole round the projecting rock to make sure he was unobserved by the bridge-makers. Having satisfied himself of that, he removed something that was hidden in the coils of matted hair that, after the manner of such ascetics, formed a sort of crown upon his head.

Seen in the moonlight it showed a tiny cup apparently of lacquered wood such as any Indian bazaar produces by the million as a receptable for medicaments, or as a child's toy.

It was, however, of somewhat unusual shape, being like a small dumpy dice-box, both ends equal, with but a slight attenuation in the middle.

This the *jogi* filled with milk, then held it to the child's lips. They seized like a vice on the rim, the cries ceased, and all was peace.

Once, twice, thrice, the cup was filled, a certain satisfaction showing on the faces of both nurse and nursling, and the former was meditating whether the infant could contain a fourth jorum when he fell forward with one awful gasp. The little cup flew from his hand, buried itself in the folds of the fur coat, which in one last convulsive struggle to rise, he ruckled so that it hid the child's face.

"Quick!" said a low guttural voice, "I hear steps! Quick! Search, brothers!"

Not more than a minute later Zamân Shâh, followed by a trooper, turned the protecting rock.

"Allah roast the infidel!" muttered the Convoyer of Caravans. "Why did he not answer when I called? But he hath appeased the *churail* of a child. Let that stand to his credit."

Then he gave an exclamation, for in the very centre of the kneeling camels showed a ghastly, contorted, naked figure, its faced turned to mother earth, the hilt of a dagger showing just under the left shoulder blade. Given a long enough weapon, it must have pierced the heart.

"That is no bungler's work," said Zamân Shâh, "but how? And wherefore?"

"It is thieves' work, master," replied the trooper, bending to examine more closely. "See—they judged it concealed in his hair; it is all undone."

And indeed, the whole superstructure of tow, wool, rags and indescribable filth which had gone to make up the *jogi's* crown or turban of plaited hair lay in confusion, each tangled mass torn to bits in hurried search.

The Convoyer of Caravans looked down thoughtfully at the body. "Thou'rt right, Ahmed; and those who did the deed have gained what they sought. What was't, think you? Some jewel, doubtless, since even yonder wig would not carry gold enough to tempt such attack. Ay, a jewel—some idol's eye likely."

Both he and the trooper spat thoughtfully. It was as well to prevent the poison of such infamy from defiling their orthodox throats.

Suddenly the Convoyer of Caravans spoke, and he spoke hurriedly. "See you, brother, this is best not known save to those to whom Providence hath imparted the secret! Lend me a hand. The gorge will hide the man, be he saint or sinner."

Without one word the hand was lent. There was a dull thud among the rocks below, and the two men looked at each other with satisfaction.

"So much for saintship," remarked Zamân Shâh coolly. "And now to return whence we came. The idolatrous dog, mind you, hath given us the slip—as in truth he hath—so being quit of all responsibility for safety—as I am—praise to the Prophet!—I will get my supper sooner than I deemed possible."

And they both laughed. His saintship had been to them anathema, and his death seemed to them but fitted to his crimes against the Most High. They would not even have yielded him the prayer for mercy they would have repeated to the dying ears of a mouse!

"He hath gone," said Ahmed to the other troopers when he joined them at the bridge, leading the camels. "Taken the quick pony-path likely; it joins in but round the corner. So we are well quit of him and a weary night's ride into the bargain."

"God be praised! as the cat said when the tiger escaped by the door," cried one of the five as he mounted and turned his camel on the backward path.

So through the moonlight once more they retraced their steps, laughing and chattering. But the Convoyer of Caravans was silent and preoccupied. To begin with, he was alarmed lest the infant, whom he carried on his saddle-bow, wrapped up as it had been in his fur coat, should begin to cry again; and then he was wondering what it was that his saintship had had concealed in his hair. If it was a jewel belonging to some princely house, there might be trouble with the banker, who possibly had held it in pawn.

On the other hand, if it was a treasure belonging to some shrine, the owners would likely say nothing publicly about a loss which might injure their prestige, and therefore their capacity for gaining money from the ignorant. He inclined to the latter belief; for he was an optimist and a fatalist combined; a most convenient admixture in his trade.

So he set the very idea of the infant aside till he had had his supper, leaving it happed up in the fur coat in the corner of the tent. It was not till he had washed a prodigious portion of quail curry and pillau down with a prolonged draught of good Shirâz wine—for, like so many Mahomedans of his time, his orthodoxy did not extend to the foreswearing of fermented liquors—that he ordered the servant to bring him the bundle, and not to drop it. For he had no notion of doing dry nurse himself, and he wished to make some arrangement for the infant's welfare before tackling the belated report of the day's doings which the yawning assistant invoice-master had been waiting to give for some three hours; his superior having incontinently retired to sleep when the Convoyer of Caravans started on his night ride.

So, as luck would have it, Ghiyâss-ud-din's eyes were amongst those which opened wide in astonishment when, the fur coat being unfolded, disclosed a naked new-born babe fast asleep.

The surprise was so great that he might easily have betrayed himself, but for a slight incident which distracted Zamân Shâh's attention. As he opened out the coat, something fell out of its folds.

Brought to him by an obsequious attendant—one of those lick-spittle servants which attend all officialdom in the East—it proved to be nothing but a little lacquered cup, and Zamân Shâh's eyes, which had lit up with sudden interest, dulled again. Yet he looked over the cup curiously. Black and red and yellow as usual showed in lines, with a hint of green below where the graver, at work on the rough and ready decoration, had cut deep into the first substratum of lac. A quaint work, this, to watch, as the rapid lathe wheel covers the object with coating after coating of coloured sealing-wax, till black or yellow or red obscures all the others, leaving box or cup dull, uninteresting. Then a swift touch of a chisel; the superimposed colour peels off as by magic, leaving a contrasting band. A slightly harder pressure of the tool and a ring—maybe of purest white—appears. But the crowning glory of the whole marvellous creation is when, graver in hand, the workman with dexterous flourish maps out curves, tendrils, sets them unerringly with flowers, leaves, fruits, cutting almost imperceptibly down to the green, the purple, the yellow, the blue. So, surely, does the Great Creator work at His lathe; so surely does Fate bite deep into man's nature, bringing to light what lies in him.

This particular cup was, however, of very ordinary workmanship, and if it had belonged to the murdered man, as it must, he had evidently set but little store by it, since there were traces of milk in it. He must have been using it to feed the babe withal when—— Mayhap the charitable deed might save him some torment!

So he set the little vessel aside and turned to look at the group of bearded, eager, astounded faces that, in the ill-lighted tent, were peering at a baby's face. And even in those early days something about that face held them.

"Lo!" murmured one, "how white it is! 'Tis of good parentage, I warrant me."

"Saw I never the like, so prim, so pretty as new-born," protested one with grey hair and possible experience. "It hath not a wrinkle. And it looks young, not old, as they all do."

In truth, the age-long look had vanished, leaving the child plump, placid.

But one man, a tall lank fellow with a philosophic face, said nothing. He was looking on his child's face for the first time, conscious of a great yearning in his very vitals towards it, admitting that his sons had not been half so attractive, wondering whether to confess his desertion of her or——

All this time Zamâd Shâd was telling how she had been found, fed by a camel, forgotten, and found again. How she had been left in charge of the *jogi*, who, before absconding, had fed her with Pir Khân's sour milk; all of which, told in his best style, elicited roars of laughter.

"Yea! Yea!" he ended. "But 'tis no laughing matter, see you! 'Tis true the child hath no stomach-ache through camel's milk and *jogi's* milk, but 'twill not do for permanence. And 'tis pity she should die, since her lungs portend long life. A wet nurse is beyond hope; but hath none of you a woman who for a consideration—since I will pay—would tend the babe?"

Ghiyâss-ud-din's head span round. Here was his chance. He had no time to calculate; to add, subtract, divide, after his wont. A vast longing seized on him to hold in his arms this little daughter of his; this daughter twice born to him, as it were, and that had suddenly become the dearest, the most desirable thing on this earth. His voice positively trembled, he had to clear his throat ere he could say hastily, lest others should be beforehand:

"If it please my lord, his slave has young children, and they have a nurse. A stalwart woman, used to babes, who could mind this one also, if my lord desires——"

Even in the turmoil of his mind he realized it was wiser not to mention a possible foster-mother; that would provoke explanation, and he was not sure how this autocratic patron might receive it.

Zamân Shâh heaved a sigh of relief.

"That settles it," he cried joyfully. "So I have not to appease her hunger myself, I care not who has the task, if that it be properly done. For look you, she is my daughter. God sent her to me, not to any other man. So take her quick to thy woman—and this"—he threw a gold *ashrafi* on the fur coat—"it may help find milk, though how—save camel's—God wot! And stay, the cup also. 'Tis the little lady's by right of gift—a gift of saintship truly, since the giver——" He paused, and covered what he had been about, ill-advisedly, to say by his usual method of quoting a *ghazel* from Hafiz:

"I'll drink from a smagdarite cup my wine of the roses' hue,
Till Death makes a flagon of clay out of me and of you."

The rollicking echo of his voice, attuned to cynicism, followed Ghiyâss-ud-din, as, scarcely believing in his own luck, he cuddled the child closer and closer as he made his way back under the stars to the tattered tent which was all the protection he had been able to afford his family. Bibi Azîzan and the boys monopolized every inch of it, he slept where he could, and Dilarâm—stalwart Dilarâm—how would life be possible without her?—rolled herself into a cocoon in her cotton blanket, and so, with every atom of air excluded, managed to keep up her own heat and become comatose within reach of a call from her charges.

It took some time to rouse the unrecognizable bundle; but finally it sat up, unhapped a face, and gave a tremendous yawn.

"What is't, master?" she asked sleepily. "Hath the Bibi megrims again, or what? If the Huzoor would but recognize that she is herself and naught else, this slave would have better sleep. Lo! the soul of a fool is dear at any price."

At another time Meeân Ghiyâss might have taken exception to Dilarâm's sleepy estimate of her mistress, but he was too much in a turmoil of joy and excitement to mind anything save the child. His hands shook as he held out the bundle he carried, and uncovered the little face.

"Look, woman! Look! The Lord hath given her back to me!"

For an instant Dilarâm stared like a stuck pig. Then, quite unceremoniously, she reached out her stalwart arms and appropriated the bundle.

"The master mistakes," she said coolly. "The Lord hath given her back to me, who am woman, and who loved her from the first. Did I not say she was lusty—ay, and pretty too? And did not my lord say, 'Peace, fool!' Ay! Ay! 'Peace, fool! Peace, fool!' And he comes to me in the middle of the night with the babe he discarded at dawn." Then with an air of resignation, as who should say what a man might or might not do, she added, "Didst go back all the way to fetch her, master?"

It was on the tip of Ghiyâss-ud-din's tongue to say, "Peace, fool!" once more; but he refrained, and told her briefly how the Convoyer of Caravans had made the babe over to his charge. "He must have found her likely," he added gravely.

"Ay! Ay! Likely he did, unless the babe walked. But there! If the cat kittens, who tells the father? The child is here and it should have been dead in the desert." Once more she looked down at it with approbation. "Yea, 'tis a lusty one! Bibi Azîzan would have died of the dose. But how 'tis to be fed God knows!"

For answer Ghiyâss-ud-din held out the *ashrafi*, and Dilarâm clutched at it.

"Why not give it with the babe, master?" she asked reproachfully; "'twould have saved me somewhat of thought—but there! a blind mouse doesn't see its own tail——"

"And thou wilt buy milk!" suggested the father anxiously. "But where? Lo! in the whole camp I know of none—save camel's milk——"

Dilarâm stood up and laughed a loud laugh. "Bah! I will feed the cow we have. Bibi Azîzan shall suckle the child, for all she is so like a grey crane with a toothache. Yea, she shall eat, and that heartily, for see you, the babe is lusty, ay! and pretty too!"

She held the child close as she spoke, and Ghiyâss-ud-din stood helpless, feeling that even as father he had very little to say. And yet, had he been equal to the situation, he would have liked to sit and nurse the child himself!

Bibi Azîzan, roused sternly to her duty as mother, was half inclined to cavil at Fate, half disposed to welcome a new interest. But the child was pretty, of that there could be no doubt.

So the days passed to a week, the weeks to a month; and every day Zamân Shâh would ask, "How goes my daughter, Mihr-un-nissa?"

And every day Ghiyâss, with an inward squirm at his own deceit, for he was an honest fellow at heart, would say constrainedly that there was no fear of her dying from the cause of not drinking milk, that being in India the recognized reason for death in all infants under three months of age. And indeed there was none.

"She will kill me," wailed Bibi Azîzan, when Dilarâm, tall and domineering, brought the child to her at stated intervals.

"So that she be not killed, I care not," retorted the nurse, "and with good savoury lentils and sweet pillau the mistress will come to no harm."

"But I shall get too fat! I shall not be able to waddle," poor Azîzan protested with more tears. "Then the Meeân-Sahib will want another wife, and I shall have to kill myself."

Dilarâm, seated on the ground watching, with the complacent, never-failing interest of all motherly women, how Mihr-un-nissa imbibed her breakfast, said nothing for a second, then mechanically, as if her words needed small thought, said sagely, "Trouble not thyself, mistress. The man is no fool; one wife is sufficient."

And Azîzan had to accept the doubtful comfort.

As Zamân Shâh had hoped, no claim regarding the murdered *jogi* had come from either money-lenders or saints; and there was no reason why they should come.

Ahmed, the only person who knew of the murder, had consented to silence for the modest sum of ten rupees, and he could gain nothing by treachery. Thus the incident seemed over, and the caravan having reached the Panjâb, where the Emperor Akbar's autocratic rule made safe conduct unnecessary, Zamân Shâh had leisure to settle up the somewhat tangled accounts of merchandise received or convoyed. In a sort of slap-dash way he was no bad totaller up of dues, but the more intricate ciphering on paper had ever been beyond him, and he had felt himself more or less in the hands of his Hindu accountants. So the marvellous rapidity and precision of the ci-devant mathematical professor was a delight. Day by day Ghiyâss-ud-din grew to favour, and when the caravan arrived at Lahore the Convoyer thereof incontinently sacked the Hindu and *nolens volens* promoted Ghiyâss to the higher state and pay; much to the latter's disgust, for he had cherished the hope of breaking loose and once more feeling that his child was his own. As matters now stood, he told himself, he was no more than an outcast. The women seemed to have joined forces in pinning him down as the chief offender in the matter of desertion, whereas he had acted in accordance with logic. But Dilarâm never let him touch the child, and his wife went so far as to veil the baby's face when he came near, as if he had the evil eye. What did for his patience, however, was the Convoyer of Caravans' remark in promoting him, that as he, Zamân Shâh, intended to marry Mihr-un-nissa so soon as she was old enough, it was as well to insure her being brought up under his own eye.

Ghiyâss-ud-din, proud, aristocratic, could not stand this; so he up and out with the whole story, much to Zamân Shâh's disgust.

Despite immediate anger, however, the latter was a good-natured man, and after a few round curses laughter prevailed.

"Ho! Ho! By all the twelve Imâms! A goodly trick indeed! To take the child and my gold *ashrafi* too—nay, twain, for I have given thee one since!—and then to restore the child to its proper mother to suckle! Truly a cake for thee, dough for me!"

"My lord," pleaded Ghiyâss in extenuation, "she was nigh starving. She could not have suckled the babe without food! Eight rupees go not far in five months, and my little sons are lusty."

"Ha! Ha!" laughed the Convoyer again; "thou begettest lusty children, though thou beest but a poor lank piece thyself. But see you, sirrah! How hadst thou the heart to leave that beauty to the jackals? By the Prophet! the first blink of her was enough for Zamân Shâh. But then I am connoisseur!" And he twirled his moustache arrogantly.

The much abashed Ghiyâss attempted explanation. "I—I saw her not, my lord! I feared to be undone. 'Twas Dilarâm the nurse who—who laid her aside!"

Zamân Shâh shook his head sagely. "Stick to thy figures, brother; there thou art supreme. But it needs more than *Al-jabr** to manage women; 'tis *jabr-dust*† they require, as these Panjâb folk have it. I must see this nurse and trounce her."

He saw her; but the trouncing scarcely came off.

Dilarâm duly appeared before him, bearing the baby cuddled on her right arm, her left hand dangling over its nose the little lacquered cup, which she had ingeniously converted into a rattle

* Algebra. † *Lit.*, strong hand.

by putting peas inside, covering the top with a piece of sheep's bladder, and tying a string round its middle.

Despite her tender age—a bare two months—the child's fat arms were struggling blindly for the prize, making vain shots at it, touching it, and setting it still further a-swing. It was a breathless, purblind pursuit in which helpless legs joined helpless arms, mouth half open, eyes puckered to a frown. Every action of the small person intent on something, what it scarcely knew.

Truly an entrancing sight, ended by Dilarâm deliberately lowering the cup on to the open mouth, which closed on it and began to suck vigorously. Whereat Zamân Shâh laughed.

"My lord sent for this slave," suggested Dilarâm tentatively. "What can I do for my lord?"

"To ask thee, witch-of-the-evil one," said Zamân Shâh, all the more sternly in that he knew his appreciation of the past little comedy had been noticed, "how, in God's name, thou didst dare to expose to wild beasts a soul and body He had sent to *my* caravan?"

Dilarâm sat down full flounced, laid the infant before her on her skirts, and folded her arms over her massive chest.

"Which end shall I swallow first? asked the pelican of the fish, master. Because I had no choice. Even beauty without dower is a prey to many men—yea, even such men as my lord is."

The blood flew to Zamân Shâh's face, turning it dusky.

"How now, slave?" he began, but Dilarâm fixed him with a calm eye. "The child is princely born, master; though Ghiyâss-ud-din claims not his right. And what is life without marriage to a woman? 'Tis but the half-split of a pea to a dishonourable marriage—and that is God's curse. And then "—she had taken the measure of her man astutely—" death the first day is easier than death by starvation, and without the master's gold *ashrafis* Mihr-un-nissa (we call her by the name the master bestowed—with life—upon her) would have tugged in vain at an empty breast. So I did well; but my lord has done better."

And, unfolding her strong arms, she swept the most appreciatory of salaams.

"Thou hast a ready tongue, woman," said Zamân Shâh, "but mark you, I renounce not my claim on the child!"

"Nor I mine," retorted Dilarâm, gathering up her charge to her capacious breast. "Lo! master, she may need us both, for the gods have given her beauty—that is a curse to women-kind!"

It was an even more fatal gift than mere beauty that the gods had bestowed on little Mihr-un-nissa. They had given her, charm. Ere she was three months old she was the darling of the camp. Everyone vied with the other to make her toys—wriggly snakes out of curled bamboo slips, yellow and black tigers out of painted mud, beautiful snow bears out of cotton pods—but she would none of them. Her rattle contented her, and if it rolled out of her reach she rolled after it, to the intense amusement of the spectators; for never was infant endowed with greater tenacity of purpose than this one. Every atom of her dimpled body worked hard to achieve her object, and when it was gained, the content on her dimpled face was all-pervading.

So the long caravan crept its way peacefully through the Panjâb plains, and Zamân Shâh had almost forgotten the very existence of the murdered *jogi* when one night Dilarâm sought a private audience with him, her little charge, as usual, in her arms.

She laid it down, asleep, among her flouncing petticoats, and began her tale.

"We are being watched, master, the child and I. Yesterday an ash-smeared abomination came begging. To-day there were two from the town. Idolaters with hair-crowns like the one whose cup is the child's rattle. And one admired it, asking whence the child had gotten it."

"And what saidst thou?" came the instant query with quick interest in the tone.

"That I purchased it for a pice in the Rawul Pindi bazaar, seeing that the one the babe had before—which was gotten from a naked abomination such as they—had been stolen from her by another naked wretch who wore his hair long and whose ears were whole. Theirs were split, see you," she replied imperturbably.

Zamân Shâh gasped, and looked at her with stupefaction. And he had ever decried woman's wit!

"Why didst lie—so nobly?" he asked.

Dilarâm settled herself down more comfortably, and began with a prodigious yawn:

"Because a snake goes crooked to its own hole, master. And the men looked sly, to match the untruth. Besides, the ash-smeared idolater who owned the child's cup had his ears split even as these. So I count them as friends; but they, the long-haired, whole-eared sort are foes; so I set one against the other, and that is good doing. Then"—she paused and fixed Zamân Shâh with her eyes—"who knows what really became of split-ear? The master says he ran away—and fair riddance too—but Ahmed——"

"What of Ahmed, woman?" put in the Convoyer of Caravans sharply, on the alert for any babbling.

"Naught, naught, my lord," replied Dilarâm airily, "save that he has been oft drunk. Now no leech sticks to a stone, and wine comes not save from a long purse. Besides——" She paused.

"Besides what?" asked Zamân Shâh angrily, for he felt the woman was turning him inside out.

"Only that we women love by lies to confound the strength of men," she replied coolly. "Thus I sent them away with fleas in their split ears!"

Zamân Shâh felt irritation overcoming his interest.

"Thou hast done well," he said in lordly fashion, "and I will see that the beggars come not into camp again."

Dilarâm laughed scornfully. "Seeing to it when sight is gone is blind man's work, master, and I follow not that path. These ash-smeared ones are by repute passed thieves; so I have taken steps along the road of stratagem. For, see you, the child shall keep her luck. As the adage runs, 'Birth and Death together in one bed make a long life for the one not dead,' and she was but just born when *jogi-jee* met his end."

"Who told thee he was dead?" interrupted Zamân Shâh hastily.

Dilarâm stared affably. "None—till now, master, though I

guessed it. Not that I care one pin's point who lives or dies so that the child keeps her luck. Thus sniffing danger, I took steps." She drew back the covering from the child. "See you, she clasps the string of her rattle as ever. Dost see any difference, master? Yet the true one is here in safe custody." She drew out a lacquered cup from her capacious bosom and laid it beside the other. "Lo! the lacquer-maker in the bazaar had it done in a trice from the pattern and charged me a pice for it. And I rubbed it in dirt to take off the newness. So if the ash-smeared abominations steal, they shall steal—naught."

Zamân Shâh looked at her admiringly. "Verily thou hast wits in that stout body of thine. Truly 'tis a trick; for if they steal and find not what they sought, they will deem thou didst speak truth about the theft—and so follow after the straight-haired, whole-eared one! Ha, ha!"

Dilarâm caught up the child and salaamed resignedly. "Yea, master; thy wits have it now. But have a care for thyself; these God-forgotten idolaters stick at nothing."

So she returned to the tent where Bibi Azîzan and the boys slept peacefully, and cuddling the child close to her for safety, lay down to rest. For some time she remained awake listening to every sound; but as the night wore on the effort became too great, and she fell asnoring.

When she woke day was glinting bright through the slit of the tent curtain.

Her first thought was for the rattle. It still hung from the child's fat wrist, and as she rose, yawning, to prepare the morning's food, she told herself that she might have saved herself a pice; still, better lose that than be caught napping.

It was not until she brought little Mihr-un-nissa out into the sunlight that she started, looked closer, then muttered to herself: "Prayers are over! Up with the carpet!"

For the cup which was carefully threaded on to the original string was not the one she had put there the previous night.

Truly the ash-smeared ones were clever thieves; but they had been foiled this time by a woman's wit.

CHAPTER III

"Life's scale tips up, then settles down again;
'One *rati* more!' the Jeweller cries. In vain
Our Purse we ransack. So the Treasure goes
Back to the Store of Things we cannot gain."

"KEEP thy cursed beasts from this ways," said Dilarâm angrily, shifting backwards a little as she sat with Mihr-un-nissa in her arms, watching a snake-charmer make his cobras dance. For the third time one of them had dropped down and commenced a quick wriggle towards her side of the gathered semicircle of spectators.

The man—he was extraordinarily small, extraordinarily agile-looking, with slender dark limbs and restless dark eyes—caught the offender by the tail, dexterously slipped his other hand up behind the hood, and so returned it to its round basket, where, as he slowly dropped it in, it curled itself round in an obedient coil.

"'Tis not this slave's fault," he said with a salaam. "'Tis the fault of queenship. The *nâg* is wise—it recognizes royalty."

The crowding semicircle tittered at the retort, and Dilarâm snorted. "Cease flattery, fool!" she remarked superbly. "If I'm a queen and you're a queen, who'll bang the butter?"

And the crowd laughed at the proverb. It was easily amused; but, the second snake refusing to dance without its comrade, the show was over; so the audience melted away to other distractions. For the Caravan had come to the town of Thanêswar, and there was more than enough to please all and sundry. Even on ordinary days the "City of God" is quaint beyond compare, with its high pink walls scalloped with white like a frosted cake, the multitudinous gilt spires of its temples, and its sacred lake formed by a deep pool of the Saraswati river, that mysterious stream which not so many miles southwards loses itself once and for all in the golden sands of the Rajputâna desert. Yet, quaint as the city is, its interest pales before that of the country in which it stands. For all around it lies "Kuru-kshetra"—in other words, the great Field of Battle where, ever since those half mythical times when the Kauravas fought the Pandavas on the plain of Paniput, the fate and fortunes of every alien conqueror of India has been decided. Strange, almost beyond thought, it is to wander on some moonlit night over the wide stretches of young green wheat that hides the bones of innumerable men—millions on millions of them—and listen for the far-off echoes of strife which folk say are still to be heard by those who choose to hear. And they say true; for to those who have imagination the past is even as the present. But the people who drifted away elsewhere when the snake-show was ended did not even remember that but a few years before Akbar, the Emperor, now reigning in the plentitude of youthful power at Agra, had secured his crown on that same plain; did not even realize that the blood of the thousands slain there was still enriching the soil, still giving colour to the young wheat.

They had, however, more excuse for forgetfulness than usual, for Thanêswar was in gala dress. There was to be an eclipse of the moon that night. Now the legend runs that at such times all the sacred waters of India, north, south, east, and west, come to renew their holiness in their sister Saraswati's breast. Pilgrims to the pool, therefore, gain the absolution of many ablutions; so the shores of the little lake were crowded, and jugglers, dancers, musicians, sweetmeat-sellers set up their shows on all sides to amuse the people. *Bairâgis* these, for the most part clean, sleek, well fed; none the less religious mendicants and so-called ascetics.

In those days Thanêswar was one of the richest shrines in the country; indeed, Zamân Shâh had come some way out of the direct road to Delhi in order to deliver a consignment of rich stuffs and spices to the head Gosain, a man of repute and power, who at the moment was showing himself to the pilgrims at the further end of the pool.

This affording a diversion, the snake-charmer and Dilarám were left alone.

After a quick glance round, he edged his way towards her on

the soles of his feet as he squatted. Then, without raising his voice, he said:

"The royalty is not thine, sister—it is the child's; but have a care of it. There be thieves abroad."

"What mean'st thou?" asked Dilarâm quickly.

He pointed to the child's rattle, then shifted a step nearer. "There was a *jogi* once. He died by the hands of bunglers; had they trusted—others—they might have found what they sought."

Dilarâm drew in her breath hard. "That one was stolen," she muttered, reverting to the old lie. "I purchased *this* in the Lahore bazaar for a pice."

The snake-charmer did not laugh, he chuckled. "And the royalty, sister, that the snake saw? Whence comes it? Didst pay a pice for it also?" His voice, jeering, but not insolent, told her the time of lies was past, and curiosity overcoming her, she asked rapidly:

"Then it is *talismân*? I ever thought it was."

He shrugged his shoulders as he rose to adjust the yoke to which his baskets swung.

"*That* know I not; but that it was prized is certain, else why send bunglers to kill him who carried it? So hide it away, sister; anyhow, while the caravan remaineth at Thanêswar!"

"Wherefore?" she began; then comprehension clutched at her. That chance shot of hers of rivalry between the split-ears and long-haired must have been true; and at Thanêswar they were *bairâgis!* The thought held her for a second or two, and when she recovered herself the snake-charmer was already many paces away.

She hesitated about calling him back, decided against it; but, taking the rattle off the child's wrist, hid it in her bosom and made her way back to the tent.

It was best to be on the safe side.

But here trouble of another kind met her; trouble that had already vexed her more than once. But this time she found Bibi Azîzan exultant because after many attempts she had succeeded in persuading her husband that, with his larger emoluments, it was only fitting the child should have a wet nurse;

therefore Dilarâm had orders to see about procuring one without delay. As they were halting by so large a town, this should not be difficult.

Possibly it would not have been so, had that stalwart woman desired it. But she did not. With Bibi Azîzan, who was only too glad to get rid of her little daughter on the slightest pretext, Dilarâm was certain of the child's affection; with another woman, in whose arms Mihr-un-nissa would be day and night, matters would be very different.

So she fought tooth and nail against the suggestion.

"I care not," insisted her mistress, between anger and whimpering. "'Tis not the custom in high-born families for mothers to suckle their infants, and the child is hungry as a wolf."

"The mistress should bethink her of the days to come, when half Hindustân will be craving to send the betrothal dates," suggested Dilarâm artfully. "Lo! she is beauty incarnate, as all can see."

"Yea! Yea! If the smallpox come not nigh her," argued the mother fretfully. "Who looks at a bride with one eye?"

Dilarâm flared out in a white heat of rage.

"What! Art not afraid to even the darling to such a fate? Lo! 'Twould be just punishment were the evil to befall thy sons!"

"'Twouldn't matter so much," protested Azîzan, now full of tears. "Who asks of the grooms beauty or health?"

This was true. Besides, these tempers of the mother invariably resulted in a stomach-ache for the child, who, in truth, was hardly getting enough for her strong frame. So Dilarâm flounced away, irate.

She would get a goat, she told herself, and some boy or old man to tend it; the child was healthy, and would thrive doubtless. If not, there was always the wet nurse. So she sent word to the *kotwali*, or police-station, of her wants, and judging discretion to be the better part of valour, decided on remaining in seclusion for the rest of the day. There were too many *bairâgis* about for safety, especially until she could see Zamân Shâh in the evening and tell him of the snake-charmer's warning.

At the moment, both he and Ghiyâss-ud-din were busy delivering their tale of goods at the Chief Priest's store. When that was satisfactorily finished they passed through the narrowest, darkest, filthiest alleys imaginable, to the Chief Priest's house. It stood close to the temples, backed by the indescribable squalor of the town, but open in front to what was generally the still levels of the sacred pool. To-day, however, the margin of the lake flashed in the sunlight as the multitude of bathers sent the water eddying and rippling in silver waves. The perfume of spent jasmine and marigold mingled with the incense that floated out from the temples, and the insistent yet separate clanging of bells from within the various shrines seemed as if the very pulse-beats of life were being counted—counted and appraised by Something Unseen, Unknown. To the imaginative mind this Something shrouded all things in a veil of mystery. Both the laughter of the crowd and its eagerness for re-generation and absolution, seemed pitiful beside that ceaseless counting of the heart-beat of humanity.

The Mohunt, or Chief Priest of the shrines and monastery, however, was not imaginative. He was oily without, oily within; everything slipped off him, soul and body, save personal gratification. The outcome of a long line of hereditary so-called ascetics, who lived to prey on the ignorance of pilgrims, he was corrupt to the core, and as he sat solemnly flattering the Convoyer of Caravans while *atar* and *pân* was handed round, he was telling himself that now the outcast had performed his task of delivering certain valuables, it was time he should pay for another treasure, which in some mysterious way had disappeared from the camp.

For the *jogi* who had joined the caravan at Kâbul had had the treasure. Of that there could be no doubt. But when *jogi-jee* had been murdered by the emissaries of the shrine nothing had been found upon him—nothing.

So Râmanund, Chief Gosain, flattered the Convoyer of the Caravan and artfully led the stilted conversation of a ceremonial visit to a point, till he could say abruptly :—

"And has his honour heard no more of the split-ear *jogi* who was murdered near his camp?"

For one instant Zamân Shâh was taken aback. Then he recovered himself. "The Maharâj," he said, "speaks of things beyond this slave's knowledge; nathless, the Maharâj may know more of the murder—if there was one—than other folk; thus, he may be able to say who did the deed—if it was done."

And the two men sat looking steadily into each other's eyes in the pause which in Eastern interviews of ceremony always follows on each remark.

"This slave knows but by hearsay," continued Râmanund. "One of the split-ears passed the shrine not long since, and said the deed was done by thieves for something the man carried in his hair—a worthless but a holy cup—so he said."

Flashes of inspiration come to most men at times. One came in the pause of etiquette to Zamân Shâh as he remembered Dilarâm's trick, and when it was time to talk again, he laughed aloud:

"Lo! by the twelve Imâms! Maharâj, make me excused. But I have enough of such cups. A woman in the camp who nurses a child made a disturbance about such an one which she found, and gave her nursling as a toy. And she has it that it was stolen from her by a split-ear at Lahore and another put in its place. Mayhap the Maharâj might like to see and question her. I will send her to my lord on my return."

Râmanund's watchful eyes glittered during the pause. "Wherefore should I put His Excellency to trouble?" he replied oilily. "I will return with my lord and see for myself."

There was the faintest note of irony in the last words, and Zamân Shâh felt himself trapped. There might be no time to effect the exchange which, in emulation of Dilarâm's previous trick, he had intended; at least, not without a delay which might arouse suspicion.

All this time Ghiyâss-ud-din, who was innocent as the babe unborn of all the secret intrigue concerning Mihr-un-nissa's rattle, had, in accordance with etiquette, sat mumchance; but now he spoke deferentially.

"May pardon be mine," he said in courtly fashion, "to

neither of my lords should this labour come. I, with permission, will return and send the woman and the child hither."

It was well meant; but Zamân Shâh hastily cut him short.

"Nay, friend," he said. "'Tis better Mohunt-*jee* should take the woman unprepared; the truth comes uppermost in surprise, does it not, Most Religious?" And his haughty stare nearly imposed on the Mohunt; nearly, not quite. Those watch ful eyes had noted Zamân Shâh's first start.

As they made their way to the camp past the margin of the lake, the latter's mind was busy as to how the business of exchange was to be carried through. Frankly, he did not know. If the worst came to the worst he must risk some delay. And after all it was a triviality. But for the desire to outwit this man who had tried to outwit him he would have told the truth about the cursed little cup. Meanwhile he backed his luck. Was it, he wondered, about to desert him? for there at the door of the tent sat Dilarâm, the child in her arms. He felt helpless. There was nothing for it but to be straightforward and leave deception, if it were possible, to the woman.

She was equal to the occasion.

"So the Religious wishes to see the child's rattle," she said calmly in answer to Zamân Shâh's halting tale. "Nay, but he is welcome. Mayhap the touch of holy hands may make this even as the last that the hell-doomed, split-eared thief stole from me at Lahore." And with that she took the string of the toy off the child's wrist and handed the cup affably to the Mohunt.

"May God help us!" murmured Zamân Shâh under his breath. "Women are beyond us men!"

Meanwhile the sudden flash of interest on the Mohunt's face was dying down to disappointment, and after a very brief inspection he handed the toy back.

And here Dilarâm's curiosity once again got the better of her. "Yea, yea," she nodded. "'Tis of no account—but the other?—the other was *talismân*, was it not?"

And once again the answer was evasive. "Of that I know not! But 'twas prized, anyhow, else why should it be stolen?"

The Mohunt looked from one to the other face keenly; but the woman's showed stolid, the man's bewilderment.

"Wherefore indeed," echoed Dilarâm coolly, "save that if, as the master sayeth, it once belonged to split-eared *jogi-jee*, 'tis his brethren belike that have it now. So that ends it."

But when the Gosain had swept away, dissatisfied, with his attendants, she sat down suddenly, laid the child on her skirts, and, lifting her hands skywards, gave a heartfelt "God be praised!"

"Yea, yea!" cavilled Zamân Shâh, "God is above all—but how didst do it?"

Then she told him of the snake-charmer, and how for safety's sake she had hidden the real rattle and given the child the false one instead.

"Thou hast the devil's own luck, woman," said Zamân Shâh, "but play no more tricks with fate. Drop the cursed cup down a well and trust to Mihr-un-nissa's own fortune."

But Dilarâm shook her head. "Nay, master, I will keep both, for see you—the split-ears believe the long-haired have it, and the long-haired think the split-ears have secured it, so we good folk set free of suspicion and harm—Sobhân Allah!"

Could she have followed Râmanund, however, she might have rescinded the last word, for as he sat secure from interruption, save from his own immediate entourage, in the darkest recess of the most holy of holies, his face showed an almost ghoulish ferocity. Before him crouched a very small man of such dark complexion that he seemed scarce seen in the obscurity.

"There are the fifty rupees," said the Mohunt. "Thou didst fail in thy last mission—the cup for which we hazarded so much hath gone back, it seems, to the split-ears—so see that thou fail not in this. Those three must die—the man, the woman, and the child."

A faint chuckle came from the darkness. "Lo! I have done more than that in half an hour," said a low voice. "The Noose of Death is swift, my lord."

"Hurry it not, then," was the reply. "Wait till suspicion cannot lie here; but they reach not Agra."

After that a chink as of money being counted mingled with that ceaseless yet intermittent clang of the bronze bells that hung before the idols in the sanctuaries.

For it was to be a great night in Thanêswar. But everywhere that chink of money mingled with the call to grace. The alms-bags began to bulge; folk, seeing it so, judged that salvation must be bought by this time, and having perambulated every sacred spot, paid toll at every sacred shrine, squatted down on the margin of the lake to await the rising of the moon.

And all around them, aiding the lush growth of the young wheat, lay the countless dead who in life had yearned after and waited for the forgiveness of sins, even as *they* yearned and waited.

But the camp of the caravan was busy striking tents against the forward march next morning, for Zamân Shâh had had enough of Thanêswar; but Dilarâm would fain have tarried, since the bespoken goat had not arrived. Not that the heart's darling would suffer, since will-he nill-he Bibi Azîzan must continue her duty till a substitute was found. So there was whimpering and anger and protestation; but Dilarâm had her way. And after all, the penance was not long, since at the very next camp a milk-white goat in charge of a very old man appeared and proved to be all that could be desired. A very old and a very small man, with no teeth and a two days' beard frosting his lank cheeks. He wore no clothes save a small waist cloth and a crimson strip of some kind of stuff, neither cotton nor wool, that did duty as turban. So his old anatomy was plainly visible. But at times he was agile enough, and his bright bead-like eyes were always watchful. Still, he also was all that could be desired, and as the days passed Dilarâm set aside a curious distrust that she had seen him before, and more than once she gave the babe to his keeping whilst she was busy with other work. He seemed to have a knack of amusing her, for when Dilarâm gave the pair a look to see that all was well, she would find the child sitting large-eyed, grave, watching the fingers that were so agile, despite their age, as they looped a bit of string this way and that and then with a jerk undid the knotted thread.

"Thou art conjuror, for sure," said the woman, graciously enough, and the old man chuckled.

"Yea, yea," he mumbled. "For sure I am conjuror! I

make changes that are beyond wit. So shall the *baba-sahiba* in years to come; but in a different way."

Once again Dilarâm looked to discover where she could possibly have seen him before, and failed to find a memory. Still, he seemed careful and inoffensive. By his own desire, he and his goat slept close beside the tent, so that they might be at hand should occasion arise; and more than once, coming out during the night, Dilarâm had found the old man squatting wide awake by the tent-flap.

"Dost never sleep?" she asked carelessly.

"Yea, mistress, yea," he mumbled; "when work is done we sleep—and so do others." And again he chuckled.

Thus the days and nights passed. They were dark nights, so the camp was quiet. So quiet that when Dilarâm woke one time she leant over to see if Mihr-un-nissa were indeed breathing, since such alarms assail all true nurses. And as she listened she heard a faint noise. It was like a whispered chuckle. Then suddenly a low voice said in command: "Thou hast a light—strike."

Scarce knowing what she did, she obeyed, and would have screamed but for a sharp "Hist!"

She held her breath, gazing at what she saw. Before her, one behind the other, lay two dark figures, so slender, so lithe, they were like snakes, and both held in their right hands a noosed strip of crimson cloth. The noose of the first lay loose around Mihr-un-nissa's baby throat, but the noose of the second was tight round a man's.

"God and his Prophet!" she almost moaned. "What?"

The man behind sat up. It was the goat-tender; but the years had fallen from him. Ay, the goat-tender, but the snake-charmer also! So her voice tailed off into a whispered "Who?"

"I am the Strangler," came the calm reply. "Yonder is the Bungler," and a lithe finger pointed scornfully to the still figure in front of him. "He will bungle no more." He leant over, loosened the noose about the man's neck, and coolly untwisting the silken stuff, wound it round his shaven head. But the figure lay still.

By this time Dilarâm had recovered from her terrified stupefaction. "Thou art a murderer," she exclaimed. "I will call——"

The deft hand was on the end of the noose that lay loose about the child's throat. "Best not, mistress," came a warning voice. "Did I not say I was the Strangler? Ere help could come, thou and the little queen yonder would have suffered change! And I would not do her evil. The world will do that all too well. Yet she hath Luck with her, and for that I watched for you and her, and that cursed fool of a Convoyer, who were as well killed."

"But wherefore?" began Dilarâm tremblingly.

The small, scarce seen figure was terrible in its calm, as, with a twitch which brought a half uttered cry from the woman, the noose about the child's neck unhitched itself and seemed to coil into his hand as the snake had coiled into its basket.

"Wherefore?" he echoed. "Because yon carrion stole my task. Look you—he was Bungler, I am Strangler. So it was mine by right, and he being of my tribe knew this; but he hath learnt his lesson. Yea, I let him slip past me, I let him cast the noose of Death, and then——" A faint chuckle came from his lips as, standing up, he stooped and lifted the dead body of the Bungler in his arms as easily as he would have lifted a child; but the flickering light of the cresset Dilarâm had lit fell and glistened on muscles tense and strong as steel, whence old age had vanished utterly.

He paused with his burden for a second. "Say naught, and there is safety for all. Speak, and there is danger," he whispered rapidly. "By dawn the Strangler will be goat-tender!"

For a full hour Dilarâm sat shivering, the light still in her hand. Then, through the rifts of the tent, faint dawn began to show, and she summoned up enough courage to rise and look out.

The old goat-tender, old as ever, was beside his goat, and he was fast asleep. There was no further need to keep awake; that at any rate was comforting; but Dilarâm's head was in a whirl. The day passed, however, as other days, and none knew of the tragedy that had been enacted save one woman who shivered despite her stalwart strength and one old, half palsied man whose watchful eyes held youth in them.

Dilarâm felt as if she could have thrown away the brimming *lotahs* full of milk he offered her; but something calm and calculating in those eyes made her keep control over herself.

And she was rewarded. The caravan reached Delhi that night, and the next morning a bright-faced boy appeared as goat-tender. The old one had gone.

"Whither?" asked Dilarâm, feeling a grip at her throat.

"To Bundelkund, mistress. He belongs there, so he said. And he is a kind man. He gave me this to tie the goat with."

This was a long twisted slip of what had once been crimson silk. It was worn and frayed by use. Dilarâm shivered again. But she was acute enough to see that the episode of the cup-rattle had ended. Both the long-haired and the split-ears were confident it had been stolen; and now revenge had passed harmless, thanks to that Strangler who was not a Bungler. So she breathed again.

CHAPTER IV

> 'As Earth is decked in Spring by Him who knows,
> For life's great bridal so the maiden grows:
> Gems without price within her heart He hides,
> And on her green branch hangs His crimson rose."

It was late March when the caravan reached Agra, and Mihr-un-nissa was six months of age; for these old-time journeyings were leisurely. She was a picture of strength and beauty; so strong, indeed, that by the help of Dilarâm's finger she could stand upright, and more than once had launched herself forth into the world recklessly in pursuit of her beloved rattle; for it never failed in its attraction. Nor did she. People stopped to notice her always, and as they passed called down blessings on her little life, lest it should be thought that her great beauty had aroused envy, and so brought the evil eye.

As Zamân Shâh had predicted, his recommendation had been sufficient to procure for Ghiyâss-ud-din a post in the Finance Department, where he was already gaining golden opinions from his superiors; so the cup of Bibi Azîzan's content was almost full. Restored to her proper position, well housed, well fed, with money wherewith to buy dress and cosmetics, the only thing wanting was an entry to Court circles.

And that came in this wise.

The gardens which the dead Emperor Baber had planted with his own hands, and which pleased his grandson Akbar in more detached and dilettante fashion, were ablaze with flowers. Roses straggled over the marble pathway, the tall cypresses were wreathed with double jasmine, the white and scarlet hibiscus were beginning to show on their dense thickets, while over all, through all, the scent of the orange blossom that starred the burnished leaves, beneath which hung the round fruit that was fast yellowing to gold, made the air heavy with perfume.

Now Mihr-un-nissa was wilful to no common degree. There was already strife between her and her small brothers over toys. They held, naturally, that as male creatures they should have all the best of everything. She denied this; her baby fingers held fast to her own, her rosebud of a mouth, when opened wide in distress, emitted a vast volume of sound. So it came to pass that, for peace sake, Dilarâm would oft leave the boys behind in charge of one of the other servants whom Ghiyâss-ud-din's emoluments made possible, and take the little lass to the "Gold-scattering Garden" that lay close to their house.

She did not know this, but it was a garden haunted by the memories of happy children—Baber, grey of hair, a child in soul; Târdi Beg the darvesh, world-worn in body, a veritable urchin in mind; sedate little Gulbadan and Alwar, the marvellous boy destined to early death. Here had the four played ball together; here had they chased each other and laughed—laughed the whole long summer day.

Perhaps that was why little Mihr-un-nissa was so happy there; for she was of their tribe—the tribe of wanderers through the desert of life, the tribe that sits free even in this world.

So one day, as she sat playing with a red rose Dilarâm had plucked for her, the Emperor Akbar, in one of his moods for solitude, came adown the orange-enarched path. A tall broad figure of a man still in the prime of youth, alert of body, dreamful of eye; but the dreams just then were happy ones, for they centred round his two-year-old son Prince Salim—the son for whom he had waited so long; the son in commemoration of whose happy birth the rose-red walls and palaces of Fatehpur—the City of Victory—were rising like magic on the rocky ridge of Sikri. So the whole strong soul of the man who swayed all India with his little finger as easily as a weathercock is swayed by the faint breath of dawn, was preoccupied, not with himself, not even with his power, his Empire, but with the future of his son.

The day was warm. The yellow glare of the sunlight seemed to hold and imprison the myriad colours, the myriad scents of the garden. The perfume-laden atmosphere seemed in its turn almost a visible link between flower and leaf, between blossom and fruit—ay, even between the man and the little child, who, set quickly on her feet by Dilarâm as the Emperor passed, stood holding on to her nurse's strong finger, and staring at him. The daintiest little figure, clad after Bibi Azîzan's own heart and with all the good taste that lady certainly possessed. A quaint little figure, too, in full petticoat and veil, holding a red rose tight in one fat little hand.

The Emperor paused, hesitated. Dilarâm's head was almost on the ground in lowliest fashion when the child suddenly let go the upholding finger and lurched forward, the rose in her outstretched hand.

"Have a care, little one," cried the Emperor, and the next instant she was in his arms. Even so her purpose did not waver. She stuffed the rose under his nostrils for him to smell, sniffing vigorously herself the while.

And he sniffed too.

"*Ah ha! Ah ha! Ha ha! Ha ha!*" So the twain were for the moment as one—the man who had come to the fulness of life and the woman who was to come to it in the future. And the whole savour of that life, blinding sweet in its griefs as well as its joys, its failures as well as its successes, seemed—so far as the man was concerned—to mingle with the aromatic perfumes of flower and fruit, and shut out sense of all but beauty incarnate.

But the child went on sniffing at the rose.

"*Ah ha! Ah ha!*"

"Whose is the little lass?" asked the Emperor curtly, setting her back in Dilarâm's arms. "What—*Meeân* Ghiyâss-ud-din's? I remember. Bid her mother bring her to the palace to-morrow. She may amuse my son."

So he passed on. Dilarâm looked after the autocratic figure vexedly. There had not been one word of praise for the heart's darling; the daintiest, sweetest, prettiest little marionette the world had ever seen or was likely to see. Nothing but his son, forsooth!

The child, however, was content. She had achieved her object; the rose had been duly smelt. She could now pull it to pieces, which she did remorselessly.

Even Dilarâm's embittered reminder that the introduction was due to the despised daughter could not dull Bibi Azîzan's almost frenzied delight at the invitation to Court. She lay awake all night devising how best to appear to advantage; and as she was really a very astute little person in a worldly way, Mihr-un-nissa came in for no small share of her planning.

"She must look her best," she nodded, full of wreathed smiles, "for, see you, 'children's plays bring wedding days!'"

Dilarâm snorted. "Set not aims so high, mistress, or falls will come; then 'twill be 'Who wants to get up? as the sluggard said when he fell into the well!'"

"High?" echoed Bibi Azîzan indignantly. "Is not the *Meeân* of a princely family, for all he feeds on paper like a fish insect? I tell you it shall be an auspicious day."

Fate, however—and Mihr-un-nissa—willed it otherwise; for she was cutting her back teeth, and was contrary to a degree. So much so that she refused to yield her pet plaything to a boy, even though he was the heir apparent; and when her indignant mother reft it from her by force, she let loose such yells that the great Emperor himself came in to see that was wrong in the nursery.

"Your pardon, mother," he said good-humouredly as Bibi Azîzan hastily veiled herself. "I wist not there were strangers; and verily I thought someone was being killed."

A chorus of explanation from the ladies, and tearful protestations from behind the veil, mingled with Mihr-un-nissa's appeal for justice, while Prince Salim, a fat, heavy-looking child of nigh three, sat triumphantly beating the cup upon the floor.

The Emperor, man-like, saw his opportunity for a display of moral power. "Lo! Shaikie, my son," he said in his deep full voice, "all men—and kings especially—must learn to respect the property of others."

And with that a peremptory hand annexed the toy. Whereupon Mihr-un-nissa's howl found fit second in a roar from the Prince, the two making such brain-splitting noise that Akbar clapped his hands to his ears and beat a hasty retreat.

"God gives the reward of silence!" he laughed. "Here"—

he flung the plaything towards the children—" let them fight for it like puppies."

" For shame, nephew !" came a thin silvery voice from a little lady whose abundant white hair showed under a rose-coloured veil. " They be not dogs, but man and woman; and 'tis the woman's part——"

Here she also burst into a laugh. Indeed, anything more comical than the race between the babies could not be imagined. Prince Salim began well, being on his feet with wonderful celerity considering his stoutness; but Mihr-un-nissa, disdaining even to crawl, cast herself on the ground and rolled over and over with such appalling swiftness that Shaikie, seeing himself outdone, cast himself upon her in turn. Whereupon there arose, not shrieks of anger, but shrieks of laughter as the tussle went on, until Mihr-un-nissa, grabbing the cup, sat up and deliberately banged Prince Salim's head with it, thereinafter offering it to him with a complacent smile which converted the outrage into an honour.

The tears of laughter were running down Akbar's face. " Said I not truly they had best fight it out? Lo! the little lass is true woman; she gives of her own free will."

And a little pair of hands belonging to the rose-coloured veil clapped loudly, and the silvery voice cried, " Well done! Well done! but blows should never be taken on loan, Shaikie! Give it her back, child! Give it her back in a kiss."

Whether in unwonted obedience to his great-aunt Rosebody's suggestion, or because it fitted in with his own wishes, Prince Salim did as he was bid. Mihr-un-nissa received the salute with chill dignity, and thereinafter there was peace; though the ladies of the harem were scarcely pleased.

Bibi Azîzan when she got home hardly knew whether the visit had been a success or a failure.

" For look you," she said tearfully, " it was a portent—most as good as a betrothal."

" Traa!" retorted Dilarâm. " What's a snippet or snippet broth? There be more than kisses to a betrothal! Nay, Bibi, sing your own song and play your own pipe, for, mark you, many a thing that falls from the sky sticks in a palm-tree.

Meddle not with things that be above you. But what will you! The camel drowned and the frog asked if the pool was deep!"

When Dilarâm resorted lavishly to the hoarded wisdom of proverbs she was quite unanswerable; so Bibi Azîzan held her peace.

But this incident was the beginning of a considerable intimacy between Ghiyâss-ud-din's household and the Palace. The little Prince began it by loudly demanding the return of the "cry-baby and her rattle," whereupon Dilarâm, always wily, took care to substitute the imitation cup for the real—a trick which enormously improved Mihr-un-nissa's temper, since, curiously enough, it was only the real cup that she would yield to none. So Prince Salim was allowed to possess it, and the ladies of the harem complimented Bibi Azîzan on the effect of good society on the child's manners.

"And they were most of them Hindus," wept the Bibi, "who know nothing of real etiquette."

But she swallowed her dignity for the time. And as the months passed it grew until it could no longer be ignored. Zamân Shâh, returning the next year with another caravan, found his protégé promoted to Assistant Treasurer. By this time the Court had moved to Fatehpur, and the camel loads were full of jade, cornelian, and agates for inlaying work, besides rich carpets and stuffs for the new palaces. And still Akbar the Emperor dreamt his dream of the race that should come after him and reap the benefit of what he was sowing.

So the years passed on. Ghiyâss-ud-din rose to be Lord High Treasurer, and Bibi Azîzan, by repute and consent, became the recognized leader of fashion in the outermost Court Circle. In the innermost the Beneficent Ladies stuck to their old Chagatâi modes and customs. One of these permitted of far greater freedom amongst boys and girls than was countenanced in strict and orthodox Mahomedan households. So Mihr-un-nissa and her brother Asof Khân continued to be playmates with the heir apparent and his two younger brothers. There were other princelings and princesslings too, so that the party was a merry one. And they all chanted the Korân together, and drew huge black letterings on white chalked writing-boards, and learnt their tables up to sixteen and three quarter's times sixteen and a half. At least, the boys did, and Mihr-un-nissa picked it up easily by hearing them.

"She hath my head for figures," said Ghiyâss-ud-din. Though he was very silent and undemonstrative, his little daughter was more to him than all the world beside.

"Traa!" replied his wife scornfully. "Of what good are figures to a woman? Praise God she hath inherited beauty—yea, a figure and a face too—from my side of the family. Leave ciphering to the boys!"

Ghiyâss pulled a rueful face. "I would if I could, wife; but when I asked Asof what ten times nine was, he answered me thirty-nine; and when I upbraided him, he maintained that the Prince said it so, and the tutor agreed. I misdoubt me they are spoiling the boy between them."

Bibi Azîzan bridled. "Princes cannot be spoilt. But 'tis time, *Meeân-jee*, that Mihr-un-nissa retire from playing with boys; 'twill make her unmaidenly. Besides, the Prince will become accustomed to look on her as a sister, and that——"

She paused before Ghiyâss-ud-din's sudden anger. "And wherefore not, woman? Emperor though he may be in the future, he is half Hindu; besides, I like not his looks. My daughter shall mate with one of her own class. And that reminds me. 'Twas ever arranged between me and mine ancient friend and cousin, Khizy Shâh, that should he have a son and I a daughter they should marry. Nay, make not a turmoil; nothing is settled, but the lad comes from Herat with Zamân Shâh next year, as I would fain see him; besides, he must join the Emperor's service. Meanwhile, the child shall run free. She but touches six, and to cage her would be to cage a young gazelle——" He paused and smiled. "Besides, 'tis good for the boys——how she queens it over them; even the Prince."

Here Bibi Azîzan's irritation overcame her whimperings—for, though her husband seldom laid down the law as he had been doing, experience taught her that when he did so he meant to take his own way.

"Yea, yea," she interrupted wrathfully, "even the Prince!

Why, she twists him round her little fingers! Is that to count for naught?"

Ghiyâss-ud-din eyed her sternly. "Ay, unless he be good man; and that remains to be seen."

What her father had said about caging the little lass was true. Tall for her age, lithe, slender, graceful, Mihr-un-nissa seemed the embodiment of youthful freedom. Her large nut-brown eyes sparkled with sheer vitality, her long, slightly curly brown hair, no matter how deftly plaited, had a trick of becoming undone and floating in the sun-bright air, and her dancing feet found a path for themselves anywhere, and everywhere. And it was true also that she queened it over the Prince, as she queened it over all the boys. The girls she treated with indifferent calm. Their ways were not her ways. They shrieked at a mouse, but when her favourite white Persian cat, that Zamân Shâh had brought her, caught one, she snatched it from the claws of death and kissed it and cuddled it, weeping salt tears when she found protection had come too late. And despite all opposition and outcry she insisted on "*kufn-duffn*," or funeral obsequies.

"*Moulvie-jee* made us all learn the text about animals from the Holy Book because Shaikie pulled the legs off flies," she said defiantly; "and a mouse comes from God even as thou dost, Dilarâm." So in her clear childish voice she intoned those notable words, so little known in the West, so little remembered by the East:

"Lo! every beast that walketh upon the earth, and every bird that flieth with wings, is a people like unto you. From the Lord they came, to the Lord will they return."

The echo of the soft Arabic sibilants and curiously liquid gutturals rang out into God's sunshine and seemed to match it.

So the mouse was buried with honour in one corner of the huge garden where, one after another, the red sandstone palaces and summer-houses, which still remain to show what the glories of the City of Victory were in the olden days, rose, each in itself completely marvellous, intricate of design and workmanship. One of these palaces at the highest point of the garden where the roach back of the Sikri ridge trended away on either side, was not yet finished; and folk wondered at it then, as they wonder at it now; for the "Palace of the Four Winds" is a puzzle for all time.

Was it really built as a playground for an idolized son? People nowadays ask the question incredulously. Was all that cube, not of solid masonry, but delicate, intricate stone-carving, built to please a child? Were those four wide low stories—open to all the four winds of heaven—with their innumerable arches, innumerable pillars, no two of them alike, really designed so that an Imperial heir should, on rainy days, find the wide air and infinite variety of Nature in his playground? What devotion, what infinite fatherly care, if it were so! And how rewarded! The mind shrinks appalled from that father's disillusionment. Small wonder that in the years to come Akbar deserted the City of Victory as a City of Dead Dreams.

Meanwhile, the children played hide-and-seek and blind man's buff amid the wide arches. First on the lowest story, then in the next, and the next as the quaint gnome-like structure grew to its completion. And Mihr-un-nissa, between the whiles of play, would trace with her delicate, dainty little fingers the carvings on the multitudinous pillars, and name the birds and beasts, the flowers, the fruits thereon; for she was of the tribe who are at one with such things.

She was just seven years of age when the topmost story of the Palace of the Four Winds was completed. The children had arranged quite a festival for the occasion. Others were to be invited: Akbar himself, possibly his ministers, Birbal and Abul-fazl, were to be present, and a little coign of vantage duly screened off had been arranged for Auntie Rosebody—who dearly loved children's games—and such of the Beneficent Ladies as chose to accompany her. Mihr-un-nissa was full of the occasion. She was to do this and that and the other thing, when a bomb fell which left her for the moment quite speechless with indignation.

She was not to go. She was now seven years old; it would be unmaidenly, immodest, especially as strange men might be there. So, at any rate, said her mother, and this time her mother was backed by her father's reluctant opinion.

The state of the child's mind is difficult to describe. Absolutely innocent, as such natures as hers ever are, of any thought of sex, surprise was the first feeling; then anger. What right had they to say she was different from a boy? She was cleverer than most of them, of course, but some boys doubtless would be cleverer than she was. She did not put it in so many words, but she felt it was but a difference of degree, she felt that she could hold her own alike with boys and girls.

Then she wept passionate and scalding tears of resentment, and her whole being went out in one vast "why?"

"It is a lie," she sobbed vindictively. "I'm not weaker than Shaikie, and I have a right to play if I choose, and I will."

Her mother, however, was obdurate, the utmost concession being that she should be allowed, if she was very meek and virtuous, as befitted one entering maidenhood, to sit with Auntie Rosebody behind the screen and watch the boys play.

"Lo!" cried the child with infinite disdain, "God did not make me to be a caged monkey or an old cat."

So she sulked; but Dilarâm, keen of observation, noticed a look of determination grow to the young face.

"If the mistress means what she says," remarked the sturdy woman to Bibi Azîzan, "she had best take steps. Those who mean to dance don't wear veils. Though for my part I doubt me if there be a pin's choice between the gadabouts and the cornered ones in virtue. And as for character, give me the former! The potter makes, but the world fills!"

So on the eventful afternoon Mihr-un-nissa, who had refused her dinner for two days, was shut up in disgrace with hearth-cakes and water in an empty room.

It did not in the least disconcert her. She had expected it, had even made her plans—whether with devoted Dilarâm's connivance or not, who can say?—to escape from durance vile. A rope lay coiled in one corner; she was agile as a young monkey, the room was but one short story from a solitary corner of the garden, where a dense thicket of pomegranates would have hidden a company of soldiers.

Here she had already concealed what she wanted, and ten minutes after the house had emptied for the "*tamasha*," she had reached it. Ten minutes more, and clad in some of her brother's garments, her beautiful long hair snipped off remorselessly by the ears, and her fair complexion darkened by a rubbing of red Sikri earth, she emerged, as bold as brass, and made her way to the Palace of the Four Winds.

She gave her younger brother Sharif's name to the doorkeeper. It was a deft deceit, for the boy, being delicate, did not often join in the Palace plays, and was not therefore easily recognized. Thus she passed in unchallenged.

It was a brave sight indeed. Crowds of boys of all ages, with the Emperor and his Ministers looking on, and a tinkle of jewels and high laughter from the latticed corner, where she ought to be, according to her mother!

Well, she was here, and she had little fear of detection, for both her brothers were away with her father on tour for a day or two. One or two of her playmates looked at her curiously, but the short hair and darkened complexion ended their doubts. And everyone was half wild with excitement, Mihr-un-nissa most of all.

"Look at yon lad-ling with the green turban," said Akbar to Birbal. "He outdistances all in reckless life. He should make a fine soldier by-and-by."

Birbal's lip curved. "He should make something, Most High. What, God settles, so they say; for myself, I hold it matters naught if one be strong or weak, timid or bold, man or woman, so long as one has brains!"

"Nay, nay, friend," laughed Abul-fazl; "woman needs more than brains; she must be beautiful."

Birbal flashed round on him. "Not so! If a woman has brains, her greatest foe is beauty, for men take her at her face value."

"Look! Look!" interrupted the Emperor, pointing to the children, who were now playing a sort of blind man's buff. "Green turban hath challenged Shaikie, and he is as a fish in deep water for slipperiness. But Shaikie will have him yet."

And truly there was an unwonted air of determination about blindfolded Prince Salim, who, having had the tail of his turban tweaked with an impudent imitation of a sheep's "baa," was now bound to catch the imitator, who in his turn was bound to keep on bleating. In and out, round about, the pair ran, both becoming breathless, and it is doubtful if the Emperor's prediction as to his son's success would have been realized within the appointed time had not an obsequious courtier put out his foot and so brought green turban to the ground. Up in a second, it was yet too late, and the pursued stood captive.

"Who is it, Shaikie?" said the Emperor, delighted.

The young Prince's hand sought the face beneath the green turban.

"Mihr-un-nissa!" he said instantly.

A roar of laughter followed; even the Emperor joined in it.

"Nay, Shaikie," he cried. "Thou hast made a mistake. Girls are not admitted. Try again, my son!"

Shaikie's heavy face flushed crimson; he tore the bandage from his eyes. "I have made no mistake," he shouted angrily. "It is Mihr-un-nissa—Mihr-un-nissa in boy's clothes."

A faint shriek came from the screened corner where Bibi Azîzan, as usual, was currying favour with the Court, but the rest of the company were too much astonished for anything save silence as they crowded round the culprit, who stood calm, defiant.

"Yea," she cried, "I am Mihr-un-nissa! I said I would do it, and I've done it, so there!"

And with that she dived—verily like a fish in deep water for slipperiness—under Birbal's very arm, and was off and away ere anyone could stop her.

"Why didst let her through, Birbal?" asked the Emperor reproachfully.

"Because she desired it, sire!" he replied, and Akbar laughed.

Meanwhile, Mihr-un-nissa, unpursued—for without royal order naught could be done, and Bibi Azîzan in the screened corner was helpless for the time—flitted through the gardens like a lapwing guarding its nest, covering her flight from thicket to thicket. And as she ran her brain was busy. If she went home straight to the women's apartments, her mother would find her at once, and being angry, might beat her. Better, therefore, to give her time to cool. Her father being absent for the day, she would be comparatively safe in the men's side of the house, which would likely be empty. So she dashed in through the tunnelled archway and then at right angles to a small sunny courtyard, where, to her surprise, a tall youth of about eighteen was cleaning his matchlock. He sat on the stone steps of the inner rooms, and at his feet lay a brace or two of black partridge.

He nodded his head carelessly.

"God speed thee, cousin," he said good-humouredly. "I have arrived before my time. Zamân Shâh and his camels should be here on the morrow; but having come so far in pursuit of these," he indicated the partridge with his foot—"I deemed it foolish to return only to ride the same road again; so I have sent the servant to buy food."

Mihr-un-nissa eyed the young fellow from head to foot. Very tall, with a pleasant, rather ugly face.

"So you are the cousin from Herât," she said slowly. "God speed thee!"

The lad laughed. "Cousin, as God will! I know not if it be so in reality. But our fathers were friends, as we shall be doubtless, for I like thy looks, though thou'rt most too pretty for a boy—should be a girl." And he fell to whistling and frowning over his work; for it was a troublesome job. The matchlock had failed to go off; something had stuck in the channel leading from the powder-pan.

Mihr-un-nissa squatted down beside him and eyed him again, this time almost malevolently.

"Why should a girl be pretty and a boy ugly?" she asked.

He shrugged his shoulders. "God knows! My mother was ugly, and she is the dearest woman in the world; but folk say so ever."

"Dost thou say so?" she persisted.

"Why, no!" he replied as he worked. "So long as both be good company, that is all I ask. And see you! 'Tis the other way round with the beasts and the birds—the cock yonder hath the gayest feathers."

She stroked the bright plumage gently, thoughtfully. "I

like thee, cousin," she said suddenly; "thou hast a good, ugly face!"

His laugh was long and loud as he stood up. "And I like thee, cousin; thou hast a good, pretty one. So are we quits? And now thou shalt have the first shot of thy life, for the channel is clear, and I would fain clean the barrel. See yonder black crow with its gaping black mouth. It deserves to die. It hath just swallowed a young squirrel. So—let me hold the weapon too. Be not afraid—'twill hurt a little, mayhap, but not much."

He was standing over the slim little figure which, nothing loath and with eager inquisitiveness in its eyes, followed his directing hand.

"Hast a good aim? So! Now pull the trigger——"

There was an overloud explosion, and the flare of a back-fire nipped at Mihr-un-nissa's long eyelashes. Luckily, the recoil had sent her flat on her back.

She sat up wrathfully, rubbing her shoulder, but tearless. "Wherefore didst that?" she asked imperiously. "Thou mightst have killed me."

"Traa!" said the youth, covering his relief that no harm had been done by assumed lightness. "That sort of thing does not hurt boys."

Her wrath grew; she forgot all but fact. "Traa thyself! I am not a boy, but a girl—so there!"

He stood and stared at her for quite a considerable time, looking a trifle sheepish.

"So," he said at length, "thou art Mihr-un-nissa, of whom Zamân Shâh boasts."

But the mind of the little lass had drifted to a bigger matter to her than the question of sex. "Did I kill the crow?" she asked anxiously.

He burst into a peal of laughter. "Now of a surety," he cried, "whether thou beest Queen o' Women or a boy, and whether I be Ali Kul the God-sent One or a girl, matters little—we have both good pluck—so there!"

CHAPTER V

'Love passes swift, and leaves no trace behind.
On yonder trellis, swept by winter wind,
Who knows if 'twere a white rose or a red
That in past summers clasped and clipped and twined?"'

MIHR-UN-NISSA'S escapade was considered by her mother sufficiently serious to warrant immediate steps being taken to prevent any possible recurrence. It was all very well for the men to laugh over it; but that sort of thing was fatal in the marriage-market. The best thing for the girl's future, then, was that she should be forgotten. To this end, therefore, she had better be sent away from Agra. Persia, of course, where all her relations lived, was too far off, but a suitable house could easily be found in some quiet country place not too far away for vigilance, whither she and Dilarâm could retire. For instance—and here Bibi Azîzan's voice dropped to a confidential whisper—there would, she felt sure, be a most desirable possibility in a few days. It was an open secret that Khanzâda Râcquiya Begum, the Emperor's first and childless wife, had come to loggerheads with Maryâm Zamâni, the heir apparent's Hindu mother, over her insensate spoiling of the boy. Doubtless Khanzâda Râcquiya, as undoubted head of the harem, would have held her own had not Maryâm Makâni, the boy's grandmother (the Emperor's blessed and beloved mother, Hamida Bânu Begum), sided with the Hindus, and Auntie Rosebody with her quick tongue been betwixt and between. Anyhow, the Emperor, who, to give him his due, was always doing his best for peace, had permitted Khanzâda Râcquiya to retire from Court for a while on pretence of finishing her book of verses; also to give change of air to his beloved little imp of a daughter, Arâm Bânu Begum; though why anyone should care for a child who, though but five years old, was a compound of unpoliteness and impudence, Heaven only knew. Still, Khanzâda Râcquiya

Begum was the person above all to instil moralities and manners, so, if she would consent to take Mihr-un-nissa as companion to the little Princess, it would be a combination of educational advantage with just that slight connection with the Court which might be useful in days to come.

The good little lady nodded and becked over this gossiping confidence, and poor Ghiyâss-ud-din felt that it would be waste of breath to dispute a plan which in truth held many advantages; for he did not want his little daughter to have much to do with the life her mother led; a life which was made up of pretty pettinesses. Then, even his short experience of the young Herâti Ali Kuli Khân had shown the father that here, if anywhere, he would find Mihr-un-nissa that fitting mate, strong, sensible, kindly, straightforward, which he desired she should have; and the girl's absence from home would not only give him more opportunity for seeing into the lad's character, but would also make it easier for him to manipulate the vague promise of betrothal, so that it could be carried out if necessary. He would thus steal a march on his wife Bibi Azîzan's objections, which were sure to be vehement.

As for Dilarâm, anything which would give her full and undivided possession of her heart's darling was welcome. This being so, and Khanzâda Râcquiya Begum approving, the plan was carried through, and ere a month had passed little Mihr-un-nissa found herself seated on the corner bastion of a high-walled garden, appraising the spot where she had come to live, and finding it good. And, indeed, few folk would have found fault with Gulâbpur, or Rose-town.

To begin with, for miles and miles the air was filled with the scent of the roses that grew in long set lines between the high cactus hedges. That, however, was before you came to Rose-Garden proper, which surely was the most wonderful place in the world! Around it a huge hundred-acre field of roses, fenced about with an impenetrable twenty-foot wall of prickly pear; grey-green, fleshy leaves and pale yellowish and pinkish blossoms, over which lemon-coloured butterflies and metal-blue dragonflies flickered, and flitted, and fluttered all day long in the sunshine. Then the sea of roses, so prim, so ordered in their lines, with a water runnel between each six rows; and every bush so like another! Grey-green, velvety leaves all set thick with Persian pink roses, distractingly sweet. As Mihr-un-nissa sat dangling her legs over the parapet of the inner wall, she seemed to feel the perfume with her toes. Then it crept up and up until it assailed her nose, and then, of course, it went right up into the sky, right away where Paradise grows, and the *peris*—silly useless creatures by all accounts—scented themselves with sandal-wood oil, as if the flowers were not enough!

This same wall was a favourite spying spot of the child, partly because it was out of Dilarâm's reach, and it annoyed her nurse to find her perched beyond her grip when she came toiling after her charge up the steep one-foot-each-way steps that, built flat on to the wall, led at each corner of the garden to a little cupolaed bastion.

"God keep the child from harm!" she would mutter, breathless, as she sank down overcome on the ledge of the eight-sided sort of birdcage where there was room, at most, for but three persons to sit. "A wild bird, she, who will never be caged; but He counts even the crows, they say."

Then she would scold and wheedle to no purpose until Mihr-un-nissa was tired of sitting astride the wall and sniffing the rose scent. It was quite different from the perfume of the inner garden. Khanzâda Râcquiya Begum called that the "Garden of Roses" in her poetry; but in reality it held every sweet-scented thing you could imagine. Lilies and jasmine, orange-blossom and sweet pandanus, trumpet-flowers and bignonia creepers, to say nothing of a wonderful unknown tree with ugly greeny-brown flowers high up in the sky. Lucky it was so, for, though afar their perfume was entrancing, quite near they smelt horribly; but when they dropped on the ground, *pouf!* the scent was gone from them at once. The little lass used to gather them up sometimes, and hold them in her hand, wondering what sort of a thing scent was, and whither it went.

But there were a thousand things in the garden to excite her young imagination. The corner palaces all floreated within with mirror inlay. The marble summer-house in the centre shaded by lace-like tracery, the lotus pink and white, in the marble water-courses where the fountains splashed. Then the water-maze! It was simply heavenly! Even Dilarâm could not object to your flying, with dancing feet, along its four-inch marble footway that criss-crossed and angled here, there, everywhere, into intricate patterns, with shallow squares and oblongs of water between them.

If you fell in, as you invariably did, she had to pick you out and dry you, since the water-maze was a recognized game in the highest circles of virtue and seclusion.

The Khanzâda herself, it is true, did not attempt it; but that was because she was slightly lame. Besides, was she not a poetess? This fact inspired Mihr-un-nissa with a certain awe and a great admiration; for, alive to her finger-tips, the child reached out instinctively to all things new in both the material and the spiritual world. So she would imperiously haul away her small companion, Princess Arâm, from any of the pleached alleys in which they came upon the poetess pacing up and down in a fine frenzy of composition.

"Hsh! Hsh!" she would say, with a forceful hand on the other's mouth. "If thou willst not I will make thee. One should never interrupt that thou canst not do thyself. And God did not make thee poetess."

"Neither did He make thee, stupid!" Arâm would reply with the cosmopolitan *tu quoque* of childhood.

And Mihr-un-nissa would look contemptuous. "Did He not? Who knows? I could if I would. 'Tis all '*fadala-toon-fadal-a-ta*'; I saw it in her book!"

"Traa!" jibed Princess Arâm. "I say thou couldst not; for, look you, she is *my aunt*, but she is nothing to thee."

This was conclusive, for the time; but after a while, as Mihr-un-nissa sat dangling her feet over the sea of roses; while the sun set cloudless behind the butterflies and the dragonflies, the music of beauty began to surge through her child's brain, and she composed a quatrain—strictly according to "*fadu-la-tun fadu-la-ta*"—which completely disposed of the little Princess's argument; at any rate, in Dilarâm's opinion. She was, in fact, so elevated by her darling's cleverness that after having the verse appropriately flourished out by the children's writing-mistress, she carried it—and the reluctant yet triumphant composer thereof—to the Khanzâda herself for approval.

Râcquiya Begum put on her horn spectacles and read as follows:

> "Under my toes there lies a sea of roses;
> Their scent comes up and tickles both my noses,
> Then flies away to feed the breath of God,
> Who sends it down again to feed the roses."

Now Khanzâda Râcquiya Begum was the great Emperor Baber's granddaughter; therefore, despite her old-maidish ways, she was bound to have two things—humour and sympathy; so she kept her smiles kindly.

"The idea," she said, "is of the best. All poems by the young should contain allusions to the Creator, since love is not decorous for them. But noses! Nay, child, noses are not poetry."

Mihr-un-nissa flushed visibly. "Wherefore not?" she protested. "God made them as well as the roses; and He must have made them first. To what purpose scent if there is nothing to smell withal?"

The Khanzâda took off her spectacles and looked hard at the speaker. She saw a tall lass with an eager, alert, childish face poised, oval, above a slender throat.

"How old art thou?" she asked. "But seven? Then hast thou time for many things; and methinks thou wilt use it too. Meanwhile 'noses' is not poetry, neither is toes—or toeses."

The joking hint of a possible rhyme was too much for Mihr-un-nissa's indignation. She burst into a peal of silvery laughter in which Râcquiya joined; and this was the beginning of a curious friendship between the vigorous young life and the disappointed older one, which lasted till the latter ceased to be.

It was of enormous advantage to the child, for Râcquiya Begum was unusually well educated, and she found in Mihr-un-nissa a pupil who bade fair to overmatch her ere long.

"She is worthy all that can be given her," said the Khanzâda, when, discreetly veiled, she gave audience to the Lord High Treasurer when he came to inquire of his little daughter's well-being. "She will have the mind of a man in the body of a beautiful woman. That will make life somewhat of a problem, so I would teach her Euclidus and Aljabr (mathematics and algebra), since she has taste that way."

"She takes it from me, Highness," replied the gratified father. "Lo! with permission, I will send an ancient master. He can live in the village, and the child can learn in the Rose-Garden."

So, except when it rained, when a shrivelled ancient-of-days was permitted as a favour to pass through the inner gate and give his lessons in the marble summer-house which centred the garden, Mihr-un-nissa, and Dilarâm, of course, went out to an arbour amid the sea of roses, where the child learnt solemnly that two parallel lines continued for ever-and-ever-a-day will never meet, and that *a* plus *b* may equal *x* or any other letter of the alphabet. And her eyebrows, with their faint slant upwards towards the nose—strange, almost invariable sign of great beauty—would slant still more, giving a puzzled, wistful, yet eager look to the hazel eyes below, and she would argue, "But if there was something outside, it might be different."

To which *munshi-ji* would reply sententiously, "There is nothing outside," and Dilarâm would bid her not ask foolish questions, but learn her lesson like a good girl.

So months passed by. In the next season of roses Bibi Azîzan came out to visit her daughter, and was simply enchanted with life in the Garden of Roses—for a month or six weeks! After that she hungered for the town again. But while the novelty lasted it was paradise. To rise to the scent of roses, to go to bed with it, to spend the day eating rose comfits, and watch, from a marble cupola, roses being picked; sometimes, decorously veiled, to go down gingerly to where the great rose-water stills were set in the shade of tall jamun trees and have fresh, still warm, rose-water poured over hands and feet—this was idyllic! Bibi Azîzan waxed enthusiastic over it, though she never could understand Khanzâda Râcquiya's and little Mihr-un-nissa's regret for the poor yellow residuum of roses that was left when the sweetness had been extracted from the petals. Of the two sympathizers, the child was the keener. She refused to have any rose-water poured over *her*. God had given the perfume of the rose to the rose, and no one had any right to take it away. She wanted nothing but the roses themselves; so while the others watched the distilling, Mihr-un-nissa would wander, on the sly, among the rose-beds; much to Dilarâm's alarm; for the black cobras would slip out at dawn and dusk from the high cactus hedge to cool themselves and drink in the runnels of water. So much so that before the rose-picking began, the dawn-bright air would echo to the hollow fluting of the snake-charmer's pipe as he sat half asleep against the fence—one to each long side of the square they had, so that "*nag-ji*" might have his music and remain at home.

But Mihr-un-nissa was fearless, and in troth the long black ropes of things fled from her steps as a rule.

"Yea, yea, she is safe enough from them," muttered a toothless old man who, they said, had blown his pipe in the garden for years; "but let her not bring the infant's rattle she plays with at times with her, nurse-*ji*. She carried it the other dawn, and lo! had I not nigh burst my lungs, the king cobra would have slid after her."

Dilarâm, who had been listening superciliously to the old dodderer's mumble, sank among her flouncing skirts all of a tremble.

"What knowest thou?" she asked fearfully. "Art thou the Strangler again?"

"Nay, nay, not I," dissented the ancient one. "I am only of the Bunglers; yet for all that, this slave knows a charm when he feels it."

After that Dilarâm never allowed Mihr-un-nissa to carry the rattle into the Rose-Garden; but in truth the child was not so set on it as of old, and only asked for it occasionally, as it were, to assure herself it was still there.

So the years passed on. Sometimes, for a month or two she went back to her father's home; but Bibi Azîzan, in her periodical visitations, found all so satisfactory that the question of removing the child altogether never arose. In fact, the smart, wily, worldly little woman began to trade on the "Rose-Garden" as an asset, talking of it to her fashionable friends, and declaring town life would be intolerable without the possibility of a retreat thither and a return to country occupations. And, to do her justice, this was not all talk; for she was a notable housewife, and many were the conserves and pickles and essences of which she supervised the making. She went further, indeed, and actually during those years invented the method of making attar of roses by collecting on tiny swabs of cotton the oily scum that rose on the vast vats of rose-water, and afterwards extracting therefrom an almost priceless essence, one drop of which would not only perfume a complete suit of clothes, but perfume it for years and years.

Even Khanzâda Râcquiya, though too much immersed in intellectuals to care for such mundane things as scents, gave full meed of praise to Bibi Azîzan's ingenuity; but Mihr-un-nissa was sternly logical, and held to her view that it was unkind to take away the scent from the poor flowers. They should be allowed to remain as God made them.

"Traa!" declared her mother. "If we women were to remain as God made us, without falsities and cosmetics, we should be ugly indeed!" Then, as she glanced at her little daughter, she hesitated; for here was an exception to the rule. For the little maid was growing increasingly and exceedingly fair, and about her, like a perfume itself, hung charm indescribable. There was a dimple in her cheek, not where dimples usually lurk, but higher up, closer to the nose, which made her smile a thing never to be forgotten. Dilarâm would sit and gaze at her, and shake her head in a sort of helpless admiration, and Zamân Shâh, when he came once or twice to see the little lass whose life he had saved, became speechless from all save Hafiz, and murmured of roses and thorns, of changeless Love and the Dust of Chance, while Mihr-un-nissa looked at him mysteriously under her levelled brows and played with the white Persian cat, or the talking mynah, or the little gazelle fawn he had brought her; for she was passionately fond of animals. And she was still a child, though she was nearing her twelfth year. She still loved to sit dangling her toes over the sea of roses, though she had given up straddling the wall out of deference to Râcquiya Begum, who told her she was too tall to wear anything but maiden dresses, and though, by this time—

having a distinct taste for easy versification—she could have written quite a respectable ode to the beauty of Rose-town.

So life passed full of scent and savour, till one evening, as she sat perched in the little octagonal bird-cage of a bastion, she espied her father coming up the roadway which led to the great arched gate of the inner garden. She would have called welcome to him, but for the fact that he was accompanied by a tall young man whom in an instant she recognized as her cousin Ali Kul. She had not seen him for years, but there was no mistaking his long length and a certain merriness of feature, even though he did wear a bandage over his left temple and there was an ugly streak further down the cheek. He must have been fighting; likely enough, since he was a captain in the Emperor's service.

Now Mihr-un-nissa knew that Dilarâm would instantly summon her to meet her father, whose coming was indeed one of the girl's chief pleasures, but when she saw her cousin part company with him and stroll along by the wall, she hastily swung her legs inside, slipped down behind the low latticed parapet until only the very top of her head was visible and watched. Ali Kul was evidently admiring the roses while waiting for her father, and if he kept on as he was doing, he must pass right under her perch. And she was consumed with curiosity to know how he had hurt himself. So she disregarded Dilarâm's calls, which began immediately to arise, and finally, craning over the parapet, said in a silvery whisper:

"What hast done to thy face, cousin?"

Ali Kul, mind and body surcharged with the sweetnesses of the roses, looked up and saw—— Most likely he saw the dimple.

For an instant he stood too surprised for words; then they flew to his lips. "Mihr-un-nissa, is it thou really, my boy-girl cousin?"

"Lo!" she replied superbly. "What dost matter if I be boy or girl? I am Mihr-un-nissa, for sure. So tell me—how didst hurt thy face? Hast lost an eye? Quick—they come!"

And indeed the sound of a heavy body breathlessly ascending

the narrow stairs became audible, accompanied by fitful gasps of indignation.

"Nay!" began the young man hastily, "my eyes——"

"Oh, waste not time with eyes," interrupted the questioner, dropping her voice to an indignant whisper; "who cares about your eyes? I asked who did it. Quick!"

But it was too late. Dilarâm's broad face showed above the level of the bird-cage floor, and the culprit had to wheel round almost ere she caught the one word "Tiger," with which Ali Kul fled round the corner as for dear life.

Dilarâm sat herself down on the topmost step and essayed to be sternly composed despite her lack of breath.

"Wast talking to thyself, child?" she asked.

Mihr-un-nissa had drawn her veil decorously over her face, but it was sparkling with mischief. "Nay, nursie," she replied coolly. "I was asking my cousin Ali Kul how he had lost his eye?"

Dilarâm gave a little shriek and beat her hands over her head. "Would he had lost both ere he came prying," she said vindictively; "and he is not thy cousin, nor anything to thee at all."

Mihr-un-nissa's eyebrows levelled themselves to a frown. "He can be my husband, anyhow, if I choose," she remarked, as, skipping lightly over Dilarâm's big body, she flew like a mountain fawn down the perilous stairs.

She was sitting on her father's knee, cuddling close to him, ere Dilarâm arrived, and the latter, despite her indignation, had not the heart to disturb the family group by a recitation of the enormity that had been committed. The more so because the good man was in full swing over the tale of his favourite Ali Kul's prowess, to which Mihr-un-nissa was listening somewhat disdainfully.

"Lo! child," reproved Ghiyâss-ud-din. "Even if 'twas but, as thou sayest, a tiger, and though Heaven be praised, he hath *not* lost an eye, yet 'twas a brave deed; for look you, the Prince was in danger from the savage brute when Ali Kul turned on it with bare arms and a stick. Yea, and when the stick broke and both arms were bitten through, he struck it on the jowl with his bare fist and gripped it by the throat, so that they rolled over and over together like two wrestlers. So, through being too near, the savage beast could use neither claws nor teeth, and fear fell upon it. And doubtless Ali Kul would have strangled it had not consciousness left him. Whereupon the tiger gladly left him lying and made off."

Mihr-un-nissa's disdain had gone; her eyes were shining.

"Did it get away?" she asked almost in a whisper.

"Nay!" replied her father; "and here comes in courage. For Ali Kul, regaining sense, followed it and brought it to bay once more, holding it so until others came up to despatch it. 'Twas a brave deed."

The little lass upon his knee said nothing, but that evening as she sat holding her knees tight to her chin after eating her supper, she suddenly announced: "When I marry I shall marry a brave man."

Dilarâm, outraged, scolded her best, but it was the beginning of a new outlook on life for Mihr-un-nissa. She was not always at play now. Sometimes she would sit and dream for hours, and nothing pleased her more than to learn by heart the versicles of Hafiz, or, with Khanzâda Râcquiya Begum's help, to imitate them; for the embargo on love in favour of the Creator had been withdrawn.

So the day of departure from the Garden of Roses came when she was nigh fourteen. At this time she herself, nurtured amid scent and colour, sweetness and beauty, was like some fragrant bud about to open. If all who saw her, even when youth had passed, are agreed upon her extreme beauty, she must indeed have been a "sight for sair een" as she sat for the last time in the birdcage cupola overlooking the sea of roses.

It was dawn, for she had spent a wakeful night thinking of the new world of men and women into which she was about to step, and with the first blink of light she had stolen up for a last look on the world she was leaving.

The sky was clear as a topaz; not a cloud. The great cactus hedges, devoid of their flickering satellites, showed pearly-tinted. It was still so dark that in the sea of roses the grey-green leaves seemed to obliterate with shadow the pale pink of the flowers.

But all was so still, so soundless, that you could hear the faint bursting of the rosebuds as they opened. It was just a sigh—less than a whisper—telling of an entry into the lists of beauty.

Mihr-un-nissa held up her hand instinctively to listen.

As she did so, the little lacquered cup with which she had played as a child, and which for the last day or two she had insisted on carrying about, slipped from her slender wrist and fell into the sea of roses below. She craned over to trace its course if possible; but she could see nothing—nothing, unless that shadowy rope of a thing was a black cobra. What matter? When day came Dilarâm would go and find it.

And sure enough, when that good soul heard of the loss, she was for searching at once. Vaguely, at the back of her mind, the orthodox Mahomedan woman credited the *jogi's* cup with all sorts of heathenish sorceries that, impious though they were, still brought luck, and she was determined her darling should not be deprived of it; especially now when womanhood awaited her.

So she ambled forth on the sly, taking tent to her steps when she neared the place by reason of the old snake-charmer's caution regarding the attraction the toy had for snakes.

And sure enough, just under the cupola's bastion, coiled round something like a bird upon its nest, was a huge black cobra. She had to summon up courage to curse it solemnly in God's name and her best Arabic; but it obeyed the mandate of the Most High, and slid away.

Dilarâm, coming up to see what it had held so precious, sat down helplessly in sheer surprise. For there lay, like a broken shell, a lacquered mould, as it were, of the red crystal cup that lay beside it! She took it up curiously. Was it crystal, or could it be a real ruby cut to cup shape? She could not tell. But it was the child's, and no one else must have it. Yes, it was the child's; for there lay its hiding-place, which must have been broken by the fall.

Did this explain the desire of the split-ears and the long-haired to get it? Was it really ruby, therefore without price? Or was it also *talismân* and luck-bringer? Both, maybe. Anyhow, it was the child's. Yet if it was given to her, and if it proved valuable, it would be taken away from her.

Half an hour afterwards, Dilarâm, all grunts and grumblings, gave back to its owner a little lacquered cup, bidding her be sure and not lose it again, since in the finding of it she, Dilarâm, had nigh been bitten by a cobra.

Mihr-un-nissa took it carelessly. "Why didst trouble, nursie? I could do without it better than without thee."

And she threw it aside with a laugh. Dilarâm chuckled to herself as she went off. The child knows by instinct 'tis false; so, the real is *talismân*, for sure. And she holds it firm through me, who would give my heart's blood for one breath of her body!"

CHAPTER VI

"The clamorous cry of birth is but the Voice
Of Self's command; 'Set wide the Door of Choice,
That I may enter! I, and I alone,
Choose that for which I sorrow or rejoice.'

"Oh Foolish One! Know that the Door of Choice
Opes not for you or me. Long since a Voice
Bid it be shut or open at His Will
Who sends man tears, or bids his heart rejoice."

PRINCE SALIM was fighting quails in the topmost story of the Palace of the Four Winds, where he had so often played as a child. It was given over, as it had been then, to his desires and delights; and they were not all innocuous. A big, handsome, lazy-looking lad of sixteen, he lay on an embroidered quilt watching with yawning indifference the savage fury of the brave birds pitted against each other.

"'Tis three to 'Cock-o'-the-Walk,'" said Lâla, the Prince's most intimate companion, as, with a feeble flutter, one of the combatants fell over on its side, spent to death, while the conqueror gave shrill cries of victory.

The Prince frowned. "Match him with 'War-King'—'tis the best bird we have, and the upstart needs a lesson."

The hot air seemed to quiver; the quail in the hooded cages echoed the cry of conquest; the tiny victor, breathless but complacent, strutted up and down the white cloth that was spread for the fight—it was spotted with blood—and waited for renewed fray.

But this was a very different antagonist, older by a year, sleeker in plumage, knowing the ways of warfare. Overmatched from the beginning, the younger bird fought desperately, helplessly, and a roar of reckless laughter from the group of lads who were watching the game followed on a sudden spring which brought it to the ground, fluttering in surprise. But at the same time a grave voice came from behind.

"Art not ashamed, Shaikie, to lounge idle, watching God's creatures suffer for thy amusement?"

Prince Salim rose sullenly; it was his father, the Emperor Akbar.

"Death is the right of all, sire," he replied, not without wit.

"Ay," retorted his father sharply; "but death as God sends it, not as man. Of a truth, wonder holds me how thou canst be son of mine to take pleasure in such cruelties."

He pointed to the beaten bird, whose blood flowed freely from the vicious wounds given by the silver spurs worn by its antagonist. Akbar's scorn grew as he marked that the younger bird was not so armed.

"Lo!" he said, and his voice was thunder. "Such is not sport—it is devil's work."

The bird, all its courage gone, fluttered, reeled round, died; and Akbar, waiting for no further excuse, strode away. This boy of his was at once his pride and his grief; for, spoilt from his earliest day, Salim was anything but a satisfactory heir to Empire. And yet, mayhap, he was nearer to his father's estimate of what that heir should be than Akbar, ever sensitive to the least failure, was willing to allow. At any rate, he cut short the somewhat ribald receipt accorded by his companions to his father's words with a round curse, seized the strutting victor, wrung its neck, and flung its body far from him; then gave curt orders to the attendants to do likewise to every occupant of the hooded cages.

"His Majesty cannot again say that the death I deal is not as merciful as the Creator's," he remarked amid the silence which had fallen, alike from bird and human voices.

"I will have quail-curry for supper," quavered the professional buffoon of the party; but Prince Salim sat glum.

In truth, his whole habit was sullenness. Like all spoilt natures, he seemed to have a quarrel with fate. Selfish, yet dissatisfied at self, he viewed all things with reference to himself, so found small pleasure in them; not even the adulation showered on him by a certain Court faction which honestly held that the lad would make a better ruler than the present ascetic occupant of the throne, who would wink at no injustice, no malfeasance, and was not to be bribed by luxury and pleasure.

In truth, the Court was at variance over the young Prince, especially in regard to his on-coming marriage with a Hindu bride.

Auntie Rosebody, to whom the Emperor sometimes listened when he would listen to none else, protested against this, almost with tears in her silvery voice. "Nay, nephew," she urged, "a truce to policy! 'Tis doubtless well to 'grind millet and sing the song of wheat' if you can impose upon folk, but to give the boy a Hindu to wife because 'tis advisable for Empire that Rajput and Mahomedans be friends is rank foolishness. See you, the torch-bearer sees not his own steps, so I, his ancient aunt, tell the Emperor full plain that he is wrong. All God's strength is truly not put into one man's body, but inside and out, that man's body is his own. So give the lad a wife of his own faith, who will know how to hold him. These Rajput maidens are high-spirited, I grant, but they know naught of our etiquette—and care not for it neither. And Salim needs etiquette to keep him straight."

Her wisdom, or unwisdom, was, however, lost upon Akbar, who had laid his plans and meant to keep to them, though others besides Auntie Rosebody objected strenuously. The Prince himself sided with neither party. In truth, he was not much interested in the coming marriage except as an opportunity for greater licence in the drinking of wine and the eating of sweets; in fact, he met the coarse jesting of his boon comrades over his coming nuptials with a sullen recommendation to mind their own business; it was nothing to him.

Despite this aloofness of the principal party, intrigue was rife, especially in the Mahomedan harem, where Bibi Azîzan held an assured position as general newsmonger. It needed but a little deft management to show herself the unbiassed partisan of other people's daughters. "Lo!" she would say with unction, "I am told the Nawâb of Futtehgarh hath a daughter of incomparable beauty, and he is Syyed too! What more suitable?" And all the while she knew that, charm for charm, beauty for beauty, wit for wit, there was no maid in all Islam to touch Mihr-un-nissa, her daughter.

But the girl was difficult. Taken to Court, she would not show to advantage. "Let me be, *amma-jân*," she said as she played with a litter of Persian kittens. "I care not to rub my forehead in the dust before the Beneficent Ladies. They are good and kind, but they love me not, and I love them not—save dear Aunt Rosebody, who laughs at me, and I laugh at her. Lo! I could sit at her skirts for hours, she is so comic."

Bibi Azîzan sighed as patiently as she could. "'Tis not manners to call a high-born one comic," she replied firmly. "But there! Water runs off a bald head, and teaching runs off thine. Thou wilt not understand till thou art married, so we must see to it without delay."

This vague threat was held over the girl's head like any sword of Damocles; but she took no heed to it. Once, indeed, she had retorted that her father would have to be consulted, and that he would most likely choose his favourite Ali Kul; but this had only produced hysterics in Bibi Azîzan and bread and water for herself, so in future she simply sat and smiled. And in truth, the astute little lady had no intention of marrying Mihr-un-nissa to any of the numerous aspirants whose mothers decorously approached the subject of betrothals.

"The child is over young," she replied. "In high Persian families 'tis not the custom to marry early, and the *Neean*, her father, being princely, will not hear of it."

So she set them aside, while in a hundred tentative ways, by a thousand tentative words, she was insinuating to the innermost Court circles that it would be quite easy to find a suitable bride, and so prevent the beauty and youth of the young Prince from being sacrificed to his father's ambitious aims. She even persuaded that honest man, her husband, into broaching the subject to Rajah Birbal, the Emperor's confidential friend; from whom, however, he got small sympathy, since Birbal was renowned for sterling common sense.

"Look you," he said, "were the youth in love, or did he even show inclination that way, I might cry halt, since love is a master, and the lad needs mastering. But, as I judge, he is not made that way. He drinks, he gambles, he plays fast and loose as he chooses, and he is sullen as a crocodile. But women touch him not, and one is as good as another, so be she is fair and comely; and *that* this Rajput maid is said to be. This being so, and the marriage pleasing the Most High, I, for one, am for letting an eldest son, like a bad penny, be useful for *once*."

And the memory of his own dissolute spendthrift darkened the Minister's face; for Lâla, the chief of Prince Salim's evil companions, was Birbal's son—his only son.

Ghiyâss-ud-din came away from the conversation discouraged; but Bibi Azîzan received the report of it gladly, for it gave her an idea—a bold one, a dangerous one, but one worth trying if it could be compassed.

"Leave all to me, Bibi," said Dilarâm succinctly when she was consulted. "What use is a duenna if she cannot conduct a clandestine interview? Leave it to me, I say, and if I manage not—ay, and without talk—weave my shroud."

And in reality it was simplicity itself. Mihr-un-nissa, accustomed to outdoor life, had the run at certain times and seasons of that self-same garden where, long years before, the eighteen-months-old child had held out a crimson rose for the Emperor Akbar to smell. What more easy then for Dilarâm to take her charge there at an unauthorized time? What more easy than to find out when the Prince was likely to be there?

However managed, by what underhand conniving, by what bribes, certain it is that one sun-setting, Mihr-un-nissa, discreetly veiled in the usual thick creamy veil worn by all women when out of doors, was left for a moment or two sitting beside a fountain while Dilarâm, apologetic, hurried off on a forgotten errand.

The girl, more independent than most of her age and station, was nothing loath. The garden was full of scent and flowers, the fountain splashed and made little rippling of wrinkles over the fair young face reflected in the water. It set her laughing, then dreaming of the quaint disaster which seems so impossible to the young—her own old age, when she would indeed be wrinkled. And what would have happened in the interval? For the first time in her life she realized that perpetual youth was hers indeed, that as woman she was custodian of the immortality of the race. So to her dreaming came an imperious voice:

"Hold my birds! I am tired of them."

She looked up to see a tall lad, heavy of brow and face. Instinctively she shrank back, pulling her veil forward; but the birds—two doves—were already transferred from his wrist to her lap, their owner had turned away, and she could but hold them as desired. In truth the task was less distasteful than it might have been, since, with her instantaneous recognition that the lad was none other than the Prince heir-apparent, Mihr-un-nissa became eager for adventure. Yes, that was Shaikie, her playmate. Memories of past supremacy swept in upon her; she saw herself domineering over the indolent, passionate, but good-natured boy—he did not look so good-natured now!

In truth, at the moment Prince Salim was in a very evil temper. He had covered his half-hearted shame and angry retaliation on the fighting quails by a heavy drinking-bout.

He had a sore head, possibly a sore heart, though he would have laughed the insinuation to scorn. He had refused to join his boon companions and had chosen solitude in the garden. Having failed to amuse himself with his pets, he was now trying to get pleasure by ruthlessly picking flowers and flinging them away after one short second of possession. To no purpose, for everything seemed savourless to-day, and he was back before the crouched up, shrouded figure, so slender, so childlike in its outlines, demanding his doves again.

But there was only one. The other had escaped from Mihr-un-nissa's listless hold, and was now cooing its delight at freedom from a neighbouring orange-tree.

The lad's face, still sodden with last night's debauch, darkened at the sight; his eyes, too engrossed with self for quick observation of others, saw nothing but his loss.

"Only one?" he queried angrily, sharply.

The reply came as sharply, with as much arrogance but without the anger.

"Ay, my lord! One has flown away—yonder."

The calmness of the answer roused his instant passion.

"Fool!" he cried. "How?"

He spoke as he was accustomed to speak to man, woman, or child; since, save his father, there was none in the land to whom he owed, or chose to give, courtesy. But in the slender girl he met more than his match.

"How?" she echoed, and her voice was disdain itself as she rose swiftly and flung out her arms. "So, my lord!" she said superbly, defiantly, as the remaining dove, thus loosed, flew to join its mate. In her quick uprising the thick veil had fallen from head and shoulders leaving her free, ablaze with indignation, beautiful exceedingly.

There was no sound save the happy cooing of the doves as Prince Salim stared helplessly at what he saw. It was daintiness incarnate, a creature instinct with life, fulfilled with all that makes life perfect, noble, worthy; and every atom of good that was in him followed his eyes, every atom of his coming manhood held out its hands to her—the one woman in the world for him.

A moment in a million! Love at first sight; most mysterious of all things on God's earth.

"Mihr-un-nissa!" he said in a low voice at last. "Yea, surely thou art Mihr-un-nissa, Queen of Women!"

Truly the mind, as it travels over the lad's subsequent life, cannot help wonder as to what that life might have been had the love which came to him that sunsetting in the "Garden of Scattering Gold," been throughout the long years their guiding star; for it was Love intangible, unspeakable, as it is known but to few, and they seldom of God's best.

Anyhow, it was a moment in a million millions, in which his past seemed to slip from him, leaving him alone with her, while the skies flamed red with the dying of day, and the bewildering scents of the garden, outwearied by the caresses of the sun, filled the air.

But the moment came and went, leaving Mihr-un-nissa coldly critical, if a trifle startled by the look which came to the lad's eyes, reddened though they were by last night's carouse. Yet she spoke kindly enough.

"Yea," she replied. "I am Mihr-un-nissa, thine ancient playmate. And thou art Mahomed Salim, whom we called Shaikie. God speed thee well, my lord!"

And with that she gathered up her veil in stately fashion and turned to go with dignity. But, seeing Dilarâm emerge from a pomegranate thicket hard by (where, Heaven save the mark! she had been hiding all the time, ready, if needs be, to come to the rescue), a sudden desire for safe shelter with another woman overtook her, and she flew like any fawn towards the duenna, leaving Prince Salim, his soul in his eyes, too bewildered by what had befallen him for speech or action. Possibly, had he known how persistent this was to be, had he guessed that it was to last till the hour of death itself—ay, and beyond death doubtless—he would have been more bewildered still.

Meanwhile, the first glance at Dilarâm's face, whence radiance would not be dismissed, told the shrewd girl something of the truth; but with characteristic comprehension she said nothing until, seated in the cool quiet of her own balcony, she had the delinquent face to face and eye to eye, without possibility of interference.

Then she rounded on her calmly.

"Thou and *amma-jân* art fools and noodles thus to try and deceive. Yet I grant 'twas well prepared. And my veil slipped to a nicety. What didst tie to it to make it so heavy?" And she held up one corner, where a distinct bulge showed carefully knotted up in Indian fashion.

Dilarâm caught at it. "Nay, child, 'tis nothing—'tis but sand. Give it me, heart's darling. Lo! 'twas not for heaviness—I swear 'twas not," she cried; "'twas only for luck!"

Mihr-un-nissa's face was almost malevolent in its acuteness. "Is sand luck?" she asked. "'Tis the first I've heard of it. Besides, 'tis hard." And all the while her deft fingers were busy over the knot.

Dilarâm tried whimpering. "Thou hast no right to say such things. Thou hast no right to suspicion me—and thy mother—oh, fie!—so foully. It was chance, pure chance!"

Mihr-un-nissa's malevolence grew cynical. "Yet, yea," she jeered. "Chance is as good as any other father to such stupidity! Chance that I had to put on my best robes because t'others needed mending. Chance that thy memory was befogged! Chance that 'twas not women's time in the garden.

Chance that Prince Salim, being sullen "—here her silvery laugh rang out—"nay, that is not chance. He is ever so, they say——"

At this moment the knot loosened, disclosing a small red crystal cup. Mihr-un-nissa turned it round and round in her hand, then looked at Dilarâm, who sat shaking her head in mingled negation and annoyance. "'Twas only for luck, I swear," she mumbled tearfully; "and God knows, the veil falling may have been that."

The girl, however, was too curious to listen. "What is't?" she asked imperiously. "How didst get it? Tell me quick, or I go to my father—and that, thou knowest, is bowstrings or a sack!"

Thus adjured, Dilarâm told the story of the *jogi's* cup from beginning to end, while Mihr-un-nissa, holding it in her hand, listened and laughed and thrilled. "'Tis as good as Alif-Laila (Arabian Nights)," she said, when it was ended, "and truly, nursie, thou art a clever old thing, and deservest pardon." Then she became serious and lifted the blood-red cup daintily with both hands; so, suddenly, held it to her blood-red lips and made as if she drank from it.

Thus for a space the reds mingled and glowed.

"'Tis the Cup of Life—my Life," she said, smiling, "and, as Hafiz hath it, I will take it with a laughing lip, even if with a bleeding heart."

So saying she tucked it away in her bosom. "And look you, pander-procuress," she continued in mock heroics, "one word of this to anyone and I tell my father, and that, thou knowest right well, is bowstrings!"

Dilarâm, who was still sitting fruitlessly shaking her head, began to nod it instead.

"Of a truth," she mumbled, her voice half tears, half satisfaction. "I hold there is none other with a right to know, since thou hast come to woman's estate. Yea, I see in thine eyes thou art child no longer. Things have been made plain to thee, and thou must keep thy luck thyself."

And she was right in a measure. The moment in a million had not left Mihr-un-nissa untouched, even though it had not brought her what it had brought to Salim; but she had been made to realize the existence of some undefinable, mysterious Power which at any moment might touch her own life. So after Dilarâm, full of assurances of secrecy, had left her, she sat with the red crystal cup in her hands, dreaming of what might come in the years, even in the immediate future. And, vaguely, she felt a sort of disdainful pity for the lad with the sodden face.

In regard to the immediate future matters marched with a celerity that was fair bewildering.

For Prince Salim, like any child crying for the moon, went straight to his father and demanded to be married forthwith to the only woman in the wide world, Ghiyâss-ud-din's daughter, his ancient playmate, whom, by chance, he had seen that day in the "Gold-Scattering Garden." There had been no question of his earnestness, or the intense selfish desire which had overlaid that first spontaneous giving of himself and all that he was worth into another's keeping.

And Akbar, surprised, had for the first time hesitated in his plan. Whereupon a turmoil had arisen in Court circles. Bibi Azîzan, beside herself with joy at the success of her stratagem, faced her husband with unusual indifference to his opinions.

"Talk not to me of the Prince's character," she said scornfully. "A man is ever what a woman makes him. Besides, he is but a lad, and dead to-day gives birth to another to-day."

"Ay," retorted Ghiyâss-ud-din dryly, "but a rope once burnt keeps its twist. Besides"—and here he took the final plunge—"the child is already betrothed to Sher Afkan, as they call Ali Kul nowadays."

Though this brought about the finest attack of hysteria to which he had ever been treated, he stuck to his point. What is more, he repeated it when Rajah Birbal, by the Emperor's desire, came to sound him, as father, regarding the possibility of a secondary marriage.

And all this time, according to the custom of the country and the age, no one thought of inquiring the opinions of the girl herself.

Only the Emperor asked of it when Rajah Birbal made his report. The latter shrugged his shoulders. "That, Most

High, I could scarce ask with courtesy. But inquiry is needless. There breathes not a girl to whom the heir-to-Empire would not be welcome husband."

Akbar's face darkened, yet lightened. "Think'st thou so, friend? Of that I am not so sure. There be some women I wot of——" And he paused. Perhaps he was thinking of one woman, a mere singer of pedigrees, to whom Empire meant more than passion. Anyhow, he was silent for a space; then he said autocratically, "I would see this girl. Bid her father bring her to me this evening."

Birbal stared. "'Tis out of the common, sire," he began.

"Nothing is that in Akbar's Court!" said the Emperor, cutting him short. "Am I not the father of my people?"

So that same evening, in the light of the seven-wicked lamp, a slender figure in white stood before the Emperor-of-all-the-Indies, while Ghiyâss-ud-din waited without.

"Wilt not unveil, my daughter?" said Akbar courteously. "I would fain see the face that Shaikie loves."

Without a word the girl threw back her veil and faced him. For a moment Akbar was silent; then he said quietly: "My son hath good taste, but not better than his father."

Mihr-un-nissa flushed slightly, but her words were simple. "I am glad I please the King."

"Wherefore?" came the quick query, but the answer was as quick. "Because they call me Queen o' Women, sire, and the duty of the Queen is to please the King."

"Thou hast a ready wit too," he said. "Dost wish to be a Queen in reality?"

She paused, and her clear eyes met his. "It depends, sire, upon the King."

His grave eyes took her in from head to foot. He recognized that here was one who might be all things to a man, and, taking her by the hand, he led her to the royal divan.

"Sit there, Queen o' Women," he said, "and give me thy desire. Dost wish to marry my son Salim?"

Her lip trembled a little. "I wish to marry no man, my lord."

"Yet thou art betrothed to Sher Afkan, they say. Is this so?"

"My father says so—and he is a brave man. I like him." She spoke quite fearlessly.

"Better than Shaikie? Wherefore?" Akbar's parental pride was in arms at once; but Mihr-un-nissa heeded it not. "Because he is better man. The Prince is but a boy."

"And thou art but a girl. So if it came to choice, thou wouldst choose the tiger-slayer?"

"It cometh not to choice," she began; but he interrupted her with a wave of his hand. "Nay, child, it doth. Either thou must marry Sher Afkan or Salim must have thee. Thou canst not hang like a ripe fruit within his reach; 'twould not be fair to him. Thou must choose——"

It was the turn for her pride to be in arms. "Then I choose my cousin," she said coldly as she rose.

Akbar stayed her by a gesture. "Lady," he said almost pleadingly, "wilt not try and love my son? This marriage to the Rajput Princess must go forward, but with all honour would I welcome thee—as daughter-in-law."

Her look almost made him quail. "Sire," she said, "they call me Queen o' Women, and I will be that to a good man, if I am not Queen in reality."

"So thou art ambitious?" he broke in.

"Of my rightful place," she said, and her small hands clasped together so tightly as she spoke that he could note the strain she put upon herself. "Great King, you bid me choose, and I have chosen. I love no one; but love is not all, and none shall say I did harm to anyone—least of all to the son of the Emperor Mahomed Jalâl-ud-din Akbar."

And with that she swept him a salaam than which no Court lady of mature age could have done a better, and asked leave to retire. Which he gave, feeling that he also had met his match, and vaguely regretful that it was impossible to secure such beauty and such wit for his heir. For instinct told him that force, even had he been inclined to try it, would have availed him nothing. He could capture the body, but the mind was beyond him, and, in truth, it was too like his own for him to think of coercion.

Nevertheless, the maiden must be given her freedom of limited choice with the least possible danger to Salim. Ghiyâss-ud-din, nothing loath at a speed which put a definite term to his wife's outcries, nothing loath at a secrecy which curtailed ceremonies, fell in with the idea of a hasty wedding, and so, ere a week was over, Mihr-un-nissa found herself in bridal scarlet with her hand tight clasped in one that gave her confidence, and as, through the long strings of thread jasmine blossoms which formed her bridal veil she looked calmly at the scar upon the bridegroom's face, she knew she was giving herself to a brave man. Seated on the Persian carpet beside him, her garments touching his, she could feel the tense earnestness with which, when the dower was named, he broke in on the legalities settled beforehand with a sum extravagantly beyond all power to pay, as evidence that never, never would he consent to part with her; and she knew she was giving herself to a loving man. So, when the time came for her to repeat after the Kazi that she took him willingly for her husband, a smile was on her lips, and the bewildering dimple showed itself half revealed by the loose strands of the flower veil.

Bibi Azîzan, of course, was in tears, but that could be put down to natural emotion, and not to chagrin. Dilarâm, at heart a woman pure and simple, could not help, like Juliet's nurse, rejoicing that her darling had found at least so proper a man. And of good rank too, since Akbar, to facilitate matters, had appointed him to the Governorship of Bengal. Therefore she was smiles and tears; mostly the former, since she was to go with the bride to the new home.

And when the marriage contract had been duly signed and the circled ceremony broke up, Sher Afkan stooped to his new wife's ear and whispered:

"Good-bye, Queen of Women! I deem it best to go at once. We shall meet later on in some Garden of Roses. Farewell, my heart, for a time."

She gave him one grateful look through the flowers, and he took the memory of the bewildering dimple with him.

And as through the darkness of the night her *dhooli* followed fast in the wake of the knot of horsemen that were galloping hard on the Bengal road, she took out of her bosom the blood-red crystal cup and held it to her blood-red lips with the hand on which shone the ring new given her by her new husband. So once more the reds mingled.

She gave no thought at all to what she left behind her. A lad, passionate, young, sullen, lying face down on the embroidered cushions in the Palace of the Four Winds, muttering to himself :

"I bide my time! I bide my time!"

BOOK II

CHAPTER I

> "Lo! as the taper wastes and wasting burns,
> So happy Life lives on itself, nor learns
> Aught of the Lesson that each Soul must know
> Till Death steps in and good from ill discerns."

How long does it take to live twenty-two years? Not long when the heart is happy; and the Queen of Women had been very happy. Perhaps not supremely so, since her nature had never been raised to its heights nor plumbed to its depths; but those heights, those depths, were so immeasurably superior to those of the ordinary woman that in the phraseology of normal life she would have been set down as one of the fortunate few who lacked nothing.

At six and thirty, history hath it that she was far more beautiful than she had been at sixteen. The extraordinary charm of face, figure, voice, manner had increased with the experience of those twenty-two years, and the dimple had become more adorable in contrast to the greater gravity of the eyes, the firmer lines of the mouth.

One regret—and that grew fainter with the passing of the years—was hers; she had no son. One had been born to her in the early years of married life, and had died when still an infant. Then had come a long period during which, comforted by her husband's absolute content in things as they were, she had schooled herself to childlessness. Finally, a girl had been born to find its way into some empty niche in its father's heart (which he must have kept concealed from her sedulously), and so round up his life into perfection.

"Talk not to me of sons, wife," he said. "See you, the whole world, as you know, is bound up for me in one woman; so I welcome this one made in thy very image."

It was not true, for the child took more after him, outwardly at any rate; but he believed it as he put his arm—his great strong arm—round her; so she smiled up into his kindly, scarred face.

The question as to whether she really loved the man she had chosen in preference to Prince Salim, whether the mysterious something she had once seen so clearly in a lad's eyes had ever touched her life, never occurred to her; partly because, kindly, loving, affectionate as he was, it had never really touched her husband's life. He was one of the many who, being made without moods, without unevenness of temperament, never feel the need of an over-mastering passion. Clear as crystal, strong, sensible, affectionate to a degree, he was so dear to her, as a friend, a son, might have been dear, that she thanked God he was no different. In brains she could not help seeing her superiority, but with this knowledge came the certainty that not one man in ten thousand would have surpassed her; thus both her own cleverness, and his comparative lack of it, sank into insignificance. Indeed, for one so palpably more intellectual, she relied on his judgment almost curiously, bringing her paintings, her embroideries, her sonnets to the bar of his opinion. If he approved, she was satisfied, for she knew his verdict to be quite unconventional and natural; while as for her achievements in conserves, pickles, jams, and the like, she trusted his taste before that of her brother Asof Khân, who was a noted gourmet of the Agra Court, and who, on his occasional visits to his sister, invariably brought with him some recipe for a new dainty. These Mihr-un-nissa concocted with infinite care, to her brother's entire satisfaction; but, as often as not, her husband would make a wry face and set his portion aside. "There be too many savours to it," he would say, "and I like them all! So my palate quarrels as which be first, and there is war in my inside also, since turmoil, once begun, invades all things!"

That, indeed, showed the most salient point in his character. He loved peace as he hated war or pain of any kind. A mighty hunter, he would yet grieve over any wounded buck or bird that escaped to suffer, though he would cut the throat of the one or wring the neck of the other without a qualm. Yet the tale of his slaughter was enormous, for his great recreation was sport, and he taught Mihr-un-nissa to shoot as straight as he did, always maintaining, indeed, that she was a surer, steadier shot at winged game than he was himself.

"'Tis a question of temperament," he declared. "Thou art far more alert than I, and it shows in the hitting of black partridge as in all else."

Asof Khân, her courtier brother, was inclined to demur to his sister's prowess in the field, though he was forced to admit that the outdoor life with its varied interests kept her wondrous young. He himself, though but a few years older, was already portly; a greasy-looking middle-aged man with loose curves about his mouth and a great flow of conversation. He came primed with all the gossip of the Court, and they heard from him—their only link with it—of the town life they had left so far behind, and regretted so little. And there had been much to chronicle, for those twenty years had not been peaceful ones. Prince Salim had drifted further and further from Akbar's ideals, had more than once actually rebelled against his father. He had been forgiven more than once also, but the minds of many were already alert over the question of the succession. Would Salim finally be chosen as heir, or his young son, Prince Khushrau, a promising lad of whom Akbar the Emperor was very fond? Not so fond, however, as he was of the still younger Prince Khurram, who greatly resembled him in many ways.

Possibly, had the Emperor been quite free to choose, his choice might have fallen on the latter; but Akbar was ever dominated by a sense of duty, and to oust an elder brother for a younger, from no cause but personal liking, was not in his code of things to be done.

So it lay between Khushrau and Salim. Asof Khân plunged boldly for the latter, and waxed hot with indignation against his young brother Sharif, who was an adherent of Khushrau's.

"He could scarce be worse as a monarch than Prince Salim promised to be," Mihr-un-nissa would say coldly, while Asof Khân sat looking at his sister with curious eyes.

"Why dost stare so?" she asked petulantly. "Art taking an inventory of me?"

"Ay!" he replied jestingly. "Dost forget that *amma-jân*—and mayhap others—will question me as to thy looks on my return?"

For Bengal being a far cry from Agra, and Bibi Azîzan never having forgiven her son-in-law for removing her daughter from Court influences, the good lady had never brought herself to pay his house a visit.

So matters stood twenty years after Mihr-un-nissa had laid her hand, not unwillingly, in that of her cousin with the scarred face. Griefs had come to their peaceful wedded life, but they had passed. Friends of her youth had died; among them faithful Zamân Shâh, who more than once had travelled conveying a caravan as far south as Burdwân in order to see one whom, with a sort of delighted diffidence, he still called his daughter. Many were the strange gifts and pets he sent her, and ever they came, accredited by some *ghazil* of Hafiz, to which Mihr-un-nissa would reply with her ready wit and easy versification, while those two, Zamân Shâh and Ali Kul, would look at her admiringly.

It had been when on the return journey from his last visit to her that he met with his death. The caravan which he was guarding to Kâbul had halted but a few miles from Thaneswar. No noise, no outcry was heard, but when morning came Zamân Shâh was found strangled in his bed. Revenge, not robbery, must have been the motive; but the whole affair was mysterious, since Dilarâm, who might perchance have given a clue, kept a close tongue.

It was safer for her heart's darling.

But though griefs had passed, joy and luck had come and had remained. So had the little red crystal cup, though for the most part it now held memories of pain, since Mihr-un-nissa, in half reliance on its talismanic properties, had ever used it as a medicine-glass when dear ones were ailing. So the mere sight of it set Sher Afkân making wry faces, and swearing that *jogi-ji* must have sent it to be the fly in the honey-pot of his life!

Thus matters stood when one day he came back from his work at Burdwân and sat him down sadly in the marble summer-house which Mihr-un-nissa had caused to be built in the middle of the garden she had had laid out in imitation of that Garden of Roses where she had spent so many years of her young life.

"It is all over, wife," he said. "Akbar is dead—the best king India has ever had—the finest man—in a way our best friend—hath found freedom."

Mihr-un-nissa left her occupation of conserving rose-leaves and came to stand beside him. "And who succeeds?" she asked after a pause. "Did the Emperor keep his promise to Khushrau and make him his heir?"

Her husband shook his head. "Nay, at the last Salim's father forgave his son once more; and—and he may do better than folk think."

Mihr-un-nissa's lip curled; she went back to her conserves. "Then must he have changed much since he was a lad. God send he may!"

Something in her tone made Sher Afkhân give her a quick glance as he echoed the wish.

"God send he may!" he cried, and with that caught up his child, a wee girl of some five years old, and went racing with her on his shoulder through the garden. Down one alley, up another, ducking his great height for the most part to avoid the branches of the flowering trees, which sent showers of multi-coloured petals upon child and man, both full of laughter.

Mihr-un-nissa watched them, now in sunshine, now in shade, and a troubled look crept to her eyes. For she was shrewd enough to see that this change of Kings might mean much. As a Prince, Salim had ever been revengeful, and from one or two things her brother had let drop, it might be that he had not quite forgotten. Anyhow, her husband was not likely to be a *persona grata* at the new Court, and his faithful service of years would count for little in his favour. So dismissal from his office might occur; not that it mattered much, since they could live on, these dear ones, quite happily without the pomp and circumstance. For Ali Kul, as she still called him in their intimate life, had never been one to care for luxury, and the child, little Gladness—who, despite her father's dictum, was growing to be his living image—would be as wholesome and as happy in the garden as it was possible for any child to be. And for herself?

She paused in her work and smiled; for she knew herself to be capable of earning a livelihood—should it come to that—in many ways; even as confectioner! And it would be strangely satisfactory to feel that those two dear ones were dependant upon her, though in a way they were so now, since it was her beauty which had brought their present luxury. And her lip curled again at the thought of the payment that had been made; for she was clear-sighted to a degree.

So she lifted out the rose-leaves from her syrup and set them to dry on the marble slab, noting with pride how they had kept their colour, how crisp, how fresh they looked. Old Dilarâm, now grown fatter than ever and rather deaf, was seated a little way off, packing the dried ones in small silver-fringed baskets, that were destined as an offering to Mihr-un-nissa's old friend and teacher, Khanzâda Râcquiya Begum; this occasional interchange of trifling presents and somewhat ceremonious letters being the only link Mihr-un-nissa had cared to cherish with that past life of her youth.

"Hast heard the news, nursie?" she said, going over to the old woman with a fresh batch of rose-leaves ready for packing. "Our lord the Emperor hath found freedom!"

Dilarâm threw up her hands. "May he rest in peace!" she exclaimed; then her shrewd, strong old face wrinkled itself in sudden anxiety. "And who hath the throne?" she added.

When she was told, she sat shaking her head and mumbling to herself. Mihr-un-nissa stamped her foot impatiently. "Out with it, nursie; what thinkst thou?"

"This!" said the old woman suddenly, unhesitatingly. "May God save the master's life!"

Her hearer stepped back, the hot blood leaving her very lips. Then she turned away angrily. "Say not such foolishness, slave!" she cried hotly. "Men are not made so—they forget!"

Dilâram, packing the scented rose-leaves away in their silvern boxes, mumbled again over her work. Men might forget some things, but not all. And why had Asof Khân ever been so curious?

Mihr-un-nissa, returning to her rose-leaf syrup, tried to set the old woman's words aside, but failed to do so. Mere revenge she had herself imagined; but this was different, and brought with it, not for the first time in her life, a sudden distaste for herself, for the beauty which makes men fight for the possession of a woman—as if it were possible to gain possession by blows!

Then her whole self, body and soul, rose in revolt against the thought that she might be the cause of danger to her husband, and she told herself the idea was incredible. Still, it remained with her, though, as the next few months passed, bringing no sign of any interference from Agra, it lessened greatly; and she was just beginning to scoff at her own dread when something occurred which was at one and the same time a relief and an insult.

Sher Afkân received, by a duly accredited envoy, a clear-cut proposition from the new Emperor that, in consideration of certain benefits—one a large sum of money—he should consent to divorce his wife, as every Mahomedan is able to do at a moment's notice, and send her to the Imperial harem.

Mihr-un-nissa read the precious document, which her husband put into her hands without comment, and felt, above all, relief. Here was legality and sweet reasonableness with a vengeance. No hint here of violence or even of calculated revenge. Salim was willing to strike a commercial bargain; the goods would be paid for when delivered. Then the insult of the proposition made her once more think of her own beauty with abhorrence, and she glanced at her husband almost piteously. He showed calm, unmoved, only a tightened grip on his sword-hilt telling of uttermost tension.

"Well!" she queried at last passionately. "What sayest thou to the transfer? 'Tis a big price!"

"What I say—or think," he replied in even tones, "counts for naught. That is why I refer it for the woman to decide. I stand in no one's way."

"And if I say no! A thousand times no!" she burst out. "If I say that death is preferable, what then?"

His whole aspect changed. Calm was gone, and the fury of the wild beasts he had so often slain informed every inch of his great height, every atom of his honest soul, as he shouted: "Then may God curse him for ever and ever to the nethermost hell, and may this hand of mine be the one to send him thither, Emperor though he be!"

His face was black with pure passion; he literally quivered with sheer anger.

Mihr-un-nissa went up to him and laid her beautful head on his breast. "Hush, my heart," she said fondly. "Walls have ears, and he is Emperor!"

He held her to him with a grip of iron, covering her the while with hot, burning kisses. Then he gave a half ashamed laugh. "'Tis not often thou seest me thus, sweet wife," he whispered, "though thy beauty is enough to madden any man."

She shrank, even in his arms. "Talk not of my beauty, husband," she almost sobbed. "'Tis such a little thing. So many have it."

"Not as thou," he protested, "and when I think—— By the Prophet! I could send my sword through his heart when I think——" He renewed his kisses, and she gave a little sigh.

"Think not, dear heart," she said almost resignedly. "'Tis not worth a thought, since thou and I art agreed on this matter. See, I will write a rejoinder in my best style and with my best pen, and thou wilt be satisfied with it."

"I am satisfied with all things that thou doest, Light of mine House!" he replied fondly. "Sure, none but a fool could be otherwise!"

Her answer was half smile, half sigh.

So the letter was written, and a full stately one it was, though Ali Kul objected to one argument therein set forth—namely, that the woman in question was now of an age when her sex ceases to be desirable. To begin with, he said it was not true; she might say what she liked; besides, Asof Khân must have reported otherwise.

"Thinkst thou," asked Mihr-un-nissa hotly, pausing in her scribe's office, "if that were so, I would——" Then her mind flew back to many a vague hint of her brother's which, viewed from this standpoint, betokened ulterior motives, and she sat silent, asking herself bitterly if even brotherly affection could not withstand the fatal lure of her beauty. But there were other arguments in the letter which pointed out that with the writer honour stood before mere greed of gain, and ended by stating curtly that apart from these considerations of the man concerned, Mihr-un-nissa, as woman, declined to be bought and sold!

It was duly besprinkled with scent and gold-leaf, placed in an embroidered silken bag, and given to the courier who had brought the Emperor's missive. He carried another packet too, a far more bulky one, being nothing more nor less than Sher Afkân's formal resignation of his office and his papers of commission.

There was no reference to his wife as to the sending in of these. He simply told her what he had done, and when, somewhat taken aback by his promptitude, she suggested time for consideration, he cut her short by saying firmly: "I remain not one other hour in the service of a man who hath so grievously insulted me—and thou also. I am no longer Governor! Nay, more: I hold no rank in the Emperor's army. I owe him no service of sort or kind. I am free. Here, slave!" he called at an attendant outside. "Take my sword; and thou—burn all my uniforms and accoutrements—dost hear? Henceforth I am no longer Sher Afkân, since that title also was given me by the Mogul. I am Ali Kul Istalijii, by birth Persian, gentleman at large."

"'Twas as that I first saw my lord," said Mihr-un-nissa softly.

Ali Kul's pleasant ugly face was irradiated by a smile. "When thou wert boy! In truth, my life, I see small difference in thee now, save that thou art taller—and better-looking."

"Naught of looks, I prithee, husband," she answered, smiling also. "Others may count them, but we—heed them not!"

So cheerfully, happily, they set the insult aside, and hand in hand strolled off into the garden to see how some new lilies a Chinese traveller had brought from the far-off hills were growing.

There were plenty such interests for these two, and the next few months passed for them even more happily than heretofore.

Ali Kul was indeed swordless, but his guns remained; so he and Mihr-un-nissa, with the little Gladness, duly carried from camping-place to camping-place in a little dhoolie all hung with bells, had many an expedition after big game and small game.

News of the Court drifted down to them slowly, yet surely, but none of it seemed to affect them in any way. They heard the new name which Salim assumed—Nur-ud-din Jahângir (Light of the World and World conqueror)—and smiled to themselves that one who was a light to nothing, and who could not even govern himself, should arrogate to his person such a title. They heard also of the harshness with which Prince Khushrau's ill-considered attempt at rebellion had been treated, and pitied the lad, who, without doubt, had been incited thereto by his father's rebellion against Akbar, and the consequent indecision of the latter as to the appointment of his heir.

"God send Sharif doth not mix himself up in it," said Mihr-un-nissa anxiously; "but he is ever hasty, and hath such an enmity to Asof that he will act contrariwise to him if he can."

"Ay," assented Ali Kul, "but I like the fellow better than his elder brother, for all his hastiness. Asof is too calculating. He hath thy father's turn for figures, but uses those of thy mother, and they are not mine."

So, after a time, they heard of the Emperor's intended shooting excursion to Kashmir and Kâbul, whereat they breathed more freely, feeling that he would be unlikely, when occupied there, to turn his thoughts Bengal ways; he would have enough pleasure without seeking for more.

Herein, though partly right, they failed to allow for a very important factor in the case—namely, that the attraction Prince Salim had so suddenly developed for the girl who had held his doves was less of a pleasure than a necessity of life. Furthermore, they did not realize the effect which his Rajput wife's recent death had had upon a mind that, with all its faults, was imaginative, romantic, and superstitious to a degree. Briefly, it seemed to him to offer a recommencement of life. He was now free to place the one woman in the world where she would have been twenty years before, had not his father thwarted his desire—to that father's own injury, be it said, since from that day when he had passionately declared he had been tricked, Salim had been at ill concealed enmity with Akbar. Then the mere method of the poor Rajput lady's death bore out his feeling that Fate was at last on his side. For it was not a natural death. She had poisoned herself, in grief, it was averred, at her son Khushrau's evil deeds. Whether this be so or not, it is difficult to say; but that the event made a great impression on her husband Jahângir is evident from what he writes of her in his memoirs.

"Her mind," the passage runs, "had been several times disturbed, such feelings being hereditary, her ancestors and brothers having shown signs of madness; but each time she recovered. However, when I had gone ahunting, she in her agitation swallowed a quantity of opium, and quickly passed away. In consequence of her death I spent some days without any kind of pleasure in existence, and for the space of four days (which amounts to twenty-four watches) I took nothing in the shape of food or drink."

Whether the latter sentence conveys truth or not, certain it is that just as Jahângir came to the throne he found himself unexpectedly free to offer the most honourable form of all marriages to the love of his youth. That this must, given his emotional nature, have had a profound effect upon him cannot be doubted, though whether it was the determining cause of his first offer of a divorce is a mere matter for guess-work.

Be that as it may, just as the roses in the Burdwân garden were beginning to blossom the next year, a bolt out of the blue fell upon the contented married pair who lived therein. A *firman* from the Emperor requiring their instant appearance at Court in Agra was followed almost immediately by the news that Jahângir's own foster-brother and most approved tool, one Kutb-ud-din Koka, who had lately been appointed Viceroy of Bengal, was approaching with a large following on Burdwân.

For what purpose? Those two looked into each other's fearless faces, knowing in their inmost hearts that it boded no peace to them.

"I misdoubt me 'tis for evil, not for good," said Ali Kul,

as with his arm round his wife's waist he read and reread the missive which bade him repair to the Viceroy on his arrival for orders. "Yet this," he continued, smiling into her eyes, "is beyond doubt! I can defend thine honour and mine own better than most."

Nevertheless, Mihr-un-nissa, even as she looked at his long limbs, his broad chest, and the still youthful poise of his whole figure, felt her heart sink. He was man indeed; but what did strength and courage avail against treachery? What even did her wit avail against autocratic powers? Yet that they were face to face with both she felt sure. A sense of coming disaster brooded over her very soul; which stood apart from her, as it were, looking down on the beauty of body in which at times it revelled, condemning it utterly. Had she only been as other women, life would have gone on peacefully. So, as she sat thinking, she took the *jogi's* red crystal cup from the silken bag in which she always carried it strung round her neck with a fine row of seed-pearls, and laid its brim to her lips.

Once more the reds mingled, but it struck cold, and she laid it back in its hiding-place with a sigh.

Was her luck leaving her?

CHAPTER II

"O Sâki! Save the Cup of Life, what Gift
Hast thou to bring us blind ones? Canst thou lift
The Veil that hides Ourselves from our own Selves?
Canst thou show Light beyond Death's dreadful rift?"

ALI KUL decided to write courteous reply to the coming Viceroy hat, having no official standing of any sort, he must ask on what business his attendance was required; to which had come answer that the Emperor desired him forthwith to leave Burdwân, and with his wife and family repair to the Court at Agra.

Again a courteous request for a reason had gone forth, to be met by a temporizing invitation to a private and unarmed meeting, when the position would be fully explained.

"I must go, wife," said Ali Kul decidedly. "Mayhap hey mean ill, but 'tis writ fair, and no brave man can refuse."

Mihr-un-nissa stood looking at Kutb-ud-din's message of nvitation with a sinking heart. But she did not attempt to over-persuade her husband. She knew him too well for that; knew that when once he had made up his mind as to what an honourable man should do, nothing—least of all personal danger—would turn him from his purpose.

"When is the hour?" she asked dully.

"I have fixed dawn," he replied briefly. "So we have he night before us, O Queen of Women!"

A night of nights, velvet-still, moonless; but the fireflies howed them the paths of the garden as they wandered up and own by the light of the stars. Their low voices were the only ound to be heard, for the very cicalas were silent. And they ad much to say to each other, much to arrange calmly, quietly; or they were both brave, and faced possibilities with firm earts.

"If, as may well be," said Ali Kul, "'tis a plot to murder ne, remember, dear heart, death is a thing decreed by God, nd 'tis His province."

She stopped him with a swift gesture. "Peace, husband!" she replied in a low deep voice. "If thou goest, which God forbid! then am I left to judge alone, and before God I will avenge thee!"

"I will avenge myself," he answered lightly. "For the man lives not who will send Ali Kul to find freedom in Paradise without journeying to Hell himself."

"Yea, yea," she assented, and there was a trifle of impatience in her tone, as if she were being tied down to something of little importance, while her wonderful eyes took on an intensity of look beyond this world. "That way doubtless thou wilt take vengeance for thyself. But there be other methods——" She paused and smiled a marvellous smile. Held in it was all the wile and wisdom of womanhood, all its infinite cunning and patient skill. "Yea," she went on, "thou shalt be avenged! The uttermost enemy shall pay the uttermost farthing."

He smiled back at her almost deprecatingly. "Be not too lavish of thy blame, then, dear heart; for, see you, 'tis never fair to judge poor men folk by what they seem to do. 'Tis only the evil they really do that merits punishment, and what that is, God only knows. Let Him decide!"

She flung her arms around his neck in a sudden passion of love. Never in all those twenty years of wedded life had she been so near the Mystery of Love as she was then.

"Nay, nay, dear heart," he whispered; "this is not like thee. Quiet thyself! There is naught worth a tear."

Was it not? she wondered, as she controlled herself, and hand in hand they passed on into the shadows of the garden.

The night slipped by; a primrose dawn followed, without a cloud. A greyness came first, then suddenly a glory of golden light stretching to the zenith. A bulbul was singing to a rose as they walked down the marble-edged path leading to the high-arched garden gate.

"Farewell, wife," said Ali Kul as he vaulted on to his bay Arab. "I return when God wills. Life has been joy; it may be joy yet."

Holding little Gladness in her arms, Mihr-un-nissa from the

corner bastion of the garden watched him ride adown the road, a simple, manly figure, unarmed, unattended, save by two running grooms. He looked what he was, a well-bred, high-born Mahomedan gentleman, conspicuous chiefly for his physical strength and bravery. Her mind went back to that first time she had seen his scarred face from the bastion of the Garden of Roses, when she was still a child dreaming of childish things, and it travelled onward until now; yet in all the long years she saw nothing in his treatment of her that she would have changed. So, with a sigh, almost acquiescent in the evil she felt was coming, she turned away.

Meanwhile, Ali Kul rode on cheerfully, though he also cherished few allusions as to the future. They might, though they would scarcely dare so much, murder him; on the other hand, the semblance of legality might be observed.

At the entry to the Viceroy's camp, a bevy of horsemen fully armed met him. He shot one quick glance at them, raised his eyebrows slightly, then, following the directions given in answer to his curt order to be shown their master's tent, rode on. But that one look had been enough for him. Mischief of some kind was meant.

At the entrance to a large *shamiâna* tent he dismounted, gave his horse to the running grooms, and strode in for his interview alone, unattended. He found the tent packed with armed men, and he set his teeth. This was to be more than a war of words!

The Viceroy, a black-bearded man of about his own age, made feint to greet him suitably, but Ali Kul waved his phrases aside.

"The meeting, my lord," he said bluntly, "was to a private interview. I was bidden to come unarmed, as I have come. Bid these men depart, or I go."

Something in his bold bearing compelled compliance. With a hasty mumble of forgetfulness, Kutb-ud-din gave reluctant orders to retire. The tent emptied save for three men, who moved close beside their master. Ali Kul's eyes fixed themselves on these contemptuously.

"My body-guard," began the Viceroy almost apologetically. Ali Kul gave a quick laugh.

"If thou needst a guard against an unarmed man," he replied curtly, "they have my leave to stay," and he gave back their angry scowl with interest; so, turning to the Viceroy, made a courteous salaam as he put the query:

"What wishes my lord with this slave?"

"Obedience to my orders," retorted Kutb-ud-din sharply. "I demand the instant attendance of thyself and thy house at Agra. The Lord of the Universe, the mighty Jahângir, ordains it. Thou hast already slighted his command in one way—see that thou slight it not again."

Ali Kul drew himself up to his full height. The tent was dark, but through the shadows his eyes flashed fire, though he still spoke in quiet, measured tone.

"My lord mistakes. I slighted the desire of the Emperor, not his command. Not even Jahângir the Mighty can order a man to divorce his wife."

"What treason, what defiance is this?" began the Viceroy, seeking a quarrel.

"Neither treason nor defiance, my lord," returned Ali Kul, still quietly. "Give to me the authority by which such demand can be made, either from the Holy Book or the Unwritten Law, and I yield. Divorce is the right of the husband, not of the King. The command could not be made; therefore treason is not, since there is no disobedience."

So far he had followed the line of argument thought out by Mihr-un-nissa, and the Viceroy was outwitted.

"Then see," he said sullenly, "that thou disobey not the lawful command to attend the Most High's court without delay. Thou *and thy house*."

Ali Kul smiled. "For myself I am at the command of the Most High. For my house, I crave the reason of this outrage; without it I refuse. Lo! even Majesty interferes not between a man and his lawful wedded wife. Death alone does that. So, if Jahângir the Mighty desire this slave to die, let him do murder here upon an unarmed man—ha!" He turned quick as lightning at a step behind him. Almost too late. The fall of a flashing knife grazed his right arm.

"So!" he shouted, and his voice was that of a tiger at bay. "If 'tis to be death I begin at the beginning."

And with the words, disdaining the assassin behind him, he sprang at Kutb-ud-din as a tiger springs, clipped him round the middle, tore him from his feet, and, flinging him high in midair, as a terrier does a rat, dashed him to the ground. The blood spurted from nose and mouth; he lay still.

The onslaught had been so swift that until now the assassin's knife had been Ali Kul's only danger; but it came again, this time gashing in on his shoulder. With another fierce cry, another lightning turn, he was round on his foe, and one blow from his closed fist literally stove in the murderer's skull.

And now, with teeth clenched and shortened breath, he faced the three men who, for a second, had stood appalled by the incredible swiftness of his attack. Their swords were drawn; he was unarmed; but to wrench one from its owner's hold by the point—though it cut his fingers to the bone—and turn to against his adversaries was the work of an instant. But to do this he had had to retreat across the tent almost to its outer wall, ere he could engage his opponents. Then it took but short time to stretch one at his feet and disable another; but the clash of arms had aroused those outside, and they were in on him ere he had finished the third.

Ay, the time of Death had come, but he meant to sell his life dear. So, his back against the tent wall for shelter, he defied them.

A terrible sight truly. All the noble nature of the man turned to the ferocity of the wild beasts he had so often mastered, every drop of his kindly blood afire for slaughter, every atom of his gentle strength given over to death-dealing.

How many he had killed he knew not, cared not. Others remained. His tally of vengeance was not yet complete. He had strength left yet——

So, half awed, they pressed round him as the dogs press round a wounded deer, scarce daring to meet his furious assaults, when suddenly, with one hideous shout of "Coward!" he lurched blindly forward, and the point of his sword, driven on by the weight of his falling body, spitted his nearest foe, overbore him, and they fell together. But as he fell his hand-grip loosened on his sword, he turned over, and lay face upwards, with his empty sword-arm outstretched as if in appeal to High Heaven, his head pillowed peacefully on his enemy's breast. He had avenged himself.

And someone outside the canvas tent wall withdrew from it a long pointed dagger red to the hilt with heart's blood, and said gleefully: "That got the hell-doomed one. He fought like a mad dog till this finished him."

They had stabbed him from behind. But what mattered it? His dead lay around him.

The Viceroy still breathed; but his skull was fractured, and Amba Khân, his deputy, was dead. Likewise the assassin whose knife had started the quarrel, and two others; while the grievously hurt were many. So Ali Kul Istalijii, even while in sheer despite they hacked at his dead body with their swords, lay content with a smile upon his lips. He had not even had time to think of Mihr-un-nissa or his little child; he had died fighting.

But over in the Garden he had never left Mihr-un-nissa's thoughts. After leaving the bastion when he disappeared from view, she had attempted to occupy herself otherwise, had failed, and had returned to watch for a coming which in her heart of hearts she knew would never come. She was so sure of this that as she walked, dry-eyed, her mind wandered over what should be done if he were dead. Like all women of her calibre, she was highly strung, what nowadays is called neurotic. So the unknown future, even for a few hours, was ever peopled for her with possibilities both of evil and of good, and as she watched she saw him lying dead, she anticipated her own grief.

She had not long to watch. A riderless horse, broken loose from the groom's startled hold, told her instantly of disaster. Yet only for one minute did she give way, only for one short minute did she sink, a cowering heap, upon the ground, moaning in her sudden anguish: "God, why didst Thou give me Beauty? Why, oh why? Lo! we were content with happiness—we were content—content!"

Suddenly she rose, grief lost in desire for vengeance. This

was no time for tears, no time for regrets. Her mind must be at its best, to piece out vengeance. She sat for a minute or two for thought, then, hurrying from the bastion, bade the servants lock the doors and still their outcries; for by this time the running grooms, following fast upon the horse, had brought word of their master's death. Doubtless, she said, he was dead, but he had died a brave man, and there must be no cowardice in his house, or in hers. So swiftly, knowing her time might be short, she set them arranging a fitting bier in the outer court of the palace. This she decked with flowers; then putting on a widow's white robes, she shrouded herself in the coarse veil till nothing but her face showed. A face beautiful exceedingly, but as terrible in its desire for revenge as her husband's had been ere death came to make it peaceful.

So, standing at the head of the bier, she waited, until a knocking came to the outer door, and voices cried:

"Open! Open, in the name of the Emperor!"

"To whom?" Her voice, strong, clear, silvery, echoed out, and could not be mistaken for that of a servant.

There was a low-toned colloquy outside; then someone said with more politeness:

"To the emissaries of the Viceroy, honoured lady."

"Bid him come himself," she replied curtly.

"But he is dead," came an incautious voice.

"For that may God be praised!" she called exultingly, adding in colder tones, "Then let his deputy come in his place."

This time there was a faint chuckle, for paid mercenaries and jealous courtiers have few regrets.

"He lives not either, Bibi," said someone evidently in authority. "Neither do half a dozen of our best men, for Khân Ali Kuli Khân Bahâdur sold his life dearly, as became—himself. So we desire his house no harm; but we have royal orders to enter and arrest. We invite compliance peaceably. If not——"

"Slaves, set wide the doors! We of this house are loyal to the law!" came sharp command in interruption.

The servants obeyed, and a party of troopers hustled in, then stood doubtful before what they saw. It was an empty flower-decked bier, at its foot a child, wide-eyed, curious, at its head a widow calm and stern.

"I claim my husband's body," said the latter, addressing the man who appeared to be in command in full, clear tones. "When he hath been laid to his rest, but not till then, I obey. God knows I will go gladly, since life here has no more to offer to the widow and the orphan."

Something in the very simplicity of the claim, its stern justice and reasonableness, struck home, even to those rough soldiers, and after a brief consultation the leader consented to delay. So, leaving a guard in possession, the rest retired, discussing amongst themselves the events of the day.

"By God and His prophet!" said one, "here is a pretty coil! The Viceroy and Amba Khân—whom we can well spare—to say naught of half a dozen good men whom we need—and that counts not Ali Kul himself, the first of fighters—all stiff and straight because a woman's fair!"

"Fair!" echoed another. "For my part I saw naught of fairness! Her face struck me cold; but 'tis the full stomach that sees God, and mine is empty as the Emperor's wine-skin; so, by Allah! let us back to fill it."

Whereat there was a noisy laugh, and they jingled back to camp merrily. Yet were they not without bowels of mercy, for when, later in the day, a slower procession came along the same road, the rough bier carried the body of a brave man decently disposed for burial, and the scarred face was bare of bloodstains and showed placid, smiling.

"Nay, let him be," said Mihr-un-nissa tearlessly when Dilarâm, wailing and moaning, would have undone the shroud to see where his wounds lay. "They stabbed him in the back. The grooms said so. That is enough for revenge."

Her calm was almost appalling in its stoniness; it was as if a marble statue spoke and walked and acted. So they laid the dead man on his bier in his own home, and she went off to superintend the preparation of a grave in the summer-house. For she had thought it all out with those clear-seeing, imaginative eyes of hers, and had realized that she would have no time to raise a suitable mausoleum for the husk which had held so brave, so dear a man; yet it could not be left to lie unsheltered, uncared for, beneath storm and wind and rain. But in the centre of the summer-house there would be security; and if she worked hard all night she might be able to cut the name Ali Kul on the marble slab that would lie over his heart; for amongst her many gifts she had somewhat of the carver's art.

"Ali Kul" over his heart. That would be enough. The rest would be graven upon hers.

All the moonless night through, therefore, she sat chiselling by the light of a flickering lamp beside her husband's bier, while the fireflies still danced along the shady paths where they had walked together but the night before.

When the dawn came—another cloudless primrose dawn—the tablet lay ready.

She would not look again on the dead face, though Dilarâm, her features swelled out of all recognition by pent-up tears, that had had to be shed in secret, urged her to it as a duty.

"Nay," she said quietly, "there will be no forgetting. His scars are graven on my heart."

Finally, the shrouders came with their monotonous chant, and the Kâzi, with his texts and choristers to give back the responses, and all went in orderly procession to the grave, in the side of which a niche had been hollowed out coffin-wise. Such a long niche! but it was a long length that was laid to rest within it, while Mihr-un-nissa watched, holding little Gladness by the hand, and the wail of the hired mourners echoed out into the garden. She stood silent without one tear till the earth was shovelled in and the marble slabs set back true and level, with the one which she had chiselled with his name just above where his heart should be.

Then she turned away, leading the child by the hand.

"Send word to the camp," she said, "that Khân Ali Kul Bahâdur's house will be ready at dawn, if fit and proper escort be sent."

Dilarâm would have had her spend the night in packing up valuables, but she would not hear of it.

"Let the murderers and thieves take all. The greater their

sin the greater their curse. Such things are of life, and death is my portion."

And in the darkness of the night she crept over to the marble summer-house that was now a mausoleum, and crouched down on the cold stones above the heart which had beat truly, not for her only, but for many. And suddenly the full meaning of the tragedy forced itself upon her, and she sank prone on the marble, laying her hot cheek upon it, while her hot hands beat themselves together unavailingly.

"Oh, curses!" she moaned—"curses on the beauty which hath wrought a brave man's undoing!"

And a great contempt for that which till then she had cherished, and a still greater contempt for the men whom such beauty made mad, rose in her, to remain for the rest of her life.

CHAPTER III

> "Ere the Stars were, my Life was set and planned;
> So to the Tavern while I give command
> God's messenger comes, and, knocking at the door,
> Shows the real order in his veilèd Hand."

It is a far cry from Burdwân to Agra; further still to the city of Kâbul, where the Emperor Jahângir was seeking pleasure.

And surely, no more pleasant place could be found. Surrounded by snow-clad hills, watered by many streams, set in the midst of enchanting gardens, it showed, this middle-June-tide, a perfect Paradise of sunshine and blossom. The presence of the great Imperial camp brought additional liveliness to its multi-coloured bazaars, while the soft undulations of the gardened lawns on its outskirts were dotted, as with flower-beds, by groups of gaily-dressed sight-seers enjoying the, to them, novel sensation of walking upon grass that was soft as velvet under their feet.

"Lo!" said a tall, stout man of about forty, plainly dressed, but bearing from head to foot the dignity that doth hedge about a king, "to traverse this with even sandalled feet would be an outrage on propriety and good manners!" He spoke easily in a sweet full voice, and smiled indolently, carelessly.

"The Most Mighty speaks truth," acquiesced an obsequious courtier; "yet even the feet of Majesty must tire after such perambulations as hath been ordained this day."

Jahângir gave a self-satisfied smirk.

"Ay!" he assented. "I do not think I ever walked so far before; but truly the body forgets fatigue while the mind is so entranced. See yonder cherry-tree. Do not its fruits, hanging like globes on the branches, seem like round rubies!" And there was a reality in his admiration which gave additional softness to his eyes and the contours of his face; a heavy face in itself, in which expression seemed over-burdened by fleshiness; yet the expression was there.

"Write that sentiment down, Record-master!" ejaculated the elder, Asaf Khân, ecstatically. "It is worthy of immortality."

And the Record-keeper lingered behind a second to set down the Emperor's remark in black and white, while the Imperial cortège moved on at the rate of a funeral procession; for Jahângir was corpulent.

It passed on through the City-Adorning gardens, first laid out by one of the great Baber's (Jahângir's great-grandfather) many aunts; and paused awhile outside it where a stretch of fallow ground sloped down to a stream. Here a gold-covered chair was set, and one by one the Emperor gave audience to architects, builders, designers; for here he proposed to lay out a new garden to be called the "World-Adorning," which should be so made that for beauty and sweetness there should not be, in the inhabited world, another like it.

And herein the whole nature of the man showed itself. What his great forbears had done that would he also do, and, as it were, go one better to boot. Since he had been in Kâbul, the spirit of his mountain-bred ancestors had risen strong in him.

He had delightedly studied the priceless memoirs of his great-grandfather, he had ordered his life according to the old pattern, and as he, somewhat laboriously, made the round of the gardens, he was tuning his very mind to that keynote of almost exuberant delight in Nature which gives us the harmonies of Baber's delightful book. He did it unconsciously, whole-heartedly; given the *milieu* of hardy soldiers and kindly friends his ancestor had had, who knows but Jahângir might have touched reality in his pose? for he was easily influenced. His *entourage*, however, was against him. The very contractors for the garden hid their greed under the sycophant's guile.

Majesty must be tired; Majesty had bestowed his soul-inspiring feet sufficiently long on the thrice-blest earth; Majesty should enter its golden *dhooli* and repair to the scented shadows of the private apartments. Wheedlings, coaxings, flatterings, while in the centre of the posturing courtiers sat the monarch, heavy of feature, *blasé* of heart, yet fulfilled withal with desire to act up to the present ideal. A pitiful enough spectacle, not without its pathos.

But there was one thing more to be done, ere drugged rest was his. He must, in company with a select circle of innermost Court ladies, visit the tombs of his ancestors. Khanzâda Râcquiya Begum, for instance, had never before visited her grandfather's grave. He must go thither with her in approved fashion. So, surrounded by worshipping females, dispensing his sad smiles like a sacrament amongst them, he journeyed to the simple tomb overlooking Kâbul city, where Baber rests.

"HEAVEN IS THE ETERNAL HOME OF THE EMPEROR BABER."

So runs the legend that uplifts itself into the empyrean, as if for all worlds to see.

A noteworthy group, this, above the resting-place of one of the most lovable men who ever lived. A man of many faults, but with a heart large enough to hold them all and leave enough for charity—the greatest of all virtues. The small bowed figure of old Râcquiya Begum, her heart full of conventional regrets, her kindly mind, under all its pious reverence, working away at the ode she meant to compose on the occasion. She brought a stiff posy of tight-packed flowers to lay on the grave. Jahângir, fresh from the reading of the Memoirs, had a bunch of mountain tulips as his offering. Runners had been sent to fetch them from distant uplands, and Jahângir felt a thrill of pride at the appropriateness of his own offering. For the moment he was the man he wished to be; for the moment he was the Light of the Faith, the Encircler of the World.

There were tears in his eyes as he looked out over the glorious panorama of hill and dale, of forest and stream, of earth and sky.

So his great ancestor had stood, radiant with admiration; so Jahângir stood, for that ancestor's attributes were latent in him. But only for a moment or two. The time for drugged rest had come. As the gold-encrusted *dhooli* of state jostled through the bazaar to the Bala Hissar palace he was already half asleep. He scarce opened his eyes upon the scented women-folk who crowded about his couch in the private apartments; he yawned faint pleasure at a pet monkey's antics as he munched an aromatic comfit heavily laden with opium. So to the sleep almost of the dead, inert, helpless. But there were guards to watch it. Stalwart Abyssinian women with drawn swords at each door and stealthy footsteps of spies in the Persian carpeted corridors; for despots need guards, and Jahângir was despot if ever there was one.

So to wake, yawning, at sunset and ride under a royal umbrella, scattering rupees, half-rupees, and quarter-rupees to indigent persons on both sides of the road, till he reached the Shahâra gardens, which, in the evening light, looked green and fresh.

Being Thursday, the Emperor was giving a wine-party to his intimates, and they were all awaiting his arrival in the twelve-doored marble summer-house that stood on the very bank of the stream that ran through the middle of the garden. A pellucid stream, no more than eight feet wide, that rippled over a pebbly bottom with a tinkling babble. The summerhouse was hung with gold tissue, and set with thick silken rugs, and littered with embroidered cushions. Tall eunuchs with jewelled fans stood ready to whisk away intruding flies; bare-footed, obsequious servants flitted about with gold and silver beakers; from behind a screen came the fine whinging of a *satara* and a man's voice chanting a love-song. Every now and again a tiny boy dressed as a girl came round with a silver dish of rose-water and a heron's plume brush, with which he sprinkled the air to make it cool and perfumed.

Of enervating luxury nothing lacked; the very guests in their stiff brocades, their faces set in flattering smiles, seemed as it were mere stage properties to the heavy figure lolling on the divan, its restless eyes roving about in search of pleasure.

"If the Lord of the Universe consents, his slaves have arranged a cooking entertainment as a preliminary, and *arghushtak* dances to follow on the opposite bank of the stream," said the Master of the Ceremonies, touching the ground with his forehead. "Is it approved?"

"*Manzur*," murmured the monarch, handing his golden beaker to be refilled.

So, over the water, a crowd of men and boys appeared; small portable braziers were brought, filled with glowing charcoal, and ranged in two rows; sides were chosen; and swiftly, with laughter, singing and dancing, the *bughra*—a kind of long, very slippery macaroni—was cooked. Then the fun began. Each side flung the slithery comestible at the other side's open mouths, and loud was the merriment both amongst the competitors and the spectators as the macaroni was caught or missed. Even when caught it was no light matter to swallow the long length.

"Quick, slave, quick!" chuckled the Emperor, as one vainly tried to bolt a yard-long piece that in the throwing had coiled itself round nose and ear. "Quick, or thy last chance is over!"

It was a booby game, but it pleased, and many a cup of good Shirâz had gone down ere it ended. Then came a quieter entertainment. Twenty young men, and the like number of young girls, each with great bunches of oleander blossoms stuck behind their ears, circled themselves in couples round a group of musicians and awaited the signal to begin. But custards and confections were being handed round to the guests, so there was a pause. Jahângir's full voice rose on it with all the solemnity of the half intoxicated.

"'Tis a fine flower-bed. Mark you, chamberlain! Who loses his oleander in the dance hath his turban taken off to show his bald head."

"Ha! Ha! Ha! Ha! Witty beyond compare!" cried one of the intimates, while another said unctuously, "And if the offender be a female, what punishment hath the Crown of Intellectuality ordained?"

Jahângir thought for a minute; then said thickly, "None. Woman, being the flower of—of this world—is—is exempt."

A chorus of praise went up, and the Court Recorder's pen was called into use once more. Meanwhile the dance went on—a stately sort of circling measure, with rapid shiftings of feet and clappings of hands.

Jahângir yawned, once, twice. Then suddenly he held up his forefinger—the finger of majesty. The music ceased, the dancers disappeared. With cups in their hands the onlookers were left staring at the empty lawn, across which the moon, new risen, was beginning to throw long shadows.

"If it pleases the Shadow of God," came the voice of the impresario rather quaveringly, since the last entertainment had fallen somewhat flat, "there be a poet here who, though he be of the Hindu faith, hath composed an ode in honour of the Most High, and craves leave to recite it."

The Emperor, now half full of wine, gave an assenting hiccup, and a thin old man came forward and began to chant as follows:

> "If the Sun had a son the world would ever have day;
> Night would be no more known for ever and ever alway.
> For when one gold-crowned head sank out of our sight
> The other would take his place and keep the world still light.
>
> "O King! like the Sun, your father was given a son
> To sit on his throne after he went to his rest,
> And illumine the world as brightly as he had done,
> Driving the night of mourning from every breast!"

Atrocious doggerel though the verses were, they were received with loud, fulsome acclamation by the courtiers, while Jahângir sat solemn, almost tearful, thinking of his own virtues and his father's. Contrasted with the chill purity of the world outside, now bathed in the light of the new-risen moon, there was something almost revolting in the artificial atmosphere within the summer-house, where a dozen or more of men conspired to pander to every weakness, every vice of another man. The air was heavy with adulation, poisoned by insincerity, infected by intrigue. From the applauding sycophants to the toothless old man bowing and grinning over his rhymes, the miserable victim of these wiles could not hope for one helping hand to aid him in self-government. It says much for him, therefore, that his mind, refusing to dwell on himself, passed to memories of his father.

"'Tis ten years since I sat here with that blessed one," he said, after having awarded an elephant to the poet as reward for his eulogy—"ten years since he, laughing, bade me follow him over the stream yonder. Could I jump it now, I wonder?"

"Wonder is unnecessary," said an intimate rather thickly. "The Lord of the Universe can do all things."

It was an unfortunate remark, for Jahângir was in that preliminary stage of drunkenness when everything seems cause of quarrel.

"How knowest thou, slave, when I know not myself?" he asked angrily, and rising unsteadily to his feet, he looked out over the water, shaking his head.

"Lo! I will try," he continued, "and thou shalt try also. Stay! we shall all try in turn, and thou shalt go first—go!"

The wretched man tried to excuse himself. At the best of times he could not have compassed a six-feet jump, and at the moment he was not sure of his own feet; but the fun of the thing had seized on Jahângir's mind, half sobering him, and he was eager as a boy over the idea.

"See now!" he cried. "Thou shalt be starter, Mohabat! thou art too old to compete—but the others be all under forty—now, Dilawari, 'tis your turn first—jump!"

Down by the banks of the stream they stood, the bevy of courtiers in their stiff brocades, Jahângir, towering above most of them, while Dilâwar Khân, after two futile runs, took the leap. A roar of half-drunken laughter greeted his ignominious fall in midstream.

"Swim! Swim for thy life, man!" almost shrieked the Emperor, beside himself with delight as the miserable man, wet through, scrambled out of two feet of water. Another and another followed, one escaping with a wet foot only, while one cleared the jump easily, amid frantic plaudits, led by Jahângir, who shouted, "Captain of 1,000 horse for that, Afzul!"

Last of all came the Emperor's turn. By this time a dozen or so of more or less soaked sycophants were sitting on the opposite bank, half sobered by their dip, shivering with the chill, but ready still with flattery, as Jahângir, with a very creditable effort considering his corporation, took a wild leap and precipitated himself on all fours amongst them, amid cries of "The Emperor wins! Long live the Pillar of the Faith, the Agility of the World!"

As they helped him to rise, he looked round on them distastefully.

"Yea, I have jumped it," he said, "but now that I am nigh forty years of age, I did not jump it with that activity I showed when I was thirty in the presence of my revered father. So, gentlemen, to bed, for ye are wet!"

The royal litter crossed the stream at the word, the bearers wading knee-deep through the shallow stream, and the atmosphere of adulation and sycophancy and flattery seemed to come with it, as the dripping courtiers crowded round obsequiously, bowing, prostrating themselves, calling on High Heaven to bless His Imperial Majesty, the Greatest Monarch on Earth (and, incidentally, the best jumper!). So Majesty ambled off, preceded by linkmen, followed by a posse of troopers, and flanked by those unfortunates whose duties were not yet over.

Thereinafter peace reigned in the garden and in the rest of God's world. But far away down the valley on the road that trends from south to north there was a jingle of bells, and a man lithe of limb, guiltless of clothing, with a pike over his shoulder, and a hoopoe's feather in his rag of a turban, was running for all he was worth; for he was a Government *harkâru* bringing news.

From hand to hand it had come through long nights and days, for—as has been said—it is a far cry from Burdwân to Kâbul city; but when a royal messenger is waiting every six miles upon the road, ready equipped to seize the packet and start off with it at full speed, posts travel more quickly than one would deem possible, without the aid of metalled roads or railways.

And the Moguls were ever particular as to their posts. By field pathways, across hill and dale, through flood and tempest, rain and snow-storm, they might have to go, but go they must and that quickly. Moreover, night and day they must be delivered. And so, ere Jahângir the Mighty retired to rest he listened to a letter which had never paused a second since it was written in far away Burdwân. And this is what it said, after the usual salutations:

"On the 3rd Sufar, after the 3rd watch, Kutb-ud-din Khân, foster-brother, obtained the Mercy of God in this wise. Having orders from the Most High to bring Ali Kul, commonly called Sher Afkân, to Court, and if he showed any futile seditious ideas to punish him, the said Kutb-ud-din Khân, immediately the order was received, went hastily to Burdwân. Sher Afkân, becoming aware of his arrival, went to receive him alone, with two grooms.

"The aforesaid Khân, knowing Sher Afkân's character, immediately surrounded him. This proceeding raised doubts in Sher Afkân's mind, to relieve which the aforesaid Khân gave him a private interview, when the vicious fellow, drawing a concealed poniard, stabbed him in several places. Amba Khân Kashmiri, with loyalty and manliness, rushed to his defence, but also received a severe wound. Whereupon the troopers fell on Sher Afkân, cut him to pieces, and sent him to hell. It is to be hoped that the place of this black-faced scoundrel will always be there——"

So far the Court reader had read without interruption, while Jahângir, the little cup of aromatic opium he had been about to take still in his hand, reclined heavily on the divan, listening. The more potent effects of the wine he had swallowed had passed, leaving him dull in intellect, alert in emotion. Now, with a sudden gesture of abandonment, he tossed off his potion and flung the cup away. It crashed and shivered on the wall.

"Enough!" he cried. "Enough for to-night!" Then he leant forward, his dull eyes ablaze. "Write, slave, write and return by swiftest runners. Jahângir commands that the rebel's house be treated with all reverence. So now for dreams—for by God and His prophet I am tired—yea, weary of many things!"

CHAPTER IV

> " Friend, play no Game but Love within the House
> Of Life's illusion! Let the fool carouse
> Over the wine-cup! Keep thou to the Arch
> That shelters Sight upon the loved one's brows."

THE journey from Burdwân to Agra was necessarily slow, yet its very slowness served to dull the tragedy which had preceded it. Day after day Mihr-un-nissa's tearless eyes looked out upon new scenes, day after day she knew that, even physically, she was leaving those twenty years of happy life behind her. Every rhythmed footstep of her *dhooli*-bearers along the dusty road told her that she was being sent forward by Fate. Sent to what? She asked herself the question over and over again, and the easiest answer seemed death. If the worst came to the worst she could always kill herself; but to her intense vitality it seemed a miserable thing to do. It seemed a confession of failure. Even the revenge of plunging a dagger into the real murderer's heart seemed poor. It would be over in a moment, and her soul craved long drawn-out punishment. So the days passed. With an armed escort the *dhoolis* jangled on through the hot nights, the bearers chanting their monotonous appeal to keep step, to amble straight, to think nothing of the burden, to trust in God, which by degrees seemed to sink into her mind and still her nerves. During the scorching day they found shelter in some friendly official's house; for, even without the direct instructions, those who were in charge treated her with every distinction. To them the position was simple. The Emperor had heard of her great beauty. He desired her, and she, being woman, would jump at the connection. She might, of course, stand out for honourable marriage, but the result was the same. With her great charm, which every man in the troop felt through her enshrouding veil, she would likely be favourite; therefore powerful. So they treated her as if she were already their mistress, and allowed her such freedom as was consistent with safety. Sometimes in the bright moonlight nights that had succeeded the dark ones, they would order the bearers to set down the *dhooli* at her desire, and allow her to walk up and down under the enshading trees for half an hour, while they smoked their pipes; for, after her outdoor life, she felt the need of action sadly.

One night, just outside the city of Cawnpore, where they were to rest some days, and where she knew she would necessarily be shut up within four walls, she asked for this privilege, and it was granted. She had chosen her ground well, for an avenue of glorious *shishum*-trees stretched level down to the river. But for the intensity of the white moon-shafts that barred the road in lessening lights it would have been dark beneath the over-reaching branches. To one whose past was so bright, whose future loomed so black, there was something exhilarating in passing at a step from shine to shadow, and then back again from shadow to shine. She wandered on to her tether of two hundred yards or so, and was about to turn in a longer break of light than usual when a faint hissing sound in the shadow beyond made her step forward curiously, fearlessly.

A snake, certainly! Nay, two! Two huge black cobras half erect, swaying with expanded hoods; the light caught their glistening eyes every now and again. And between them on the ground, what was that? Her sight, becoming accustomed to the shadows, made out the form of an old man lying face downwards on the ground. From his position it was evident he had fallen forwards. He had been carrying a *bhanghy*, for the yoke lay beside him, the baskets at either end jarred open by the fall.

It struck Mihr-un-nissa in a second that he must have been a snake-charmer, and that the two cobras were likely his stock-in-trade; therefore harmless. It was as well, however, to be on the safe side, so, seeing the gourd flute of his trade lying beside him, she took it up and blew into it; for the desire for adventure, for action, was ever hers.

The hollow note echoed out true to tone, for she had not forgotten lore learnt in childish days from the old snake-charmer in the Garden of Roses. At the sound the swaying hoods wavered, sank, and like long black ropes the creatures slid quietly back to their baskets.

Ere they reached them, some troopers, roused by the sound, came running, and stood amazed.

"The Bibi hath the charm of the snake also," said one almost fearfully as she coolly held the lids over the reptiles, pressed the latter down as if she had been accustomed to the task all her life, and then fastened the snicks.

She was on her knees by this time examining the fallen man. "He bleeds still," she said, "and 'tis from a wound in the back. There hath been treachery," she added with a sudden inrush of sympathy, "but he still lives——"

"Ay," said a trooper callously as they turned the wounded man over. "He breathes still; but not for long, since there are none to succour his wound here on the high road."

Mihr-un-nissa stood up, autocratic. "There be travellers, as he was. How far is't to the city? A mile, or two, or three? Then I walk, he has my litter."

There was no gainsaying her; indeed, admiration for a courage rare—nay, almost unknown—to their experience of womanhood would, anyhow, have prevented opposition.

So through the moonlight, wrapped in her thick veil, Mihr-un-nissa walked by the side of the litter that held Dilarâm and the child. Ere she had gone a dozen yards, however, she turned back suddenly.

"The snakes!" she said. "God's creatures must not starve!"

"Nay, Bibi," remonstrated the Captain of the Guard hurriedly. "Wouldst let loose death upon the world?"

She gave a short laugh. "Ay, that would I," she said bitterly; for she was of two moods. One, open resentment at all men; the other, pity for those who suffered.

Dilarâm would have got out and walked herself, but her mistress was firm; they would never reach Cawnpore at her rate; she had better stay where she was and let those who could walk.

Thus it came to pass that, more light-hearted than she had yet been, Mihr-un-nissa, invigorated by the welcome exercise, found herself in the early dawn attending to the wound of the man she had picked up on the road; for she was learned, as her mother was also, in the use of simples. He was still unconscious—or nearly so, for he swallowed the medicament she gave him in the red crystal cup—but this appeared to be due more to a blow on the head, or his fall; for the wound seemed to be that of a knife, which had glanced off his ribs. So she left him in the care of a door-keeper, and later on in the day sent Dilarâm to see how he fared. The latter found him greatly recovered, propped up against the dark corner of the cell where he had been left. Her first glance at him brought her disturbance. Where had she seen that face before? She was puzzling her brains when the old man, salaaming down to the ground, said quietly:

"Hath the milk-white goat served its purpose, O! nurse of royalty?"

Then she sat down amid her flouncing skirts in breathless recognition.

"Strangler!" she gasped. "What doest thou hither, after all these years?"

"Thirty and five;" he answered. "Lo! I was not young then. To-day I am old beyond most men's years; yet am I fit for my work—ay, more than most men, though the Bunglers think not so."

"Dost—dost strangle still?" asked Dilarâm in a tremulous whisper.

He nodded. "Ay, when I have the chance; but it comes not often when one is full of years. Yet was I the Head. That is why the Bunglers would have killed me; but they bungled, as ever."

Dilarâm snorted; she was beginning to lose her dread of the man. "Traa!" she said. "Bungling would neither have been in three or thirteen had not my mistress rescued thee from snakes and wounds, and dust and death, and God knows what! So there!"

He salaamed again to the very ground. "This slave knows that," he replied. "He knows also that royalty still holds the *jogi's* luck. He drank of it last night. It brought life to him; so he owes life to the holder of it for ever, and ever."

He droned the last words out as if sleepy, laid his head back against the wall, and closed his eyes.

Next morning he had disappeared, rather to Dilâram's relief.

"Bungler or Strangler, I like not the breed," she said as she told the tale to her mistress. "Hadst the Bibi seen done what I saw that night in the tent she would find a difficulty in swallowing even as this slave does." And she cleared her throat ostentatiously.

Mihr-un-nissa, looking listlessly out of window, said dryly: "'Tis pity he hath gone. He might have proved useful." She was thinking of the future which she knew must be coming.

After that, the journey onwards was without incident, save that more than once a trooper in the escort would say to his neighbour:

"Hark! the black partridge cry once more! I like it not. There be Stranglers* about!" And his neighbour would look keenly through the tufts of tall tiger-grass and tighten his grip on his sword.

Arriving in Agra, Mihr-un-nissa, her child, and Dilarâm were, as the former had expected, given over to the care of the Keeper of the Royal Harem. Practically they were prisoners, though they were allowed to see visitors. Ghiyâss-ud-din was away with the Imperial camp, but Bibi Azîzan came in hot haste, full of gushing if somewhat insincere sympathy. She found herself repelled. Mihr-un-nissa could not forget her lack of it for her husband. Almost fortunately, however, there was a common grief which they could bewail together. For news had just come from Kâbul of a conspiracy against Jahângir's life in which Mihr-un-nissa's brother Sharif was heavily implicated, and for which—quite justly—he paid with his life.

"Lo!" wept Bibi Azîzan, "I have told him full oft what would be the end of his favouring Prince Khushrau. But he hath had an ill spite at the Most High, ever since he was Prince Salim, and ——" The good lady paused in her tears. The reminiscence was, under the circumstances, scarcely tactful, for her heart was high with hope.

* The Thugs or Stranglers use the call of the black partridge as their warning cry.

Her pause, however, was too late, for Mihr-un-nissa said quietly: "Ay, he ever favoured me, did Sharif, even as a lad. And Heaven only knows what 'twas that made him thus rash—now!"

She sat silent, her eyes travelling over the distant landscape of curving river and wide plain which was visible from the balcony of her turret room. It might well be so, she thought. Yea, it might well be that her brother, hearing in Kâbul, whither he had gone as attendant on the disgraced Prince, of Ali Kul's murder and her capture, had with his usual hot-blooded resentment resolved to compass Jahângir's death in revenge. If this were so, she could not blame him; and circumstances favoured this explanation. The Emperor had left Kâbul city, averring that he had tasted all its pleasures, and was anxious to go on his desired way, almost immediately after the news from Burdwân must have reached him. He had, in fact, commenced the return journey with unwonted haste. At the second march out, the conspiracy to kill him during one of his daily hunting expeditions had been discovered, condign punishment had been meted out to three of the ringleaders, but without fuss, for fear of delay, while Prince Khushrau had reverted to the chains from which he had been released while Jahângir, in Kâbul, had been imitating the clemency—amongst other things—of his great-grandfather Baber.

Mihr-un-nissa, wearily awaiting developments, felt that once again her beauty might be responsible for death. She had not seen Sharif, her brother, for years, he had ever been unreliable; but he was her brother, and the possibility that he had died in defence, as it were, of her husband, made his death all the more grievous; though with her usual clear-sightedness she admitted his punishment was just, inevitable.

Majesty could be maintained no other way.

Dilarâm, returning from the bazaar with her purchases of food—for from the first Mihr-un-nissa had refused to eat the Emperor's salt—found her mistress in the balcony at her tambour-frame. She had set to work at once on embroidery as a means for making money, and being keenly alive to the necessity for quick return, was hastily turning out cheap, easily sold caps in preference to more elaborate work which would take time in preparation. That could come after, meantime it was food she required, and must have. Even in such small things her mind was curiously clear; even in commerce she would have made her way.

She counted out a dozen of the caps and flung them across to Dilarâm.

"That for thy purchases," she said lightly—"two annas each beyond the cost of stuffs. The rest I keep to pay——"

"For the mistress's shroud mayhap," retorted Dilarâm crossly. "Lo! the Bibi grows thin, and 'tis not becoming."

"Thank God for that!" replied Mihr-un-nissa with sudden, almost overpowering earnestness; for that coming interview with the Emperor which she foresaw was ever at the back of her mind. Not that she was afraid. If the worst came to the worst it was but death. And through that Great Adventure Ali Kul had already passed. She would find his lost companionship there.

Meanwhile, all her care must be to secure safety and freedom for his child. But here a difficulty arose. If little Gladness went to her grandmother, which was feasible, since none wanted to imprison the poor child, Dilarâm must go with her; to none other would Mihr-un-nissa trust her. This, however, would leave the Bibi without anyone on whom she could rely, without even a faithful messenger between her and the world, and to this the old nurse would not agree. Yet it was difficult in Agra to find a substitute. In Burdwân it would have been easy; there, all were devoted to Ali Kul and his house.

So matters stood when one day the harem door-keeper reported an old woman, ancient servitor of Ghiyâss-ud-din's house, who desired to kiss the feet of her patron's child.

"'Twill be old Amina, the cook-woman," said Dilarâm, nodding approval from the carrots she was scraping for a stew. "I saw her, seeking this servant a while back, and she said she could not virtuously die in peace till she had sought dismissal from the Bibi whose first food she cooked."

"Bid her in," said Mihr-un-nissa, smiling. But it was not old Amina; it was a stranger neither of them had seen before. A quaint, wrinkled old woman, scanty of teeth and hair and veil, but withal respectable to a degree, who prostrated herself on the ground, then rose to stand with bent head and hands joined after the most approved etiquette.

"What will'st thou, mother?" asked Mihr-un-nissa kindly.

"This slave seeks permission to pay back what she owes to the noble people," came the answer in a high cracked voice. "Being past work as maid-servant, she seeks service as market-woman and messenger."

"But who and what art thou?" asked Mihr-un-nissa again.

The old woman gave one sharp look round; the harem servants had retired, leaving them alone. Then she advanced quickly, squatted down close to the tambour-frame in full light, and said quietly, as a deft twist was given to her veil:

"If the Bibi will look carefully she may see."

Mihr-un-nissa's needle hand hung arrested over her work in sheer astonishment. The face before her changed as if by magic from woman's to man's, every feature seemed to alter, the very dress seemed different. Dilarâm, who was looking also, gave a gasp and sat transfixed.

"The Strangler!" she muttered helplessly. "The Strangler! God help us all!"

"Yea," assented the latter cheerfully. "That am I, by caste and occupation. And we are men of many faces, for we need the trick in our trade." He gave a little low laugh, drew down the veil, and was woman again. "If the noble lady will listen, I will tell her why I come. It is for service—to the death if need be. And the noble lady is in danger—more than she knows. After she gave me to drink out of the Cup of Luck—yea, though I was not in the body, I saw the gracious act—I found out the danger. There are those here who wanted her not, who would she died on the road. So the cry of the black partridge"—he gave it suddenly loudly, with such deadly accuracy of tone that both women started—"was heard many times from the watchers. For I am still Chief of the Tribe, for obedience, though I grow too old for execution. And now there is danger still"; his dark eyes fixed themselves on the beautiful face before him. "Lo!" he continued with a faint smile, "beauty is ever in danger from the world that is ugly, and many things are ugly in the world. So I come to sit in the outer room, and watch, and buy the food and cook——"

Dilarâm, who, half hypnotized by the low chanting voice, had mechanically resumed her work of scraping carrots, here interposed, as she scraped harder than ever:

"Traa! Cook, indeed. A likely story. Thy kind are like the glutton—eat all things with legs or wings save a paper kite and a bedstead. Not so the noble people! Besides, thou art too old—if ever thou hadst skill it hath gone—with thy teeth and hair—in relics, mayhap, like the saints beard. Ah. . .!"

She finished with a little shriek. Something long and crimson had shot out—how, Heaven only knew!—from her hearer's hands, and there were hers noosed tight round the wrists, clipped together, helpless, while the carrot and the knife fell clattering to the ground.

"The skill hath not gone altogether, sister," said the Strangler affably. "Let the Bibi judge if I am too old to be of use."

Mihr-un-nissa's brows levelled themselves thoughtfully; her face grew hard, almost savage, and something in her seemed to leap out gladly to the deadly instrument of death.

"Show me the Noose," she said imperatively. But in her hand it showed merely a worn strip of silk stained by much use, though as she slipped it, soft and compressible, through her fingers, she felt, as Dilarâm had averred, a tightness about her own throat.

"Thou canst stay," she said suddenly, briefly.

So in the old woman's guise the old man was installed as door-keeper, messenger, and general go-between. Dilarâm came at first every day to see to the cooking, but after a time acknowledged that she was but a tyro in the art, while in marketing the Strangler was far beyond her.

"Likely," she would say, darkling. "He steals the things."

But it was not so. It was only that, as one of a secret guild extending everywhere, he had a thousand avenues for power open to him.

Long before the Palace had heard anything, Phusli*—for by that name the old man had suggested, with a grin, he might be

* *Lit.*, "entangled."

called—would come back from the bazaar with news of this, that, and the other; news that was always fairly correct. "The Emperor is hurried; but he is delayed. There is time yet," he would say, and it was true.

So the days went on. It had been nigh a two months' journey from Burdwân, and now five months passed, and Mihr-un-nissa, still in her white widow's robe—for she resolutely declined the fine clothes and jewels offered her—sat in her balcony embroidering and thinking. She knew, or thought she knew, what lay before her, and prepared for it solidly; though how revenge was to come, whether by the dagger she carried herself, or the Noose which waited day and night in the ante-room, depended upon chance.

And in the end she was completely taken by surprise. Phusli had spoken of a halt at Delhi, and a hunt for game, yet as she sat in her canopied balcony one evening watching the distant lights of the city, she heard a step in the room behind her, and a voice, assured yet cautious, said: "Has Shaikie permission to interview his old playmate?"

The moment had come at last! Drawing her white veil round her closely, and at the same time unsheathing the dagger she always carried hidden in her breast, she rose to her feet.

"Prisoners have no choice, my lord; that lies with those who have power," she replied coldly, though his address had startled her.

The next moment Jahângir stood before her.

The light of the cresset by which she had been working played on the silver tissue of the robe about his feet; the light of the moon showed on his face, over massive but handsome. Fraught with terrible possibilities as the hour was, she was yet conscious that her first thought came thus: "He is taller and bigger."

Such trivialities will intrude themselves even upon tragedy.

Apparently he was startled by her appearance, for he stopped abruptly some paces from her, and passed his hand over his forehead as if to brush away some unwelcome thought. Then he spoke, one word:

"Meru!" It was the childish abbreviation of her name.

Startled again by something in his tone, she did not reply, and he stood silent, his face all broken up by passionate emotions. Then she said bitterly:

"My lord might tell his slave what he desires——"

The taunt seemed to unlock his lips, give him the clue to action.

"When there has been but one woman in the world for a man these twenty years," he said, stepping towards her arrogantly, "and she stands before him, 'tis idle to ask what he desires."

"Stand back, my lord!" she cried, stretching out her left hand in negation, the right gripping the dagger beneath her veil. "Seest thou not the corpse of a murdered man between us? Go not near it, lest it rise and kill thee."

He obeyed her gesture, but narrowed his eyes as if in perplexity.

"Dost mean thy brother?" he asked quietly. "Sure, if ever death was justly meted to a man, it was to him. Thou canst not think otherwise."

Her scorn, her passion, flamed up, her voice vibrated harshly.

"Art thou a man, O Nur-ud-din Jahângir, thus to seek escape from thine own deeds? Thou knowest 'tis the dead body of Ali Kul my husband, foully murdered by thine order."

There was a second's silence, then the answer came quietly:

"I gave no order—I——"

"Thou liest! Yea, to thy face, Salim, I say it——"

"Nay! By God and his prophet I swear! I bade them bring him hither—I——"

The passion died from her voice, the scorn remained. "Thou badest! Yea! Yea! Thou didst bid him give up honour, give up manhood, and he gave up life instead. Better that than live as thou dost, drunken, debauched, dishonoured——"

Jahângir stood, his chest heaving, his face terrible in its sudden rage, his hands stretched out towards her, clasping and unclasping themselves as if they would clutch at her throat.

"Peace, woman! Peace!" he muttered in a hoarse whisper. "Peace, or I kill thee!"

Like a flash her hand sped out with the dagger.

"Take it!" she cried superbly. "Yea, take it and kill the

wife as thou didst kill the husband. Take it, or I do the deed myself!"

With a cry he was on her, but only to snatch the dagger from her grip and fling it from him. Then he stood back once more.

Ay, he was strong enough, this drunken murderer—this——

"Mihr-un-nissa, wilt not listen?" his voice, suddenly appeased, came in almost agonized appeal. "Lo! all these years I have loved——"

"Defile not love's name with thy lewd lips," she interrupted roughly. "What dost know of love save what the wine-cup teaches? Thou hast thy one woman in the world at thy mercy here—here in this palace-prison—here amongst thy wretched minions. If thou desirest Mihr-un-nissa, O Emperor of the World, O Light of the Faith, O miserable man, why dost hesitate? She stands before thee, woman—and thou art strong man!"

Beside herself with hot resentment and passionate anger that she should be, as she knew herself to be, the weaker in body, she flung her veil from her with a superb gesture, and stood revealed in all her beauty, all her charm.

But her mind, her soul, herself, were far from him. They were with the Noose of Death that waited, she knew, beyond the closed door.

For one instant Jahângir stood as it were blinded by what he saw. Then, his face set, he shrank back into the shadow and was silent. When he spoke his voice had a break in it.

"That ends it all!" he said. "Thou dost not—nay, thou canst not understand. Yet shalt thou listen, woman, who knows not what love is, yet dares to talk of its defilement. Yea! Yea! I am drunken, I am debauched, mayhap I am dishonoured! Let that be—I care not. Thou hast said I lie. I care not for that either. It doth not change me or thee. For twenty long years, against my will I have remembered, I have regretted, I have resented. Then, when power came, I spoke the trickster fair——"

"Thou didst ask him for his honour," broke in Mihr-un-nissa coldly.

"I asked, as King, for what the King desired," replied

Jahângir, his tone changing to one of arrogant power. "Have I no right to that? Then, when he refused I sent for him——"

"What need, my lord, to repeat the falsehood?"

A fierce sigh like that of an angry tiger came from the shadows; then the strong man turned his face to the cool marble pillar for an instant and rested his hot forehead on its chill hardness. So standing, he spoke more quietly:

"Thou canst not understand, Meru! Thou hast no pity—love is far from thee; would to God it were far from me! All these long years I have dreamt of thy companionship. I have dreamt so often that we played together as we played as children. And now—oh, woman, woman! Thou dost tell me thou art at my mercy, when I would die a thousand deaths rather than touch the hem of thy garment against thy will. Yea, that ends it for ever. Thou dost not understand. Farewell!"

He turned to go, but she, remembering the Noose of Death at the door, arrested him. "And afterwards?" she asked.

He glanced at her sharply. His emotion was passing, his heart was hardening. "Thou remainest in safe keeping like other high-born ladies," he replied. "And none—not even the Emperor Nur-ed-din Jahângir—shall molest thee."

She was at the door now, opening it for him to pass through. As he did so, he bowed slightly in acknowledgment. Something in the dark corner of the anteroom stirred softly like a sleepy snake, then settled to rest again. The Noose of Death was not required that night.

And Mihr-un-nissa watched the tall figure disappear in the shadows of the arcade, then shut the door and returned stonily to the balcony. Once there, however, her calm gave way. She fell on her knees, rested her head on the balustrade of the balcony, and with arms outstretched to the stars that twinkled on so relentlessly overhead, gave way to a perfect passion of tears.

They were the first she had shed since her husband's death.

CHAPTER V

"Seek not Life's story from the painted art
That decks the cloistered Walls, or secret Heart
Of Drunkenness from those of sober mind.
Cloister and Wine-shop lie not far apart."

"Lo!" said the Strangler mournfully as he sat by the marble summer-house in the Garden of Roses where Mihr-un-nissa had played as a child. "I be of little use nowadays. Save for the hell-doomed thief who would have stolen the Khanzâda's jewels, my Noose lies idle—except as a child's plaything."

And once again the curved crimson rope shot out in the game that was being played, this time to twine round little Gladness's legs and set her a-shouting with laughter.

She ran off down the garden path, up which her mother was coming with a basket full of rose-leaves, calling out delightedly as she ran, "*Amma-jan, amma-jân,* Phusli caught me! Yea, verily, Phusli caught me!"

Dilarâm, once more packing candied rose-leaves into silvern baskets, looked up and frowned reprovingly. "Thou mightest have made the child fall. Why canst thou not miss always?"

The old man in woman's clothes shook his head deprecatingly. "Art will out at times, sister," he replied submissively. "And if I keep not my hand supple, what use to live? Why not die at once? Yet," he added, indicating his womanly garments distastefully, "no true man could die in these—not religiously!"

Dilarâm bent her brows at him contemptuously. "Traa!" she said. "Better nor thou hast died in petticoats and gone to God. But men are ever so. Lord! how we apples swim! A farthing of *bhang* and a curl to the moustache! And as for true men dying religious, look you! When the time for freedom comes at last, 'tis ever, 'Not to-day, as the saint said when God really called him.'" Then her manner softened; she looked at the spent figure before her more kindly. "'Tis being woman one moment and man the next that wearies thee. A body could not stand it long, though he be born without bones like an acrobat and have learnt to throw back somersaults like a beggar-boy. And there be no use in it, see you, since we are safe in this garden. So why not let Phusli die?"

The old Strangler stared at her. "What meanest thou, sister?" he asked.

"But this," she replied: "As snake-charmer on the cactus-hedge thou wouldst be more free to come and go, so be of more use, for 'tis news my lady desires nowadays—news, always news! And old Bisrao is dead, they say, so thou couldst get the place. The Bibi would speak for thee."

"But Phusli?" queried the Strangler dubiously. "How is she to die?"

Dalarâm grunted impatiently. "I care not, brother, so she die not here, and I have not to sing psalms. Take her away with thee, fool, and do the deed outside."

"The deed?" echoed the Strangler blankly. "Dost mean with the Noose? Nay, sister——"

Dilarâm gave a short laugh. "Out on thee, stupidity! Wouldst noose thyself? Nay, ask for a space wherein to visit a father's grave or a mother's great-uncle, and die on the road! 'Tis quite simple. But the mistress must give her consent. Mayhap she may see error in it, and she is wise beyond compare. Were she but a man——"

"Sister," interrupted her hearer solemnly, "think not such things; wouldst have her as I, neither one nor t'other? God forbid!"

Nevertheless, Dilarâm was right. After nine and thirty years of a normal woman's life Mihr-un-nissa was just beginning to find out that she was not normal. Three years had passed away since that first storm of tears she had shed in the balcony of her prison after her interview with Jahângir, yet, as she looked back on it, she felt as if it had been yesterday, so fresh, so poignant were the emotions it had brought her. Instant realization for one thing, that this man, debauched, drunken, had something she had not; something it was unlikely she would ever have. Yes, she would pass through life as girl, wife, mother, doing her duty by that life, enjoying it, and yet she would pass to the grave without tasting of life's greatest gift.

Why was it? With all her beauty, all her wit, all her charm—the effect of which she saw on almost everyone's face—why was it that the womanly instinct to give herself wholly into a man's keeping had never been hers? Perforce alone for long hours while she worked, she argued the point with herself until she saw that men never gave this love to a woman really; they reserved something always. Even Jahângir, whose love was evidently an obsession, only proposed to give his emotions. Perhaps that was what most women did also; only, since by common repute they were made up of emotions, it might be that in so doing they gave themselves.

So she analyzed herself and her world, coming finally to the conclusion that, had she been in a man's position, she could have loved as easily as they did.

Passing to considerations of the present, she saw with joy that a bitterer revenge than even she had dreamt of was hers in regard to the Emperor. A desire that had outlasted two and twenty years, that still desired a woman of six and thirty, would not be appeased by the object of that desire being free and within reach.

That is to say, if he kept to his passionate declaration that without her consent he could not claim her. This remained to be seen, though in her heart of hearts she felt that he would. He was not without force of character, misdirected though it was.

So when at the end of the first month she sent back, with a curt refusal to take blood-money, the pension he assigned to her as to all other inmates of the women's quarter, she waited anxiously for a sign; yet fearlessly, for the Noose of Death was at her door.

Yet none came. And when Khanzâda Râcquiya Begum, now a white-haired old woman nearly seventy, suggested to the Most High that she and Mussumât Mihr-un-nissa might retire as before to the Garden of Roses, and live there in the scented seclusion that suited their tastes, she fully expected a refusal of permission. Yet again no sign came; to all intents and purposes the Emperor appeared to have forgotten her. He even set about contracting a new marriage for himself. She smiled when she heard the news, as a mother might smile over the efforts of a child to gain its own way; she was beginning to follow the vagaries of this man's mind, though she still held him anathema. But when New Year's Day came round, amongst the small offerings that old friends, seeing a certain position assured to her, began to send her, there was one small bunch of campernelle jonquils for which she could find no donor. It was a north-country habit, that simple ceremonious sending of good wishes with a few stalks of the nodding, bright-eyed, sweet-scented flowers. It might well be that the Emperor himself knew nothing of their sending, save the general order that the courtesy should be shown to all and sundry in the harem at Agra.

But why send twenty miles out to the Rose-Garden?

The first year she threw them aside, the second she bade Dilarâm place them with the other flowers, and this third anniversary she was sitting with them in her hand, when Dilarâm came to ask permission for Phusli the message-woman to die, and Phusla the snake-charmer to take up office at the cactus-hedge.

She laid them down somewhat hurriedly on that fresh basket of rose-leaves she had just gathered; for the New Year in India is really the Feast of Spring, and falls ever in late March or early April.

When the suggestion was put to her, she accepted it at once with a curiously capable, comprehensive keenness. "Ay," she said. "'Tis well thought of! I shall gain thereby more knowledge than most; for thy gang, O Strangler, is far reaching. So go thy way—I will assure thine acceptance—and remember, no news is too trivial to report. I seek to know all."

This was true. The narrow range of the normal woman's life was fast widening. She was nine and thirty now, and though untouched by time as yet, was nearing the great climacterie of womanhood; for in the East maturity comes early, and by forty most women look and are old. She had few illusions; she knew that time was against her in one way; but she was conscious that fresh capabilities, fresh powers, were rising in her.

And she had exceptional opportunities for exercising them. Years before, Jahângir had entrusted the upbringing of his favourite son, Prince Khurram (afterwards to reign as Shahjahân), to Khanzâda Râcquiya Begum, his grandfather Akbar's childless widow. The lad had now almost come to man's estate, but, being devotedly attached to his step-grandmother, he came constantly to visit her from Agra, where he was finishing his education. And with him came tutors, guardians, professors, grave men of learning and political insight, to whom the Khanzâda (now past the restrictions of absolute seclusion) would give audience, while Mihr-un-nissa, more decorously veiled, would sit a little apart, yet join in the conversation. And Râcquiya was a shrewd politician of the old type, as so many of these Mogul women were.

Then Mihr-un-nissa's own father, Ghiyâss-ud-din, was a frequent visitor. An able man, now one of the greatest powers in the State, who found in his daughter a companionship denied him in his sons. For Asof Khân, though high in the Emperor's esteem, did not satisfy either his father or his sister; there was ever too much of mere personal advantage in his thoughts and actions. But she and her father discussed all topics of State, and from him she learnt how the Emperor was degenerating into a mere drunkard, and how advantage was being taken of him on all sides. And she listened with set lip; this was revenge indeed.

"Lo!" said her father to her one day, "thou seemest to have small pity—yet has the man good qualities enough, would he but use them—as thou dost, child! Truly thou hast keen wits. They clash with mine at times, but it does but show the temper of thy steel. Sure, there is naught comparable to the tie between us, save that of poor Queen Content and her father. God send her fate touch not thee!"

"'Tis not likely," Mihr-un-nissa replied coldly; but in truth the story of the only Empress India ever had, who was foully murdered after three years of admirable rule, and whose only fault, according to historians, was that she was woman, was rather a favourite of hers. It was so unlike all other tales of womanhood; so unlike the womanhood which frequented the Garden of Roses.

First the Emperor's mother, Maryâm Zamâni, a dear good soul, but a stupid, who constantly came to talk over her beloved grandson and still more beloved son with Râcquiya Begum. The long years had healed the jealousy which had existed in youthful days between these respective heads of the Hindu and Mahomedan harems in Akbar's time, and the two old ladies were ready and willing to mingle their tears over the transgressions and excesses of one who had been their idol ever since his birth. For even they could not deny the fact that year by year, day by day, the Emperor's behaviour became less and less imperial. So, when any fresh outburst of insensate anger, any fresh outbreak of mere foolish debauchery, became public, poor Maryâm Zamâni would hasten to find consolation from the childless old poetess in the Rose-Garden. The two would sit hand in hand while Râcquiya, mayhap, would quote the verse that heads this chapter, and say softly:

"He knows, sister! He knows! The lad hath a kind heart at bottom, and things went wrong in the beginning."

And she would give a side glance at Mihr-un-nissa, for they had few secrets between them. But the mother would go away comforted for the time.

There was another constant visitor to the Garden—Ârjamand Bânu, Mihr-un-nissa's niece and Asof Khân's daughter, a charming girl of sixteen who, by a strange coincidence, had been formally betrothed, with great carousing, to young Prince Khurram just at the time of Ali Kul's death. That was three years ago; both parties to the contract were of full age, yet there had been no talk of marriage. Both these facts excited Mihr-un-nissa's wonder. First as to the service Asof Khân had rendered to make a royal bridegroom for his daughter an equivalent reward, next as to the reason for this delay in the nuptials; a delay, unusual, unaccountable.

Unless, indeed, her aunt's refusal to fall in with the Emperor's plans had made the latter determined to have nothing further to do with what must give her pleasure. Or perhaps, again, it might be pure, unreasonable resentment that his young son should have what he desired when he, his father, had been denied it in his youth; for it was common knowledge that Khurram and Ârjamand were deeply in love with each other.

By dint of thought Mihr-un-nissa was beginning, without pity, to follow the wayward workings of the Emperor's mind, and the more she understood, the deeper became her conviction that the best thing that could happen for himself and for his Empire was an early death from drink, leaving the way clear for the Prince to reign in his stead. To this end she encouraged the young couple in their attachment as far as was possible with the strict etiquette of seclusion; perhaps a little more, since her outdoor life with Ali Kul had freed her from many conventionalities.

Naturally enough, a close bond of union sprang up between the young Prince and the woman, double his age, who was so infinitely his superior in wit. She used to rally him on his sober face, and say that his name, which means "joyful," was the most inappropriate one she had ever heard, for in truth he had the look of a disinherited knight as he roamed moodily about the garden paths hoping for some indiscreet glimpse of Ârjamand.

"Show him thy little finger with the ring he gave thee on't, child," Mihr-un-nissa laughed when, one day, the girl had been manœuvring to give her young lover some sign of her presence. "'Twould be more soothing, see you, than the sight of six-swathed yards of Dacca muslin, which is all that is possible with the Khanzâda looking this way."

And the girl, blushing, had waved her hand with the betrothal ring on its little finger from the balcony, and both she and her young lover had felt grateful for the suggestion.

Meanwhile, outside the pleasant haven of the Rose-Garden, matters were going ill with the Empire.

An expedition sent to quell disturbance in the Deccan failed in its object. Another army had been despatched to the seat of war, more money had been raised and sent; but the Amirs were quarrelling with each other, and grim tales of starvation amongst the troops, from lack of proper supplies, were beginning to filter up country.

One order after another was given, the Generals were changed, this one promoted, that one degraded, while Jahângir, half fuddled with wine and opium, signed the *firmâns* right royally. The rest of his time he spent in collecting rubies from far and near. Every petty Amir, knowing his craze for them, included one or more in his *nuzzer*, or offering of entry.

"Take it back; 'tis the colour of an onion," he said sarcastically to some, and the presenter thereof would slink away ashamed, knowing that a black mark stood against his name. But often the Emperor tired even of rubies, and would go off on hunting expeditions, away from his capital for four or five months, slaying animals by the thousand.

But ever round his camp the cry of the black partridge would be heard as the secret guild of Stranglers watched and waited, silent and slippery as snakes; and at nights the chattering laugh of the hyæna would echo out, giving some signal to the stealthy forms that slunk in the darkness.

For Phusla had kept his promise, and news was being gathered; trivial news, yet in a way important to the woman who listened to them by the cactus-hedge.

"Yea, yea," mumbled the toothless old man; "Majesty, having had a surfeit of rubies (there was one that weighed five *tanks* six *surks*—the giver thereof got commission of 500 horse as reward; look you, none get aught without rubies), decided on hunting. He hath killed fourteen hundred head—yea, he shoots straight when he hath not too much wine in his eyes. Lo! the chase fills his head and he forgets all else. Ahrah! But he was an angered when the tiger cubs slipped past by reason of the thickness of the scrub. Majesty is ever fond of young things, and he had set his heart on these. So orders came to search and find without fail. All that night the camp scarce slept, and we also, being expert, searched, yet found not the right ones; but having knowledge of another, we fetched one, and his Highness Prince Khurram appeased Majesty with it next morning. So anger died down somewhat. But that same evening Mohabat Khân, counsellor, sent foot in hand to us for another, ere the king would cease cursing; for see you, he had been in his cups for days. And even so wrath remained——"

Phusla the snake-charmer paused as he sat retailing his yarns to Mihr-un-nissa in the shadow of the cactus-hedge, while unwinking eyes stared at them through the prickly leaves.

"Ay?" she queried sharply. "And even so—wrath remained—what then?"

The old man coughed deprecatingly. "Even so, being but man, and that man largely absent through drink, wrath remained. It was a big blue bull, *Bibi;* Majesty had crawled within just range. Mehtu, one of the Tribe, *Bibi*, being passed *shikari*, had got him up to it when by mischance an owl of a groom and two misbegotten bearers, thinking they had been called, appeared; and pouf! the blue bull was away. So——" he paused again.

"So," re-echoed Mihr-un-nissa impatiently, "what happened? If all ill deed be done, to tell of one is not hard!"

The snake-charmer rocked himself to and fro as he did when blowing at his gourd flute, and he spoke in a hollow sing-song tone to match.

"Nay, 'tis easy," he replied. "Yet the tongue trembles lest it tell not the exact truth. That is known to God only. But the Emperor being away, *as Emperor*, and what remained of the rest of him being fuddled with wine, ordered that the groom be killed upon the spot and that the bearers be hamstrung and so be paraded on ass-back through the camp, that none ever again should have the boldness to do such an evil thing as deprive Majesty of pleasure."

"And was it done?" asked his hearer sharply.

"Ay, that was it. 'Twas Majesty's order, though Majesty was not there, being half drunk. Mehtu saw the groom's widow wailing. She hath three young children."

Mihr-un-nissa rose swiftly, her right hand clenched.

"May God curse the murderer!" she said with terrible intensity, and turned to go; but the Strangler arrested her.

"Nay, Most Excellent, there is more," he called. "That was Mehtu's news—he is of the outdoor tribe; but Lâl, who is of the indoor, hath other. He spreads the carpets in the royal tents, Huzoor, and he bade me give the mistress this, which he hath found where the blest bed of Majesty had honoured the lean earth!" He fumbled in his breast and produced a torn bit of crumpled paper, which he gave into Mihr-un-nissa's half reluctant hand. "Lo! the Most High had been marvellous drunk, seeing that he shows it but little as a rule. They could not guide his sainted footsteps, so they lifted his divine body to his honoured couch, where he lay. But afterwards, waking, he sat up crying, so they say——"

"A drunken cry, set to the drunken laugh," commented Mihr-un-nissa coldly.

"Mayhap!" assented the old man. "Yet was the man drunk, so not there. Then, as he recovered himself, he called for pen and paper and spoilt much. So when dawn came, and Lâl had to spread the carpet elsewhere, there was much litter. But *that* he found; so sent it, deeming it might be worth perusal."

Mihr-un-nissa glanced at what she held. Badly written, blotted, half torn. Her first impulse was to throw it away unlooked at. Then she crushed it in her hand, waited till she was alone, smoothed it out, and read:

"Oh, turn thine eyes from me, Beloved one;
Let me burn rue to cloud what I have done,
And drive the devils from my aching heart.
Lo! I am mad to meet thee—mad to part!
Yea, take thine eyes away, lest they should see
My foolishness. Frenzied and mad for thee
The World is; and thou movest frenzied too
With Anger at me. God! what shall I do
To ease the arrow that has pierced my soul!
Thine absence brings despair, and yet the goal
Of union would be worse. Jahângir, know
The time for tears and prayers is morn! Then go
Down on thy knees and pray God send some light,
Even a spark, to cheer thy darksome night." *

She sat looking at it for some time; then, with a faint sob, folded it up and hid it away.

* From Jahângir's "Memoirs," written 1610

CHAPTER VI

"Oh, if thou beest True Lover, wash not hand
From that dear Stain of Love! From worldly brand
Of Self and Pleasure wash it. In the End
Ye Twain before God's Judgment seat will stand."

JAHÂNGIR, in the balcony of his palace at Agra, lay somnolent among cushions of gold tissue. Beyond the marble fretwork of the low balustrade the sun shone buoyantly on fresh green leaves and blossom buds.

Beyond that again the level wheat-fields and shimmering cane-brakes stretched away to the opalescent line of pale blue which marked where the distant ridge of Sikri lay; and over all the crisp cool air of a North Indian early spring morning swept on the wings of a light breeze, which kissed the cheek softly, caressingly. An invitation to be up and out, to leave even the trappings of royalty behind, seemed to filter through to the Emperor's drowsy mind; but he had not the initiative to accept it. He lay inert, vaguely content, vaguely discontented. Just outside, in a curve from the battlements of the Shah-burj to a stone post fixed on the bank of the river, hung the heavy chain of pure gold, weighing over three hundred pounds, all set with sixty golden bells, which it had been Jahângir's first act after his accession to place there, and which he had named the "Chain of Justice, so that if those engaged in administration should delay or practice hypocrisy in the matter of those seeking justice. the oppressed might come to the chain and shake it so that its noise might attract my attention."

Excellent in conception; at first, possibly, in execution. But it seldom rang now, or, if it did, the monarch was in no fit state to hear it.

At the moment his mind was far from the affairs of State, and he frowned when he was reminded of them by a servant, who, with his forehead in the dust, chanted in modulated voice the information that the Khân Khânum—in other words the Lord of Lords, the Commander-in-Chief—awaited the Emperor's pleasure.

The frown settled deeper, became almost a scowl; for Abdur Rahmân the Khân Khânum was in disgrace. The army in the Deccan had fallen into even greater confusion. Men and horses were dying by the hundred; finally a sort of peace had been patched up with the rebels, and the troops had been withdrawn to Burhanpur. But even this move had not relieved the tension. The Amirs of the Army were quarrelling bitterly; orders and counter orders came in quick succession; finally the Second in Command represented that "all the division of counsel had arisen from the treachery and want of arrangement in the Khân Khânum, and that the only possible way of success was to recall him, and give the absolute control to the writer, who, on consideration of a further force of 30,000 horse being immediately supplied, would engage in two years' time to settle the affair under pain of dismissal from the good graces of the Most High."

When this letter had arrived, Jahângir, in hot indignation, had summoned the offender to court. Now that he had arrived, sheer indolence counselled delay.

"I receive him not; bid him kick his heels elsewhere;" came the verdict. Then satisfaction at having made up his mind gave an impetus to Jahângir's will. "Bid the astrologers," he added, "find a propitious hour for a hunting expedition. I go to-morrow. Bid the Head of the Tent Department see to it. And to-night, as farewell, bid the Stewards of the Household prepare a Feast of Intoxication. The guests have choice as to what drink they affect, so let them see to it that all kinds are ready. Dost hear?"

The servant slid out backwards, and Jahângir lay back among his cushions. He was not drunk, nor near it; simply mind, soul, body were poisoned with narcotics and stimulants.

That night after dark the Feast of Intoxication was held in the Mirror-Room of the Palace. It was not large, this room, and its wall space was reft away by the twelve arched doorways, three on each side, which led to outer slips of rooms where the servants in their gold liveries hurried up and down, bringing aromatic comfits and strange exhilarating drinks to all who asked for them; but the roof was inlaid in bold arabesques, with floriated gold tendrils bearing leaves and flowers of looking-glass, each reflecting in its own small world the scene that lay beneath it. So there were thousands on thousands of befogged Emperors looking down on the real one, who lay in the centre of the room, his figure half hidden by the soft contours of the pillows on which he rested.

It was a handsome face that showed faintly, sullenly amused at the antics that were going on. A handsome face with large, well-opened eyes, a fine forehead, and a heavy moustache hiding the full curves of a mouth that was curiously at variance with the weak lines of the lower part of the face. The balance of power was, indeed, absolutely in favour of the upper part, there being very little, either for good or evil, between the long nose and the chin.

As to the brain that lay behind the forehead, who can say what it might have been? Adolescence had brought such an excess of alcohol to it—he himself confesses to twenty cups, or about six quarts, of double distilled spirit in a day—that it had never had a chance of showing its true metal. It had been sodden from the commencement. Yet the same sullenness that he had shown as a boy testified to discontent. Discontent with what?

Not with his surroundings, surely. Never in this world has man been placed more favourably both for power and pleasure. Succeeding to an Empire wisely regulated by a wise father, he had the wisdom to continue government on that father's lines. His own additions to the State code were humane and statesman-like. He was surrounded by many sycophants, it is true, but he had men beside him by the score, who, given a hearing, would have brought him sound advice. Despite all this there was a warp somewhere; despite all these advantages he had not the resolution necessary to choose between good and evil, and so on this day, some six years after his accession, he lay, his massive form half hidden by silken softnesses, watching the buffoon of the company mimicking a Sufi religious dance to a tune—a very undevotional one—sung by a choir of Delhi singers who had been amusing the company with their doubtful repertory.

It was really rather funny! In a large white sheet and a high cap made of paper twirled to a peak like a dunce's, Sayyidi-Shâh spun and twisted and pirouetted while he improvised a topical verse about everyone present; and every time the refrain came round he cocked his cap a different way, first over one ear, then over the other, over one eye, at the back of his head, finally putting it over his nose and continuing to spin gravely, amid the roars of his audience. And this was the refrain:

"A dervish's cap is oft awry;
Sometimes it pointeth to the sky,
Sometimes to earth; but—let me tell:
It pointeth oftenest to Hell.
'Tis all awry!
Ah, fie!"

Absolutely banal as it was, there seemed to be something in the cadence that was catching, for more than one drinker of "exhilarating drinks" got up, whirled and span for a minute in imitation of the improvisation, then subsided unsteadily, amid the immoderate laughter of his companions.

"'Tis going round that makes my legs giddy," explained one solemnly, after, by a narrow ace, he avoided sitting down on the top of royalty.

Jahângir was the first to weary of the silly game. He held up his finger despotically, and it ceased as if by magic.

"Why canst not be original, fool?" he growled to the singer. "Why parody a decent verse?" And he quoted the couplet of Amir Kusrao', concerning the Saint Nizâm-ud-din Auliya whose cap was awry. "Yet for my part I have not gripped the hidden meaning of the verse, though there is one doubtless," he added; then as if a thought struck him, he gazed round his intimates almost contemptuously, and said: "Mayhap one of you gentlemen have a reading. If so, out with it—dost hear! Out with it!"

The words were not a request, not a permission, but a command, and the most sober of the lot rose with a bow.

"An it please royalty, the hidden meaning of the verse—is—is"—he looked round helplessly—"is that it hath none."

There was another roar of laughter; but Jahângir frowned.

An older man, and a fatter, stood up to appease the storm that threatened. "'Tis this way, Majesty. He beginneth by saying each man has his own faith, his own religion, his own shrine. Then he passeth on to the next hemistich——" He paused as if the word was a difficulty, and like a cork out of a bottle the most noted toper of them all shot up with a hiccup:

"And I s'hay he has none! I shay that the hemi-hemi-hemi-stich referreth to women's garments, an' not to poetry. I shay that the world is in a cocked hat——"

As the words were uttered the speaker suddenly threw out his arms and fell, amid yet another roar of laughter.

"Pick the drunkard up," began Jahângir; then something in the lax inertness of the prostrate figure struck him, and he was at its head before the others had recovered from their surprise. He turned the face upwards, stood for a second petrified, then raised himself, every trace of blood gone from his face, his hands trembling visibly.

"He is dead," he muttered hoarsely. "God hath called him! He is dead!"

Others, crowding about the prostrate man, sobered by the incident, swore it was but a fit; he would come round ere long. Physicians were called, but Jahângir was right. Even as the mocker fell with the ribald words upon his lips, the spirit had passed.

"He hath delivered his soul to the hands of his Creator!" said the Emperor, and his eyes showed fear. He had never seen death in this guise, and the sharpness of the contrast unhinged even his apathy.

"My nightly cup, slaves," he called suddenly. "And you, gentlemen, get you gone, and pray Heaven morning find you not dead like this one." And tossing off his nightly potion of an elixir containing six grains of opium, he retired to the women's apartments.

A sorry life indeed; but this incident had for the time sickened him of debauchery, and he turned with unusual interest to thoughts of his hunting expedition. He would get away from temptation and from the cares of State for three months. He would go to his favourite reserve, where antelope and partridge abounded, he would leave behind him the companionship of fools. Ay, even that of the wise men who bored him with advice he never took—it was so wily, so considerate. But out in the open he was taken at his face value. If he stumbled in his stalk, the quarry fled before he had a shot at it. If he missed a bird, he missed it. Out in the green wheat-fields or the sandy desert dunes he felt freer. The very thought of them made him more a king, and he spent the day in safeguarding the city during his absence by appointing a suitable custodian and in issuing orders that, to avoid the unnecessary destruction of crops inevitable from the passage of a large camp at that season of the year, the equipage should be limited to things absolutely necessary, and that none but his own personal servants should accompany him. Doubtless his desire to get away from the Court atmosphere shared, with kindliness, the honour of the thought; still when all is said and done, the kindliness remains.

The astrologers, somewhat hurried in their horoscopes, professed themselves unable to find a lucky moment for departure until late in the evening, so daylight had almost departed ere Jahângir rode through the city to the Dahrah garden, where he was to spend the night. This being so, he made it a sort of farewell procession. Heralds with bags of small coins preceded him, scattering the money broadcast among the expectant crowds. The royal banner floated, the royal kettle-drums clashed, and over the head of the tall, massive, indolent figure the royal umbrella swayed and waved.

A fine figure of a man truly, with all the pomp and circumstance of Eastern etiquette between it and the realization of what it was in essence—a drugged, discontented voluptuary.

He was a different being, however, when the next morning he shed his royalty, and, attired in a plain hunting suit, left civilization behind him for his small camp on the wilds. Ere evening came he had forgotten he was Emperor in a patient stalk of a blue bull which, when brought to the scales, weighed more than any other he had ever shot; an immense consolation to the man whose Imperial troops were at starvation point in the Deccan. Yet again he did a kindly thing. He had the flesh roasted and given to the poor and needy.

Meanwhile, what of the city, the Empire he had left behind him? When times are troublous the immediate presence of absolute authority, undivided, unassailable, is a potent factor. This being removed, small wonder was it that, during the next three months, while the Emperor was killing fifteen hundred head of game, matters should come to a crisis.

Even Mihr-un-nissa, away on the peaceful Sea of Roses, heard of one cabal after another from Phusla the snake-charmer. With the thousand eyes, the thousand ears of his tribe, he was the best of newsmongers, and of late he had been more assiduous than ever, and as he retailed his budget, his soft eyes would fix themselves on the beautiful face with curious intentness.

"The Empire is slipping from the Emperor's grip," he said one day, "and that is not well. If my grip on the Noose slackens, that is the end."

She heard much also from Prince Khurram, who, now past eighteen, was that unusual thing in the East, a son devoted to his father's interests. He came often to consult with his grandmother, the Khanzâda, and each time he came he was more rueful.

"If my father had but some wise head beside him 'twould be well," he said. "None has a softer heart than he, as I know full well, but he has ill friends about him, and he will not listen to the advice of the wise ones. Mirza Ghiyâss-ud-din, for instance, would be a tower of strength; but the Emperor will scarce see him these last four years."

And he looked to where Mihr-un-nissa sat, unveiled to him as betrothed to her niece. Extraordinarily beautiful still, but the adorable dimple did not show. She sat grave.

"It's the pity of the world," assented Râcquiya Begum. "These last four years have changed Jahângir much; and yet I pray for him each day, though what to pray for I scarce know." And she also looked at Mihr-un-nissa. The latter rose vexedly and left them. She knew what was in their thoughts; knew that the reason why Ghiyâss-ud-din's advice was spurned was that he was her father; knew that the long unusual delay in the marriage of the royal lovers Khurram and Ârjamand was due to the fact that the bride was her niece. As she walked away she heard the young Prince's voice: "Even if he had such a counsellor as thou art to me, O Most Wise——"

"Or as Ârjamand will be, O my son!" broke in the old spent voice sympathetically.

"Ay, when it comes! But I weary, grandmother. I waste my youth in longing."

It was all true. Yet what could she do? They could not ask her to forgive the man who had wrecked her life. But had he wrecked it? She made her way to the cupola'ed bastion which had been her favourite station as a child, and seating herself there, looked out over the Sea of Roses and asked herself the question. Had her life been wrecked? No, a thousand times no! That past was gone, but, with her clear sight, she could not but see that her life was fuller, more complete. She was independent as she had never been before. Her embroideries, her paintings, her confectionaries were known far and near in the women's world. "'Tis Mihr-un-nissa's making," was a *cachet* that admitted no criticism. And she was happy; undoubtedly she was happy, even though as she leaned over the parapet she seemed to see Ali Kul's kindly scarred face as she had first seen it.

The thought brought her no tears; only a fiercer spirit of revenge against the man who had cut her husband off in his prime. Yet how different that revenge of hers, so sweet, so complete, had been from the crude killing she had conceived at first? Four years of gradual degeneration; four years of discontent; that was something like revenge!

She gloated over it, setting far from her the thought that this degeneracy involved the ruin of an Empire. Yet, as ever in the midst of her exultation, her husband's kindly words came back to her: "Be not too lavish of blame! 'Tis never fair to judge us poor men folk by what we seem to do. 'Tis what we really do that merits punishment, and what that is God only knows." True enough! But even if Jahângir had not lied when he said he had not ordered the murder, even if he had only meant to take her, if not legally, at least peaceably, it made no difference. He was still blood-guilty; he should have known, he must have known, his tools would have no scruples.

The sound of a step on the foot-wide stair that clung to the wall made her peer over, to see Phusla the snake-charmer, Phusla the Strangler.

"I have news, *Bibi*," he said in explanation, "and seeing the Most Gracious from my station by the cactus-hedge, came to impart it—in private."

She bade him come up and sit, which he did, squatting as far from her as the narrow limits of the bastion would permit.

"'Tis had from the Deccan," he continued. "The Royal troops have been routed. They were but half-hearted, see you, since sedition grows apace. Prince Parviz hath the army with him, and God knows if he be loyal or not. He is older by two years than Prince Khurram, and, now that Prince Khushrau hath no chance of succession, might well put in his claim; being as he is full Mussulman, while Khurram is half Hindu."

"Peace, slave!" interrupted Mihr-un-nissa imperiously. "Thine office is to bring news, not to comment upon it. Hast any definite knowledge of conspiracy?"

In an instant her ready mind had seized on the idea that if her favourite Prince Khurram were to have his succession disputed, it might be well that a crisis should not come quite so quickly.

"Nothing, Most Gracious," replied the snake-charmer submissively. "'Tis talk; but talk turns to trouble in a night."

"No other news?" she asked, her mind with what she had heard.

"Only that His Majesty the Emperor hath to date killed twelve black buck, forty-four gazelle, five bears, 108 blue bulls, beside 1,126 partridges."

She roused herself angrily. "Peace, fool! What care I for the Emperor's slaughter-house?"

The old man gave a grim chuckle. "The Most Gracious was not brought up to love the Noose of Death as I." As he spoke he slipped off the soft strip of crimson silk he wore ever as a girdle and passed it through his fingers caressingly. "Lo! it hath given freedom to many, and the hand that holds it hath dealt death to many; yet the *Bibi* shrinks not from this slave. That is because he hath not dealt it to one she loves. That is all the difference. The act is the same." There was a curious expression on the wizened face, half mocking, half sympathetic.

"It is ever so with women-kind," he went on—"ay, and with most men also. 'Tis how it touches them that makes right and wrong."

She looked at him, dissenting.

"Murder is ever wrong, slave," she began.

"Ever?" he queried, interrupting her almost cavalierly. "Say not so. Lo! I will give case, and the Most High shall judge." He settled himself comfortably ere he commenced in the sing-song of the story-teller: "There was a Bungler once who killed a brave man by stabbing him through a tent wall with a long dagger that reached the heart."

Mihr-un-nissa started. "What dost mean, slave?" she exclaimed.

"Naught, Most Gracious," answered the old man, whose face was imperturbable in its calm. "'Tis an old trick of the assassin. Lo! for myself I hold the Noose"—he paused—"but of that, nothing! And there was another man who ordered a Strangler to kill the Bungler for his deed. Wouldst say that his crime equalled the Bungler's crime, or that the Bungler's crime equalled the crime of those who gave him the order to stab through the tent wall?"

Mihr-un-nissa's breath came quick and fast. "Cease prating of thy Bungler and Strangler, old man," she cried fiercely. "Whose was the order?"

The old snake-charmer gave a mirthless chuckle. "Which order, Huzoor? Lo! they were both to kill, and some think 'twas the same mind that fathered both thoughts. Yet I know naught but this. The order to kill the killer came to me, the Head of the Tribe, and I obeyed. A life is such a little thing, Most Gracious. It is so easy to take. If the Huzoor gives orders they will be obeyed."

His soft eyes looked up into hers with gentle deference.

"Strangler!" she cried suddenly, "thou art an awesome man—go, get thee to thy snakes!"

After he had gone she sat till dark fell, thinking over what he had said. If it was true, if, as he had hinted, the Emperor had meted out death to the death-dealer, what then? Was the crime the same? Yes! A thousand times the same. The Emperor was guilty; and yet—— She gave a fierce sigh, and, leaning on her elbows, looked out over the darkling Sea of Roses. Her woman's life was almost over; that she knew was inevitable; but surging up within her came a consciousness that something better, something more germane to her real self, might be possible in the future. So far, she had never yet met her match, not for brains perhaps, though hers were good enough, but for general capability, for keen vitality. In those old days she had been able to outweary Ali Kul, strong man though he was. Her nerves were iron, her slender muscles as steel. What was there then between her and a man's life save sex; and sex was going. And suddenly all the past seemed to slip from her like the chrysalis from the dragon-fly, and for a moment she felt new wings, shimmering, iridescent wings.

So with a little sob she rose up and went down the foot-wide stairs to the garden. It might be a perilous path, she thought, that path she saw opening before her, as, carefully in the dark, she found her footing; yet in a way it would be a greater revenge on Fate—ay, even on the man who had done her such a deadly injury—than the more obvious one. To save an Empire was better than to ruin one.

She found the Khanzâda and Maryâm Zamâni, who had come over with Prince Khurram, waiting, in a marble-domed room set with floriated tendrils of gold and looking-glass like the one at the Palace in Agra, for the evening reading of poetry; for Mihr-un-nissa was a practised elocutionist. By the light of the cresset lamps, their fine old womanly faces showed worn and anxious.

She took up the volume of Sa'adi that was lying by the reading-desk and began, the Persian rhythms falling softly from her lips:

"There lingered still some little of the Night
When one of faery face put out the Light;
Like a spent soul, its smoke arose and sighed.

Look down! Ah! Now, indeed, Love endeth Right;
This is the Road! Ah, take it! Learn of me;
Dying, thou gainest Love's best ecstasy.
Art thou afraid? Ah, then I say to thee,
Launch not thy boat upon Love's boundless Sea;
But if thou venture—then hoist sail, quit anchor,
To storm and wave trust thyself hardily!"

Her voice found echo in the vaulted roof, where myriads on myriads of tiny mirrors reflected the scene that lay below. Myriads on myriads of women listening to those words:

"Dying, thou gainest Love's best ecstasy!"

listening with all their ears, and understanding—nothing!

The sound died away into a murmuring as of many bees. Then there was silence until Jahângir's mother spoke.

"If thou couldst forgive him, daughter? He might listen to thee. He hath never forgotten——"

"Wash not hand
From that dear Stain of Love! From worldly brand
Of Self and Pleasure wash it,"

quoted Râcquiya Begum with a break in her voice.

Mihr-un-nissa stood for an instant looking at them, superb in her extraordinary beauty, almost terrible in her set determination.

"He killed Ali Kul," she said, and left them.

CHAPTER VII

> " With Woman's veil and turban Man-ways tied
> A Vision came—most fair to me. I cried,
> 'Lo! art thou Man or Woman thus arrayed?'
> 'Nay, I am neither. I am Love, it sighed."

ÂRJAMAND BÂNU sat in the marble summer-house of the Garden of Roses, teaching Gladness, now a bright-faced girl of nine, how to weave a bridal chaplet of jasmine stars and rosebuds.

" Thou must give it to thy dolly and prepare a wedding-feast for her," said the elder girl lightly. She was a very pretty girl, very sweet-looking, but she lacked the animation which at her age—just eighteen—should have been hers.

" Nay, cousin," replied the little maid solemnly. " Dolly is married already."

" Then wear it thyself," smiled Ârjamand, flinging the finished flower garland over the child's head.

" Nay! cousin," protested the small maiden, still more solemnly. " I am too young yet for weddings. *Amma-jân* says so. She says I must wait years and years before the dates are sent. It is a pity; but thou must wear it thyself."

And with that she tried to transfer the chaplet, Ârjamand resisting with almost unnecessary vehemence. " Nay, nay!" persisted the latter. " If thou art too young, I am too old. 'Tis true, dearest, I grow far too old."

And then suddenly, causelessly, it seemed to the child, she burst out crying, and sat covering her face with her hands to hide her tears.

" What is't, dearest?" asked Mihr-un-nissa, coming at the sound of sobs from the inner arcade, where she had been at work, and laying a sympathetic hand on the girl's head. " Hath Gladness hurt thee? She is over rough, I fear. Thou shouldst be more gentle, child——"

Gladness pouted. " Nay, *amma*, I did nothing to her. I

but tried to put the wedding garland round her neck, and she said she was too old. And on that she began to blub. If she be too old to marry she can be a canoness. 'Tis a lovely life, with none to worry you. Ah, fie, Cousin Ârjamand! That is not courageous!"

And with that the little maid stalked away, indignant.

Mihr-un-nissa, with a pang at her heart, sat down beside the girl, and drawing the hand that bore the gold betrothal ring away from the tear-stained face, stroked it consolingly. "Doth it hurt so much as that, child?" she asked pitifully, yet in a measure uncomprehendingly.

"Ay," sobbed the girl, and then suddenly she burst out almost angrily. "Oh, if thou wouldst but be kind, we might be happy! *Nanni* says so, and father says so—and—and—*he*, I am sure, thinks so."

Mihr-un-nissa released the hand, rested her elbow on her knee; so, with chin upon her palm, looked steadily away from the girlish figure, all trembling with its trouble.

"And what says grandfather?" she asked suddenly.

Ârjamand, drying her tears furtively with her veil, answered in doleful accents: "Grandfather says thou art the best judge——"

"For which Heaven be praised!" put in Mihr-un-nissa devoutly. "But see you, dearest," she went on kindly, "though 'tis doubtless true that the Emperor took umbrage at me in years gone by, what warranty have I he cares for forgiveness? Wouldst have me offer myself to a man?"

Ârjamand sat up now, looking at her aunt with sombre eyes. "Wherefore not?" she replied, "since there lives not one on God's earth but would be proud to take you. Dost know, aunt, that thou hast never reckoned with thy surpassing beauty? Lo! when I saw thee last night fresh from the bath, with all that glorious hair of thine enshadowing thee from head to foot, I thought—nay, I knew—no man would ever forget thee—for ever and ever and aye thou wouldst be his vision of beauty."

Mihr-un-nissa's face grew stern. "And if I despise him?" she began."

"Thou canst not despise the King," interrupted Ârjamand

with a tinge of horror in her voice. "He is God's Viceregent upon earth." And she joined her little palms together and bowed her head between them in respectful homage.

This argument was new to Mihr-un-nissa, and she admitted its validity to a certain extent as she went back to work. Undoubtedly Jahângir was the Lord's Anointed, but that was no reason why she should forgive his trespasses against her, why she should forgo her revenge. And if no man could forget her beauty, there was the less virtue in Jahângir's faithfulness—if indeed he was faithful.

As the days went on the little coterie in the Rose-Garden became increasingly sad, for increasingly bad news came from the Deccan, where one trouble after another followed in quick succession. Even the advent of the New Year scarcely sufficed to raise their spirits. Yet it was an auspicious time. Majesty was returning, as ever, to celebrate it with pomp at Agra, and everyone must be in attendance. Mihr-un-nissa begged to be excused, but the old Khanzâda was firm.

"Thou needst not join in the rejoicings," she said, "but thou art of the Court, even if thou refusest the pension the Most High awards thee, and which he, of his bounty, bestows upon the poor."

For once in her life Mihr-un-nissa gave a feminine reply. "More likely the overseer takes it as perquisite," she suggested bitterly.

Khanzâda Râcquiya Begum looked at her mildly. "Yet were Majesty's orders otherwise. So it counts for virtue to him."

Her hearer bit her lip to keep down the retort that Majesty's orders were responsible not only for good, but for evil. What was the use, however, of argument? The plea urged by old Dilarâm that the Emperor was the Emperor, and the rest of the world his subjects, was much more to the point. So one morning the whole party started in *dhoolis*. They were to rest at a half-way *sarai* for the hot hours of the day and reach Agra that evening. The ceremonial entry had been fixed by astrologers for the next morning, March 21.

Late March is probably the time of all others in which Northern India is at its best; and this year of grace 1611 the winter rains had been good, while further showers in February had conduced to a bumper crop. Once the little party passed the seas of roses, leaving even the scent behind them, they came out into a wide, open, fertile plain, a sea of corn fast ripening to harvest; the fields—guiltless of fences, and relying for demarcation only on little cones of unbaked mud hidden by the stand ing crops—stretching away to the horizon in rich promise for the future. But as they neared the half-way house the aspect of affairs changed. Here much of the tall wheat was beaten to the ground; the green crops had been cut for fodder, and great tracks as of the passing of men or animals showed everywhere. The headmen of the half-way village were in readiness to receive the cortège, as in duty bound, with offerings of sugar-candy, raisins and nuts. They were white and black bearded men, profuse of sad smiles, and with almost preposterous deference for the Court ladies. The old Khanzâda interviewed them in right royal fashion, calling them her children, and making the usual perfunctory inquiries as to the prosperity of the village. To all of which a chorus of assenting voices proclaimed that under the rule of that Pillar of the Faith, that Light of the World, Nur-ud-din Jahângir, all villages, all men, were prosperous. Yet Mihr-un-nissa, sitting silent behind her veil, watched their eyes wander to their ruined crops even as they spoke. In a flash she made up her mind. Passing rapidly out through a side door into the cloistered *sarai*, she came upon Dilarâm contentedly smoking her pipe. To seize the ample veil of the good woman, cast it round herself, bid the startled owner retire out of sight without an instant's delay, and sit down in her stead, did not take long. She knew perfectly well what the old lady had been awaiting, and as the headmen trooped out from their interview, she was ready with outstretched palm for the *douceur* to which, as attendant of the Beneficent Ladies, she had a right.

The eldest of the men, a veritable pantaloon with a white beard, who was evidently the purse-bearer, advanced towards her and held out a coin.

"Traa!" she said, imitating Dilarâm's rough tongue as nearly as she could. "That be too small."

The old man muttered something about poverty, which she

interrupted with a laugh. "Lo! then I take naught," she said; then lowered her voice. "I am not as the others"—she tossed her head backwards to indicate those within—"who grab at all things. I am daughter of the fields! Sit down, father, and tell me, how comes it that the village is poor?"

The old man pocketed the offered money in haste; he could say he had given it, and, as such expenses came out of the general fund, be, by that, the richer.

"Dost ask why?" he answered, "and thou a daughter of the fields? If thou hadst eyes thou wouldst see. Our crops are ruined. The Emperor's camp passed hither yesterday; it is as a horde of locusts."

"But thou hast compensation," she said quickly. "Ay, and in full. 'Tis the command of the Emperor!"

The old man smiled the peasant's mirthless smile. "Of a truth, daughter, thou knowest little! Yea, yea! The Emperor gives the order, but the overseers heed it not. Yea, yea, the money is paid, but not to us. So goes it ever when the eye of the Most Mighty is turned away from his servants. Lo! when he turns it on, there is gladness, yea, even in the littlest things. See you, but yesterday the Most Exalted—may he live for ever—came on a child crying because they had taken his pet lamb—for *pillau*, they said, to the Most Mighty, but I misdoubt me it was for some underling. And he waxed wroth, and had the man who took it beaten with staves, and gave ten rupees to the child—he is my grandson, daughter—as consolation."

"Then thou art not so poor!" commented Mihr-un-nissa dryly. "So thou canst give me back the coin thou hast put in thy pocket."

But pantaloon-*ji* had risen at her first hint, and was ambling off. Mihr-un-nissa, having assured herself of what she needed to know, had dismissed him cunningly.

All that afternoon, as she was jogging along to Agra, her thoughts were busy. A vague indignation, not against but for the Emperor, made itself felt. Was there no person about him capable of seeing that orders which sprang from innate kindness of heart were carried out? A man like her father, wise beyond most—but he, alas! was useless——

So she circled round and round the old question restlessly.

It had been arranged that she should spend the first night with her mother, in order to leave Gladness in her charge before she went on to the palace ceremonials. She felt glad of this now, since it would give her an opportunity of speaking to her father, and every moment of time she was feeling more and more the need of someone on whose judgment she could rely.

Yet when she found herself face to face with the grave, grey-bearded man whose every thought came with almost mathematical precision, and who would no more make allowance for frail humanity than he would make an allowance for a fault in arithmetic, she found herself tongue-tied to all but everyday questionings as to the real state of the Empire. Here Ghiyâss-ud-din had not a very optimistic tale to tell.

"In the Deccan," he said, "things be as bad as well can be. Orders have doubtless been given, but in the plentitude of executants naught is carried out. The Emperor hath sent more than enough money, and troops sufficient. But he hath not the leaders in his grip——"

"Hast heard if Prince Parviz be disloyal—to his father?" asked Mihr-un-nissa curtly.

"To his father, I misdoubt me. With all his faults Jahângir hath the knack of dutiful sons——"

"Except Prince Khushrau!" put in Mihr-un-nissa.

"Even Khushrau hath no enmity to him now; but were the Emperor to die, those three, Parviz, Khushrau, and Khurram, would be at each other's throats."

"And which would win?"

Ghiyâss-ud-din shrugged his shoulders.

"Khurram hath advantage, being his father's nominee. Parviz has that of orthodoxy. 'Tis a powerful lever, since even now folk are not yet reconciled to believers and unbelievers being as one. And Khushrau hath pity to his share, and primogeniture. Yea, he hath a bigger following than most think, witness the strange affair at Patna but the other day, when a mere impostor, saying he was Prince Khushrau escaped from custody, rallied enough adherents to take the fort. So there would be disturbances and oppressions and strife. But God send the Emperor be wiser in the future than he hath been in the past! Sure, no man can stand such potations for long."

Mihr-un-nissa felt she had heard all this before, and what she needed was to know exactly, not what the courtiers thought, but what the people, who crowded the bazaars and who to-morrow would pack in dense multitudes to see the show, were suffering. There was but one way to find this out, and it was simple. She must continue what she had begun that afternoon, and go herself, as the Caliph Haroun-ul-Raschid had done, to see with her own eyes, hear with her own ears.

Already the city was all agog with preparations for the morrow; now, then, was the time!

There are many high-class Mahomedan houses where the screened women, on occasion, adopt the habit of men, and so pass, in the gloaming or at night-time, where they would not venture in women's garments. The style of dress makes this easy. A big turban hides long hair, the loose shawl covers feminine contours. So—not without objections from Dilarâm, who, however, was appeased by being allowed to accompany her mistress—the two slipped out on their adventure so soon as darkness made this possible. Dilarâm's face was of a type sufficiently common to pass muster. With a wisp of unbleached cotton-wool to do duty as a beard, just showing under the throat-encircling folds of a heavy brown blanketing, she looked the peasant in for a holiday. Mihr-un-nissa, dressed similarly, obscured her beauty with a dirty bandage under her chin and slanting across one eye, as if she had a toothache. Both were quite unrecognizable, and mixing with the crowd that was surging through the streets, were soon lost in it.

The whole city was *en fête* for the morrow's ceremonials. Everywhere Court officials were busy hectoring unpaid workmen over the putting up of rich brocades, the laying down of carpets, the setting of the thousand and one tiny oil lamps which on the following night were to illumine the Palace. It was perilous work in some places, and Mihr-un-nissa watched with a sickening heart one old man, urged by threats from below, climb the topmost pinnacle of the Fort Mosque. She seemed to know what would happen, and when it did, when the sudden slip came, the quick scream, and then the dull thud, she struggled as one possessed not to be dragged towards the spot by the inrush of the crowd of which she formed part.

When the pressure was over, when the back-draw of satiated curiosity began, she found she had been separated from her companion. So much the better, she thought, for her blood was up. She meant to see everything, hear everything she could, and Dilarâm hampered her.

That night was an education in itself. Up and down she wandered, sitting at times beside a sweetmeat-seller, munching a farthing's worth of *batâsa*, listening with all her ears. Then out on to the levels by the river, where a fair was being held, drifting along with thousands of others through the lanes, all edged with little lights, behind which sat sellers of every kind of toy and trifle—glass bangles, little brass gods, rosaries, charms, betel-boxes, lacquer-work—all things and everything. But folk were too much interested by these trivialities to talk much save for rough jests and laughter, while the sound of many voices and the banging of cymbals and tom-toms drowned all confidential whisperings. So she drifted away again to the city, where the more staid of all sorts and kinds sat in little knots on the outside edge of the shifting, merry-making crowd, and discussed village politics and town gossip.

And everywhere she overheard the same tale of orders neglected, or kindness of heart frustrated by disloyalty. Some of the stories made her clench her hands and long for revenge—not punishment, but revenge pure and simple; for she was true woman in this—she admitted no compromise.

Once and once only she came nigh detection, and that was in a narrow street where flower-decked balconies and an all-pervading scent of musk told the profession of the painted women who sat at the receipt of custom. It was here, if anywhere, Mihr-un-nissa knew, she might come upon things worth hearing, and she had been hanging about for some time in the stream of idlers when she apparently attracted the notice of a somewhat fat, somewhat elderly female, whose artificial allurements covered the loss of natural charm.

"Thou art too pretty a fellow to pass pleasure by," came her voice, raucous with long years of the singing of indecent songs. "Come hither, my charmer, and I will comfort thee." And she laid a clutching hand on Mihr-un-nissa's shoulder and leered at her.

"If thou hast no money she will give thee credit," jeered a half-drunken habitué. "Come, show thyself a man!"

Mihr-un-nissa gave one look round, realized that her only safety from those evil-looking, sensuous men lay in immediate flight, wrenched her shoulder from the painted grip, and fled, pursued by deafening laughter and coarse jokes.

She had heard much that night to leave sharp mark upon her very soul, but this was almost too much. Sick with absolute loathing of womanhood and manhood so debased, she would see no more of life, and made her way home, to find Dilarâm half distraught with fear.

"Of what?" asked Mihr-un-nissa contemptuously. "Of myself, likely! Leave me, I say; I would rest awhile ere I go to the Palace."

When she was alone, she threw off in disgust her man's disguise, discarded all garments that told of womanhood, flinging both into a corner in a disordered heap, and, wrapping herself in the coarse outside shawl that belongs to both sexes, sat down by the window.

"So!" she muttered. "There goes humanity! Now for thought!"

What was she to decide? What was she to do?

The rising sun found her still thinking. Then thought became impossible while the glorious pageant of the light went on. She sat still, almost unconscious of her world, while the light grew on her beautiful face; but when the miracle of sunrise was past, when the gold had changed to turquoise, when the rosy clouds had paled to fleecy snow, she realized that her mind must have been working all the time, for her way seemed clear before her.

Revenge she wanted, and revenge she must have; but it must be of a different kind from that in the past. For the last four years she had lived, rejoicing in the gradual decadence of the man who had done her so grave an injury. Now, if it were still possible, she would make that man the slave of her will. He should, as it were, live through her; her vitality should overbear his apathy and indolence. She would at last be Queen not only of Women but of Men!

And this would bring with it other advantages. Conscious as she was of a growing power in herself, a power undreamt of in her youth, this would give her a free field. At first, doubtless, she would have to rely on her womanhood for influence; she would not be able to escape from her own bodily beauty; but she could sit apart in her soul as she sat now, and let it slip by unnoticed.

A half savage delight at the prospect swept through her. Doubtless, the wrongs of a people misgoverned, and the intolerable disloyalty of those in authority, were factors in her decision; but they were almost forgotten in the thought that here before her was possibly a revenge undreamt of, a revenge such as no woman had ever had before.

But it might not be possible. What should she do towards making it so? She must see the Emperor, of course; that was certain. Sick as she was of the unerring effect of her rare beauty on all men, she admitted she had no better weapon. In the meantime she would send Jahângir a New Year's bunch of campanelle jonquils. So much she was in a measure bound to do. So much she could do without forfeiture of self-respect.

As dawn passed to day, she resumed her white widow's robe, and was carried to the women's apartments in the Palace, where she was lodged in her old quarters. Dilarâm and Phusla accompanied her. The latter had only been prevented from resuming the rôle of Phusli by Dilarâm's stern refusal to assist at a resurrection before the Day of Judgment.

"Traa!" she snorted. "God knows His own work. Phusli hath been in His keeping these three years, and were He to see her walking about His earth once more, He would ask why. Nay, nay! Stick to thy sex which thou hast lost, old man! See, I will make thee a scarlet coat, and thou shalt wear a sword and a badge like the best o' them."

"So I may keep the Noose, sister, I ask no more," replied the old Strangler submissively.

So when Mihr-un-nissa repaired to the palace he took up guard in the ante-room as before, while his mistress belaboured her brain as to what message she was to send with the jonquils. Something that was quite ceremonious and yet—no! there must be nothing of appeal about it; her pride forbade that. Finally, after tearing up many attempts, it stood thus in her fine elegant caligraphy:

"Humble greetings to the Most High, the Pillar of Faith, the Representation of the Most Merciful, Nur-ud-din Mahomed Jahângir, Emperor of all the Indies, Encircler of the World, from his slave and servant, Mihr-un-nissa."

Then she added as an afterthought, "Daughter of I'timad-daulet Ghiyâss-ud-din, widow of Khân Ali Kul of Burdwân."

That, at any rate, told the truth; that, at any rate, showed that if she meant to forgive, she had not forgotten.

After she had sent it tied to the regulation bunch of jonquils, she sat in her balcony listlessly waiting for the time when with the other ladies of the harem she would go behind the screen in the new building which had been devised for such rejoicings and watch the ceremonious weighing of Majesty against gold and silver and precious stones. Last time he was weighed he had tilted the scale at fifteen stone. It was expensive for Majesty to weigh so much, but good for the poor, who benefited by the distribution that followed. Yet he might well be lighter this time, after close on four months of a hunter's life.

So the trivial thoughts ran, till the blood flew to her face, then left it colourless at old Phusla's sudden interruption:

"The Emperor craves admittance."

So soon! He could hardly, as yet, have received—— She curbed her rising thoughts, stood up, threw back her veil, and gave permission in a low voice.

Undoubtedly he was thinner, as he stood where he had stood four years ago; not in golden tissue and jewels as before, but in the simple morning garb of a Mahomedan gentleman.

"Nur-ud-din Mahomed Jahângir, Emperor of all the Indies, Encircler of all the Worlds, hath come," he said, and his voice betrayed no emotion, "to tender thanks in person to Mihr-un-nissa, daughter of I'timad-daulat Ghiyâss-ud-din Khân, and widow of Khân Ali Kul of Burdwân, murdered—but not by the Emperor's orders."

She could not speak. His words woke all the past; she could only wring her hands together and say in a muffled voice: "Leave that to God. He knows!"

Jahângir took a step forward. "Yea, He knows!" he cried vehemently. "And He knows how all these years—all these long, long years—I—have waited." His voice failed him suddenly; he held out his hands appealingly.

"Meru! Meru!" he whispered, his whole face breaking up with the intensity of his desire. "Wilt not forgive?"

"Yea," she answered firmly, holding out her hand. "I will forgive; but even the Emperor must not ask me to forget!"

Two months afterwards they were married; married so quietly that no mention is made in Jahângir's autobiography of the most momentous act of his reign.

BOOK III

CHAPTER I

> "A ruby cup filled up with ruby wine
> Of Love's best vintage is this Heart of mine;
> Drink of it as thou wouldst, dear one, nor fear,
> When it is empty, that thou wilt repine."

"MIHR-UN-NISSA art thou to me alone, my Queen of Women," said Jahângir fondly. "To the world thou art from this day Nurmâhal, the Light of Palaces."

"As my lord please," replied the woman who, dressed with a splendour befitting her rank as Empress of the Emperor's whole life, occupied a seat on the royal divan. It was a question whether she was more beautiful in this guise than she had been in her widow's shroud, but of the beauty, the charm, there could be no question at all. The fame of it remains to this day; she is the Eastern Helen.

"Art not satisfied, my life?" came the quick query, and she had to smile and lay her hand on his to appease his solicitude. They had been married close on a year, and no woman with a heart could have experienced such child-like devotion, such absolute trust, without a growing affection for the donor. Wayward as he was, spoilt child of fortune, semi-savage in his treatment of many, to her he was ever the diffident lover. What he had said years before, when he upbraided her for her lack of understanding, was true. Whatever he was to other women, his passionate love for her was reverence itself. That touch of her hand on his was needed to give him courage to lay his lips to it.

"Yea, I am satisfied in most ways," she replied. She would have been *exigeant* had she not been so, for those twelve months had wrought many changes. Within a month of her marriage her father had been honoured and promoted, within three he had been appointed Grand Vizier of the Empire on account of his previous services and his great sincerity and ability. The result of this had been immediately seen in a complete readjustment of the Government. The campaign in the Deccan had been started afresh, the outlying Amirs had been called to order, and the rules which Jahângir had promulgated on his accession had been once more put in force. These rules are curiously far-seeing and just. Number one forbids the levying of any but Imperial cesses, thus putting a stop to extortion by petty chiefs and landholders. Number two provided for the creation of State-managed and safe rest-houses on all roads infested by thieves. Number three forbade the opening of bales of merchandise on the public roads without the leave of their owners. This again was a side stroke at imposition by high-placed officials. Another provided for the rights of property in all, unbelievers or Mussulmans. Only if no heirs were to be found the State might employ property in charitable and religious works.

Yet another was absolute prohibition of the making or sale of any intoxicating liquor or drugs. Officialdom was further restricted by the order that in Crown lands no one was to interfere with the peasants' right of cultivation.

Finally, the punishment by cutting off nose or ears was abolished, and the founding of hospitals in great cities, with efficient physicians for the healing of the sick, ordained; the expenditure, "whatever it might be," to be defrayed by the State.

Not bad rules, as additions to those made by his father Akbar.

Last, but not least, the young royal lovers had been made happy, to Nurmâhal's great and unceasing delight. It seemed as if the intensity and closeness of the bond between these two gave the woman who in both her marriages had missed the perfection of the tie a vicarious satisfaction. This was accentuated by the fact that she whole-heartedly accepted Prince Khurram as the future Emperor. It was for him, as for his father, that she laboured to set things right. Naturally, the personal feeling of power had stepped in to make such labours easy, but the record of this first year of her ascendancy shows that she used all her influence for good. Two very womanly ordinances stand out from the mass of rules promulgated or reinforced, as proof that she did her best to keep Jahângir in the right religious path. One is that all the antelope skins—and there were thousands of them—that the Emperor shot should be cured and given as prayer-mats to the various mosques—a quaint imaginative way of identifying him with the devotions of his subjects. The other is the abolition of the *sijdah*, or uttermost prostration before royalty, so far as judges were concerned, since they should be considered the pivot of the Divine Law that is above Kings—another imaginative and purely feminine idea.

So the woman who had given up the revenge of destruction for the revenge of reconstruction had every reason to be proud; and yet her eyes, as they sought the Emperor's, were dissatisfied.

"Most ways?" he echoed reproachfully. "Why not all ways?"

She was quite fearless with this man; she answered him fair and straight.

"Because my lord hath not kept to his promise," she said. "In the matter of wine, it is true that he seldom takes more than the half of what he did; but in the matter of drugs!" She smiled, and her distracting, adorable dimple made mince-meat of the Emperor's rising vexation. "Thou dost take too much, dear friend," she continued affectionately. "It's not good for soul or body; then thou goest into the women's apartments, and they give thee more."

He gloomed as he sat there holding her hand. "Wouldst have me give up all my pleasures?" he asked almost pitifully.

"Not all, my lord," she whispered archly, as, deliberately taking the reins as it were, she guided his hand round her waist; so, with her head on his shoulder, looked up at him laughing. "Am I not a pleasure, my lord?"

He kissed her passionately. "Truly thou art a witch-woman," he said, and his voice trembled. "Were all as thou art there would not be a drunkard in the Empire! But see you, Light of Palaces, Queen of Women, 'tis hard to baulk a man of sleep when he hath been thirsty all day! And the slaves give me even more than I ask."

Nurmâhal's brows levelled themselves sternly. "That can I

well believe," she said dryly. Indeed, she was becoming accustomed to these efforts on the part of his *entourage* to drug Jahângir back to a slavery which brought others freedom and power. "Therefore, my lord, I have a plan, and if my lord permits I will unfold it," she continued; "but since it is long to recite, I will do it in proper fashion."

She slipped from his hold to the step of the divan, took up a *cithâra* that was lying to hand, and in a second had assumed the air and tone of the professional story-teller.

Jâhangir laughed delightedly. "Thou art all things in turn! Truly a man can never have a dull moment with such a companion," he said, little dreaming that she had rehearsed the whole scene beforehand, and was ready with apt reply for all possibilities. So in a moment she had paraphrased a couplet of Hafiz:

> "One good companion and a cup of water—
> For these I'd give the world and what comes after."

She chanted the doggerel with infinite verve, and went on to her tale in approved fashion.

"It telleth," she said, "of a *jogi* and an infant's toy, of luck and misfortune, of life and death."

So, admirably, losing no point of humour or pathos, she told the tale of the red crystal cup. More than once Jahângir, fascinated, broke in with admiration.

"'Tis better than *Alif Laila!*" he cried. "I shall have to call thee Shahzâdi; but in truth, as I said, thou art all things in one."

She swept him a mock salaam, and replied: "The Presence had best wait till this slave hath finished; then, mayhap, 'twill be off with her head!"

Thus the story went on. She spared him nothing, or herself either; though when she described how her dying child, Ali Kul's child, had lain in her arms unbettered by the magic cup, her voice broke a little, and he, with tears in his eyes, bent down to say, "Tell me not, if it hurt thee, dearest."

Finally, with a laugh she rose swiftly, drew the little cup from her bosom, and held it up.

"And this—and this," she cried, "I gift to my lord the

Emperor—may he live for ever! This much, no more shall he drink, from this time henceforth." She turned to him quickly, sinking to her knees. "Promise but this, my lord, and it is thine, my Luck is thine."

She looked divinely beautiful, her face all soft with a pleading that came from her heart; for those twelve months of intimate companionship had brought into her life a new feeling; the feeling of a mother for her wayward son.

Jahângir reached forward and held the cup she held; but his eyes were on her face in passionate delight.

"Most beautiful!" he said almost triumphantly, "Most beautiful, I promise! Nay, more—this Luck of thine shall measure all my pleasure. All—all—all shall be thine."

"Then take it, my lord," she replied softly, and stooping to the cup laid her lips to it. So the blood-reds mingled once more ere her slim fingers loosed their hold, leaving the crimson cup in the man's hands. He held it at arm's length for a second, every atom of him tingling with fierce delight. At what he scarcely knew—at her beauty, her wit, the cleverness of the whole incident, the entrancing romance of it all.

"Yea, I promise!" he cried, and took her kiss from the cup's lip as he spoke. Then he started suddenly; his eyes took on a new expression. He turned the cup about and about, scanning it narrowly.

"Crystal, didst say?" he exclaimed at last. "Nay, 'tis a ruby—before Heaven 'tis a cut ruby, and I ought to know." Quick as lightning his diamond ring was off and scoring the cup forcefully. Not a sign showed on the polished surface, and he laughed exultantly. Then as quickly his face grew grave. "Lo! it is fate," he murmured; "all these long years I have sought—I have waited for the gem of gems—and I have found both—in one!"

"Art sure, my lord?" asked Nurmâhal curiously. "Is it not over large?"

"The largest in the world," replied Jahângir, once more exultant. "And it hath no flaw, save this small one here—and 'tis pure pigeon's blood—a gem without price, without fellow! 'Tis worth millions."

But Nurmâhal was silent. Was this, then, the secret of the Luck—the ultimate end of all things—money?

"I wist not it was so valuable," she said dully. "I gave it thee—for luck."

"And it shall be for luck!" cried the Emperor, pleased beyond measure—"our luck—not mine or thine, but ours." He clapped his hands together, and when the servant waiting outside appeared, bid him go fetch the Court jeweller and his scales without delay; he must see at once what his treasure weighed.

"Were it to weigh the world's weight," said Nurmâhal suddenly, "'twould mean no more to me."

But Jahângir had thrilled to another note, and scarcely listened. So her brows levelled themselves, her eyes darkened as she left him. Even so, ere she passed into seclusion, she paused to say:

"Remember thou hast promised, my lord!"

He glanced round quickly. "Yea, yea! God keep thee, dearest! I shall be over busy, showing this to the jeweller and taking counsel regarding its past, for more till to-night. If aught be lacking, thy father can ordain it—or thou thyself—Queen amongst women!"

She did not sigh over his quick absorption in novelty. She knew him too well for that. Yet the discovery of the cup's value was unfortunate; but for that she could have impressed him more with the responsibility of his promise. And there was need to impress it upon him. At first, in the glamour of his devotion to her, he had kept to her rules; rules so carefully made, so well strengthened by a thousand and one wiles. But of late, since they had returned to Court life from the hunting expedition designed especially to free the Emperor from the temptations of the old routine, lapses had occurred; and they must not occur; that was certain. Her reign must be absolute, her power omnipotent; that she knew. She had called to her aid all her charm, all her wit, her versatility, her knowledge of Jahângir's emotional nature—briefly, his temperament; and then the pricelessness of the cup she had held all these years as worthless, save as a talisman, had stepped in to cloud her appeal to the man's better self. There was the irony of fate about it! That it should be a ruby, of all gems, was in itself an injury; placing her on a par, as it were, with the numberless applicants who had sought to curry favour by pandering to Jahângir's craze for the stone.

She felt depressed; more so when she found her mother, *Bibi* Azîzan, awaiting her in her own apartments.

The good lady was now an old woman, and age had mellowed her somewhat. Besides, her delight in at last seeing her daughter in what she considered that daughter's rightful place was almost touching in its whole-heartedness. And when the Emperor, as a reward for her discovery of the rose essence (also, doubtless, for being the mother of Mihr-un-nissa!) presented her with a valuable string of pearls, remarking that she had "by her ingenuity bestowed a blessing on mankind for all time by her invention of a perfume which restored hearts that had gone, and brought back withered souls with a scent as if many red rosebuds had opened at once," she purely wept for joy, and agreed with the poetess Princess that it should be called "*itr Jahângiry.*"

Since then she had taken to coming to her daughter with long strings of petty requests, long tales of petty intrigues, most of which Mihr-un-nissa set aside, much to *Bibi* Azîzan's despair. To what purpose, she argued, was a woman the favourite sultana of a mighty monarch if one was not able to give with the right hand and with the left, too, just as one chose? And to Nurmâhal's gentle reminders that monarchs and monarchs' wives had responsibilities, she would reply with a snort that such talk might do for her daughter, but *she* did not find dew a satisfying diet!

On this day Nurmâhal sat patiently enough and listened. She even temporized, for she felt closing in around her that net of fine-spun conventional estimate of what a woman ought to be, will be, must be, from which all clever women have to suffer; briefly, she knew herself condemned unheard for all purposes outside that conventional estimate, not because she failed, but because she was a woman.

After a time her dressers came in to apply cosmetics, and braid her beautiful hair with fresh pearls and other jewels. To this also she submitted. This she had anticipated; but after her five years of freedom from the necessity for attraction, it was more irksome than she had reckoned upon.

Still, she could not forgo it. Her power over Jahângir was not sufficiently consolidated, as yet, to allow her to neglect any means of enhancing it. So, attired to perfection, the very quintessence of beauty, she waited until the hour chimed when Jahângir, finished with his day's work of audience, should come to her once more for rest and amusement.

And he did not come.

Even as she waited, she gripped the possible reason. When an hour had passed, she sent for the Chief Eunuch.

"What ails His Majesty?" she asked.

"He rests, Most High."

"Where?"

"In his own apartment. There is naught wrong, Most Gracious."

"Peace, fool! I asked not thine opinion. Slaves, my veil."

Despite the protestations of the official, she stood the next minute beside Jahângir's couch. He was hopelessly, blindly drunk, snoring like a hog.

With face set like adamant she returned to her apartments without a word. She did not even think. She knew that the great fight of her life lay before her, that if she lost ground now she would have no foothold soon. The man over whom she meant to have absolute sway had weakly succumbed to temptation—doubtless to treacherous temptation; that made it all the worse.

"When the Emperor craves admittance," she said briefly to her janitors, "tell him I do not receive!"

That night the whole Palace was astir. What new thing was this?

"He will trounce her, doubtless," said the women servants; but the men looked scared.

So did the Grand Vizier Ghiyâss-ud-din, the culprit's father, when, after an agitated interview with the Emperor, now sober, but sullen, he came to interview his daughter.

"I receive him not, father," she said in reply to all his

exhortations, " without an apology. Let him confess his fault, and I will forgive. Otherwise he hath the sack and the bow-string at his command."

Jahângir, by this time squirming, face downwards on his couch, heard the answer which Ghiyâss-ud-din, honest man, had the courage to give in its entirety, with mingled anger and anxiety.

" Hath the Emperor of all the Indies ever yet confessed himself in the wrong?" he asked plaintively, and Ghiyâss-ud-din, beginning to realize the importance of the struggle in which his daughter had embarked, was forced to admit that such a suggestion had never before entered into the head of mortal man—or woman.

Then ensued a tragio-comedy in the whole Court; for, naturally, such a piece of gossip could not be concealed. At first absolute incredulity prevailed. That anyone, least of all a woman—one raised from the dust, too, by the Emperor's clemency, as the scandalmongers, with their usual exaggeration, took care to proclaim—should dare to dictate to Nur-ed-din Mahomed Jahângir, monarch of the whole world, was preposterous, inconceivable. Then, as truth dawned, resentment became rife, and cabal against the offender grew. Stern old Mahomedans, with their beards dyed black or red, hinted darkly, as Nurmâhal herself had suggested, at sacks and bowstrings. The high Court ladies came and upbraided their sister with grave dereliction from duty. As for poor *Bibi* Azîzan, she wept and moaned. Why could not her daughter be content? She had more jewels and more power than any other woman in the world, and if she wanted more, a woman could always wheedle anything she liked out of a man. And then in her despair she let out a secret she had hitherto guarded jealousy—namely, that though she herself had always posed as a meek, down-trodden, obedient, dutiful wife, she had invariably had her own way in everything about which she really cared!

" That is no news to me, *amma-jân*," remarked Nurmâhal a trifle bitterly. " The difference lies here. I care not a split pea for the things thou carest for, and thou carest not one for those things dear to me."

And through the whole imbroglio she kept her head calm and

collected. She even sent back her regal jewels to the Treasury and began once more on her broidery frame.

"Thou hadst best not go too far, daughter," said Ghiyâss-ud-din warningly. "'Tis three days now, and the panders are busy devising fresh amusements. There is a Georgian beauty——"

"Thank God for that, father!" retorted Nurmâhal with a smile. "She is welcome to that side of him. I like not animals, that are not true animals, but men-beasts!"

Sitting there, a perfect vision of extraordinary, captivating beauty, the man who had begotten her, looked at her helplessly. Vaguely he felt that what she said was true. Here was womanhood, even motherhood, without one touch of feminine jealousy.

Suddenly she softened. "Entreat me not, father," she said; "I must be firm. Thou knowest not—none know save he and I—what promise passed between us ere we wedded. Were I to yield now, both he and I are condemned utterly. Let him make his choice between me and drunkenness. He must acknowledge his fault."

So she met even the pleadings of her dear old friend Khanzâda Râcquiya Begum, now almost an invalid, who sent for her and first upbraided her, then wept pitifully as she predicted Jahângir's return to his old bad habits. Then it was that Mihr-un-nissa set a trembling lip, and kissing the old withered hand, said almost appealingly: "I prithee trust me in this. Did not I launch my boat upon love's boundless sea? Must I not therefore quit me hardily?"

And the old poetess, hearing the familiar words, murmured their sequence: "Now indeed, Love endeth right; dying, thou gainest Love's best ecstasy. God send it may be so, daughterling!"

By this time Jahângir was utterly miserable. The Court functionaries had tried every form of distraction, and he in his turn had tried them all; but everything was Dead Sea fruit without that for which he had longed all his life. Everyone was at his or her wits' end, and still the man's pride of position and the pride of the whole Court was up in arms. Yet, when one venerable pantaloon delicately suggested a return to ancient methods of dealing with refractory females, the Emperor flew into a rage, dismissed him from Court, took away his salaries and perquisites, and was only saved from saying, "Off with his head!" by the bitter consciousness that he would make a fool of himself thereby.

And then the Emperor with his own hand wrote a letter to his tormentor, upbraiding her with cruelty and sending her a couplet he had written in his dark sleepless hours:

> "Turn not thyself away; without thee life is naught.
> For thee to break my heart—will it avail thee aught?"

And it went on to say that even if he had done wrong she also was in the wrong in demanding that the Shadow of God should lay down his crown at her feet.

The letter was in itself a confession, and it was pathetic in its helpless, hopeless pride.

Nurmâhal thought over it for a while, and then she sent for her father; he was her stand-by in all her difficulties.

How arranged, history says not. It only says that on a certain dawn Jahângir, alone, happened to be standing by one of the arched pillars of the twelve-doored marble summer-house which, after the fashion of India, centred the crossed aqueducts that divided the garden into four quarters. The marble flooring, edged by a low lattice-work of carven marble, raised him some four inches above the path outside; but four inches, yet enough for dignity. And history further says that Nurmâhal happened to be walking in the garden at dawn-time, and alone, also that, plucking roses as she wandered, her footsteps led her past the summer-house but four inches below the feet of the man.

A fascinating picture this for the mind's eye. Jahângir waiting a-quiver to give the humble salute which had been arranged was to presage forgiveness; Nurmâhal hovering between laughter and tears, ready to respond with a lowlier one. While all around the rosebuds were bursting and the birds singing, careless of such trivialities as a lover's quarrel.

And after all the programme was not carried out according to arrangement. Jahângir, it is true, attempted to be dignified, but his conventional salute suffered from his sight of the adorable dimple, and degenerated into one of supplication. Whereupon Nurmâhal replaced her courteous acceptation by an effort after the "*Tasleem*," or Court homage. Too late! At the first sign Jahângir was over the low lattice, and beside her, raising her to his arms.

"Queen o' Women! Queen o' Women!"

The bulbuls sang it to the roses, and the roses sent the perfume of love into the air, but only those two in the garden knew what it really meant.

Later on in the day Ghiyâss-ud-din stood looking at his daughter regretfully. "Hadst thou but been man," he said, "thou wouldst have ruled India well."

She pursed her lips, but made no reply. Even here she had to combat the belief that a woman could do next to nothing, and that in what she did do she must be actuated by purely personal considerations.

But in her heart of hearts she knew that though the verdict of her world might be to call her unscrupulous, cunning, ambitious, she had gained her end, and meant to keep it. That night she sat by the Emperor's couch and told him stories like any professional *raconteur* until the regulation dose of drugs given in the ruby cup had its effect, and he slept.

CHAPTER II

> "Lord, if I—sin-stained—rest a moment here
> Within Love's cypress shadow, wilt Thou sear
> My soul with vain regrets? What matters it
> Which Paradise I choose—the Far or Near?"

"APPLE of mine eye! Core of my heart!" murmured Jahângir fondly to his three-year-old little granddaughter, as he sat playing with her in the Garden of Splendour on the edge of the great Anasâgar Lake at Ajmere.

Four years had passed since he—the Shadow of God upon Earth—had apologized to a woman, and he had never regretted his humility. In truth, he had small cause to do so, for things had gone smoothly since then, both in Court and Empire; in addition, those four years of constantly recurring evidence of her husband's unbounded, almost unreasoning confidence in and love for her, had brought about such a softening of her woman's heart that as Nurmâhal sat smiling, watching the man and the child at play together, she felt that both were equally dear to her. And that meant much, for little Chamni, or Princess Parterre, was the darling of her relatives' eyes. The first-born child of the royal lovers, Khurram and Ârjamand, she was a perfect flower; or rather, not a single blossom, but a whole wealth of colour, scent, and sunshine. Hence her name, given her by her grandfather, who had inherited from his, that almost unbalanced love of beauty which goes to the making of a poet.

Nevertheless Nurmâhal had discovered in those four years of intimate association with the man whose personal destruction she had once vowed, that this love of beauty was not his most salient characteristic. That, strangely enough in one so given to ungovernable impulse, was love of justice, and she had long since acquitted him of having connived at Sher Afkân's death. It had been an unforeseen consequence of one of those uncontrolled exhibitions of autocratic power which his *entourage* commended, and about which he himself was of two opinions; for that he was indeed the Shadow of God upon Earth Jahângir never doubted for a moment. That conviction, indeed, lay at the bottom of his confidence in Nurmâhal. She had the power of making him what he should be, more easily than he could make himself; for he was extraordinarily indolent in mind. This, however, may have been due to his health, which even now was but indifferent; he would, indeed, sometimes remark regretfully that temperance did not suit him so well as excess, though his Empire had doubtless greatly benefited by the change.

How could it be otherwise? he would add with a smile, "when its whole fortune was consigned to the disposal of so highly endowed a family as his consort's?" Her father, without a rival in arithmetic; without a competitor in critical knowledge of every species of ancient and modern poetry; without an equal in facility of quotations. And what was even better than all this, with a countenance ever beaming with smiles and an intellect which insured that every measure of State unconfirmed by his counsels had, by reason of its inherent imperfections, small chance of remaining long on the statute-book. Then her brother, Asof Khân! The best cook in the Court, an excellent *raconteur*, to say nothing of his admirable qualities as Lieutenant-General of the Imperial Forces under Jahângir himself as Generalissimo. A trifle too stout perhaps, but that was doubtless due to the super-excellence of his quail curries!

Finally Nurmâhal herself. Here Jahângir's lightness would die down, and his voice would tremble. "Of my unreserved confidence the Princess is in entire possession. She is the incomparable companion of all my cares. I do not think anyone is fonder of me than she is."

Not a bad character, on the whole. And it was a true one; so, as he played with little Chamni, he looked back at the woman who had so taken possession of him thirty-two years before, when he was a lad of sixteen, and said to her affectionately:

"Dost think me foolish, wife? But see you, she is our child by rights. Khurram is mine, and Ârjamand is thine, and hadst thou not gifted thyself at long last to me, those two would never have come together. So she is God's gift to us for our wasted youth."

She could not but thrill to his thought. Yet it was not true. Had they indeed married in those old days they would have missed much. Yet she went over to him and laid her jewelled hand on the long thin fingers with their one signet of royalty.

"Mayhap, my lord," she replied. "God knows we could scarce love her more were she indeed ours!"

Jahângir smiled. "I could not, for sure. And thou? What says the proverb? 'No woman is mother till she be grandmother.'"

"Wouldst have me as old as that?" she said lightly.

"Old!" he echoed. "Of a truth I care not so that thou art *thou*. And she is like thee, I swear—she hath thy dimple." He held her hand close; but he clasped the child closer. Truly it was an adorable little face, but something in the absolute adoration of the man's expression made Nurmâhal say warningly, "'Tis not wise to set thy heart so strongly on any mortal thing. And Khurram may call her back."

Jahângir shook his head gaily. "That is not likely, with Ârjamand so fruitful. He hath son and daughter already, and God knows what the next may be—or the next—or the next. Lo! there is one each year!"

Nurmâhal smiled back at him. "Of a truth she is busy. Yet tempt not the Powers with love so lavish. God calls the little ones to Paradise more oft than he calls us older folk——"

"Lo! she is of heaven already," interrupted Jahângir. "And, so that He call not thee, I will be satisfied."

So he sat playing with the child. Prince Khurram, coming in a little later to pay his morning respects to his father, found him so employed and seemingly oblivious of his Imperial position, careless of all the magnificence which surrounded him—the silken carpet spread on the ground, the gold brocade screen set up to ward off the morning breeze, which on the Ajmere plateau, 3,000 feet above sea level, is apt to be chilly. The pearl-embroidered cushions on which Nurmâhal reclined, the posse of eager, expectant servitors waiting discreetly at a distance, all seemed forgotten in the flowerful face of the little child.

Khurram's usually discontented-looking countenance relaxed. Why it should be so grave, so proud, was somewhat of a perplexity. He was admittedly the Emperor's favourite son, almost the acknowledged heir apparent, and he had the full favour of the Emperor's counsellors. Then he had but just returned from a successful campaign in Rajputâna, where he had had the honour and glory of finally reducing the Rana of Udaipur to submission; a task which had hitherto defied the Imperial troops and their leaders—ay, even the great Akbar himself.

This he had achieved more by diplomacy than by force of arms; and he had come back, not with booty, but with the Rana's free gifts; and what is more, with his son Kunwar Kâran, who that very day was to make willing obeisance at the great New Year durbar. Thus there was no apparent cause for a gravity which even in those days set Nurmâhal's quick wits awondering.

"She hath been good child, I trust, during her mother's absence?" he said, somewhat primly, of his little daughter, who by this time was lording it over her grandfather's knee as cock-horse.

"She hath been as the angels of God," replied the Emperor decidedly; and cuddling the child he walked with her to the latticed marble balustrade that overhung the shining levels of the lake.

A marvellous view, this, from the domed pavilions of the Garden of Splendour—at one's feet, rippling lightly against the massive stone dam that hems in the gathered waters of the huge reservoir-lake, the breeze-stirred waves, green, pellucid, reflecting in quivering light and shade what lies above them, behind them; the Emperor of all the Indies with the little child in his arms; the golden screens, the orange groves, the rose thicket, the pillared minarets of the distant Mosque; and, crowning the rugged, isolated, rose-red hill, the Goatherd's Fortress, grim, inaccessible.

Forward, beyond the glittering lake, like blue tents rising out of the green plain, the Aravâli hills.

Curiously peaceful, curiously serene, seeing that for centuries

Ajmere had been the centre of strife for the most warlike nation in the world, the Rajput race.

Curiously domestic, curiously simple, considering that the man who stood there, absorbed in the child, was the object of the ambitions, the intrigues, the hopes, the fears, of his whole world.

The beautiful woman reclining on the pearl-strewn cushions felt the strangeness of it even while she set herself, as ever, to please; to keep her hold on things that Jahângir himself might have let slide.

"And Ârjamand and the two babes? How go they after their fatigues?" she asked in her full round voice; for Prince Khurram's wife—to whose memory he, as Shahjahân, was in after years to raise the Tâj Mahal—never left him in all his campaigns, all his wanderings.

For an instant the young man's habitually clouded face lightened and brightened.

"Well," he replied—"wondrous well, considering. And the lad is strapping for his nine months. Yet do I think it almost unwise of Ârjamand to follow the drum as she doth. Better she had stayed at home, woman-like, under thy kind protection."

Nurmâhal laughed a trifle bitterly.

"Yet doth she her duty as wife and mother nobly. And as for women being born to idle! So say all men, believing not in woman's strength and skill, till we teach it them. Ârjamand can withstand fatigue better than thou. Nay, 'tis true. To bear children as she doth needs more endurance than to win a battle—but of that no more. Since we be alone, I would fain have thy opinion on thy father's looks. To me he seemeth thin and colourless. His illness tried him much. The change of remedies—for at first he would seek no counsel, have no medicine, save mine——"

"This have I heard already," interrupted the Prince dryly, his dour face hardening.

She shot a glance at him of disdainful defiance.

"Thy newsmongers are worthy of praise, Highness," she said scornfully, "but mine are better."

And with that she leant forward and whispered something in

his ear. He started, and the dark flush flew to his face at what he thought none knew but himself and one other.

"But how didst hear?" he stuttered vaguely.

She rose, clapped her hands for her attendants, then swept him a royal salaam.

"From thy father-in-law, my brother—mayhap," she said imperturbably, "or mayhap from my newsmongers—but—I have heard it."

So saying, she crossed to where the Emperor stood to tell him it was time to be preparing for the festival, leaving Prince Khurram to digest the fact she wished to impress upon him—namely, that it was unsafe for him to count on secrecy for any of his doings.

Half an hour later, as she passed through from her attiring-rooms to the private audience-hall where she received her father and such high officers of State as desired an interview, Phusla the Strangler, attired now in a uniform positively encrusted with gold, stood with the other servants of the seraglio, his head bent over his breast; beneath, his joined hands showed in reverential salaam. She shot one look at him to see if the secret sign that he had news to impart showed also on the thin old hands; then swept on, satisfied that there was none.

This man, head of an organization which existed all over India, was literally her eyes and ears. Even her father wondered how she learnt so much, and often, as she sat musing over past events, it seemed to her as if the chance which had brought her this man's devotion was the greatest piece of luck in all her life. And it had come to her, in a way, from the *jogi's* cup. But secrecy, absolute secrecy from all save Dilarâm—and as much as possible from her—was the very essence of its value. None must know how she got her information.

She found her father awaiting her in the audience-room, his hands full of papers: an old man now, with a long white beard, his face was full of affection, full of pride.

"'Tis even as thou saidst, daughter, not as I thought," he began. "Truly thou art wise, and extraordinarily knowledgeable. So orders have been duly issued in the case."

He passed on to other business, and she sat down beside him

listening, consulting over the affairs of State. Seemingly she deferred to his opinion, yet a keen observer would have noticed the skill and tact with which she held command over her father's mind when she differed from him; but this was not often. For those two had but a single aim; to manage the Empire as it should be managed, and at the same time to keep up the Emperor's dignity as Supreme Ruler. It was not an easy task, but it grew easier as time went on, bringing to Jahângir greater and still greater trust and confidence.

When business was finished she rose to go, then hesitated, was silent, finally spoke. "Father," she said, "let not Asof Khân, my brother and your son, learn too much. Nay, I mean no complaint, but see you, things are different for him. Thou art heart-whole devoted to the husband of thy poor daughter Mihr-un-nissa Nurmâhal! Wherefore should he not be so to the husband of his daughter Ârjamand? Dost see? So far Prince Khurram's interests are as ours; but in the future—God knows! So ignorance is wiser than knowledge."

Ghiyâss-ud-din looked at his daughter almost awesomely. "Thou art far-seeing," he replied, "and the wisdom of thy speech is manifest. Yet, saving Asof, whom wilt thou have when I am gone?—and I grow old."

She took his hand and kissed it affectionately. "Not so old for all thy wisdom," she said brightly. "And God knows I may meet the bowstring ere thou meetest fair death. Nay, seek not to deny it, revered! For all the peace, all the power I possess, I live in danger of my life from day to day. What woman in my position doth not? And were it known that I, and I only, hold consent or denial in the hollow of my hand, my shrift would indeed be short. Yea, thou, with thy wisdom, thy accredited power, standest between me and possible death, certain shame, every hour of my life. So long, that is, that none know how I decide; only so long as that—shake not thy head, revered! 'Tis so, and I—woman though I be—have the wit to see it. So let not the cat out of the bag even to Asof! Farewell! All is arranged for the durbar, I trust. The entertainment being my portion is prepared—and thou hast a truly acceptable offering?"

Ghiyâss-ud-din smiled a little sadly. "Yea," he replied, "there is a fine ruby——"

She interrupted him with one of her sudden bitternesses.

"Oh yea, yea! And Asof hath another, and Khurram, and the Khân Khânum, and the whole string of you. All to curry favour with one who counts but in name—who is as a child, pleased with a new toy—like the Englishman's coach."

Ghiyâss-ud-din puckered up his face. These Englishmen, who had come on the first real accredited embassy from a European sovereign to an Eastern monarch—and who were to be formally received that morning—were no favourites of his. He preferred the Portuguese Jesuits who had hung round the Court for years.

"The Englishmen have nought of worth," he began; "I have seen their offering, and 'tis contemptible."

Nurmâhal smiled grimly. "All but the new coach, the like of which was never seen. And novelty ever pleases menfolk—ay, even to new women."

Her father held up his hand reprovingly. "Nay, daughter! Thou of all women needest not to say that!"

She looked at him for a moment without speaking, her extraordinarily beautiful face almost pitiful in its whimsical comprehension. Then she spoke.

"Do I not work hard for such position?" she said, and trailed away, the golden ornaments on her ankles tinkling, the golden circlets on her arms slipping and clashing, the great chains of rubies and emeralds, diamonds and pearls, swaying, swinging as she walked, and a perfume of roses and orange-blossom emanating from every fold of her silken robes, every plait of her glorious hair. Truly a figure armed at all points to ensnare, to arouse the devotion and the desire of man.

An hour or two later she sat behind a thin screen at the *jharoka*, or window of audience, watching her husband Nur-ed-din Mahomed Jahângir, Emperor of all the Indies, Pillar of Faith, Shadow of God, receive the felicitations of his subjects on this the tenth New Year after his accession. The quaint old town was all hung with rich draperies garlanded with flowers, and thronged to its uttermost with nobles, courtiers, soldiers, in their gala dresses. On the roofs, peering women showed glittering with jewels, and at each post of vantage children of all sorts and sizes swarmed, full of laughter, even the poorest with a yard or so of bright-coloured muslin for turban or waist-cloth. Looking down from the balconied window of the *jharoka*, it seemed a parterre of gay flowers; all the more like because of the wide green awnings that hung midway above the narrow streets.

The noise was incessant. Not from the crowd—that swayed silent, as an Indian crowd does to-day—but from the sweetmeat-sellers, the toy-vendors, and the insistent outcries to make room for this, that, or the other notable on his way to offer homage to Kingship.

The balcony and the wall beneath it were hung with gold brocade looped by great ropes of threaded amethysts, turquoises, garnets, and jacinths. The courtyard below was carpeted with silken rugs; and here two baskets, suspended from above by silken cords, waited in the charge of gold-encrusted servants. As each claimant on the Emperor's regard approached, he laid his offering in one basket, which was immediately hauled up on a lacquered windlass from above by no less a person than old Dilarâm, now fat almost to deformity. Its contents were promptly laid before the Emperor, and if they pleased him, a return present in like kind came down by the other basket; if not, the discomfited giver received his own again.

This procedure was for the jewels, the gold pieces, the various bric-à-brac, the rich stuffs and costly curios; the horses, elephants, tame antelopes, and hunting leopards that went to make up many of the giftings being led past in strings and accepted pending the Emperor's future decision; for naught unworthy could be taken by the Shadow of God, who through it all sat impassive, irresponsive, on the black marble stool of Majesty.

A marvellous stool this, that followed Kingship everywhere; a talismanic stool with a big red stain as of blood on it, showing how it had resented the footstep of an infidel.

Once, it is true, when his son Prince Khurram, a tall, martial, gallant figure in coat-of-mail, came forward leading by the hand a taller one in the dress of Rajput chivalry, with bright soft deer's eyes taking in curiously all the novel luxuries of the scene, diplomacy so far overcame dignity as to produce a slight bend of the head, a slight outstretching of the hand of fellowship.

An immense honour, this, from the Shadow of God! But Kunwar Karân, the mountain-bred Prince of Udaipur, must have his reward for his fealty. And from behind the Queen-consort's screen came a sigh of content, as the group, well pleased, passed on. So much, at any rate, was secure, thanks to Khurram's good generalship and better diplomacy, and the way was now open to a settlement of the Deccan difficulty, which had defied all effort for so long.

And now a murmur from the crowd of mingled amusement and wonder roused Nurmâhal to fresh attention.

The English embassy!

She could scarce repress a smile. Three men in doublet and hose, destitute of flowery robes, looking like forked radishes, their heads uncovered, shoes on their feet. She had seen the like before, since the Portuguese came often to the Court, though these, being for the most part priests, did not disdain the added dignity of dress. But at a function of this sort! Still, they bore themselves well, and the great Queen's eyes criticized keenly, as she noted their frank, upstanding attitude of courtesy without servility.

Yet their offering!

Even Sir Thomas Roe himself, writing a report afterwards of its miserably inadequate attempt at barbaric wealth in an assembly where six-thousand-pound pearls and ten-thousand-pound diamonds were plentiful as blackberries, admitted that it had failed, and that if his Company "were furnished yearly from Francford on the Maine, where are all kinds and rareties and new devices, £300 would go farther than £300 layd out in England, and here better acceptable."

It was a complete fiasco, and but for a quick whisper from behind the screen, reminding the Pillar of Faith of a certain coach and four, Jahângir might easily have returned the petty offering by the other basket. But at that moment, providentially, the Ambassador of the ruler of Iran appeared with a leash of nine European hunting-dogs, and the Emperor's impassive eyes lit up with pleasure.

It was a weary business, lasting for hours on hours, and after it was over the State procession remained. But here a surprising diversion occurred. Just as the Emperor—a gorgeous figure in sleeveless cloth-of-gold coat sashed with twined chains of drilled pearls, rubies, and diamonds, his turban showing the thin heron's plume of royalty, and hung on either side by a ruby and a diamond, each as big as a walnut, and centred by a heart-shaped emerald like a field of young green wheat—just as he paused at the foot of the stairs for his esquires to buckle on his jewelled sword and hang his jewelled bow and arrows over his shoulders, not one coach-and-four but two drew up!

Sir Thomas Roe looked at his second in command doubtfully.

"By the Lord!" remarked the latter, "but they are clever counterfeitors; and so quick too! 'Twould have taken our workmen a good three months to do the like."

"'Twill not last like ours, I warrant me," said the third.

True enough; but for the present it was so like that those three knew it not save by the cover, which was of gold Persian velvet.

Jahângir, meanwhile, was delighted beyond measure. Into the first coach he got, preceded by drums and trumpeters, the insignia of Empire, and loud music of sorts, and flanked by two gigantic eunuchs carrying huge fly-whisks of long yaks' tails set in maces of pure gold all patterned with rubies. Behind him came nine spare horses gorgeously caparisoned, their furniture garnished, some with rubies, some with diamonds, some, again, with pearls and emeralds. The State palanquin came next, hooded with crimson velvet, fringed a foot long with big pearls, but empty; for Nurmâhal, who had planned everything, done everything to please, sat in the English coach, which, new covered and trimmed rich, brought up the rear of the procession.

Half veiled, looking out with weary eyes, she felt small pleasure even in the success, even though Jahângir had once again told her that none in the wide world could compare with her for beauty or for wit. Even the new title he had given her—Nurjahân (Light of the World) instead of Nurmâhal (Light of the Palace) seemed of small account. It was true enough, but what did she herself gain by it? What had she gained in the past? Power, it is true; but power gained not so much by talent as by beauty. She felt cribbed, cabined, confined by it; she felt that she could not be true to herself. So the vague wonder grew as to whether, had she realized at first the price she would have to pay for power, she would have chosen as she did. Yet the very thought brought shame. The man whom she cozened and cajoled was, after all, well worth her care. So far as she was concerned, she could have no quarrel with him. And the child? This thought brought immediate joy, and she settled to content, little dreaming, despite her warning to Jahângir against making an idol of his pet, that the day drew nigh when the flowerful face would pass out of their lives.

"Chamni's hands are hot, dearest," said the Emperor anxiously one morning, and by afternoon the little lass lay languid in his arms, as he walked up and down the terraced Garden of Splendour, where the breeze from the lake struck cool.

"The fever will pass with the night," comforted Nurjahân, calm as ever. "Fret not, my heart! I will give her medicine out of thy ruby cup. It hath always brought us luck!"

Had it? She wondered, even as she spoke, and with a pang she remembered that other sick baby who had died, despite her care, in those far-off days in Burdwân. Ali Kul had stood between her and grief in those days; and now——

But the fever did not pass. Old Dilarâm, as she sat nursing the little one on her capacious lap, crooning the old, old songs to it, caring for it as even its mother could not care, shook her head tearfully over the dazed look in the eyes that but a day before had been so full of life and laughter.

"Count not the child as thine till smallpox doth decline," she quoted, snivelling. "And they say it rageth even now in the city."

Nurjahân heard, and quaked; but she kept her even calm, standing bravely between sorrow and the man. For a few days, only a very few days. On the fifteenth of June he had to face it. Utterly bewildered, he clung helplessly to her strength. Long years afterwards he writes in his memoirs: "I was greatly desirous of recording the event myself, but my heart and my hand failed me. Whenever I took up my pen, my state became confused; so that at the last I helplessly ordered I'timad-daulat (the child's great-grandfather) to write it."

And this is what he wrote. "On June 11 traces of fever were seen in that pure daughter of Shah Khurram of lofty fortune, for whom His Majesty showed much affection, and on the 15th the bird of her soul flew from her elemental cage and passed to the Garden of Paradise."

They buried the little maid close to the grave of the great Chisti saint in the Durgâh, and flowers of every sort and hue and sweetness covered the tiny body of one who had been as the angels of God. It sleeps there still in the sunshine in the little grave that for long puzzled the antiquarians, but is now known to be the sole relic of a tragedy of love and sorrow in the life of a man who was at once passionately cruel and passionately soft-hearted.

Nurjahân took him away at once to the "Chashma-i-Nur," or "Fountain of Light," a spot amid the mountains close to Ajmere which had hitherto been his chief delight. But he hardly noticed the change, and would sit with his head on his beloved's lap, murmuring her name over and over again. "Queen o' Women! Queen o' Women!"

Even when, five days afterwards, the news came that the bereaved, distracted mother had given birth to another son, and Prince Khurram, his heart wrung as much by his father's grief as by his own, suggested that the new-born should take the place of the dead darling, he only shook his head. When he returned to Ajmere, they had walled up the palace window which gave on the quarters where the little lass had lived, but months sped by and still the man's eyes would fill with tears at every trivial thing that recalled the child.

And Nurjahân watched him with jealous, apprehensive eyes. "The Emperor must quit Ajmere," she said at length to her father. "His mind is unhinged. He sleeps not; he eats not. Thus must it be arranged. Khurram hath done his task amongst the Rajputs well. Parviz his brother hath failed in the Deccan. He must be recalled, and Khurram be given over the Deccan design under his father. The Prince will go forward with an advance guard. The Emperor can follow at his leisure, and can journey so far as Mandu, anyways. It hath a climate more equable than this, they say, and the road thither is of the best for the chase. Therefore suggest this—of thyself, I pray thee, to my lord—of thyself, remember! And I will take the infant with me. By degrees it may comfort, though it can never replace." She paused a moment, and her eyes filled with rare tears. "He would not wish that himself—his thoughts are with her in Paradise."

Of a truth she understood this man; understood the womanly passion of his affections and their sentimentality.

CHAPTER III

> "The heart of man is as a marble screen
> Behind which hides His Face who holds the mean
> 'Twixt good and evil. In that holy Shrine,
> Swept by the winds of Heaven, no man hath been."

PHUSLA the Strangler sat looking mournfully at the crimson Noose of Death. It lay inert in his hands, the hands of a very old man, with fingers knotted by age. And yet, suddenly, the twisted rope of faded silk shot out unerringly and looped itself round Dilarâm's pipe-bowl as it stood on the ground beside her frilling petticoat.

It was even more flouncy than of yore, seeing that Dilarâm had grown inordinately stout. Phusla, on the other hand, was as inordinately thin. A mere thread-paper of a pantaloon, yet his eyes were keen still, with the keenness of youth. He heaved a faint sigh, dexterously loosed the loop, rolled up the silken rope, put it in a coil on the ground in front of him as he squatted, worshipped it with appropriate gestures as if it had been a god, then laid it tenderly in Dilarâm's lap.

"To thy keeping, O revered sister, I entrust it," he said mournfully, "for 'tis not safe with me in this mine own country." He stretched his empty hands over the wide valley of the Nerbudda river, which lay below the rocky scarps of the high central plateau of India. For Nurjahân's plan had been carried out, and, after five months' journeying, the royal party had settled down at Mandu, the capital of Malwa. A beautiful, half ruined fortress-town set in beautiful scenery, and in a beautiful, temperate climate.

"See you," continued old Phusla, "I was born yonder, and I learnt my trade amid the tall sugar-brakes, the thickets of grass, and the wide opium-poppy fields. Look! Show they not like the farthing toys full of coloured glass chips, the children turn to make patterns withal? Yea, they are God's toys, and they make men dream by their colour as well as by their juice! To sit in the sun and see the Dream-compeller drop like innocent milk! Ah, sister, it maddens the brain! And I sat so but yesterday when I went forth a-hunting with the mistress as usual. Ay, and I saw others of the tribe, who knew me not, doing as I—and to-day I tell thee my hand, old as it is, itches to be at work again, bringing sleep. Lo! I saw a fat money-lender as I came homewards, trotting along solitary on his mule, and 'twas all I could do to keep the Noose quiet. Therefore, lest I bring disgrace upon my masters, for God's sake, keep it safe from me——"

Dilarâm summoned up quite an appropriate shudder. "Not I," she replied scornfully. "Take thy fat red worm away! Shall I, governess to the noble harem of the Most Mighty, condescend to the custody of a Noose that hath slain Heaven knows how many virtuous men?"

"And women, sister!" put in Phusla with malevolent accuracy.

Dilarâm coughed. "Mayhap, old man," she returned after a pause. "But thy fear of sin comes over late in the day. What is a fowl to one who hath swallowed a sheep?"

Phusla looked at her with wistful eagerness. "Wouldst have me use it, then?" he asked.

She laughed. "I said not so—and yet"—her manner changed—"I would for my mistress's sake it were round some necks I wot of; but of that no more at present. So, if thou art afraid, meanwhile, of this"—she touched the crimson coil gingerly with one fat finger—"why not bury it?"

Phusla shook his head. "I should but dig it up again, sister; then I might return to my old life, and the mistress would lose eyes and ears; and that means more than thou thinkest, woman. Yet I would not burn it, since she may need it yet. Therefore it remains but that thou shouldst take custody. Then I can do service with a heart at rest——"

Dilarâm snorted. "To beguile the Most High with tales of tigers, and my mistress into spoiling her beauty by exposure to the sun and wind and storms—to say nothing of mosquitoes, sandflies, and such noxious beasts. I tell thee, old man, I am at my wits' end to repair damages——"

"Yet do we men not see them, sister," interposed the Strangler mildly. "Nurjahân hath charm more powerful than these. I tell thee she is as beautiful in hunting dress——"

"Traa!" interposed Dilarâm. "Try not to teach an old parrot! Do I not dress her in leathern doublet like a man each day? But there! the times are upside down! Pumpkins sinking, millstones floating! And all to follow my lord like a dutiful wife, so one can say naught. And look you, fool, I admit she is even more beautiful so."

"If thou hadst seen her as I saw her," broke in the old man, his eyes aflame, "thou wouldst have called her the Great Mother of Destruction fresh from Indra's heaven. Lo! saw I never the like, and no man neither! See you—my men had tracked four tigers, and the Emperor's men marked them down close together. So they lay and so they came out. Two together, one afterwards and one again. And the mistress was in the *howdah* with the Lord of Light. Now, how it came about I know not—mayhap 'twas a game between those two. But the Lord of Light laughed and, keeping his hand on his gun, bade her fire. And she did. First one, then the other, were deprived of life utterly by one shot each. Then, ere there was time for gratulation, out came another tiger. That took two shots, and so did the tigress, which came out last. Thus we were all amazed, and she sat smiling like the Goddess of Destruction! Yea, yea, saw I never the like in all my long life! The bodies of four tigers deprived of life in the twinkling of an eye! Until now was such shooting never seen, that from the top of an elephant, from inside a *howdah*, six shots should be made, and not one miss; so that the four beasts found no opportunity to spring or move! Truly 'twas a marvel"*

Dilarâm yawned. "And thou forgettest the best of the tale, O reciter of stale news," she said scornfully. "Namely, that the Lord of Light gave her two emerald bracelets worth a lakh of rupees, and scattered 1,000 gold pieces over her, as reward."

Phusla's eyes twinkled. "Methinks she was more pleased

* From the Memoirs.

with the couplet the poet wrote on 't"; and straightening himself he mouthed:

> "In form a woman is fair Nurjahân,
> Yet slays the tigers as she smites the man."

Dilarâm frowned. "I like it not," she said; "it doth contain allusion to matters best left alone. My late master Sher Afkân (may his pilgrimage be fortunate!) was, all men know, a tiger-slayer, but——"

"His wife learnt it of him, doubtless," interposed Phusla dryly. "Meanwhile, thou hast the Noose. Keep it, I pray, against it may be wanted. Nay, woman, thou must. That it is urgent, take my word. If thou didst understand the law of the Stranglers thou wouldst know naught but death or duty parts them from the Noose."

And he got up masterfully, leaving her staring distastefully at what lay in her lap. Being, however, a woman of sound good sense, she recognized the loss Phusla would be to her mistress; in addition, she had quite an affection for the gentle, suave old man. It would be a pity if he were disembowelled for murder on the high road; yet the Lord of Light was so set on equal justice that he would not condone a fault even in a faithful servant. And the mistress was learning the trick off him too—more was the pity. A body had to do duty fairly and squarely or suffer. So she tucked the soft silken coil into her capacious bosom, where it lay comfortably unrevealed in the contours.

Meanwhile, in another part of the Palace, Nurjahân, in consultation with her father, sat looking at a paper with set lips and keen eyes.

"Whose was this?" she asked. "I'll warrant me, Asof's. Well, I like it not, and Prince Khurram must be instantly advised——"

Ghiyâss-ud-din shook his head. "Too late, I fear me, daughter. No messenger could reach ere the deed is done. And after all, 'tis not so important, being but a slight matter."

"Slight; yet one that may lead to much. It saps, see you, at the sovereignty of the King," replied Nurjahân. "Besides, I like not to be outwitted even in slight matters, and those who devised this thing have, of intent, left small time for amendment. So a messenger—the swiftest—must start at once."

Again Ghiyâss-ud-din shook his head. "The swiftest known to me may be of no avail. And even if it were important, Prince Khurram might be trusted. He is heart-whole loyal to his father."

Nurjahân paused a second ere she answered. "Ay, heart-whole loyal. Yet is he a juggler with words, and words are ever untrustworthy. Yea, he is better diplomat than swordsman, good as he is. That is why I would have all things clear as crystal. Thou knowest as well as I, father, what this Court of ours is like. There be those that favour Khurram, those that favour prisoned Khushrau—would God his father would set him free! I held it would be less evil if the people saw him; prisoned Princes are ever priceless—and there be those who even favour Parviz, who hath no brains. And they be all of one mind concerning Nurjahân, who beguiles the Most High with witcheries." She clasped her hands over her head and let them fall apart with a gay gesture. "So be it! But even Asof shall not lead into a wrong path Prince Khurram, whom I favour, partly because he is the best of the bunch, mostly because he is the very apple of his father's eye, his son of good fortune—and Jahângir—God help him!—needs good fortune in his life. So the message shall be sent—and that in time."

"But how? and by whom?" asked Ghiyâss-ud-din incredulously.

She laughed. "Knowest thou not by this time, father, that I have magic at my command? 'Tis hey presto! Abracadabra!"

"In truth, daughter," smiled her father fondly in return, "folk say so. And thou hast the knack of making men who see thee serve thee—'tis thy beauty, doubtless!"

"Ay," she answered suddenly, petulantly, "'tis my beauty, doubtless. Were I man, all could see me—and all would serve—doubtless."

There was one old man at any rate who was ready at all times of the day or night to do her service; so but a few minutes later Phusla, squatted on the ground in the servants' quarters before his earthern firehole, was busy kneading hearth-cakes. Not that he needed food ere starting on his errand, which was, briefly, to give a certain letter to the nearest outpost of the Tribe, with orders to hand it on along the Deccan road by all possible—and to others impossible—speed, by day and night, through jungle and *jheel*, by field and forest. It was over early hours for dinner; but he needed one of the hearth-cakes as a hiding-place for that same letter; a hearth cake with a big bubble to it.

So he went on kneading, though the elastic dough, soft and smooth as putty, left both fingers and brass bowl clean, showing it was ready for the fire. And as he kneaded, he watched a fellow-servant who he felt sure was watching him; who had, he fancied, been spying on him for some days past. It was as well to be sure. The man was small, slender, dark; such another as Phusla had been himself at that age. So he went on kneading until curiosity prevailed.

"Thou art early at cooking this morn, O father," came the comment at last.

Phusla smiled innocently. "'Tis because I am hurried to-day, O my son," he replied, and the expected retort followed fast.

"Not in kneading, father. Thou art particular about thy dough."

The Strangler's eyes blinked for one moment. It was as he suspected. He was being watched; doubtless by a Bungler, paid by other bunglers to do work he could not do.

"Particular?" echoed the old man suavely. "Yes, all are particular when they desire bubbles on their bread; and I am partial to them."

As he spoke he caught up a lump of the dough, flapped his first cake to due thinness and roundness between his palms, so with a dexterous twist laid it, like a large wafer, on the hot griddle which awaited it. A second or two and the cake was ready for turning; a second more, and it was toasting on edge before the glowing embers, and the heat, acting on the half-baked dough, was raising a blister which grew and grew all over the surface of the round cake, like a big bubble.

"A good one that!" commented Phusla with a sudden grin

and a stony stare. "A body might hide a letter inside, and were it deftly done by one who knows the trick, none would be the wiser."

The man gave him a quick look of comprehension, knew himself discovered, and moved away, discomfited, in haste.

Phusla looked after him, chuckled, and muttered under his breath, "Bungler!" It was clear that somehow or another the fact that his mistress was using him as messenger had, even in that short space of time, become known. How, it was useless to inquire. All treacheries were possible in that environment. His part was to devise some other method of concealment, and that quickly, and to make his escape from the palace without an instant's delay. Less than five minutes after, he started. A very keen eye used to the trade might have noticed that the strip of tinsel round the bambu pipe-stem all travellers carry had been unwound and carefully retwined to allow of a slip of paper being coiled beneath it; but there was no other sign of a secret letter.

So he felt safe. Not quite so much so when he was stopped at the gate of the Palace by no less a person than Asof Khân and accused by him of being a Strangler; in other words, a member of a secret and outlawed brotherhood liable to instant death.

"But," faltered the Captain of the Guard almost fearfully, "he is servant to her Highness the Begum."

"'Tis for that I arraign him, with her consent," replied Asof haughtily. "Lo! the Emperor sits even now in the Hall of Audience. Haul him thither; Jahângir will see justice done."

Phusla's keen eyes blinked again; he was wondering how much they knew; not much, unless he had missed seeing what he ought to have seen; and he had been very careful, especially since he came to his own country.

He walked with the constable willingly, his mind busy with his chances. Nurjahân, screened as usual beside the Emperor's throne, lost more composure than he, as she saw her old servitor in custody. That her message was the cause of his arrest was patent; but on what count was he brought to the bar of justice? The first words of the accusation opened her eyes. Truly the old Strangler stood in danger of his life, and she was powerless to help. Even if she could have gained Jahângir's ear, she knew him well enough to realize that an attempt to sway his sense of justice would be vain. Dilarâm, however, who as governess to the harem sat at her mistress's feet, after craning forward to look through the lattice, glanced back consolingly.

"Fear not for the old man, Highness!" she said. "Lo! he is cunning as a snake that ever goes crooked to its own hole. Justice will slip off him like a camel in mud."

And Phusla, in truth, looked wondrous calm as he stood before the man who had power to say "off with his head" if anything in appearance or speech proved disagreeable. But Jahângir was a fair judge; on so much history is agreed.

"What hast thou to say for thyself?" came the quiet question when the accusation was finished, and the witness in chief (the slender, dark man who had but now watched Phusla making hearth-cakes and who had straightway gone to his employers and told them that the only way to prevent some message being sent was instant arrest) had given evidence that on the previous day, being by chance in a grass thicket near the high road, he had seen the accused with the crimson Noose of Death ready in his hand, watching a traveller with evil, gloating eyes.

Phusla salaamed to the very ground. "I say, Lord of Light, Protector of the Poor, that the witness was in truth watching the traveller himself. That I watched him, so that he had to refrain, and that his story is retaliation. Lo! Most Just, it is a question of the Noose. I say 'tis he who bears it, not I——"

A faint stifled shriek, "Shâh-bash! Shâh-bash!" came from the screened balcony, but no one turned to look; all were interested in the old man's dramatic appeal. "Lo!" he went on, "let the Most High decide for himself. He knows that the Strangler parts not from his Noose till death parts him from the World! Let the Pillar of Justice decide between us. If I bear it, then let Death be my portion—if he, let it be his."

He was playing a desperate game, staking his all on his suspicion that the witness was a Bungler.

Dilarâm in the latticed balcony was rocking herself backwards and forwards in huge delight. "Lo, mistress," she chuckled in a whisper, "said I not true? He is cunning as a snake! See, here is his Noose!" She pulled it out of her bodice and laid the crimson coil at Nurjahân's feet. "There is no need for fear! He is safe—he gave it me this very morn for custody. Truly he is cunning!"

Meanwhile, the Emperor, suddenly interested, had turned to the Court referee to know if what the man said about the Noose was true. The answer came guarded, careful. Whether the Strangler parted with his Noose or not was unverifiable, such knowledge belonging to an unrecognized tribal custom; but undoubtedly, the mere possession of a Noose was in law, proof of guilt.

"Enough!" said the Emperor. "Strip the men!"

A minute later an anatomy, naked as the day he was born, stood before the assembled courtiers, imperturbably calm, a look of conscious rectitude on its wizened face. Beside it another figure, also stark, save for a crimson girdle round its loins.

"Give me mine own again, good constable," said Phusla when the inevitable verdict had been given, amid the applause of most, and the ill-concealed chagrin of some of the spectators; "and forget not my pipe-stem, friend, since I go on a journey without delay."

His voice, unnecessarily distinct, could be heard in the screened balcony, and as he passed from the Presence he salaamed twice, once to his Imperial judge, on whose crude sense of justice he had so easily imposed, and once to the woman who sat behind the screen, feeling outraged by that Noose of Death that touched her feet, weary of this tissue of machinations necessary to hold her position.

Yet it was worth while! By taking on herself, through her father, all the cares of State, Jahângir had been freed to follow his real bent and to recover his balance in the outdoor life for which he was best suited. Free to record with his own hand in his Memoirs a thousand and one facts concerning such of God's creatures as he met with, a thousand and one small details about God's birds and beasts and plants and fishes—the marvellous affection of the big cranes for their young, and the quaint look of the four-horned antelope, the "peculiarity of a bird to whom water is said to be poison (though God knows the truth)"; above all, the extraordinary beauty of a poppy-field in full flower.

And beside all this there are the records of the chase! One can see him, a tall man with sad eyes and a somewhat heavy-looking, sallow face, the stoop of coming ill-health in his broad shoulders, discussing the number of animals he himself had slain since he first began to hunt at twelve years old. Eighteen thousand more or less; a goodly total; or was it a bad one? He hardly knew, being in truth a man of two minds, one cruel, one soft-hearted; but he had, at any rate, done the world a good turn in "ridding it of eighty-six noxious tigers." And through it all, his one constant companion was Nurjahân; for, ever and always "the Princess to whom he had given his unreserved confidence" shared his pleasures and his pains. History nowhere gives us an instance of more perfect comradeship; and that very evening the heavy face lighted up into absolute beauty as he said:

"Heart of mine! How I thanked God that justice forbade punishment of thine old servant! Yea, I will remember it again in my prayers."

For Jahângir had become very devout. Eight rosaries had he of pearls, diamonds, rubies, sapphires, emeralds, amethysts, opals, and onyx, and each held four hundred beads. So at every dawn-time three thousand two hundred words of prayer were said, and said truly. The man was in earnest; yet who could say how much of his profound interest in what he called "Eternity" was not due in the first instance to a desire to emulate his father's example?

Anyhow, in the cool of the evenings in the old fort at Mandu, he held many a discussion on religious and ethical points after the manner of those which Akbar held at Fatepur Sikri. The Jesuits were there, in greater numbers than before, and the learned Mahomedan doctors still scowled at them. The more so because Jahângir had hung a Christus and a Virgin to his chaplet of beads. And Sir Thomas Roe, the English Ambassador, scowled at the Portuguese priests also; but this was because they had told the Emperor that England was, as he had divined from the poverty of presents, but a petty State in Europe. Still, on the whole they were an amicable company, and circled sedately round the Great Secret. Poor Sir Thomas Roe, it is true, bewailed the fact that he found it impossible "to convince these heathen that the Christian faith was designed for the whole earth, and that theirs, therefore, *must* be mere fable and gross fabrication." He could see no sense in their reply—"that they pretended not that their law was of universal application. They did not even say that his was a false religion. It might be adapted to his wants and circumstances, God in His mercy having doubtless appointed many different ways of going to heaven."

Such an answer he found amusing enough, but quite idle; a position in which he found himself, rather to his dismay, backed by the Jesuits.

So they sat on the silken carpets in the balconies that overlooked the valley of the Nerbudda, while silent servants glided about with comfits and sherbets, which they ate and drank as they discussed the Humanities and the Infinities. Jahângir, his weak head occasionally flustered with a few glasses of wine, would talk misty mysticism of the Sufi school, the learned doctors would prate in different terms, exactly what the Jesuits prated of the Absolute, and Authority, and Atheism, while Sir Thomas Roe would put in his word for Duty and Discipline, and the Devil take the hindmost.

And more than once, the Emperor, confused in his own conceits, would say: "Would God, gentlemen, Jadrûp, the Hindu saint, were here! Without immoderate praise he sets forth clearly the doctrines of wholesome Sufism, and from him can we hear many sublime words of religious duties and knowledge of Divine things."

Then one day, when this regret had been reiterated, a voice from behind the screen where, on these occasions, the princess who had been given the Emperor's unreserved confidence invariably sat, said gently: "Jadrûp is here, my lord! Shall I bid him enter?"

In a second Jahângir's face was as a boy's. "Jadrûp!" he cried. "Lo! this is magic indeed!"

All eyes were turned to the figure of a Hindu ascetic which showed in the shadowy archway; almost a living skeleton, yet curiously beautiful, like the figure of a carven ivory Christ upon the Cross. Hairless, toothless, clothless; yet all this forgotten in the soft eyes, lambent with a shady light, that seemed to see things unseen by others. But the whole figure seemed athrill, as it were, to hear sounds unheard, and feel things unfelt. It made no salutation, this figure showing light amid the shadows. It stood still, grave with a soft almost smiling gravity.

"Dost ask of Jadrûp what he thinks, O great King?" he said slowly. "Then dost thou ask thyself, since all are One. *Tât twâm ussi.* Thou art that. The Twain are no more twain. All things am I; yea! I am all things. Myself within the heart smaller than a grain of corn, smaller than a mustard seed! Myself within the heart greater than the earth, greater than the heavens! Lo! He who beholds all beings in himself and himself in all beings, he never turns away from it. When to him who understands, this Self has become all things, what sorrow, what trouble can there be to him who has once beheld that unity? He, the Self, encircles all; bright, incorporal, scatheless, pure, untouched by evil; wise, omnipresent, self-existent, disposing all things rightly for eternal years. He, therefore, who knows this becomes quiet, subdued, satisfied, patient, and collected. He sees Self in Self, sees Self in all. Free from evil, free from stain, free from doubt, he becomes True Wisdom. Lo! he who, meditating on this Self in Self, recognizes as God the Ancient of Days who dwells for ever in the Abyss, he hath left joy and sorrow behind him; but having reached true Life, he rejoices because he hath obtained the cause of rejoicing."

The modulated voice, falling to quiet depths, rising to still heights, ceased, and there was silence. Out in the west beyond the curved blue veil of the world, the vanished sun had left a legacy of light, clear, pellucid as a golden topaz. There was no sound. All things seemed bound in an eternal peace.

Jahângir was the first to rouse himself from the half hypnotic trance in which the Gosain's words seemed to have plunged all.

"Said I not truth?" he murmured. "Said I not he had the Secret?"

But the others woke by degrees to say anathema. Such talk was impious—worse, ridiculous—since how could the Less contain the Greater? So self-satisfied, serene, they pulled Jadrûp's words to pieces. But he himself had gone, as he had come, as if by magic; and after a time the Emperor, wearying, gave the signal for dismissal. So the Absolute and the Infinite had to play second fiddle to the whims of a man. When all the guests had departed Nurjahân came out from behind her screen and stood beside Jahângir, overlooking the fast darkening valley. He stretched his hand out to her.

"Again, truly," he said affectionately, "thou art witch indeed! How didst prevail on Jadrûp to leave his grave that he had dug for himself and come hither?"

She smiled. "Doth not my lord say how, in calling me a witch? By magic, without doubt."

The nimbleness of her mind was a perpetual joy to him. "Yea!" he said softly. "Thou art the magic box in which my life lies hid, as the children tell in their fairy-tales." And he held her to him and kissed her passionately. Yet even so, even though he was very dear to her, even though she spent her whole life in thought for him, a passionate regret and remorse that she could never feel as he did, that for her this exaltation of emotion was not and never could be, rose up within her. For him the moment was one of unalloyed content; he had forgotten his world: she remembered hers.

"I have news for your Highness," she said. "'Tis from Khurram!"

"Then 'tis bound to be good!" answered Jahângir joyously, a-thrill to his finger-tips. "Lo! I took an augury from the Diwan of Hafiz, but the other night, as to how the Deccan affair would end, and my blind finger found the couplet:

> "'The day of absence and the night of parting from my friend
> Is over, and fulfilment is the end.'

So, 'tis bound to be good——"

Nurjahân smiled as she might have at a child.

"Yea, 'tis good. The Deccan is conquered."

He stood for a second almost overwhelmed. "Baba Khurram!" he murmured. "My fortunate son, Baba Khurram! Truly am I blessed. Truly must I open my lips in thankfulness before the throne of that God who requires no return—for such a son—for such a wife!"

And over the curved edge of the shadow that held the world that lay at their feet, the sky still showed cloudless, full of light.

CHAPTER IV

> "'This world is but a bridge,' said Christ-Messie.
> 'Pass o'er in prayer; build not; for what you see
> Is but an hour, the Rest unknown. Yet hope.
> Who hopes an hour hopes for Eternity.'"

To this hour these words, carven in red sandstone round the huge oblong of the Door of Great Height at Fatehpur Sikri, send out their message of transience to the world. And on this January morn, 1619, some eight years after Nurjahân had promised Jahângir to forgive if she could not forget, they showed clear-cut in their warning; a warning that was echoed in every stone of the deserted city of disappointment and disillusionments. For even then Fatehpur Sikri had been left to solitude for long years. Its marvellous palaces had been already the haunt of bats and owls; its wide streets had been the skulking-place of jackals and hyenas, and its gardens had been given over to the parrots and the monkeys. Then suddenly the Court had decided to halt there, for plague was raging in the capital, Agra; and even in those days the danger of contagion was well known and was avoided. Yet, though but a score or so of miles apart, Fatehpur, perched on its dry red ridge, had hitherto been immune from the disease; and so the fiat had gone forth that all things there were to be as they had been; and it was so. With the almost inconceivable rapidity which comes from unbounded wealth, unlimited labour, all things had been galvanized into fresh life, and the empty palaces resounded once more to the fulsome flatteries and secret plottings of an Eastern Court. The rustle of silks and satins, the glitter of jewels, filled the wide arcades; while over in Agra the poor were dying daily in their thousands. It is a strange tale, as it is written in Jahângir's own hand in his Memoirs, this tale of how the plague appeared.

"The daughter of Asof Khân, the elder," he writes, "tells me, and insists upon its truth, that one day in the courtyard of her house a rat was observed rising and falling in a distracted state. It was running about after the manner of drunkards, not knowing where to go. She said to one of her girls, 'Take it by the tail and throw it to the cat.' And the cat was delighted. It seized it, but instantly dropped it. Then the cat became ill, but recovered. The girl, however, died next day. Seven or eight people died also, and so many were ill that they went into the garden from that lodging. In brief, in the space of nine days seventeen people became travellers on the road of annihilation." To which succinct account a contemporaneous writer adds: "If the people of that house had left it altogether and gone into the country, they would have been saved, but owing to that step not being taken, the whole town was destroyed."

Have we in this year of grace 1916 got much further than rats and segregation?

The risk of infection being thus clearly recognized, there were doubtless quarantine stations between Fatehpur and Agra, thus emphasizing the wide chasm which yawned between the glittering Court and the dying people.

Yet that message of transience and hope upon Akbar's Arch of Victory gave on the wide plain of the world and took no heed to high or low, rich or poor.

The high certainly heeded it but little; for those four years since Prince Khurram had come back triumphant from a peaceful, settled Deccan to receive at his delighted father's hands the title of Shahjahân, or King of the world, and to have gold coins showered over his head in token of uttermost appreciation, had been years of good fortune for everybody. Jahângir had recovered much of his mental and bodily health, the Empire had been prosperous, and Nurjahân, through her father, had managed all things well.

For the most part the time had been spent in travel, and everywhere those two—Jahângir and Nurjahân—had been fast companions. In his Memoirs such words as the following are frequent: "The roads being difficult, I ordained that my mother and the other ladies should remain behind while I and Nurjahân Begum went on."

Together they had seen the sea for the first time in their lives;

together they had tempted, and probably found, sea-sickness in an open boat; together they had viewed many notable places, and shot dozens and dozens of strange wild-fowl and poor foolish beasts. And together they braved sickness; for Nurjahân appears to have excelled as a nurse, and we hear of her unremitting care for her husband, her stepson, and her step-grandson, the baby who was born when little Chamani died. And here they were within an ace, these two, of another similar tragedy, but fortunately Nurjahân's care and Jahângir's vow—which he kept—never again willingly to kill any of God's creatures, were successful, and little Prince Bravery lived to delight their hearts.

So we read how the Emperor sat on the *howdah* a-hunting, and got Nurjahân to shoot the man-eating tiger, apparently quite content to see her do his part, so long as he *was* there to see, and enjoy, through her, the pleasure of the sport.

A marvellous record, indeed, of absolute self-effacement. How many lovers would be capable of it?

We read also of how Nurjahân herself fell sick, and the physicians confessed their helplessness in treating her, until by the aid of God—Glory be to His Name!—a new one found a new remedy, and in a short time she quite recovered; whereupon, as a reward for this most excellent service, this fortunate one was given three villages in his native country, and a fee of his own weight in silver, which panned out at some twelve stone.

For Jahângir had been anxious; how anxious only Nurjahân knew.

But the anxiety was over. This very day she was to give a feast to celebrate her complete convalescence. Yet as she waited in the alcove of Akbar's palace, surrounded by every luxury that unlimited love could shower upon her—waited with the certainty that her husband's morning visit would surely bring her fresh proof of his unreserved confidence—she knew that but for him and her father she had not a true friend in the whole Court; not a friend more true to her interests than to his own.

Shahjahân? Yes, so far as their views were identical he would march with her, but beyond? She did not know. Asof, her brother? She had never trusted him. Mohabat Khân, the best General of his time? He was as the others—obsequious to her face, envious of her power, scornful of her sex.

There was Fedai Khân, of course! She smiled as she thought of him, the tempter, who had been set to conquer, and had remained to serve. The curled darling of the Court, whom no woman could resist, who, therefore, might be a means of bringing a woman into conspiracy's power; for there was scarcely one net which had not been spread for her feet. Fedai Khân, "the Prince of Devoted Servants," who had been given the title by her husband for his faithful devotion to one "beautiful as she was good, good as she was beautiful!"

No wonder the Court was against her, no wonder it was hard for mortal man of those times to realize that the tie which held Jahângir absorbed in Nurjahân was not a sensual, but a spiritual one. It would have been hard even in these days to realize that a woman, still possessed of every feminine allurement, should have left sex behind her. But she had. She was close on fifty years of age. Never in the heyday of her youth had the things of sense had much appeal for her, and through all her long and varied life there never was a whisper against her chastity. A curious record for an Eastern beauty, and one of beauty so incomparable. But her whole existence was one long marvel.

So as she lay amongst the embroidered pillows, awaiting Jahângir's gratulations on this her Feast of Health, she was half weary of her power, half exultant over it.

He came at last, tall, not so stout as he had been, his hair beginning to be sprinkled with silver, his broad chest hollowed a bit with threatened asthma, his heavy face alight at the sight of her.

What did they say to each other? It is hard even to imagine; they were so different in all ways. Perhaps they said nothing save of how Prince Bravery had learnt a whole chapter of the Korân, and how the big cranes had actually hatched both their eggs. For Jahângir's life, judged by his Memoirs, was made up of such trifling things. That, the receiving of rubies, the bestowing of robes and honours, mixed up with a gentle hankering after eternal values, seem to have filled up his days. There are no more outbursts of senseless passion, no more cruelties, or overbearing judgments. Even in the business of accepting presents a change had come over the Emperor's manner. "On Thursday, the 4th," he writes, "the offerings of Mukarrab Khân were laid before me. There was nothing rare on them, nor anything to which my fancy turned, and so I felt ashamed. Finally I gave them to the children to take into the harem."

Ay, he had changed, and like a flash it came home to the woman who had bound herself to him out of a desire for revenge that she was changed also. Where was her revenge now? It was lost. She had forgotten it absolutely in her care for this man's welfare; this man who was as a child in her hands.

And this January morning he was even more childlike than usual, for he was primed with a great secret of his own devising, a secret present!

"Thou canst not guess what 'tis," he said joyously. "By all the twelve Imams! how oft have I not been tempted to ask thy advice, and so stultify myself! But 'tis done—ay, well done also! Fedai!" he called, "bid the Master of the Mint bring what he hath made, and make thy respects to Her Majesty on this her Health Day—thou hast my permission."

The figure which in answer to the call stood with lowered eyes beyond the draped curtain was one to gladden the eye. From the sole of its buckskinned feet to the tip of its turban's tassel it was perfect, simply irresistible; and a slow, kindly smile spread over the royal faces as they watched the superb salaam that sent, as it should do for perfection, just the faintest perfume of musk into the air.

"Majesty hath more than my respect," said the young man mellifluously. "She hath all God hath given to Hidâyat-ullah, so called Fedai Khân! Most Merciful, the Master of the Mint presents his work!"

A minute later Nurjahân was looking with startled, almost incredulous eyes from a gold coin that lay in her palm to the face of the man who, with a wave of his despotic hand, had dismissed even perfection, and was looking at her as the lad Salim had looked at the girl Mihr-un-nissa in the Gold-Scattering Garden long years before. She did not love him even now, and yet the look thrilled her.

" 'Tis like thee, is it not, wife?" said the man. "Lo! I had it done ten times ere I was satisfied. But now"—his voice trembled with his emotion—"now am I quite content." And he bent over and kissed the hand that held the coin.

A few of that minting remain to this day. They show a woman's face superimposed upon a man's, with the legend: "This coin obtains a hundred values from the face of Nurjahân Pâdshah Begum!" So much he who runs may read; but it needs imagination to realize the meaning of it in the year of grace 1619 in an Oriental country. Even Nurjahân herself was taken aback by seeing facts thus pictorically presented. But Jahângir was too full of his idea to face practicalities.

"Lo!" he continued, "now may God send what He will—for see you, I grow old—past fifty now. Yet if the Call comes I leave Majesty behind me. Yea, the verse is true:

" 'If thou remain'st though I am not, 'tis well.
Life's feast be thine, for me the funeral knell!
Death comes to all. I reck not when or how,
So that men say, "At her dear feet he fell." ' "

There was silence, and tears clouded her clear sight for a space. Then with an effort she smiled, and said lightly: "My Lord hath altered the verse—'tis better than Nizami's."

She spoke almost at random, urged thereto by desire not to break down, to get back somehow to the commonplace. And she succeeded; Jahângir, easily diverted even from his emotions, laughed self-consciously. "Yea, dearest," he replied. "There is in me somewhat of a poet. Thou art happier in versification than I, but I have the better judgment, methinks. 'Twas I, remember, that was amazed at the quatrain of someone we found engraved on the stone at Byâna, by the drinking-fountain. Truth, 'tis a fine verse, whoever wrote it."

And he quoted, and quoted well:

" 'For some we loved, the Loveliest and the Best
That from his vintage rolling Time have prest,
Have drunk their Cup a Round or two before,
And one by one crept silently to Rest.' "

The words, quaintly unknown, pleased mind and body; he was out of the depths and afloat once more on the easy current of life.

And Nurjahân was relieved. She wanted time to think, and after he had left her she sat looking out on her world with her usual calmness; but the tears seemed there, still clouding her clear sight.

Not for long, however. Within an hour, seated behind the *jarokha* in the Audience Hall, she was watching the effect which Jahângir's new coin had upon the Court. Never before had she fully realized her crime in being a woman. Never before had she grasped thoroughly the fact that she lived solely by reason of the beauty which had captivated a King. Yet not one word of dissent was spoken; nothing but fulsome flattery, nothing but artificial acquiescence. Therein lay the sting of it. With all her power she was but a puppet in the hand of the Emperor of all the Indies.

Had she heard the comments which passed from lip to lip when the audience was over, she could not have felt the wound of her friendlessness more acutely. Yet as the company drifted away, comment rose rife.

"'Tis the cursed beauty of her that hath bewitched the Most High," said one, concentrating the criticism of his group, "and she hath so many charms there is no trapping her! Would to God she were in Agra, to die of the plague!"

"Folk die of it in other places beside Agra," suggested a sallow-faced man, as the knot drifted away discussing the outrage—discussing, mayhap, some fresh idea of conspiracy.

Shahjahân, however, with his father-in-law and counsellor Asof Khân, who went with him everywhere, strolled moodily and silently to his grandfather's Arch of Victory. It was a spot he liked; one that suited the idea of Empire which had obsessed him, since, as a boy of twelve, he had seen that grandfather hesitate in his choice of an heir. Possibly the boy—he had been Akbar's favourite grandson—dreamt dreams even then, and was disappointed in immediate realization. Certain it is that he never wavered in his determination to succeed his father on the throne of India. It was the secret of his loyalty, the essence of every action of his life. And so far he had succeeded. At twenty-seven years of age he was Jahângir's son of lofty fortune, his prosperous and noble son, the star in his forehead of accomplished desires, the brilliancy of the brow of prosperity. He was all that, and yet, as he stood looking out over the plains of India, he asked himself what security had he that his father might not in the end revert, on his deathbed, to the claims of seniority as his grandfather had done? It was a maxim in the Timurian family that, while the eldest born still lived, the monarchy must never pass to a junior. That was the secret of his grandfather's vacillation.

And his elder brother Khushrau still lived. Nay, more; there was not wanting a cabal to end his imprisonment. The hell-doomed infidel Gosain Jadrûp, to whose opinion the Emperor was over inclined, favoured it. And Nurjahân also! Was it only woman's pity for a man wasting his youth in captivity? Or was there in it something malign?

Suspicious by nature, silent, proud, loved but by few, feared by all, Shahjahân felt that this new whim of his father's was dangerous. He had said that he would leave Majesty behind him. It was one of his many conceits, and probably meant nothing. But if it meant a woman——

"The Begum hath invited Prince Khushrau to her entertainment this evening, and Majesty hath consented. Is't the thin end of the wedge to perfect freedom, think you?" suggested Asof Khân half craftily; but, in truth, working as he did ever for his daughter and not for his sister, he was genuinely alarmed at the new turn of affairs.

Shahjahân swore a good round oath. "Would to God," he exclaimed, "that he would die of the plague! 'Twould make things clearer."

So in the streets and alleys of the red sandstone city, so lately tenanted only by the innocent birds and beasts, man walked up and down, dealing death by the Great Scourge as a remedy for their trivial jealousies; while but a few miles away in Agra Fate was meting it out lavishly on the just and the unjust.

But perhaps Nurjahân alone of all the dwellers in the City of Shelter and Victory felt the Shadow of Tragedy looming ahead. She sat in hurried counsel with her father, her chin resting on her knees above her clasped hands, her lips set fast, her eyes keen, looking out beyond the old face that showed so kindly, the old mind that palavered so adroitly of wisdom, and beyond the walls Akbar had reared, out to the future of which neither he nor she could tell anything.

"I like it not," she said suddenly. "'Tis a parting of the ways; yet will I take it without fear. Lo! the remembrance of my lord's great goodness should be a light to my path!"

The old man's wisdom flickered. "And when the light is quenched?" he asked querulously, the suggestion falling as it were distastefully from his lips.

She threw her head back suddenly and laughed. "It will be darkness," she replied lightly, "yet mayhap darkness may be more peaceful than this day of deceits and dangers. But till then"—her henna-stained fingers closed tightly on her henna-stained palm—"I hold—all!"

Small wonder if she did, for if ever woman had the will and the power to be all things, to do all things, it was Nurjahân Pâdshah Begum. She never hesitated about money; Jahângir had from time to time gifted her almost with provinces. Their revenues were well spent in maintenance, but the surplus she lavished like water in giving pleasure to the man she had monopolized. Twenty thousand pounds on a jewelled robe for Shahjahân, in order to win a smile from his adoring father: thirty thousand to enable her father's yearly offering to be, as it ever was, the best of the bunch. And only this January evening fabulous sums had been spent on the entertainment she was giving in a garden a few miles out from Fatehpur. And if Jahângir had been secret over his new coin, Nurjahân had been trebly so over her preparations. None knew what novelty was brewing.

It was January, even in Hindustân mid-winter. Fully one half of the trees in Northern India at this season have shed their leaves, and all are equally bare of flower or fruit. Scarcely a season, therefore, for what is nowadays called a garden-party.

But money can do most things in a land where there are millions of men—many of them skilled artificers—at command.

So as, descending from the Imperial dhooli, Jahângir walked through the tunnelled archway of the gate into the garden, he rounded up sharply in sheer astonishment.

For the scene was summer! High summer-tide! Every

tree had burst into leaf and flower and fruit, every rose-bush was covered with blossom. The white gardenia scented the air, the scarlet of the pomegranate bells dazzled the eyes, a d amongst the burnished foliage of the orange groves hung golden globes side by side with waxen perfumed flowers. Dark green velvet starred with innumerable blossoms covered the ground, and in the moonlight showed like softest sod, while from every tree rose the song of birds. In the cool shallows of the marble water-courses goldfish darted hither and thither, and the fountains, lit by many-coloured lights into iridescent colours, fell in spray upon huge lotus blossoms, white, pink, red. In the central four-square of the garden stood a huge golden cage, spired and domed, that rose high out of long lines and festoons of soft twinkling lamps—so high, it seemed to touch the very sky.

For one instant the Emperor stood confused; then reached, as if in doubt, to touch a flowering peach-branch that swept above his head. As he did so a well-known voice said in his ear:

> "Why risk a touch when sight says nothing lacks?
> In a king's hand the whole world is as wax!"

He turned in a flash of recognition to catch a mere glimpse of a close-veiled figure slipping away through the crowd of courtiers behind him; courtiers who for the time were forgetting conspiracy in amazement.

The quip—one of many, for Nurjahân's talent for such *jeu d'esprit* was one of her many attractions—put the coping-stone to the Emperor's delight.

"Witch!" he murmured to himself in a full flood of amusement and admiration.

A minute or two afterwards, as he entered the golden cage, however, both increased—if that were possible—by finding the witch ready to receive him, dressed as a peacock! He sank into the cushions beside her and laughed till his sides ached again.

"Thou hast no right to that, sweetheart, being female," he said, touching her jewelled feathery train that swept away, and away, and away behind her.

She replied with perfect gravity. "Has not my lord heard

the tale of the peacock, who gave his tail to the pea-hen?" she asked demurely, and then set out to relate it in her best style. Yet all the while the Shadow of Tragedy was in her heart.

For all that the fun waxed fast and furious, as it did ever on such occasions. A gorgeous repast was served under the green velvet canopies and in the golden cage, whither came, by invitation, the few who were privileged to see the ladies; amongst these, of course, the Grand Vizier Ghiyâss-ud-din, who naturally, as Nurjahân's right hand, had been in the secret of the Garden of Magic Summer.

"All hath gone well, daughter," he said doubtfully, as—for a moment off her guard—her weariness of look struck him.

"Ay!" she assented coldly. "There remains but the entertainments, and they are good."

And they were. Jahângir has given us his estimate of the juggling in his Memoirs. "Never did I see or hear of anything in execution so wonderfully strange as was exhibited with apparent facility by these seven conjurors. In truth, though we bestow on these performances the character of a trick, they very evidently partake of the nature of something beyond the exertion of human energy. It seems, indeed, that there exists in some men a peculiar and essential faculty which enables them to accomplish things far beyond the ordinary scope of human exertion, and frequently to baffle the utmost subtlety of the understanding. I dismissed them finally with a donation of fifty thousand rupees, and the intimation that all the amirs of my Court, from the order of one thousand rupees salary and upwards, should each and all contribute something in due proportion."

A quaint admixture of speculation and finance, very satisfactory to the jugglers!

So the hours slipped by. The water-clock at the arched gateway counted them drop by drop, and the old wizened anatomy of a man who stood in charge of the gong beat them out in mellow, hollow notes. For the measure of the day and night was almost a sacred duty in the Mogul Court, where the monarch learnt not to "surrender more than two or three of these coins of time to the plundering of sleep," but to be "wakeful, because a lasting slumber lies ahead of all."

So one by one the record of them quivered through the moon-lit, lamp-lit air among the waxen flowers and fruits, among the singing birds deftly concealed in cages amid the foliage, among the smiling, flattering courtiers.

It was a world of pretence, indeed, and one weary woman, even in the height of her success, longed to be far from it. Twelve o'clock! She counted the strokes even as she uttered one of her smartest, wittiest repartees.

"What new device is this?" asked Jahângir delightedly, as up the central green velvet path one of the royal *dhoolis* came swinging, borne by four men.

"'Twill be the new singer from Delhi," replied Nurjahân, stifling a yawn. "I sent for her, seeing that report saith she is even as the angels of God. Fedai, go down and receive her with due honour."

With one of his most irresistible salaams the gorgeous figure of the Court dandy stepped gracefully down the lamp-edged steps, and the Court beauties craned through the wires to watch him. The men bodies, however, were more anxious to see what sort of woman an angel of God might be! But the glare of the lamps, soft as it was, half shrouded the little group in a golden mist as, the curtains of the *dhooli* withdrawn, Fedai Khân, with a swagger, prepared to assist the fair occupant to descend. She did not move.

"Most Marvellous!" began, with another elaborate bow, the man to whom singers and dancers were over familiar; then his jaw fell: "*Allah-i-hakk!*" he muttered hoarsely, starting back.

For the sight he saw was ghastly enough. Propped up by pillows into a semblance of life sat a dead woman, bedizened, bedecked, the tawdry finery of her profession contrasting bitterly with the still majesty of the clay-cold face.

His whispered exclamation reached Nurjahân's ears, over-powering the flutings of the birds and the insistent low throbbing of the drums which are the inevitable accompaniment of all Eastern entertainments.

She was on the alert in a second, as she ever was; for life was one long round of superintendence and supervision.

"What is't, Fedai?" she called, and added imperiously, "Do what thou canst!"

The words seemed to bring comprehension to the Prince of Devoted Servitors; comprehension of danger, possibly of death. But with the comprehension came devoted service, and he pulled himself together.

"The honourable lady is ill," he said, as with a hand that, despite his effort, trembled, he stepped forward and drew the curtains. "With permission I will escort her to a physician."

So adown the velvet pathway the royal palanquin ambled, Fedai Khân keeping that trembling hand of his on the curtain, while whisperings arose amongst the guests; whisperings, and amongst some, covert smiles and sneers, while one or two looked disappointed, as if some mischief had missed its mark.

Perhaps it had! Nurjahân did not stop to think.

"Master of the Ceremonies!" came her clear cold voice, "The next item—and quickly, slave!"

It was an acrobatic performance, and greatly interested Jahângir, so far, indeed, as he could be interested, for sleep had almost overtaken him.

But the mind of the Princess to whom he had given his unreserved confidence was busy now with possibilities. What had it been? What had folks dared to do? Her keen sight seemed to have seen a dead face. Had they meant to spoil the festival? Or was it more?

An hour or two afterwards, in her own apartments, she was receiving Fedai Khân's report.

"Was it of plague the woman died?" she asked bluntly.

The strong man flushed a little. "We did not touch her, Highness. Old Phusla came, and some of his belongings carried her to the jungle and burnt her—*dhooli* and all."

She frowned, but she acquiesced. Life must be dear to the curled darling of the Court; and yet she would fain have known what her enemies had dared.

"See that another *dhooli*, alike in all points, be made at once," she said, briefly adding after a pause, "So that ends it!"

But in her heart of hearts she knew it had but just begun, that she must be prepared for endless plottings and counter-plottings.

And her very soul sickened at the thought, even while her high spirit rose up in arms against her enemies.

CHAPTER V

> "In the Serai the Travellers sit and drink
> Of Friendship's cup with many a nod and wink.
> Yet some are Murderers, and some are Thieves;
> Only God knows what in their hearts they think."

"'Tis ever wiser to have two strings to one's bow," said Nurjahân, ending a discussion with her father. "And safety lies, when there are plots, in starting others. A multitude of hares perplexes the dogs, as all know. Shahjahân hath angered Prince Parviz by his jealousy; as if any sane man should be jealous of such a good-natured boy! Therefore thou must work on the latter to see in Khushrau's release a hope of revenge on Shahjahân. And the Gosain Jadrûp can be bribed to support the release also——"

Ghiyâss-ud-din shook his head. "'Tis ill bribing a holy man——" he began.

Nurjahân laughed. "Bribe him by his holiness, father! He hath an overweening conceit of his own morality. Show him that the worldly do not wish it, and he is caught in the snare of his virtue."

She spoke bitterly, since in truth her heart was hardening under the pressure of her surroundings; for all save the man whose welfare was now so bound up in her own that it was impossible to separate their interests.

"And," she added in a different tone, "'twill be better for the Emperor's peace of mind. He is not full satisfied concerning Khushrau himself; else would he long ago have yielded to the claim of death for which Shahjahân's success calls so loud——"

"Most true," put in Ghiyâss-ud-din craftily; "but if the Timurid law of seniority doth harass the King, will it not increase this if Khushrau be set free?"

"'Twill salve the present; and I mean it not to affect the future," replied the Empress curtly; "but 'twill strengthen my hands in regard to Shahjahân and keep him where I wish him to remain, in the right path. Therefore prepare Parviz. His offering must be superb. My revenues are his, so see that nothing lacks!"

And nothing did lack. Parviz, arriving from Allahabad to pay his respects to the Emperor, presented gifts to the value, they say, of four millions of money—eighty trained elephants of the highest value; two hundred thoroughbred horses caparisoned in gold; a thousand dromedary camels chosen for their speed; to say nothing of trays on trays of the rarest fabrics and the most costly jewels.

No wonder is it that Jahângir, ever ready, boy-like, to be tickled by a straw, threw a pearl chaplet round his son's neck and instantly trebled his emoluments.

It was a good beginning; then novelty supplied an extra fillip to the growth of paternal pride. It was some years since Jahângir had seen his son, who had grown to be a fine-looking man, portly as was his father at his age, but with frank, engaging manners.

So he was received effusively and placed on the Emperor's right hand, while Shahjahân, with twice his brains and four times his reputation, was relegated for once to the left hand, where he sat glowering, wondering what the magnificence of the reception meant. He, of course, was accustomed to such welcome. His, after his Deccan triumph, had been still more effusive; but Parviz had done nothing to deserve this save pour riches at the Emperor's feet. So, cursed by his suspiciousness, Shahjahân stood aloof from the rejoicings.

It was not till a full month after the welcome that Parviz appeared one day at the private audience, bare-headed, the blue kerchief of sorrow round his neck, and casting himself at the Emperor's feet, broke out into bitter regret. It was beyond endurance, he complained, to bear the load of reflection, that while he and his two brothers, Shahjahân and young Shâhriyâr, could pass their lives in every kind of amusement and indulgence and ease, that their eldest brother should for fifteen years have dragged on a wretched existence in the solitude of a prison. It was not the lot of frail humanity to be blameless; but clemency was the peculiar and most becoming attribute of Kings!

The whole scene was probably artificial, the result fore-ordained. Jahângir asked if Parviz was prepared to accept responsibility that the unhappy Khushrau would never again commit himself by disloyal and refractory conduct; whereupon Parviz immediately committed to paper a few lines in the nature of a surety bond, and all went merry as a marriage-bell.

Except to Shahjahân. He was close to the end of the tether of loyalty. Nurjahân, with all her cleverness, had not rightly calculated the full measure of his suspicions. What she had deemed should bring him to heel, by arousing his dread of dangers to come, had awakened reckless antagonism. Something must be done, and at once, to allay his resentment. He must not be allowed to take the wrong path. She must make an effort to reassure him. But how?

She was sick to death of plotting and counter-plotting. Shahjahân had brains. She would tell him the truth.

So she sent for him, and he came to her in the small gallery overlooking the river. The whole palace had lately been redecorated by the Emperor in his lavish, flamboyant manner, the pillars all covered with plates of gold and inlaid with rubies, turquoises, pearls. The very marble of the lattice-work of the balcony was gilt and coloured. In sharp contrast to all this splendour, Nurjahân sat on a low stool simply dressed in white, as she had ever been in those first years of her acquaintance, in the Garden of Roses, with the darling of old Râcquiya Begum's heart.

"*Farzand*" (son), she began, smiling, "'tis as the friend of thy more than mother that I desire to speak to thee to-day. Sit yourself so thou canst see my face, and listen to the truth."

"The truth falls not often from a woman's lip," he replied.

She bit hers to keep back a sharp answer. "Not from Ârjamand's?" she asked, still smiling. "And she is close kin to me. I think thou dost forget that. Lo! thy children are as mine. Bethink thee, Shahjahân! Did I not nigh kill myself nursing thy nurseling? Is he not even now the apple of mine eyes? And setting sentiment aside, bethink thee again! Should I, whose brain has brought me—here—prefer a dullard to one who—despite his evil jealousy—could carry on my work as I would wish it carried on? Listen, O Shahjahân, to more than I have told others. I came into thy father's life from a desire to revenge Sher Afkân's death. Well, that has gone. I live now to make thy father happy. Do I not succeed? Answer me that?"

"Ay," he admitted grudgingly; "but 'tis to thine own advantage he is happy."

She burst out at him: "Thou speakest truth. I live but by thy father's pleasure. Without him I am lost. So I will keep him while I can. And he loves thee, Shahjahân! God! how he loves thee! Thou art his star of perfection. Yet of late thou hast been adverse to me, not seeing that without me the Emperor would—would die! Yea, that is God's truth. Ah, foolish one! Canst not see our interests must be as one, or we both fall? See here! Let us make a compact. If thou wilt be true to me, hindering me not at all in this my work, I will be true to thee. Thy father loves thee. In his private talk he speaks of thee as heir. This will I continue to nourish, if——"

Shahjahân's gloomy face gloomed still more.

"Then wherefore use thine influence for Khushrau?" he asked bitterly.

She gave him a keen cold glance. "First as safeguard for myself against thee if thou art recalcitrant. 'Tis ever good to have two strings to one's bow. There! Thou hast the truth. Next, because the Emperor was fretted in his mind. Thou knowest of late he hath taken seriously to religion—overmuch mayhap—and he feared to be unjust. He hath a soft heart, Shahjahân—and—and he is somewhat afraid—of God's wrath! As if—but no matter! Third"—here she smiled suddenly, radiantly, and the old dimple asserted its charm—"because Khushrau is a good-looking, good-natured dolt, who will harm none so long as folk see what he really is. I'll warrant me in a year the ardour of those who favour a poor, persecuted Prince in prison will have cooled. Nay, Shahjahân," she continued, "emulate not his stupidity. Thou hast the brains, man; so Shahjahân, and Shahjahân only, is what Nurjahân chooses." She held out her hand, and for the life of him, the man could not choose but take it. Ay, she was clever, and beautiful beyond compare. Confused thoughts of a change in his policy, of making this woman his friend indeed, coursed through his brain.

"So long," she added, fixing her luminous eyes upon him, "as thou keepest to the straight path. See you—I would fain end this doubt of each other—I have told you the truth—dost accept it?"

She held him by her masterful wit. In her presence, with those eyes upon him, he felt she told truth. Yet even so, his response was niggardly.

"I accept for the past and present. The future is with God," he said; and with that Nurjahân had perforce to be content.

It made the present easier, at any rate; for Jahângir, once he had made up his mind to forgive his eldest son, seized on the occasion with all the zèst of a child as an opportunity for merry-making and display.

If he was to forgive, he declared, it must be done in right royal fashion, and with no reservations. And all must take part in it. To begin with a truly magnificent entertainment must be prepared in the "Abode of Light" garden. This was one of the largest gardens in India, covering some three hundred acres of ground and enclosed by an exceedingly strong and lofty wall. A canal, passing through its midst, filled large reservoirs in each corner, and a marble-stepped tank in the middle; while round each sheet of water rose carven marble pavilions richly decorated. So much the art of man had done for beauty; but Nature had put the last touch of perfection, for nowhere else did flowers blossom in such profusion; nowhere else did the fruit-bearing trees in every variety grow so lofty, so lavishly; while all along the wide four-square paths edged by water-runnels, tall cypresses of incomparable age and size and form stood sentinel.

A place in which, amid the silence from all whisper even of the outside world, to dream away the hot hours of a summer day, forgetful of all but the flickering butterflies, the scent of the flowers, the song of the birds.

A pity, surely, to profane it with coloured lamps and gold embroidered carpetings. But this was done without regard to expense, and on the appointed day Prince Khushrau was brought thither with all pomp, arrayed in one of the Emperor's best suits, encrusted with diamonds, seated on his best elephant in a jewelled *howdah* that cost £300,000.

But nothing lacked to support the splendour of his rank as Prince of the blood royal.

In truth Jahângir had enhanced the preciousness of the reconciliation scene by every possible device, and when his son, tall and handsome, lay at the foot of the throne, his head at his father's feet, reciting verses indicative of his deep distress, and imploring clemency for the past and indulgence for the future, the Emperor felt a vast satisfaction at the display of magnificence with which, after his son had been discarded from the presence for a period of fifteen years, he was once again admitted to do homage to the Personality.

And Nurjahân? Doubtless some of the courtiers, even those who were most in favour of Prince Khushrau, had their tongues in their cheeks; but she knew the Emperor too well for that. She knew that it was all real to him, that in his heart of hearts he was glad to be at peace with all his sons.

He beamed so that he even infected Shahjahân, who did his part with a wonderfully good grace when Jahângir, ever full of ideas and conceits, ordered a rich carpet to be spread before him, then called his four sons to seat themselves on it, and pass round a loving-cup in token of their good accord.

"It shall be my cup," quoth Jahângir in his full, joyous voice, "the cup of luck! The cup from which I drink ever, the cup that hath brought me freedom from the toils of intoxication." And he looked round lovingly to where Nurjahân, barely screened by golden lace-work, sat beside his throne.

It was somewhat of an exaggeration, this statement of his, for with the years, the ruby cup had ceased to be in constant use, and the Emperor's potations had somewhat increased, though they were still moderate in comparison with what they had been, and did not interfere at all with his dignity as monarch. Still, the statement reflected his mood at the moment, the cup was produced, and the four brothers toasted each other in it, all smiles and laughter, while the courtiers craned and crowded round to see.

"'Tis a quaint cup," said suddenly a man with the level bars of Vishnu worship on his forehead. "Whence came it, dost know?" he asked of his neighbour. But the neighbour shook his head, and no more was said. Yet a pair of covetous eyes followed the servant who, when the ceremony was over, removed the beaker of wine and the cup for safe custody.

Then ensued the inevitable entertainment. The slow struttings of professional dancers went on interminably, while Jahângir yawned contentedly and the head officials sat round in adulation. But for others there were other amusements, and down in one of the corner pavilions, whither Nurjahân had retired, little Prince Bravery was getting his fun out of the show by a variety entertainment. Marionettes, jugglers, conjurors, snake-charmers, all in turn and of the very best, displayed their arts, to his intense satisfaction and that of the ladies of the Court, amongst them his grandmother and old Khanzâda Râcquiya, who, still prim, still precise, was almost bent double with rheumatism. Yet she enjoyed the performances hugely and clapped her little hands louder than Prince Bravery clapped his.

"Now, have a care, child; the next is snakes!" she shrilled as a man with his *banghy* baskets appeared salaaming.

Old Phusla the Strangler, who, in a uniform that was literally encrusted with gold, sat sleepily on the second step of the pavilion, looked up suddenly.

"Snakes! Who wants snakes?" cavilled one of the harem ladies, yawning. "Take them away and let us have something of entertainment."

"Nay, sister," remonstrated Nurjahân. "These be from the Deccan, and the Prince hath oft told me they excel there—and the child loves them, dost not, little one?"

The child, who, spoilt unbearably after the manner of Eastern children, had at first word of dissent made preparations for tears, turned to smiles instead, and his grandmothers called down blessings on his head, after the manner of fond Eastern grandmothers.

And of a truth the snakes were worthy smiles. They danced, and tied themselves in knots, and did homage in curves to perfection.

It was, a quaint scene. Just a corner of the wide garden that was filled to overflowing with pleasure-seekers; a corner screened off for the women folk, who sat chattering, laughing, chewing *pan,* and idly watching or not watching the group upon the marble steps. A group seen mistily by the soft light of the innumerable little cresset lamps that outlined the pavilions into palaces of golden light. Overhead fire balloons showed on the violet velvet of the sky, and rockets like shooting stars sped over the arch, burst, and sank in showers of coloured sparks; for in another corner of the garden fireworks were being sent up. It all seemed to centre round the dancing, swaying cobras, the lithe dark man blowing his hollow notes, and old Phusla, but half awake upon the second step; and above that, on the top one, Nurjahân, with the child upon her lap; behind the other ladies.

"Have a care, slave," cried Phusla sharply, as a snake—surely new escaped from the basket—slid swiftly upwards towards royalty, and two or three of the ladies screamed; notably the grandmothers.

"Nay!" smiled Nurjahân. "'Tis not the man's fault utterly. Thou hadst best take the boy thyself, *amma-jân,* if thou art feared; for the beasts come ever to me, do they not, Dilarâm?"

Dilarâm, who, despite her many years and increasing stoutness, still insisted on her position as governess to the harem when entertainments were going on, wheezed a long-winded reply, beginning with experiences in the Garden of Roses.

Meanwhile the snake-charmer, who had deftly made a dive after the curbing rope of a thing, caught it by the tail and run his hand up behind its hood, was standing within easy reach of Nurjahân, who had risen slightly to place the child on Maryâm Zamâni's lap.

"And there is no fear, Highness," he began in a wheedling voice, bowing down towards her as she sank back among her pillows, "since the poison fangs are drawn. If Majesty permits, I will show her—see——"

He gripped the snake firmly enough, it is true, but a hand that, for all its age, its slimness, was as iron had gripped his. Phusla had leapt to his feet and was on him, his old face demoniacal in swift passion. "See thyself, Bungler!" he gasped in the deadly struggle that ensued.

The snake, gripped hard by the double strain, writhed in helpless fury from one man's arm to the other, impotently biting the air as in the mad effort for mastery the hands that held it veered dangerously near body or face.

It takes long to describe the swiftness, the intensity, of the moment. But it was only a moment.

With a repetition, this time low, guttural, of "See thyself, Bungler!" scarce heard in the awful sob of agonized fear that broke from the wretched snake-charmer's lips, Phusla forced the open snapping mouth on to the man's chin. It was done in a moment—the fatal bite was given. He loosed his hold, but Phusla's tightened on the reptile's throat. Then with his left hand he caught it by the tail and, with one swift movement, flung it from him furiously—flung it as he would have flung his Noose of Death—and the creature, with death in its undrawn fangs, sped over the heads of the watching crowd, the lights glancing on its twining curves—shot like some deadly messenger of evil, its jaws still snapping wildly at the air, so with a dull thud crashed to death on the marble pavement at the other side of the reservoir.

It had all passed so quickly that the spectators gasped, knowing not what to think, understanding not at all the cause of Phusla's swift attack; but Nurjahân guessed, and in a second she was ready for the occasion.

"Thou art somewhat rough in thy teaching of manners, Phusla," she said; "but"—she hesitated briefly—"he deserved it!" And her voice trembled a little. "Let him nevertheless depart in peace now."

Phusla, however, had anticipated her order. The snake-charmer, too terrified at the certainty of swift death to do more than moan feebly, was being hurried away, bag and baggage, and the Master of the Ceremonies was already producing a new turn; a turn to arouse titters. Only Râcquiya Begum shook her old head sagely and said:

"'Twas well the Emperor was not here. He would have had the fellow trampled to death for his impertinence."

Nurjahân looked over to the old woman and saw vague comprehension in her eyes.

" Phusla hath punished him enough, methinks," she replied calmly, " and it but frets my lord to hear of such trivial troubles; therefore let it be as if it had not been."

But as she sat watching wearily amid the titters of the others, her mind was busy. Phusla must have been suspicious; he must have seen the poison-fangs. Phusla had possibly saved her—if indeed the snake would have bitten her. Then with a rush came the thought that it would have brought the end—brought peace. And she was very weary of it all. Her spirits revived, however, over the wonder as to whose plot it had been.

Not Shahjahân's, of that she felt certain. He was no murderer. But there were many others—many, many others.

What did it matter ? She must be careful and take her chance. One thing was impossible—that she should be turned from her purpose by fear of death.

CHAPTER VI

> "Like golden scissors cutting silk, the duck
> Nips at the azure pool; the warm winds suck
> Kisses from flower lips; my Love and I
> Lie close and pull rose petals, seeking Luck."

"HEART of my heart!" said Jahângir with a sigh, "this Kashmir country is hard to come by, hard to leave; and time passes swift therein! 'Tis but the other day we sped to see the black tulips blossoming on the mosque roof, and now the saffron paints the fields. Lo! the breeze scents my brain with the perfumes of the flower—groves on groves of it, plains on plains. Yet it needed not that for contentment, wife."

He did not look as if it did, as he lay indolently in the royal barge that was drifting down the Apple Tree Canal towards the city of Srinager. Behind them, tipped by a black marble temple of hoary age, lay the Takht-i-Sulaiman, the Throne of Solomon, quaint isolated hill whence you look out over what is surely one of the fairest countries in God's world—the Vale of Kashmir.

Nurjahân nodded assent. The past six months, since, out-wearied utterly by plague and plots, the royal pair had conceived the idea of spending the summer in the playground of the East, had sped by with scarce a cloud to mar their perfect peace, their absolute enjoyment.

"Yea," she said absently, "it hath been pleasant."

The past tense was for herself alone; for she kept all trouble from the Emperor's ears. So they drifted on, the boatmen singing their immemorial song, and marking time to it by clapping their heart-shaped paddles with their hands and so sending an arch of iridescent dewdrops over the boat.

The scene, the rhythm, the preciousness of it all touched Jahângir into a sort of frenzy of delight, as memories of those short months came back to him. Where had they not been, together, on all the pleasant places of that pleasant land? Under the plane-trees by the Dhal Lake, where the water mirrors land so clearly, that you could trace in it the wanderings of a ladybird on a blade of grass.

> "So clear the water, blind men in the dark
> Each sand-grain in its depths could count and mark."

Sitting in some boat watching the sunset flush the snows of Haramukh, or across the long levels of the lake in the shadow of the everlasting hills, lying full of laughter in the garden of the Four Winds.

They had been everywhere. Nay, more, they are there still; for go whither you will in Kashmir the royal pair seems to have been there before you, and the echo of their great content remains.

A certain English poet, by name Thomas Moore, got hold of this undoubted fact and travestied it in a love poem. Fortunately he knew so little about the matter that one need not consider Lalla Rookh as having anything to do with Jahângir and Nurjahân.

Their romance was something very different; for he was in his fifty-first and she in her forty-ninth year—somewhat aged for the conventional lovers! Yet surely in all time no two people ever made holiday more rapturously. They made the hills, the dales, the flowers, the endless beauties of the land, their very own. To this day the man's voice rings in the ear of the traveller to Kashmir.

"Truly, whatever praise may be used in speaking of this land would be permissible. As far as the eye can reach flowers of all colours are blowing. They have picked fifty different kinds in my presence this morning, and doubtless there were many more which escaped observation. There are babbling streams and whispering waterfalls beyond count. Wherever the eye looks is verdure and running water. The red rose of the hundred leaves, the violet, the narcissus, spring by the wayside, and in the soul-enchanting mountains grow all sorts of sweet and scented herbs more than can be counted, while the gates, the roofs, the walls of the houses are lighted up by the torches of the tulips. What can one say of these things, or of the scented saffron fields, and the fragrant trefoil?"

These words do not leave us moderns much room for appreciation, do they? Neither do they spare room for happiness. Even when little Prince Bravery fell out of window and nearly cracked his crown, his grandfather, after filling two pages of his diary with the occurrence, philosophically remarks that for a child of four to fall twenty feet and no harm happen to his limbs is productive of amazement; though how it happened passed comprehension, since, having regard to such dangers and difficulties, he, Jahângir, had continually kept the boy in sight and had taken the utmost care of him, never for one moment being forgetful of that little seedling in the Garden of Good Fortune. In other words, the Emperor of all the Indies had done dry nurse!

For the child's father, Shahjahân, was still the auspicious, the prosperous son to the Emperor, though Nurjahân watched him with anxious eyes. She could not forget his face when he had first seen the Nurjahâni coin, as it was called. And for all his apparent good-fellowship with Khushrau (who had, of course, accompanied them to Kashmir), she was not satisfied. The latter had fully justified her estimate of him. Probably his fifteen years of close imprisonment had weakened his brain, but he was undoubtedly a good-humoured dolt, but with just that touch of likeness to Jahângir which made it impossible to be angry at his childishness.

In truth they had been quite a happy family party, and, despite her preoccupation with affairs, she had found time to watch the little fishes in the brook as they jumped for mulberries, and help the Emperor to admire the marvellous beauties of Nature. For even in this her companionship was needful for full enjoyment.

Of late, however, disturbing news had come through from the Deccan by her secret agents.

Shahjahân's work of pacification had not been lasting. The Amirs were in revolt, and it was time someone was sent to punish them.

Mohabat Khân, the great General of the times, was already busy in Kâbul over rebellion; but Shahjahân was wasting his powers idling about the Court. Why not send him?

So she hinted to the Emperor, who fell in, as usual, with her suggestions, though it was hard to get his attention to them.

As they drifted down in the boat, for instance, she attempted to make him serious over the reported death of one of his Governors in the south; but he would none of it.

"Lo!" he remarked lightly, "if it be so, what else could he expect, being so fat? He could scarcely walk, and the giving of a dress of honour was a penance. He could not put it on for puffing. Were I as he I should be glad to leave my lump of earth in the perishable dustbin!"

Whereat she laughed, as she laughed so often at his childlike quips and cranks.

But they all laughed that autumn day when the plane-leaves were turning crimson, and the distant snows of the Pirpanjâl Pass, over which they had to make their way southwards, warned them, by the way they crept daily down the mountain-side, to be up and going ere the drifts became too deep.

Everyone was in high spirits, for it was the Feast of the Dasahra, and as it was to be the last festival in Kashmir, it was being celebrated with much fervour.

Seated in a pavilion overlooking the river, the Emperor spent the afternoon while the cup of exhilaration was passed round, and by the time the review of all the horses and camels and elephants and mules belonging to the Imperial stables began, everyone was very merry. And it was an imposing sight. Horses, grooms, elephants, mahouts, camels, and drivers, all caparisoned in their best, and humanity eager for the gold and silver roses, and almonds, and pistachios that were scattered broadcast by the almoners.

"Thou takest that one with thee to the Deccan, Baba," said Jahângir to his son, as the finest elephant in the stud passed the royal standard, "and thy stepmother gives thee its marrow."

Shahjahân bowed his thanks, with a quick look at Nurjahân's face. He never felt sure of her, never could make up his mind if she was to be trusted. In a way he was glad to be going to the Deccan, and yet——

He looked at his father, acknowledging that the rest in Kashmir had done the Emperor good. There was that to be said in the Empress's favour; her husband's health was her first consideration. Small wonder since, were his support removed, her power would not take long to undermine. Meanwhile, it seemed safe for him to leave. The Deccan had not taken long to settle last time. His father had promised him the handsomest of money rewards for success, and one must risk something, even though the oaf Khushrau might have some chance of an innings.

So he sat brooding, silent and glum, while all around him rose laughter. For the Emperor, after the review was over, expressed a desire to make an experiment. He had read in some old writer that if a man were given two pounds of saffron in one dose, he would thereafter laugh so immoderately that death would ensue. The credibility of this statement Jahângir wished to investigate, for, especially when slightly exhilarated, he was keen on abstract truth. Now there was a wicked pirate—a peculiarly wicked pirate—in jail under sentence of death, upon whom the experiment could be made with the utmost propriety.

So with the exaggerated decorum of semi-sobriety, the pirate was produced—a lantern-jawed man, to whom laughter seemed antagonistic, unknown.

"'Tis well," remarked the Emperor sapiently, gravely—for he was on the verge of a cup too much—"the result will be all the more remarkable."

So it would have been, had anything occurred; but nothing did. The pirate remained stony grave—and no wonder!—but the Court chuckled furtively.

The Emperor frowned. "Try him with four pounds," he said with deliberation. "If that will not do, 'tis a lie, and I will have the book burned."

The exhilarated Court wagged their beards, and nodded their heads, trying not to smile, while with difficulty the poor pirate swallowed the four pounds. Then there was a pause of suspense. One minute, two, three, four——

But the pirate remained stony grave.

By this time Jahângir's last cup had still more bedazzled his brain. He sat looking at the imperturbable pirate mournfully.

"It doth not even occasion a smile," he murmured; then, looking round on his company, he added, "So where is death?"

Sometimes a straw tickles, and no sooner were the words uttered than their absurdity flashed upon the speaker. He began to giggle, the courtiers' repressed chuckles rose to follow suit, and a roar of inextinguishable laughter followed, that echoed and rang, and rang and echoed, till it seemed as if it would never cease, and the laughers held their aching sides as they rocked backwards and forwards, shaken to the marrow.

"Of a truth, gentlemen," gasped Jahângir, when he could get his breath again, "the old chronicler was not so far out. It hath half killed me."

So, in high glee, he bade them commute the life-sentence on the pirate as a reward for the longest laugh of his life.

But a few hours later, startled, alarmed, distressed by his first real attack of asthmatic breathlessness, the memory of his idle words returned to him with remorse.

"Lo! this is death!" he gasped to Nurjahân, who, as ever, was foremost in remedies. "I cannot breathe—'tis punishment."

She soothed him as best she could, though it was all she could do to preserve her calm, for even the physicians seemed to have lost their wits; and as for the servants and courtiers, they crowded together talking in whispers and looking askance at Shahjahân, as if his father's moments were numbered.

"There is but one resource," said the learned doctors. "We must bleed the patient."

Nurjahân gave a quick glance at the pale, exhausted face. Her common sense rebelled.

"Nay," she said, "give him wine!"

"Wouldst run counter to wisdom?" put in Shahjahân, who, genuinely distressed, stood by helpless. "My father——"

She cut him short cavalierly. "My wisdom is greater than theirs," she said curtly; and with that ordered wine to be brought, and before them all filled the ruby cup and held it to the livid lips.

"Father!" exclaimed Shahjahân in a fierce whisper, "drink not; she knows——"

"Best," came in a faint sigh, as the agonized eyes drifted from his son's face to his wife's; and the wine was swallowed.

For a second those two stood holding each other with their eyes. The moment for the parting of the ways had come quite trivially; but each knew that never again would they tread exactly the same path.

"Madam," said Shahjahân bitterly, "you have mayhap killed my father!"

"Sir," she replied, "I have mayhap saved him!"

Whether she had or not is a moot point, but ere morning came this first and most severe attack had passed—so far as the body went, that is to say; but Jahângir came back to ordinary life far more devout than he had been. He was quite convinced the attack was direct punishment for levity. That sort of thing ran in his blood from his great-grandfather Baber, who had a like fancy after every severe bout of fever. And the piety brought with it, of course, a desire to be more conventional, to behave in all ways more after the accredited pattern of an Eastern potentate.

So Nurjahân had her work cut out for her; for, naturally, Jahângir's entourage seized upon the passing mood to gain their own ends.

Faithful to her policy of giving the man she dominated a free hand in small things, she raised no objection to the idea of his going without her for a few days' tour among the saffron-fields in order to recuperate: the result of which being, as she well knew it would, that he returned, before time, eager for her companionship once more.

"I felt, dear heart," he confessed, "as if I had left happiness behind me!"

They were standing, as he said this, hand in hand, on a spur which gave them their last full look of the Vale of Pleasure, since the journey southwards could no longer be delayed, and they had started immediately on his return from his tour of convalescence.

She waved her hand towards the valley. "Is it not so indeed, my lord?" she replied, evading the point. "Have we anywhere been so happy, so content as yonder? Shall we be so again?"

"Nay," he gave back gallantly, "I take happiness with me." And he stooped, with almost a flourish, over the hand he held.

But Nurjahân was in no mood for compliments. Only that morning her husband had carelessly enough let out what seemed to her something of great importance—namely, that Shahjahân, who had accompanied his father for those few days, had preferred a request that Prince Khushrau, his brother, should be allowed to go with him to the Deccan.

She had been too surprised at the time to make much remark, but her thoughts had been busy since.

Wherefore this request? Khushrau was no soldier. Indeed, of all Jahângir's sons he was the one most like his father, incorrigibly idle, full of talent, wilful, but most lovable. That was one reason why she had added her influence to that of Gosain Jadrûp and Prince Parviz, in order to set him free from imprisonment. Parviz's motive had been clear enough. He hoped thus to bind his brother to him and in the future, mayhap, enable him to make a stand against Shahjahân's intolerable pride and pretensions. But she herself had had no such views. It was true what she had told the latter. Ever since she had married Jahângir she had set before herself the purpose of building up the Empire first for him and next for his son. There was no question which son. Shahjahân was far the most able, far the most suitable; in addition, his wife Arjamand, the mother of all his children, was her own niece. The point was so settled in her own mind that anything that threw doubt upon it seemed absurd. But this proposition of Shahjahân's opened up new vistas.

Why did he want to take his brother with him? There could be but one answer, that he desired to have him in his power, and away from the possibility of a *coup d'état* during his own absence in the event of his father's death; an event rendered more possible by the recent illness.

Her face set and her lip hardened as she reached these conclusions, on which, as usual, she acted at once.

The passage of the Pirpanjâl Pass gave her an opportunity such as she desired. The snow already lay deep, and ere they started in the morning a blizzard began. As usual, the order came for the other ladies to await better weather, while Nurjahân, as ever, remained the Emperor's companion. In her hunting dress she followed him on horseback, lessening the discomforts of the ride for him by one half, in his delight at her daring.

After a time, however, the road became too slippery with ice for horses to pass over in safety. The path also was in many places too narrow to allow of palanquins to pass, so the Emperor and Empress, with much laughter, submitted to be carried in bag-dandies. Altogether it was a most enjoyable day, and ended in just such an amusing episode as Jahângir loved. Owing to the difficulties of the road the royal tents did not come up in time, and those two had to shelter like ordinary mortals in a dry stone shanty near the top of the pass. The shifts and makeshifts giving opportunity for the display of Nurjahân's extraordinary all-round capabilities, she regained her accustomed sway over the Emperor at once, and would doubtless have succeeded in getting her own way in regard to Khushrau but for an unfortunate accident, news of which was brought to the former ere the Empress had time to speak; for long experience had taught her to be almost over-calculating in her management of this man. So much depended on her success that this had to be, though over and over again it woke in her a contempt for herself. Why could she not treat her husband as a man instead of as a spoiled child? But she could not. And this accident was one which re-aroused in him that desire to be orthodox, as it were to save his soul, which his illness had begun. A great favourite of his, a young fellow who often acted as *mahout* in shooting expeditions, was drowned.

Nurjahân, sent for by Jahângir on their arrival at a stage, found him in great tribulation. It was a judgment on him, he said. The boy had obeyed orders and remained behind some marches in the rear. Being hot, he had started to bathe in the river, though warm water was at hand. Folk forbade him, telling him that unnecessarily to get, hot, into a river so agitated and bloodthirsty that it would roll over a war elephant was contrary to the dictates of caution.

From excessive self-will and reliance on his powers of swimming—which were unequalled—he mounted a rock and threw himself in. Immediately he fell, from the violent movement of the current he could not even try to swim; to fall and to go under were the same thing, so he gave away the goods of his life to the floods of destruction.

Ready with consolation as ever, Nurjahân felt she must be patient yet awhile, and take the Emperor in a better mood.

So it came to pass that when she did speak, Jahângir met her advice not to allow Khushrau to go with his brother with the curt reply that the promise had been made, and must be kept.

"Must!" echoed Nurjahân, her autocratic temper rising at once. "To such as the Lord of Light there is no '*must*' save his own free-will. Shahjahân wishes it, 'tis true; but Shahjahân is subject. And believe me as thou wilt, my lord, it is not wise. Wait, hear what my father says—we meet him at Lahore in a few days. Let Shahjahân go forward as arranged, since the need is urgent. Khushrau can follow, should my father—whose wisdom my lord trusts—approve of it. So much my lord can surely grant to one he loves, and who loves him?"

She had gone through the gamut of her art, she had ended by bringing her beauty to bear on the point she pressed, she had told her usual lie; but to no purpose.

Jahângir, beguiled from the subject in hand—that was ever an easy task—gave a little satisfied laugh.

"But, dear heart, Shahjahân will not go without his brother. He hath said so in so many words. Therefore let be—it wearies me, and we have so many a more pleasant subject of discourse, see you. Did I tell thee, dearest, that the religious have found me two more Names of God for my rosary? They shall be rubies, and they make up the whole to five hundred and twenty and two—or twice the number my revered father—may God's way be his!—had on his chaplet. May my wisdom equal his! Lo! when we leave Delhi I must go by Brindrabân and see that holy man Jadrûp. There is none like him—sure he is the mirror and mouthpiece of the Most High——"

So he went on, while Nurjahân sat with interested face as if listening; but her thoughts were far away.

Then Shahjahân refused to take command in the Deccan unless he were allowed the care of his brother? Evidently he was afraid of what might happen. Evidently he meant to be prepared.

Well, other folk could be prepared also. There were not lacking ways to counteract Shahjahân's caution. The Emperor had another son, young Shahriyâr. A weakling, it is true, yet as a child he had shown promise. Let him be patronized; let him be brought forward. It would at least give Shahjahân cause to think. And stay! Even as to her relationship to his wife Arjamand, she could outwit the fool! Had she not a daughter of her own? A wilful girl, Afzul's child, 'tis true, who would have none of marriage as yet, but chose to be a canoness; older by some years than Shahriyâr, who was but eighteen. Still, all the better for the quick begetting of children; children who would be grandsons and daughters, not grand-nephews and nieces only.

Did all this come into this woman's mind? Perhaps it did. She was almost terribly clear-sighted. Far down the years she saw; far down them she laid her plans. And the habit of scheming had grown day by day, month by month, year by year. It could not in her position be otherwise. It was almost a necessity of her existence. At times—lessening times—she raged against it; and ever and always she strove to let it touch her relations with her husband as little as possible. But it was there.

All we know for certain is that Shahjahân marched for the Deccan, taking with him his brother Prince Khushrau, and discretionary powers to treat the latter in any way he might think proper. It is doubtful, however, if Nurjahân or her father knew of this permission.

And in Jahângir's Memoirs we find this entry made during his stay in Lahore, immediately after the departure of the Deccan expedition.

"I demanded in marriage for my son Shahriyâr the daughter's daughter of Madaru-l-mulk I'timadu-d-daula, and sent Rs.100,000 by way of dowry."

CHAPTER VII

"A holy man once dug himself a cave,
Six feet by three, as house; a passing knave
Mocked at him for its size; he smiled and said,
''Tis big for one whose end will be a grave.'"

If Agra and Delhi are rose-red cities it is because Muttra has made them so; Muttra with her vast sandstone quarries, out of which almost every palace and mosque and temple in Northern India has been built.

It is an experience to stand amid the buttresses of ruddy rock, the wide hollows that eat into the heart of the red ridge, and think of the glories of Agra and Fatehpur Sikri; of Muttra itself and Delhi that once lay here in solid unhewn mass; dead clay that man's genius has brought to life.

It was in an outlying spur of these quarries that Jadrûp the Gosain, leaving his hole at Ujjain, had dug himself another, as small, as uncomfortable; a hole, as Jahângir describes it, "like an inkpot," in which "he could only turn round with a hundred difficulties and tortures, since the passage to it is so narrow that a suckling babe could scarce pass through." From which we may opine that the Emperor, though he often paid the ascetic a visit, never went inside; for despite constant illness Jahângir was still personable.

Jadrûp had, however, other visitors beside the Emperor, and on one evening in late March in the year following on Prince Shahjahân's expedition to the Deccan, he was sitting in earnest conclave with a man, also of the religious class, but of a very different stamp. Briefly, he was the Head Gosain of the Shrine at Thanêswar. He had come down to Muttra for the yearly religious fair, an unusually big one, since it coincided with a partial eclipse of the sun. But it was not of the money he hoped to rake in from the ignorant that he was thinking, as he leant forward, almost whispering, and watching his companion's face narrowly the while; since, if you wished to influence the great Jadrûp, saint and ascetic, you had to be careful. As Nurjahân had said, you had to bribe him by his own holiness.

"See you," continued the Thanêswar Gosain, "your saintship knows the story. How long ago the Great Mother's cup was stolen from the Shrine, though, having regard to rumour, we kept it secret, and had this made to show the faithful, if need be. But 'tis not shown to the rabble, and, since the Mahomedan came uppermost, there be few of our religion in high places."

He had taken out of his bosom a small red crystal cup, which he handed to Jadrûp, who turned it over and over.

"Yet is Jahângir most tolerant," remarked the latter somewhat evasively. "He is not far from the Kingdom. Lo! I have talked with him much, and he listens."

"Who would not listen to a voice as of God's angel!" exclaimed the other unctuously. "But thou knowest—I have told thee—how we have sought the real cup, the marrow of this one, for years; how it disappeared; how by chance one of our people saw it, so he thought, in the hands of the young Princes when they toasted each others' healths; how since then we have proved with care and trouble that it is in the hands of the Emperor. Now, harken, O saint-*ji*? Since Mai Kalí has known where her cup is held—held *wrongfully*, mind you—what has happened? The Emperor hath been ill—all the past year he hath been ailing, and his illness increases. For the cup, see you, hath undoubted charm both for evil and for good. That is why we, who guard the Great Mother, desire it back,—not for filthy lucre. This"—he touched the cup he had given to Jadrûp—"is as valuable. It also is of ruby—nay, it is more so, since it is better colour."

"'Tis bright enough, for sure," acquiesced Jadrûp as the sun, shining through the translucent red, sent a blood-stain to his hand. "And thou wouldst have me tell this tale to the Emperor——"

"Not only so," interrupted the other quickly. "See you, there is no need to tell thee what would have happened had the cup been found in lesser hands. But the Emperor is, even to the Hindu, the Shadow of God, the Lord's Anointed. We dare not kill, and we cannot steal. We have tried, and failed. So, in the name of the Great Mother, O saint-*ji*, we come to thee. Take this cup of us. It hath stood in the shrine for years. It is even as—nay, better than the original. Give it thy blessing. Persuade the Emperor that it is for his own safety——"

Gosain Jadrûp shook his head; the craft of the other had gone astray. "Nay," said the holy man, "that is secondary. I will point out the justice. Jahângir is good disciple; he loves justice, and the cup, being stolen, is not rightly his——"

"And," broke in the other, "there is yet another reason; but of this, say naught. Report hath it that Nurjahân Begum gave the Emperor the cup. 'Tis a long tale, but of this we know. There was an old woman not worth revenge—and one Zamân Shâh, who hath gone to his account—in it. Now the cup hath charm, and the woman hath bewitched the Emperor. If he were to give it up—why then——"

"'Tis not meet for any man to be under the dominion of a woman," put in the holy man sententiously. "Leave the cup with me, brother. I will see what I can do for the glory of the Most High, for justice and the Great Mother."

He held the cup up to the sun as he spoke, and a blood-red ray shot through it and seemed to pierce him through the heart. And all around him the red rocks glowed in the light of the setting sun.

"But say naught of the woman, saint-*ji*," said the other quickly, "and bid the Emperor keep his own counsel. Remember, 'tis God gives the reward of silence!"

Gosain Jadrûp looked at his companion with a tolerant smile of spiritual pride. "I need no teaching what to say, brother. The Great Spirit guides my tongue." And with that he relapsed into silent meditation.

Meanwhile Nurjahân, who, with the Emperor as ever, happened to be at Muttra on one of his constant visits there, was looking out over the river-steps from her balcony with the unfailing interest that everything in the wide world still had for her; for despite her years she was not old in mind, nor in body also, though the last year of life, since Shahjahân had departed with his brother Khushrau on the Deccan expedition, had, with its growing anxieties, brought a look of fatigue to her still lustrous eyes. To begin with, the Emperor had been constantly ailing.

Asthma in its most severe form had taken hold of him, and the physicians could or would do nothing to alleviate his distress. Hot and dry medicines, cold and wet, goat's milk, camel's milk, all were tried without profit. But Jahângir was extraordinarily patient with his unsuccessful doctors. Far more patient than Nurjahân herself was inclined to be, for since Prince Parviz had appeared hastily from Allahabad, under the impression that his father was dying, she had become somewhat suspicious as to whether the wish were not father to the thought that made the physicians so solemn, so afraid. She herself could see no ground for fear; the complaint was very distressing, of course, but did not threaten life. Between the attacks, too, Jahângir was quite himself, ready even to laugh at Fedai Khân's—hot-headed Fedai Khân's—suggestion that stringent measures should be taken to make the half-hearted doctors do their duty.

"Lo!" Jahângir would say with a smile. "See you, 'tis not their fault. If God's destiny did not at times concur with the blunders of the medical profession, we should none of us die or get better!"

The only thing that so far had seemed to do him good was stimulants. And herein was a further anxiety for Nurjahân. Jahângir had broken from her control. He not only drank wine in hitherto prohibited hours, but he drank it to excess. And he would not hear of moderation; indeed, she had hardly the heart to propose it, seeing that his only alleviation lay in the exhilaration of drugs or alcohol; an exhilaration which led to a generally exalted state of mind, in which he would sit for hours discussing eternal values with Jadrûp, or taking himself quite seriously as the Shadow of God upon earth.

Then Nurjahân had other anxieties. Her mother lay dying, and though the tie between them had never been of the strongest it was ill contemplating the breaking-up of what had outlasted long years. In addition there was the dread of how the loss would affect her father, who was growing very old, and who, despite many a rub, had ever kept his youthful admiration for his wife.

So as she sat waiting for the Emperor and looking out over the crowds that thronged the river-steps, Nurjahân's mind was ill at ease. The curious moaning surge of thousands upon thousands of human voices not dominated by one common cadence, but each giving utterance to individual, personal speech, fell on her ears mournfully. A wail it seemed to her of useless, petty desires and hopes, joys and fears.

And when the Emperor did arrive, the news he brought did not tend to give her solace. Jahângir, who had evidently had enough wine to carry, was for once loud in complaint. He had summoned a new physician, one who, being "house-born," might have been expected to have sympathy and understanding, instead of which he had positively declined all aid, professing inability to treat a disease of which he did not know the origin. It was not the first time Nurjahân had heard this plea, and her brows darkened. What did it mean? Were they plotting some new conspiracy against her? The weariness of a continual petty fight struck home to her; but she soothed the Emperor as best she could, until, with much fervour, he announced his intention of giving up all medicine, weaning his heart from all visible remedies, and placing himself absolutely in the hands of the Supreme Physician.

After which he called for another glass of wine and went off, relieved for the moment, to see Gosain Jadrûp; where he remained longer than usual, returning in high spirits, full of Gosain-*ji's* merits. God Almighty had given Jadrûp an unusual grace and lofty understanding, an exalted nature and sharp intellectual powers, together with a God-given knowledge and a heart free from the attachments of this world. A man could not choose but be bettered by the blessing. One who had it, as he, poor suppliant at the Throne of God had it, was blest indeed. What to him did it matter what earthly physicians said? Yes, though he, Mirza Mahomed, the so-called Messiah of the Age, had been honoured above all other Court physicians as more skilful, more experienced, on purpose that at any dangerous crisis he might help his benefactor, he might refuse and go to Jehannum if he liked! There would be no need for physicians again. The New Year was to bring health.

So he ran on light-heartedly. He even refused his evening

potation. He did not need it. Had he not said he was going to rely on the Supreme Physician?

So a day or two passed in comfort, and they went back to Agra, the Emperor more like himself than he had been for months, and full of his duties as monarch even to the haunts of idolatry.

"Possibly," he said, "I have in this been somewhat remiss in the past. There is good in all things, as I have myself proven." And then he went on to recount how his revered father had once answered his protest against idolaters being allowed to build new temples in these words: "My dear child, I am the Shadow of God upon earth. He bestows His blessing on all His creatures without distinction. Ill should I represent Him were I to withhold compassion from any of those entrusted to my care. With all His creatures I must be at peace. Why, then, should I molest anyone? Besides, are not five parts in six of the human race either Hindu or aliens to our faith? Were I to be actuated by the principles you suggest, what alternative would there be but to put them all to death? I therefore think it wisest to let these men alone."

To which self-evident wisdom Nurjahân gave assent. She was not greatly interested in such questions, neither were her thoughts much with things unseen. She was too busy in this world to consider the next; for she was curiously unselfish. Her own future, outside the task she had set herself, did not trouble her at all.

So things went on, until one night the Emperor was taken ill. His attendants came to her affrighted. Their master was worse, they said, than he had ever been.

She went to him at once and found him almost choking for breath. Weary of useless doctors, and remembering how he had during the last few days curtailed his wine-cups, she gave his measure in the ruby cup the attendants brought on the instant, brimming it up once, twice, thrice.

It eased him somewhat, but the attack passed but slowly, and she sat beside him as she always did, holding his hand, cheering him with words, ministering to him in every way she could.

But it was not till sunset of the next day that, fully at ease he lay back on his pillows quite himself again. Yet not quite

As a rule when an attack was over, the elasticity of his spirits caused a rebound in favour of vitality. This time he lay languid, as if disappointed or dissatisfied.

"My lord is through his trouble," said his nurse sympathetically. "Praise be to whom praise is due!"

He laughed suddenly, bitterly. "Ay," he answered, "to whom it is due—not to those who promise falsely." Then he added, "Give me more wine. I go back to that."

She handed him the cup. As she did so something about it struck her. There had always been a slight flaw near the bottom, and she could not see it. She held it up in the sun-ray to see, but all was clear, the light was nowhere refracted at a different angle.

Startled, she looked at Jahângir; he was looking at her half angrily, half dubiously. "Give it me, quick," he said; "stand not so staring at nothing."

His very voice increased her wonder. "I was looking for the flaw," she said slowly. "It is not there."

"Not there!" he echoed lightly; "that makes it all the better."

"Better?" Her voice took on a sudden seriousness. "Better is comparison, and with what does my lord compare this cup?—with itself? Then suddenly swift comprehension seemed to come to her, and her eyes narrowed. "This—this is not the cup I gave. This is not—my lord, what hast done with it?"

She held out her hand, holding the cup, accusingly, and Jahângir turned away from her impatiently.

"I might have known there was small use in trying to conceal it," he muttered vexedly. "Thou art too sharp for most of us. It was not mine. It had been stolen from the Shrine at Thanêswar."

"Does my lord think I was the thief?" she interrupted freezingly.

"Nay, nay, I said not so," he returned, and his voice, like a child's, was full of a general sense of injustice. "Sit down and I will tell thee—since it has to be told."

So he told her how the Gosain Jadrûp had urged him to restitution; how his own sense of justice had coincided with the holy man's request. Besides, he added with rather a wry face, it had seemed to him likely that the possession of this idol's treasure was indeed in some way unlucky, that it might be responsible for his illness.

"Dost give such power to their stocks and stones?" she asked sarcastically—"thou, a believer in the one true God, the one Supreme Physician?"

But he was ready with an answer there. Was there not also a power for evil?—was it not the duty of every true Mussulman to avoid the devil? He did not blame her for giving him the cup, but once he discovered the true ownership of it, his honour demanded——

She started up suddenly, her face ablaze. "Thy honour! Thy health! Thy justice! Didst have no thought of me—nor of the long years I played with it as a child—not of the care I lavished on thee with the gift—to take it all and give not one thought to me—to my luck—thou hadst no right——"

He was on his feet beside her, tall, menacing, almost bursting with rage.

"Woman, darest thou to say I have no right?—I, the Shadow of God?"

It calmed her somewhat, though she defied him even more strenuously: "Ay, thou hadst no right! Thou toldst me once long ago that I could not understand thy love. Be that so! Thou canst not understand mine! Mayhap no man can understand the love a woman gives him—by day, by night, always, at all times—my thoughts—my luck—my all—and thou wouldst exchange this for mere justice—and thy health, doubtless! Yea, doubtless they promised thee thy health!"

"And if they did, woman——" he began, trembling with anger.

She laughed aloud. "Their luck against mine—their ruby cup against my ruby cup—out on it!" She flung her hand up in disdain. The cup she held slipped from it, crashed upon the marble floor, and shivered to a thousand fragments. The shock of this sudden and unlooked for breakage sobered them both. They stood for a moment staring down at the splinters of glass, then at each other.

Jahângir was the first to speak, and he spoke in a low constrained voice.

"So they have lied to me," he said. "'Tis not even crystal. How came I not to see?—I had drunk too much wine, methinks. And yet—Jadrûp——"

His face worked; he was nigh tears, for he was still weak; and in an instant she had realized what he was feeling, and was at her place as consoler. Even anger could not prevent that. He was so much a child to her, she could not see him suffer.

"Jadrûp hath no knowledge of such things, my lord," she said hastily. "Doubtless he deemed the cup was ruby—as thou didst, my lord, being, as thou hast said, overcome with wine. But that is past. Yea, it is all past. It hath not hurt—it shall not hurt——"

He caught at her hand helplessly. "But the promise—the blessing that went with the cup?"

She smiled at him. "That shall remain, my lord, and to it shall be put my forgiveness—yea, my forgetfulness! And thine also! Come, put it past! Be patient yet a while, and the cup—ay, and my luck too—shall return." Her eyes blazed; she stood upright, her head thrown back. "It is I, Nurjahân, against the world—with Jahângir as her lord and master."

Suddenly mindful of the part she had had to play for so long, she was at his feet, kissing them.

A month later the Emperor wrote in his Memoirs: "Nurjahân Begum, whose skill and experience are greater than those of the physicians (especially as they are brought to bear through affection and sympathy), endeavoured to carry out the remedies that appeared appropriate to the time and to the condition. Although previously to this she had approved of the remedies made use of by the doctors, I now relied on her kindness alone. She, by degrees, lessened my wine, kept me from doing things that did not suit me and food that disagreed with me. As in the past year of my life I had suffered much, in thankfulness that in the commencement of the New Year signs of health became apparent, Nurjahân Begum begged to be allowed to make the arrangements for the festival of my solar weighing. Although from the date on which Nurjahân Begum had entered into the bond of marriage with this suppliant at the Throne of Grace she had made such arrangements as were becoming to the State, and knew what were the requirements of good fortune and prosperity, yet on this occasion she paid greater attention than ever to adorn the assembly and arrange the feast. All the servants of approved service who knew my temperament and in that time of weakness had fluttered round my head like moths, ready to sacrifice their lives, were suitably rewarded. And even the physicians, though they had not done good service, yet in consideration of the contempt with which they had been treated, they received various favours.

"At the conclusion of my weighing—I weighed but thirteen stone, owing to my weakness and leanness—trays of gold and silver coin were scattered in the skirts of the Ministers of amusement, and of the poor.

"At the end of the entertainment the offerings she had prepared for me were produced.

"And amongst these offerings was a ruby cup."

"Why!" said Jahângir delightedly, "'tis the very split of a pea to the other! Truly thou art a witch! And to the very flaw—how didst arrive at it?"

"Art sure 'tis not the same, my lord?" she said archly; then seeing his face fall, she added hastily: "Nay, I am no thief! Money can do much, and the Emperor has gifted me with it in such plentitude that all things are possible. Therefore 'tis not the same—yet is it the same, since it carries with it Nurjahân's luck!"

But all the time, though she kept such a brave face, she flinched inwardly from the future.

CHAPTER VIII

> "Was it God's Star or wandering traveller's Light
> That guided my lost footsteps in Life's night?
> What matters? Since it lit my path of gloom
> And cheered me with the hope my way was right."

ONE of Nurjahân's most potent remedies was change of air, and so soon as the Emperor was fit to travel, they set off on a prolonged tour round the skirts of the hills, ostensibly seeking for some spot of ground on the banks of the River Ganges where it debouched from the mountains that would be suitable for the building of a permanent hot weather residence; since there could be no doubt that a high temperature did not agree with Jahângir. So they set forth in great state, with full Imperial equipage, and taking with them the whole harem of four hundred ladies, old and young. But neither the number of these nor their varied relations to the Emperor made any difference to Nurjahân. She smiled on them all, not because she knew she stood first, but because they really did not affect her in the least, for she seems to have been singularly free from jealousy.

It was an immense move, the moving of the Imperial camp. Reading of its extent and magnificence in the Institutes of Akbar, the head positively begins to ache over the numeration of its luxuries. The audience tent that covered seven acres of ground, the miles on miles of screens, the square yards of silken carpetings. And outside this the hordes of tent-pitchers and Heaven knows who or what, and the herds on herds of baggage-animals.

But they all got under weigh, slowly, sedately, and struck off up country, regardless of roads if they happened to have a "contrairy circumbendebus" about them; or rather making their own roads as they went along; a method easy enough in the flat plains of India, especially when no regard is paid to crops.

A stately march indeed! One that lingers pleasantly in the

mind of this generation; a generation that is whisked away through God's earth at sixty miles an hour. A march that will be inconceivable in the next, when "aerobuses" will carry us at more than Ariel's speed.

In truth, a goodly, kingly march, full of dignity. Yet those who know India, and have camped there, must wonder what the nights—between eleven and twelve o'clock—must have been like when thousands of camels were being laden with that seven acres of tent; for there is enough noise over the removal of one small "*shamiana*" to drive sleep away from most eyes.

Yet from sunset to sunrise there must have been comfort in the "Lamp of Justice" which, swung high on an immense pole, always showed where the Emperor's tent stood.

There was one very heavy heart that went along with the great camp; the heart of a weary old man, who, but for the fact that his daughter needed him every hour of the day, would fain have remained behind to weep over his wife's tomb. For Bibi Azîzan had died, and Ghiyâss-ud-din, her husband, felt life was barely worth living without her, though he was brave and said little of his grief. Not like Asof Khân, her son, who mourned profusely; but then he had always been his mother's darling, as the father of that delightful Arjamand who had given—how many?—royal sons and daughters to Shahjahân the victorious—Shahjahân who in due time would become Emperor, if only Nurjahân, his wife's aunt, could be kept in order. Bibi Azîzan had been wrapped up in these royal great-grandchildren, and had rather sniffed at the idea of another royal great-grandchild through Sher Afkân's daughter.

The good lady had gone her ways, however, without seeing one, and as time went on, even Asof Khân—who was already ready to forecast evil and imagine the worst—began to think that Providence meant to put a spoke in Nurjahân's neat fifth wheel to the car of State. If there were no children of that marriage, Prince Shahriyâr was not likely, of himself, to oust Shahjahân, or, for the matter of that, Parviz, who was also a good-looking man, in the Emperor's esteem. For Shahriyâr was small and delicate.

News came from the Deccan as they journeyed northwards

that was eminently satisfactory. Once again Shahjahân was successful, once again the auspicious, the fortunate, the victorious son shines in his father's Memoirs. And there could be no question that that father's health was much improved by Nurjahân's treatment. All along the march he was "constantly engaged in the pleasure of hunting," though he still kept religiously to the vow, made for little Prince Bravery's sake years before, never again to kill any of God's creatures with his own hand. But he had grown particular also as to eating them! The sight of a tame duck swallowing slow-worms was sufficient to make him foreswear all duck-flesh in the future, and there was a perfect tragedy over a white heron which had been sent him as the most toothsome of comestibles. "By chance there came out of its crop ten bugs in a distressing and disgusting manner, the very remembrance of which was an offence," and quite prevented his tasting the delicacy.

Such, then, was the man who, plus confidence and affection unlimited, unlimitable, Nurjahân had to pilot through the dangerous waters of Statecraft—a hard task.

For her father was failing fast. Indeed, as they reached the hill country he had to be left behind in a standing camp while the others pressed on to Kangra, which the Emperor was determined to visit; since never before had it fallen into Mahomedan hands, and he wished, as it were, to take full possession of it. For of late, even though he still held the Gosain Jadrûp to be an easily-imposed-upon saint, he had been inclined to pose more and more as a Defender of the True Faith; an attitude in which he received the full-blooded assent of his courtiers. Nurjahân, on the other hand, being gifted with statesmanship, was for the tolerance of Akbar. But she had little time for minor matters, with her father on the sick list, and the urgent need to watch over the Emperor day and night.

"If thou art so anxious, dearest," said Jahângir kindly, seeing her reluctance to leave her father behind, "why not remain? I shall not like it, but what then? Thou dost more for me than I for you."

His face, still heavy despite its signs of ill-health, was loving-kindness itself. He meant what he said, yet the woman into whose face he looked knew that he might as well have suggested flying to the moon. He simply could not live—really live—without her.

So she shook her head, saying she knew her duty better than that. And yet when—having gone but two marches further—news came that the old man had taken a sudden turn for the worse and was sinking fast, she broke down for once into womanly tears and regrets that she had ever left him.

The Emperor was greatly distressed. He "could not bear to see her agitation, and gave instant orders for a return to the standing camp." The courtiers tried to dissuade him from such an unheard of procedure as the alteration of Imperial plans for a woman's sake, but he set them aside.

"Considering the affection I bear to them both," he said, the tears in his eyes, "I can do no less."

So, after a hurried journey the Emperor and the Empress, hand in hand, stood beside the dying old man. To English ears this sounds a small thing; but in India, and in those times, it means, and meant, much. Nothing could show the closeness of the tie between those two more than this.

Ghiyâss-ud-din was almost unconscious. So much so that Nurjahân was doubtful if he recognized the Emperor.

"Methinks he doth not, my lord," she said with tears.

But she was wrong. With a courtliness and readiness stronger than death the old face smiled, and the old lips murmured the well-known couplet of the Anwâri:

> "Lo! if a man born blind were here, he would feel
> Majesty even in darkness, and straightway kneel."

Jahângir, easily affected, could not restrain his tears, and remained by his old Vizier's pillow for two hours, while the courtiers outside fretted and fumed at the unusual condescension.

But, in truth, the Emperor was extremely fond of his father-in-law, and devoted quite a page of his Memoirs to recounting his virtues, the chief one of which appears to have been his unfailing courtesy.

"Though it is not within the power of mortal man to grant every request, no one ever went to I'timadu-d-daula with a peti tion who turned from him in an injured frame of mind. He showed loyalty to his sovereign and to his duty, yet left pleased and hopeful him who was in need."

There is another entry concerning the old man which, from its nature, throws light on the character of the man who sets it down. "From the hour in which his companion (his wife) attained the Mercy of God, he cared no longer for life, but melted away day by day. Although outwardly he looked after the affairs of the kingdom, and did not withdraw his hand from business, yet in his heart he was grieving at the separation; and so, after but three months and twenty days, he passed away. What shall I say about my feelings through this terrible loss?"

And what of Nurjahân? She was simply crushed. For a while she seems to have been knocked out of time, as it were. The Emperor resumed his march two days later, but it appears likely that she remained behind—partly, no doubt, to see the arrangements for the removal of her father's corpse to Agra carried out fittingly, but partly to gain a breathing-space in which to face the future.

And while she lay upon her couch, face down, silent, not sobbing at all, but tearlessly, and, after a time, fearlessly, choosing her part in the drama that had to be played to the bitter end, old Dilarâm, still flouncy as to skirts, and old Phusla, skinnier, more bright-eyed than ever, sat solidly in the ante-room refusing admittance to all stoutly.

They had served the mistress for so long together, these two, that though they quarrelled in words, as always, their hearts agreed. "Lo!" murmured the Strangler mournfully, "'tis maybe but natural; yet when the lady had borne so much so bravely, one wonders if aught of courage hath gone from her with the cup. For look you, sister, 'tis idle to say it hath not changed hands. My people know it for sure. The long-haired ones have it again."

"So thou sayest," remarked his companion; "I believe it not."

"But why, otherwise, did the Bibi move Heaven and earth to get its match—as she did?" persisted the other.

"So thou sayest," retorted Dilarâm again scornfully. "But

all saying is not truth, and the cat ever dreams of tripe—but 'tis small wonder the mistress loses heart——"

"'Lose heart, lose all,'" quoted the old man maliciously.

"Out on thee and thy proverbs!" gave back Dilarâm, righteously indignant at her province being purloined. "But there! a man ever knows best. Lo! 'the blind cow always has a separate stall.' But if thou wilt the truth, 'tis thus—Ghiyâss-ud-din gave her life in the beginning and gave it her doubly in State affairs, for, see you, one cannot beat a drum with one hand, and her right is ever occupied with the Emperor."

And old Dilarâm was right. Nurjahân felt for once the greatness of the task that lay before her. But after a while its very greatness stimulated her, and she rose dry-eyed, vital to her finger-tips, too keen to be up and doing for much thinking.

So she followed the Emperor swiftly, afraid, as she ever was, lest he might be misled without her.

And in truth he had gone a little further in his religious enthusiasm over this capture of that stronghold of the Hindus, Kangra, than she was disposed to tolerate.

He had called all the learned doctors of the law, all the exponents of the true faith together, it is true, and had held a solemn service of appropriation in the big square of the fine old fort that crowns the isolated hill above the town. So far, so good. It was only meet and just that the Kutbah, or Praise-prayer for God, His Prophet and His King, should be recited proudly where, hitherto, only idolatrous rites had been heard.

(And here, *par parenthese*, may one be permitted to wonder why some such ceremony did not form part of King George the Fourth's Great Durbar, and why, for long, long years after India was formally annexed by the English crown, the Kutbah continued to be read in the name of the Sultan of Turkey?)

So far, therefore, Nurjahân approved; but when it came to slaughtering a bullock in the Hindu shrine held in the fort, she set her lip. It had been done, however, and Jahângir was piously exultant over it, as he was bound to be; for those two hours beside the death-bed of Ghiyâss-ud-din had fanned the flame of devotion, and for the time the conviction that, as the Shadow of God, he had to set a shining example of religious intolerance came uppermost. The past, however, was past, and the only thing to be done was to see that in the future the balance was held more evenly. And, truly, the view from the top of the fort, as Jahângir took Nurjahân round to see all the merits and beauties of his new possession, was sufficient to make most human emotions, thoughts, hopes, fears, desires, disappear into the background. Backing the hollows of the town, range on range of shaded mountains rising higher and higher, losing their contours one in the other, till, without a break, like a wall reared against the sunlit sky, they merged into snowy peaks and snowy clouds, one seeming not more remote than the other. Falling from the hollow of the town southward, edge on edge of receding hills melting into the blue horizon of India that cut the sky, soft yet clear, half-way up to the zenith.

Jahângir stood, his hand in hers once more.

"Truly, dearest," he said solemnly, "we must prostrate ourselves in thanksgiving for this great gift which no King hitherto has hoped to receive. Let us build a lofty mosque to the Glory of God inside the fort."

Nurjahân, her eyes on the distant horizon, answered him absently:

"Ay, there is no harm in that."

But she guarded him against more disapproval than the remark that "the world had here wandered into the desert of error" when together they went to see the great shrine of Durga at Jwâla Mukhi, where flames burst forth at intervals from a rift in the rock. Possibly the remembrance that the temple had once already been properly and scientifically sacked by Mahmud of Ghazni may have had a soothing effect upon zeal. It is more likely, however, that the legend attached to the place, telling how the great god Mahâdeo, from the intense love and attachment he bore to his wife, had carried her dead body about with him wherever he went throughout the world, until, her form dissolving, her heart had dropped into the rift whence flames come ever to show that even the draught of death cannot quench love, may have had more to do with patience; for Jahângir, with all his faults, was "Compleat Lover."

Perhaps he clasped the hand he held a little tighter, and

wondered what he would do if the woman for whom he had so great an attachment were to leave him alone. As Jahângir himself so often says in his book: "God only knows!"

But his antagonism to Hindu superstition, Hindu miracles, remained, despite the fact that the beauties of the surrounding country roused the Emperor to an admiration which made him forget almost everything else. The delightful position of one village made it a pleasure worthy of being seen. Another was so enchanting that a lac of rupees was ordered to be spent at once in order to make lofty edifices suitable to the spot, in place of the Hindu buildings which, however much they are decorated, are never pleasant to live in; while it was decreed that in future it should be known as Nurpur, the City of Light, after both Nur-ud-din Jahângir and Nurjahân.

She by this time had gathered up the reins of State into her small, capable hands, so that, dissent as it would, the Court was not surprised when the Emperor issued his edict conferring all the powers and establishment, all the privileges and emoluments of the late It'imadu-d-daula Ghiyâss-ud-din Beg to his daughter, Nurjahân Begum, and ordering that her drums and orchestra should hereinafter be sounded immediately after the King's.

They shook their heads in secret over the guile of womenkind, and that night, post-haste, a horseman with silenced horse's hoofs rode noiselessly southwards bearing the news to Shahjahân away in the Deccan.

And all the while another horseman with silenced horse-hoofs was bringing news from Shahjahân to Jahângir away in the low hills where he was busy catching jungle-fowl, observing their habits, and remarking on the peculiarity, "that though they differ not at all in plumage or shape from the domestic fowl, they make no sound when caught by the feet and turned upside-down, but remain silent, whereas their congeners the cock and hen deafen Heaven with their outcries."

He was also observing the habits of others of God's creatures; notably a very holy Hindu, who, by repute, had entirely renounced all control over himself.

"See you, dearest," he said gravely to Nurjahân, as in obedience to his daily custom he came to her ere retiring to the society of the other members of his vast retinue in the women's quarter of the camp. " 'Tis the duty of Kings to ascertain truth. Therefore I sent for the man and examined him. I found a marvellous state of persistence. He stood, arms outstretched, in the figure of a cross. Thus he remained motionless, neither moving nor to sight breathing, but remaining like a fossil, unobservant of all. So it occurred to me that in a state of drunkenness some change might be wrought. Therefore I ordered that they should cause him to take several cups of double-strength spirits. 'Twas done, dearest, in liberal royal fashion; yet the man remained impassive; till suddenly his senses left him, he toppled over, and they carried him out like a corpse, dead drunk. 'Twas God's own mercy he did not lose his life, but certainly there is much persistency in his nature. Would God I could carry as much liquor with sobriety!"

Whereat Nurjahân laughed. But the news that Jahângir brought her was not always provocative of mirth; sometimes it held tragedy.

The camp had reached the Rawul Pindi district, and Nurjahân had been busy all day settling up details regarding her assumption of her father's office, while Jahângir had passed the time delightedly with the poet Bi-Badal, who had composed an excellent chronogram on the taking of the Kangra fort, which began:

"World-gripper, World-giver, World-holder, World-King,
With the sword of a *ghazi* he conquered the fort."

It was growing dusk, and the time for the Emperor's evening visit drew near. So, with a sigh, the woman set aside the man's work for her own, and put herself into the hands of her dressers. It is a quaint picture to raise before the mind's eye.

A beautiful woman possessed of almost absolute power, yet holding it by virtue of a man's passionate admiration.

So nothing must be wanting in allurement, nothing to mar the perfect beauty of the still supple, still youthful face and form which, dressed to the uttermost, welcomed the Emperor with smiles. But none were required. In an instant Nurjahân recognized that the man who came before her, a letter held in his shaking hand, his face full of agitation, almost fear, needed more than the solace of this world's joys. In an instant she was beside him; for the instinct of motherhood for one who had given himself so wholly into her keeping was never far below the surface.

"What is't, my lord?"

He looked at her appealingly, almost pitifully.

"Dearest," he said, and his voice shook, "he is dead—my little son is dead. Lo! how I remember when he was born, how glad, how proud we all were. And my father—peace be with him!"—he was maundering on, but the woman's wits outstripped his words; she could not wait for his verbiage. Seizing the letter he held, she glanced at it, then stood almost awful in her quick suspicion.

"Khushrau, thy son, dead!" she exclaimed. "How—and by what means? His brother's, likely!"

Jahângir stood before her almost child-like in deprecation, scarce realizing the suspicion of her words.

"Nay, wife! Shahjahân himself writes in grief. 'Twas sudden—a colic—'tis the will of God—but—he was my eldest, and——" he stretched his hands out to her as if for help. "When he was a little babe, I remember——"

Then he broke down almost into tears, and even suspicion was forgotten as she comforted him as she could always comfort and console this man who loved her so dearly.

CHAPTER IX

> "A shroud may hide the corpse of one who dies;
> Flowers may hide the lips where a kiss lies,
> And words conceal a thought; but this is sure:
> Love cannot hide the Truth from loving eyes."

"Lo! I must know the truth," said Nurjahân in a clear, hard voice, "and thou, O Phusla, must bring it me, as thou hast brought me so much before," she added in a kindlier voice.

The old snake-charmer, who crouched at her feet, touched the ground with his forehead.

"To hear is to obey, mistress most great," he replied. "But this slave is old, old quite beyond measure."

"Traa!" muttered Dilarâm, who of late had become almost the old man's double, having taken him completely under her supervision and care. "God knows His own work; 'tis waste time telling Him, and we can see for ourselves that thou art old."

"Canst not set thy tribe to work as ever?" asked Nurjahân quickly.

The Strangler shook his head. "'Tis a question of life or death, mistress," he replied. "If such things pass through many hands, knowledge filters out and clouds the path. Nay, I must go myself; and I go willingly. Yet"—he paused, and his keen, clever old eyes met hers unflinchingly—"if the Presence will consider," he went on, "'tis a long journey hence to Burhanpore, where the deed was done—if it were done at all. And I am old. Therefore let it stand thus: I go; if I return not, the Presence may know that naught has happened, and that I stay to die where my fathers died——"

Here Dilarâm gave a feeble conventional whimper.

"Peace, woman!" continued the old man magisterially. "Obscure not sound sense by foolishness. Wherefore should I journey back to a strange land? since surely my days are numbered. So I will go, Majesty; and if I find nothing—if 'tis true that Prince Khushrau died of the colic, as is reported, then I return not. I should but cumber the ground. But if I find 'tis as Majesty suspects—if poison were given—if 'twas murder, then——" he paused.

"What then?" echoed Nurjahân, her eyes on the old man's almost wistful face.

"Then I must return—I will return. Yea, death shall not claim me till I have given my message."

His head sank to his breast as he spoke; he lifted his right hand—the hand that had been so skilful with the Noose of Death—as if taking an oath to himself.

Nurjahân watched him intently. Something in the intense personal vitality of the old man, his utter disregard of all lets and hindrances in his way, had always appealed to her. Now she said with a half smile: "Thou canst not noose death from thy path, O Strangler, as thou canst noose thine other enemies. What if it take thee unaware with thy message?"

The old man rose and made his farewell salaam. "The Presence may rest assured," he said; "I will deliver my message, *if I have one!*"

"And if not," broke in Dilarâm with an angry snivel, "thou wilt remain to die, with none to bid thee God-speed—with none to spread a funeral feast, with none to—to give a decent wail," and she ended with the soft moaning howl of bereaved womanhood.

"Woman!" replied the Strangler, turning on her with dignity. "Have I not oft told thee that the ashes of my fathers will welcome me, whether it be in heaven or hell? But there! 'tis ill teaching an old parrot!"

With which parting shot of a proverb—designed possibly to change old Dilarâm's grief to anger—he retreated.

But ere he left he sought another interview, this time alone with the mistress he had served so well.

"Majesty," he said, "if indeed I go to my death, the tribe will still obey the commands of he who bears this ring." He slipped a slender signet ring in silver off his little finger and laid it on the ground before her. She stooped to raise it. It had simply a sort of caduceus of two entwined snakes scratched upon it.

"A paper signed with it will pass; but on urgency use the ring itself." Then the old face grew troubled. "I know not if they will be as true as I, but they will obey."

That night an old man on a mule, with a crimson coil hidden under his traveller's dress, started southward, guiding his course by the stars.

Two months? Yes, two months it would take him to reach Burhanpore. With luck, a month for investigation. And then——?

"God send he died as all men die!" he muttered to himself as he rode on. "'Twould be better for Majesty and better for me. Then could I die in peace, and my ashes mix with those of my race."

Nurjahân, however, as she journeyed Kâbulwards with the Imperial camp, thought differently. From the first moment of hearing the news she had jumped to the conclusion that the Prince's death was not natural. In truth, probabilities were against his dying so opportunely. Her suspicions of Shahjahân, which had been aroused by his insistence on having the custody of his brother, had insensibly grown during the last year by being dwelt upon, and Prince Parviz's sudden appearance, without being summoned, during his father's latest attack of asthma, had strengthened her belief, right or wrong, that his sons were eager for their father's death in order to wrest all power from her.

And here she was doubtless right. The appointment of a woman to the highest office in the State must have been a bitter pill for the men of that day, or, indeed, for the men of any other day. It was an incredible, inconceivable, unforgivable insult; no more, no less. It warranted every form of detraction, every sort of opposition, all and every conspiracy that could be hatched. A weak, doting, ailing monarch, a designing female; with these two characters, any illiterate fellow could write the book of the play. It would mean nothing to him that the orders of the new Vizier show a new note of tolerance and justice; that the rumours of aggression in Kandahâr by the Shâh of

Persia should be met with statesman-like calm, and a request amounting to an order sent requiring Prince Shahjahân's immediate attendance at Court, bringing with him a sufficiency of artillery and elephants to enable him—"should the rumour prove true—to start at once with an innumerable army and countless treasure, to bring home to the aggressor the result of breaking faith and of wrong-doing. Since, thanks be to God! the success of the Prince's arms in the Deccan would now allow of his taking command in Kandahâr."

It would mean nothing to him that a tried servant who had become weak and old was given a more suitable post for his years, or that, in order to ease the condition o the peasants, a certain heavy cess was remitted throughout the length and breadth of Jahângir's dominions.

It would mean nothing to him that when reliable information was received that the Shâh of Persia really had designs on Kandahâr, orders were immediately issued for the Imperial Court to quit the enchanting region of Kashmir and return to the Punjâb in order to expedite the arrival of the victorious army from the Deccan, and to arrange for the due preparation of artillery and all warlike material. It would mean nothing to him that quick foresight is seen in regard to commissariat necessities; that, "since there would be little or no cultivated land on the march to Kandahâr, the despatch of a large army to sponge on the people was not to be thought of, and that therefore a subsidy should be given to a sufficiency of *banjaras*, or itinerant grain-sellers, to enable them and their bullocks, to the number of 100,000, to march with the army in order that there should be no difficulty about supplies; but that, by the grace of the Creator, the army should be well furnished with everything, so that without delay or hesitation it might reach Isfahân, the very capital of the traitorous Shâh."

Neither would the order sent—apparently on provocation—to the General in the Punjâb that he should not give way to over-eagerness, but, undisturbed, await the arrival of the victorious Deccan army before starting on the campaign, be accepted as evidence in favour of mere woman's wit.

All this masculinity of organization is obliterated by the femininity of the organ!

So, once more, this time in August, ere the saffron-fields had come to their full bloom, the royal pair—he was fifty-four and she fifty-two—left the playground of the east, not by the Pir-panjâeb Pass, but by the one which debouches on the hill territory of Jammu, and is the quickest route.

For Nurjahân was impatient to start the Kandahâr expedition. It was too soon to expect old Phusla's return, and with her usual and most feminine sense of fair play, she would not judge Shah-jahân on the mere suspicion which lay, nevertheless, always at the back of her brain.

They paused at the spring of Achibal for a farewell feast ere saying good-bye to what—for Jahângir at least—was an earthly Paradise. A place where his great love of the beauties of nature could be satisfied without stint, where he could lead the open air, outdoor life in which his curiously simple tastes found their greatest pleasure. To hold a Feast of Cups beside the great river which gushes out of the living rock at Achibal, to look down along the wide avenue of poplar-trees edging the aqueduct that leads the water to the levels below—those wide levels of winding streams and green rice-fields, of silvery willows and the red, hundred-leaved rose—that was content.

"Dear heart," said Jahângir regretfully to the companion of all his pleasures, "'tis ill to be leaving this land of eternal spring."

"Nay, my lord," responded Nurjahân gaily, "not eternal! The winters here are hard indeed, so the report goes." Her face changed to concern. "The poor folk must suffer. They are ill-clothed. Even in the warmth of summer they carry about their clay fire-baskets within their single garment, as my lord must have noticed. So when cold comes they must suffer much—poor souls! I would 'twere possible——"

"All things are possible," put in Jahângir quickly. "Dost forget I am the Shadow of God?" he added a trifle reproachfully. "As such, 'tis my duty to see to this. So I will give——" He paused, the idea took hold of him and he went on quite eagerly: "Yea, I will gift a whole village—the rental thereof—to this purpose of providing a second shift to the poor. Ay, and heating the water for religious ablutions in the mosques, see you, since that is a goodly work. And I will entrust it to——" He looked round for help to Nurjahân.

"Entrust it not to clerks whatever," she said, "nor to contractors. 'Tis not that they are dishonest, but money sticks to them—they cannot pass it on if they would!"

Jahângir laughed. "Hast learnt that, wise woman? Stay, I have it. I will put it in charge of the poet—my Persian poet from Isfahân. Lo! he is so full of the humanities that he will not discriminate too much—and he will write me verses on it also, so that will give us the other half of the lentil!"

So they sat smiling over the farewell gift to the poor of the land they loved so well. Half an hour afterwards, however, they were frowning over the contents of a letter which a despatch-rider had brought with all haste from the Deccan. It was Shahjahân's reply to his father's summons.

Jahângir's heavy face flushed with sheer anger at its wording. Curtly and without periphrases, it was a refusal to come north until the rainy season was over.

"I like not the style nor the matter," thundered the Emperor. "And I know not the meaning of it——"

Nurjahân, her brows levelled, her nostrils distended, stood looking at the letter she held. "The meaning of it will be made manifest ere long," she said, and her voice was bitterness itself. "Mayhap 'tis fear——"

"Fear!" echoed Jahângir almost incredulously. "But wherefore? Have I ever given him cause for fear? Have I not loaded him with honours, with favours, with——"

"'Tis not what my lord hath done," put in the Empress coldly. "He sits free of blame; 'tis what the Prince hath done himself. Some deeds bring fear with them."

"Thou speakest in riddles, wife, and I care not to guess them," retorted the Emperor angrily. "The fact remains. Khurram, my son, whom I have loved"—his voice broke—"hath written me that which bears traces of disloyalty. He hath dared to do this—and—and for the moment I have no remedy——"

"Ay!" said the Empress, her mind going beyond the personal. Shahjahân's guilt or innocence, his loyalty or disloyalty, were as nothing to the check and delay this refusal would give to the Kandahâr expedition. "There be none worthy to send in his stead—save, mayhap, Mohabat Khân."

"Mohabat hath his hands full with the hell-doomed rebels beyond Kâbul," interrupted Jahângir, his anger growing to rage as the full enormity of Shahjahân's refusal came home to him. "And why should I, the Emperor, the Shadow of God, be thwarted? I summoned Shahjahân. Wherefore comes he not?" The old uncontrollable passion seized on him, his face grew dark. "My curse upon him as disloyal!—to repay my favours thus—disobedient—and I trusted him!"

The man was roused to his very depths; the darkness of his face turned to lividness—he gasped for breath, struggled to go on, then sank back among his cushions, speechless, overcome by his constant enemy.

In an instant, thought was turned to remedies; but even as she administered them, Nurjahân's resentment rose against the cause of the attack. How dared he thus openly defy his father's—what is more, her—clear orders? Whether he was fratricide or not—and that decision must await the Strangler's return or non-return—he was plainly rebellious; he had openly defied his father's and her authority. That this thought of her own power had come to her was inevitable; authority always brings with it a certain arrogance. So her thoughts turned instantly to revenge. And as she sat when the Emperor had quieted down and gone to sleep after a full dose of opiate from her ruby cup, she sat looking at the empty measure with brooding eyes.

She had passed beyond the first vague superstitious alarm which had beset her when she had found her luck-cup had gone out of her life. She had, as it were, reasoned herself out of it. Doubtless, it had been "*talismân*," but the charm had not been hers—hers only. It had been something outside herself, and life had taught her that her only safety lay in self-reliance; that she, and she only, made or marred her fate. And this recognition had come home to her with greater strength since her father's death. It had made her colder, harder perhaps to the outside world, but infinitely more capable.

So she sat, brooding over the empty cup, fully resolved to defend her position to the uttermost.

By refusing to come at his father's request, Shahjahân had done more than mere disobedience. He had for the moment wrecked all her plans. She had intended that this Kandahâr expedition, the first over which she would have entire control, untrammelled even by her father's preconceived and masculine ideas, should be a success. And Shahjahân, whom she had chosen, irrespective of his other actions, was, unquestionably, the first General of the age. He had failed her.

So the idea flashed in upon her very soul—why not vest the command in some creature of her bidding; someone who would be a figure-head to her command?

She had tried many things in her life, from cooking to statesmanship, and in all she had found something in herself which made for success. Failure seemed far from her; she could scarce credit its occurrence even in generalship. Thus she sat brooding over the empty ruby cup, until her plans took form.

It was on Jahângir's fifty-fourth birthday that she announced them. They were at the spring of Vernâg, the source of the Jhelum river. Here, when as a Prince Jahângir had first visited Kashmir, he had ordered one of his "suitable buildings" to be erected.

And suitable it was, and is, to this day. An octagonal reservoir darkly deep, reflecting the cloistered walk surrounding it, the verdure of the gardens beyond, the blue of the sky above, the semi-darkness of the domed ante-rooms on each side. A reservoir so clear that a blind man at midnight could count the grains of sand at the bottom of it; so clear that nowhere could the fishes that swam in it hide themselves.

Jahângir had spent the best half of the morning in watching them shoot from every side to the centre, if a crumb was thrown into the water, till they made a rapid star of silver, and in admiring the surpassing beauty of a water-plant that swayed about in the ripple, bearing flowers here and there, giving it the appearance of the variegated tail of a peacock. Briefly, in all Kashmir was no sight of more beauty, of such enchanting character.

But now it was audience-time, and there beside his throne was Nurjahân's filmy-screened seat. But a few threads between her and that outside world which held womanhood in such slight esteem.

It is a picture well worth preserving in the Gallery of Significant Recollections. Imagine it! A hushed audience of big bearded men, hands on the scabbards of their swords and fingers itching to be at the woman's throat. And she, supremely beautiful, supremely capable—so far as history goes, blameless of all but ambition—the very life, the soul, the informing power of the monarch who lived through and by her—a lovable, irascible, weak, affectionate creature more like a woman than a man.

So through the cloistered alleys the long-winded phraseology of the Shâh of Persia's letter and the answer thereto echoed and re-echoed. The former pointed out how Kandahâr was a hereditary fief of Persia; how in times of misfortune it had fallen into the hands of Jahângir's lofty family, who, being of the same blood, were counted as guardians; how, from feelings of brotherhood, the Shâh had awaited restitution, thinking that, after the manner of his ancestors who were in Paradise, the Emperor of India would voluntarily take the matter into his consideration; the more so because the petty country was not worthy of his notice. It went on with Persian verses to the effect that the ever-vernal flower of cordiality must remain in bloom, since between Persia and Hindustân trouble could not exist, and naught was possible but love and trust. It ended by a fervent wish that the star-brushing standards of the Emperor of all the Indies might ever be associated with the Divine aid.

The reply, though it carefully avoided all notice of the Shâh's hereditary claim to the disputed province, was even more dignified and flowery. It asserted that the glorious monarch, the star of heaven's army, had without rhyme or reason disturbed the rose-garden of love and friendship; that no mention had previously been made of any wish for Kandahâr, that petty village, but that on hearing of its occupation orders had immediately been issued not in any way to transgress the pleasure of the prosperous one. Nevertheless, when such steps were taken without the return of the letter-bearing ambassador, the question must arise, to whom will mankind ascribe the merit of keeping compact and holding in trust the coin of humanity?

It ended somewhat curtly with the bald wish that God would preserve the receiver at all times.

But it was stiff and to the point. So, whether it was woman's work or man's, the hearers accepted it heartily with fulsome flattery.

Then followed a brief outline of the Emperor's policy. Since Prince Shahjahân had declined to obey the Emperor's order appointing him to the supreme command in Kandahâr, that order was cancelled. Fresh ones had been sent to say that the Amirs and the army generally were to come north without him, while he himself might take up a permanent residence wherever he wished, as the provinces of Malwa, the Deccan, Guzerat, and Kandesh, would be handed over to his possession, in return for which his *jaghers* in the north would pass to his younger brother Shahriyâr, who had been appointed, in Shahjahân's place, Commander-in-Chief of the Kandahâr expedition, the entire cost of which would be defrayed by Nurjahân Padshâh Begum, who pledged herself, should necessity arise, to expend upon it all the moneys she had inherited from her father and whatever else she had acquired through Majesty's favour and indulgence, in order to bring it to a successful conclusion.

The Amirs, the Omrahs, the courtiers generally, stared at each other when Shahriyâr's name was mentioned. He was still a lad, not yet out of his teens, and weakly at that. Up till then he had not shown much forwardness in any way. Still, the Begum had undoubtedly made a very sporting offer, and if someone of experience, such as Rustum Khân, who knew every foot of the way, were sent with the boy, all might go well.

And as for the order concerning Shahjahân, it was an ingenious method of keeping him at arm's length, and not a few of the Court had begun to look at him askance over his brother's sudden death.

So once more they assented with fulsome flattery.

That same evening, however, when Jahângir came on his daily visit to the Empress, his mind was once more running on the extreme iniquity of Shahjahân's behaviour. It was monstrous, inconceivable, without parallel.

"He will come to evil, mark my word!" he said, half between tears and anger. "When, with a father like me, who am at least his ostensible creator, and in my own life-time have raised him to the dignity of Sultanship and denied him nothing, he acts so badly, I appeal to the justice of God that He may never again regard him with favour! And what is more," he added almost spitefully, "'tis five years since on account of the great regard and abundant affection I had for Khurram and his sons—especially Shuja, who was dangerously ill at the time—I resolved, if Providence would grant me the child's life, that never again would I sport with a gun or inflict an injury on any living thing with my own hand. And all these five years, despite my love of hunting—especially with a gun—I have kept my promise. But now—now—curse me if I shoot not, just to pay back his unkind behaviour! Ay, and no one in the camp shall dare to travel with me without a gun too—and they shall shoot. Yea, they shall shoot at everything they see." He paused, and added with an appeased smile: "But only God knows if they will kill aught!"

And the very next morning Jahângir felt some consolation for his son's disloyalty in once more enjoying the extreme pleasure of sport, and laughing at the efforts of his courtiers to shoot straight.

In such ways he was pure boy.

CHAPTER X

"In Life's long Ledger, on each passing page
Right deeds and wrong are written. When old age
Claims at Death's door its earnings, who can say
Which Master has been served, which gives the wage?"

THE Imperial camp lay at Thanêswar, that quaint old town of sacred shrines where, long years before, the little Mihr-un-nissa in her sleep had so nearly been deprived of her plaything, the lacquered cup.

And now, Empress of all the Indies. with unlimited power, unlimited resource, at her command, she lay behind silken screens, in a marvellous tent of Kashmir shawls, held up by poles of solid silver-gilt and set with precious stones.

She had rested late, for the last three months had brought the influx of a thousand new anxieties. The Emperor's health was failing fast. There could be no question but that Shajahân's behaviour was largely responsible for his father's sudden breakdown. Though the latter still found abundant pleasure in the chase, he was easily tired, and when tired was apt to be piteous. Only that very evening he had come to Nurjahân, his unfailing comforter, full of his grievances, and had kept her from necessary work.

"See you," he had said, "I write no more with mine own hand in my Memoirs. It shakes too much, so I have desired Motâmid to write notes, then submit them for verification ere transcribing them into my book. 'Tis all my son's fault. Lo! I have ordered that in the notes he shall be named 'Disloyal'; nothing else does he deserve. What affection, what interest have I not bestowed on him! My tongue fails in ability to set them forth. And now in a warm climate that is extremely unsuited to my health I have to be active, to ride and review troops. And what is worse, see you, is this! His vileness hath deluded others, and these must I punish, though heretofore they have served me well."

And when Nurjahân, as ever, had attempted consolation, he had gone on angrily: "Oh, 'tis well to say 'tis God's will, and I thank my Creator that he has given me strength to bear my burden and reckon it as light. But what lays heavily on my heart and places my eager temperament in sorrow is this, that when every loyal man should be vying with each other in my service against mine enemies, this inauspicious disloyal one should have struck as it were with an axe at the root of his own dominion, and become a stumbling-block in the path of the momentous affair of Kandahâr. For it will have to be postponed—mark my words, it will have to be postponed," he repeated, looking almost helplessly at the woman to whom he had given his unreserved confidence.

"It is postponed," she replied quietly.

And this was the truth; for events had marched quickly since that peaceful day at the Vernag spring. To begin with, there had been a fracas—nay, more—bloodshed, between Shahjahân's and Shahriyâr's agents over one of the latter's *jaghirs*. The rights of the matter are immaterial; the result was instant animosity. Briefly, the fat was in the fire. All the Emperor's passionate anger had been aroused, he had clamoured for immediate action against his son, and as a first step had ordered Mohabat Khân, his greatest General, to Court. Mohabat, a wily, astute man, had replied that he could do nothing so long as Nurjahân's brother, Asof Khân, remained at hand able to checkmate his moves. Nurjahân had seen the justice of this stipulation. In her own heart of hearts she saw that her brother must naturally favour Shahjahân, his son-in-law's cause. So as, with a view to expenses, Jahângir had sent for all the treasure in gold and silver that had accumulated since his father's time at Agra, Asof was deputed to escort it thence.

The result might have been foreseen. News of the treasure came instantly to Shahjahân, who started from Mandu at once with the object of intercepting it. So at least it was said. This had necessitated immediate effort for protection. Hence the journey southwards of the Emperor with a small picked force;

a force, however, that was joined on the way down country by many contingents. In fact, though the march from Lahore had been without previous notice—for time did not admit of delay or reflection, and there were at first but few Amirs in attendance—before the arrival of the camp at Thanêswar such a force had come together that in any direction one looked the plain was occupied by troops. Thus once more the green wheat-fields of Kurukshetra were trodden down by soldiers' feet.

So Nurjahân had her hands full. Yet still she hesitated to take decisive steps, for old Phusla had not returned. It was long past his time; and that might mean innocence. Then Shahriyâr? She could not gloze over his inefficiency. And there were no children of the marriage, no sign of one as yet.

It is difficult to get at the workings of a woman's mind when it has to deal with such absolute, yet unstable, power as this woman possessed. What thoughts, what aspirations and desires were hers it is impossible to judge; but when the tortuous ways of Eastern diplomacy were over each day, it is to be guessed that she was outwearied.

On this particular evening more than usually so; she therefore dismissed her attendants, all save Dilarâm—who, despite her great age, still clung to her duty of sleeping on the floor within reach of her mistress's hand—and simply flinging aside her veil, lay down to rest in the flowing white garments that were still her favourite dress.

So the light of the little scented, jewelled cresset that hung from the tent-pole glinted on diamonds and pearls still twined in her abundant hair and on the ropes of pearls about her neck. The distant noises of the camp filtered through the silken screens; the singing challenge of sleepy watchmen one to the other broke in on the semi-silence. All was peace and darkness; for the "Lamp of Justice" swinging in front of the Emperor's tent hard by threw but a feeble gleam across the wide enclosure. Someone yawned, a patient weary yawn, and from Dilarâm's quilt-muffled figure came a gentle snore.

What was it that in the darkest hour of the night made Nurjahân sit up suddenly and listen? She scarcely knew. Not Dilarâm's slow snore, but a faint chuckling sound from the further side of the tent. But that, surely, had come after she awoke? Before that, what was it? Something that awoke her. She waited for a minute, but heard nothing. Then, dissatisfied, she rose, took the jewelled cresset from its stand, and walked noiselessly across the tent with bare feet upon the silken carpet.

She was a brave woman, but what she saw made her give one startled cry, half checked by that desire for silence, for secrecy, in which she had learnt to look for her surest weapon. It was enough, however, to rouse Dilarâm, who, half drunken with sleep, staggered towards the light. To put down the cresset on the floor, seize her by the wrist, and gag her outcry, was a second's work, but it entailed sinking to the ground with her. So the women's flouncing skirts almost touched the outstretched arms of a naked man which still moved convulsively in a last death-struggle. For a noose was round his neck, a noose that was fast held by another figure that lay behind him, a figure that, even as they looked, slackened its hold, gave one faint sigh, and then lay still.

"Phusla!" whispered Nurjahân hoarsely. "Phusla! Not one word, nursie—not one word! Quick, the lamp! Let us see if he still breathes—methinks he is dead—ay, dead!"

The added horror seemed to slip her by as she knelt curiously beside the naked anatomy of the old Strangler.

He was quite dead. He had gone out like a lamp in a wind, killed doubtless by the effort to kill. And as she knelt the full meaning of his return flashed in on her; but old Dilarâm, grasping nothing save that her ancient friend was gone, began to whimper.

"Peace, woman!" said Nurjahân in a voice vibrant with command. "None must know. And if thou desirest not that the old man be held Strangler by all, take that noose off yonder carrion. It hath done its work surely!"

Dazed with sheer horror, the old woman loosed the slip-knot, withdrew the twisted silken rope, mechanically coiled it up, and thrust it—as she had done once before at the Strangler's command—into her capacious bosom.

"None will know now—none will know," she muttered, rocking herself backward and forward. But Nurjahân saw further.

"They will suspect," she whispered sternly, "if they find him thus. Quick! Thou hast care of his things—his braided coat—his badge. Go boldly—none will challenge thee!"

The old woman, mumbling away at charms to keep off evil between her hushed wail of grief, obeyed, as she had ever obeyed her nursling ever since that day when Ghiyâss-ud-din, repentant, confused, overjoyed, had given it back to her arms from the desert where it had been laid.

So Nurjahân, alone, crouched beside the dead men, the jewelled cresset by her side, waited in silence for her return. Such scented silence, holding so strange a scene! The woman with the light showing her braided, gem-set hair, the two still forms, one so peaceful, the other contorted in the last agony of swift suffocation, lying one behind the other on the silken carpet. Phusla's face, worn, old, inconceivably lined, the mouth open, the eyes closed, showed sideways; the other's was hidden under his arm. Poor loyal—heart-loyal—old Strangler! His skill, his contempt for other's incompetence, found vent in her soft, half-smiling "Bungler!" as she drew her white draperies distastefully a shade further from the old man's last victim.

"Bungler!" Ay, that was what old Phusla would have called him—Phusla the Strangler— !

But how had it come about? Had mischance brought the old man to the spot in time to save her?—for the Bungler was no common thief; such carrion did not risk life for a few jewels when there was loot and to spare in less secure places. Or had he become aware of some plot against her life—there were so many!—and led the Bungler on to believe he would help?

There was no fathoming the thoughts or actions of that mind, master in its way. But the question remained. Had the old man returned with a message, or had he come merely to save? She would never know, for he was dead. How peaceful he looked, this loyal old servant of hers, who had dealt death to—how many?

But what was death? Nothing! She was not speculative in mind. She was too much enmeshed in the things of this world to think beyond it; but she had read much, and the words of the Bhagavad-Gita, which she had often heard Gosain Jadrûp repeat, recurred to her:

> "Yea; but we when man layeth
> His worn-out clothes away,
> And taketh new ones, sayeth,
> 'These will I wear to-day.'
> So putteth by the spirit
> Lightly its robe of flesh,
> And passeth to inherit
> A residence afresh."

Certainly, the Strangler, despite his many crimes—ay, despite his many virtues—had slipped out of life easily enough!

As for other thoughts, time enough for them when the immediate present had passed.

Dilarâm was long of coming, but she was old. Ah, there she was at last! Between them they could clothe the old man to some semblance of his Court office. But after that——

Stay! Fedai Khân, now the Quarter-master-General. He was ever to be trusted. In a way it was his business. But to send for him in the middle of the night would be to arouse suspicion. She must wait till dawn.

"Peace, fool!" she said harshly to old Dilarâm, whose grief showed signs of becoming audible. "If thou wouldst save him from suspicion, be still! See, take up thy quilt and follow me to my audience-tent."

With the lamp in her hand, she set aside the curtain dividing the two and took her place on the cushioned divan. So, one elbow resting on her knee, the hand pressing her firm lips together, she waited for the dawn, while Dilarâm, choking in her sobs, fell after a time into profound slumber.

When Fedai Khân could be called to the Presence without fear of tattle, she would call him. Till then she had time for thought.

So when Fedai Khân, duly called through the eunuchs in attendance, appeared, as usual beautiful to behold, spick and span, perfect in salutation, he found the Empress ready with all plans.

Briefly, in private audience, she told what had happened, setting old Dilarâm at the tent-curtain to recite her morning verses of the Korân, so as to prevent outside listeners from overhearing.

"The soil within," she whispered finally, "is but loose sand. A child could scrape a grave for the carrion as it lies. 'Tis but to cover it; the silken carpet will do the rest. Wilt do this for thy mistress, O Fedai, and forget thy nobility?"

Fedai bowed low. "Nobility lies in service, Majesty. It is done," and he moved to enter the inner tent.

"But hist!" interrupted the Empress. "There is the old man—Dilarâm, thy quilt. Wrap him in it and lift him to the threshold of the outer door. Folk will deem he died in his sleep—dost understand?"

"But, Majesty," remonstrated Fedai blankly, "he hath been away these months."

The Empress looked at him coldly. "Thou dost mistake. He returned but yesterday, and sought instant and private interview with me. As ever, I saw him; privately, mind you, and——"

"Majesty's orders shall be obeyed," said Fedai, bowing hurriedly; there was something almost appalling in this woman's calm foresight.

The Empress raised her voice as he disappeared into the inner tent, drawing his broad tulwar to serve as shovel. "So the camp moves, as I said, at the third watch. Bear in mind the order, and have all in readiness. Dost hear?"

She paused for a reply, and from within came at once the orthodox reply: "Majesty shall be obeyed!"

So for the space of some ten minutes orders and answers were given duly. Then Fedai emerged, somewhat breathless; yet still, as ever, spick and span.

"Thou hadst best call thy writer and set down the order," remarked Nurjahân.

"Majesty shall be obeyed," murmured Fedai Khân, wondering at this woman's calm.

So all was in order, and the eunuchs and slave-girls waiting in the corridor discussed the sudden move sleepily.

"Lo!" said one, a big brawny fellow, "I augured ill from the

Begum's hurry. Can a body not rest in peace? And she was up half the night too. Curses on all womenkind, say I!"

"Wah!" commented a pert slave-girl. "That may be. But she dismissed us all early, and the old porcupine Dilarâm would not let us in at dawn, saying the Begum was busy. So we be not so hard used as thou—man-and-no-man! Lo! 'tis better to be woman, say I!"

It was not for a good hour afterwards that the body of old Phusla was discovered outside the back entrance to the tent, just where he was wont to sleep—found cold and stark, wrapped up in a quilt. "Why, 'tis thine *anagâh-jee*," remarked a curious maid, and Dilarâm with sobs told the tale dictated by her mistress, of the old man's late return and how she had loaned him her quilt. And as her grief, till then pent-up, was genuine, it carried the tale with it. Even the magnificence of the obsequies ordered by the Begum for her faithful old servant did not assuage the poor old lady's tears, though she took undoubted pride in the amount of sweet-scented woods and oils that went to the burning of that frail body.

Nor, though the ashes were duly put in a proper receptacle, and Nurjahân promised to send them safe to the village in the Deccan whence the Strangler had said he came, was she content. She sat weeping and shaking her wellnigh bald head disconsolately.

"Nay, nay, Meru!" she moaned, reverting to childish days. "Thou meanest well, but none can see to it save I. Look you, I, too, grow old—nay, I am old and past work as he was. Yet must my bones lie near his ashes, for, see you, we were as brother and sister. So of what use are thirty-two teeth to one rice-grain? Better to send us both by one carrier. Lo! I can sit in one basket and he in the other."

For all her sympathy with the poor old soul's tears, Nurjahân could not repress a smile.

"Thou wouldst scarce balance with poor Phusla's ashes, nursie," she said; "but if such be thy desire, thou shalt go in state."

So, two days later, a quaint procession started southwards from the Imperial camp, Dilarâm attired in scarlet like a bride, seated in a spangled *dhooli* which seemed too small for her size and flouncing garments, preceded by a *bhangy wallah*, his bamboo yoke scarce bent by the weight of Phusla's ashes in one basket, balanced by the coolie's pipe in the other.

"'Tis ever so!" remarked Dilarâm almost apologetically. "Were I burnt, which God forbid! I should not be so heavy. 'Tis so with all men. 'If I live, the world lives; if I die, the world dies!'"

And Nurjahân, Empress though she was, felt that she was more alone than ever without her two old servants.

That evening she sent again for Fedai Khân.

"Did they find the carrion?" she asked sharply. "If so, and there was the mark of the Noose——" She paused in evident regret.

Fedai salaamed as ever to perfection. "Majesty has no cause for vexation," he replied. "I cut the carrion's head off with my sword ere I buried it."

Nurjahân was silent for a second. Then she said coldly: "Thou hast done well, Fedai. Better than I, who had hours and hours for thought." Then she added half to herself:

"Lo! I grow old, too!"

She felt disheartened, uncertain; in a way disappointed. Phusla had returned, but had he returned with a message? Or, discovering one of the many plots against her life, had he journeyed back simply to save her? She had immediately caused inquiries to be made as to whether the two men had been seen together, and had traced them back as far as Agra. But beyond that——?

For if old Phusla had journeyed northward but one furlong alone she felt she would have the right to believe the worst of Shahjahân.

Yet when all was said or done, she knew, being no fool, that when she and Jahângir were dead and gone, Shahjahân was the worthiest of all the claimants to power. Prince Parviz and Shahriyâr were alike unfitted for the throne, and even Prince Dara Buksh, Khushrau's eldest son, who had been honoured by the Governorship of Guzerat and a handsome allowance, did not promise well.

She was in this curious frame of mind when news came to her which changed the whole tenor of her mind.

After three years of marriage a child was to be born to her daughter. In an instant the horizon of life altered. Her ambition—no longer personal, and therefore to one of her character trivial—centred with all the fervour of a mother round the thought of an heir who would be bone of her bone, flesh of her flesh.

A day or two afterwards the Emperor ordered his army to put on their *chiltas*, or quilted coats—in other words, to make ready for battle.

CHAPTER XI

> "O'er Life's grim battle hovers Victory
> Ready with laurel wreath. The fighters try
> To win her favour, while with bended bow
> And arrow set, their Fate stands smiling by."

THE order came none too soon, for Shahjahân and his army were marching rapidly on Delhi; with what intent who can tell? Yet this is certain: matters had at last come to a crisis.

It is true that the undutiful son had, through an envoy, made proposals to his father, but these requests were, in that father's opinion, so unreasonable that Jahângir not only refused him permission to argue his point, but actually handed the ambassador over to Mohabat the Generalissimo to be kept in prison.

It was a strong measure, and the result was ill. Shahjahân, driven to despair, fell in with the advice of those around him. Many of these were men of desperate fortune, who hoped to mend matters by a civil war; but most were those who at all costs wished to be rid of a woman's power. Such men were insidious in assuring Shahjahân that his only chance lay in immediate resistance; that in the same way as he had been dispossessed of his northern provinces, his new southern ones would be taken from him, when he would be helpless. Foremost amongst these counsellors was Rajah Bickramajeet, to whom Jahângir, at the request of Shahjahân, had given his title. A Hindu, and Brahmin of high caste, he had been the latter's right hand for years, for he showed great talent as a General. He it was who had captured Kengra; indeed, some say that to him Shahjahân owed most of his campaigning successes. An ambitious, crafty man, his sole idea was to place his patron in power as soon as might be.

His voice, therefore, was for war at all costs. Yet still Shahjahân hesitated; he would indeed have been less than human had he not remembered his father's kindness, had he not himself felt a kindness towards that ood-hearted, irresponsible, curiously vain, yet affectionate natr e. So he divided his vast force into three sections, and, re' ining one himself, counter-marched some fifteen miles to th.. east, leaving the others to do as they chose. Apparently he wished to avoid a battle himself.

Meanwhile, over in the Emperor's camp, a certain confusion was manifest. The decision to pursue the quarrel to the bitter end came like a clap of thunder on those—and there were many—who had not yet made up their minds which cause they would espouse; the Begum's or Shahjahân's. For by common consent the battle lay between those two. So men looked at each other suspiciously. And Mohabat Khân, the Generalissimo, was overbearing. A big burly man with a henna-dyed, purple-black-edged beard; a bigoted Mahomedan to whom woman was in all ways the creature of man. During Ghiyâss-ud-din's lifetime he had taken orders from him, glozing over Nurjahân's part in making them. If one man was fool enough to obey a woman, that was not his business. Now, entrusted with the task of defeating the disloyal one, he brooked little interference. Still, when, amongst others accused by him of favouring Shahjahân's cause, Fedai Khân's name was put forward, the Empress protested.

"On whose report?" she asked defiantly.

"Abdullah Khân's?" she echoed. "What warranty have we for his loyalty?"

"What warranty?" echoed Jahângir in his turn, somewhat helplessly. "Sure, dearest, he is second in command. Mohabat trusts him utterly. He hath command of the vanguard. Whoever he selects to join his corps he gets at once. He marches a mile ahead of all the other forces. He is entrusted with the intelligence department and the selection of routes. Is not that enough? Besides, each day he brings to me long written strips of news which his spies have sent him from the disloyal one's camp. In them Fedai's name was certainly apparent."

Nurjahân's beautiful eyebrows met in a frown. Now that poor old Phusla had gone, she could not be so sure of her own information. The tribe, it is true, still worked for her; but it was for pay, and she was wise enough to discredit much of the bought news. Yes, truly, she was more alone than she had been.

Still, her courage did not fail her. By-and-by, ere long, she would have something of her own flesh and blood by her, something for which, indeed, to fight. No mother could have looked forward to that coming child with more hope, more tenderness, than did this grandmother.

So she possessed her soul in patience. "Lo! my lord, think for thyself, and be not led away by other minds. Yea, bethink thee! Last week, was not Khalîl denounced? the day before yet another of thy servants? Wouldst thou not have sworn both men faithful? Have a care lest, led away by intrigue, thou shouldst destroy thy friends at the bidding of thine enemy."

Jahângir looked alarmed. "Dost hold Abdullah false, then?" he asked.

"I say not so," replied Nurjahân. "Yet if he is, 'tis better he should not suspect our suspicion. The time is not one for the removing of a veil openly from evil deeds, therefore continue to show him all attention. But for Fedai Khân! Lo! I, Nurjahân, hold him my hostage; the dust of his sincerity is pure."

And Jahângir was satisfied. Over in Abdullah Khân's tent, however, there were gnashings of teeth.

"The hell-doomed woman is too sharp for us," muttered the traitor-in-chief, Abdullah. "We must go softly, since she suspects. But I would we had decapitated Fedai and some others ere the battle came. They are too faithful, too brave!"

So, after a day or two the battle did come. It was ere day-break that a messenger came to the leader of the vanguard, bringing him as a special mark of favour Jahângir's own quiver, with a request that its possession might animate his zeal. Fedai Khân, who was standing by, not a button or a buckle ajee in all his glorious panoply of war, muttered into his twirled moustache: "'Twere better to make sure first for whom he fights."

But Mohabat was too busy making dispositions to think of aught else.

It was a fine body of 25,000 horsemen that the Generalissimo had in his grip that March morning on the sandy plain to the west of Delhi. Far as the eye could reach as the sun rose, the level beams sparkled on chain armour and lances and the bright trappings of the lean, eager little Indian horses that were never for one instant still, yet never moved a hair's breadth from their station. About their feet, showing the tense quivering of their small hoofs, lay a little cloud of dust that turned to gold in the sunrays, while the pennons and flags seemed piled one upon the other against the primrose of the dawn.

Abdullah Khân, long, thin, dark, sitting his horse as if he were glued to it, was at the head of his contingent of ten thousand; as fine a body of men as India could show. Close at his side rode Fedai Khân, beautiful to behold, on a grey Arab. But the handsome face was stern, and the eyes, lustrous as those of a woman, never left Abdullah's face for a moment. Behind him, again, rode the Syyeds of Bârha; a loyal race this, to whom treachery even to an enemy was unconceivable. Fedai was responsible for their being in the vanguard; otherwise, not one of them would have consented to follow "Lånat-ullah," or the "Curse of God," as the common folk styled Abdullah. But there they were, small, hawk-eyed, active, like the birds of prey after whom they had named their ancestral home the "Falcons' Nest."

As the dawn grew, Abdullah's face grew dark.

"Hath the messenger not returned?" he said anxiously to a favourite henchman. The man shook his head, and the commandant of the vanguard bit his lip and looked over to the distance, where two faint clouds on the horizon showed that the enemy was awaiting the onslaught.

What was in front of him? Bikramajeet's division, or Darâb's? On that hung much. And yet, if the worst came to the worst, it ought not to be difficult to distinguish friend from foe.

Hark! The kettledrums of Empire! In a second every horse was as a statue. Again the wild, rolling call, and like an arrow from a bow each flung itself forward.

The charge had begun.

On, on, right up to the very line of the enemy, and then from the mouth of almost every horseman of the ten thousand rose up the cry:

"Friend! Friend!"

Fedai, riding hard at Abdullah's heels, rose in his stirrups.

"Traitor!" he cried, and delivered a swinging blow at the head before him. But the grey Arab swerved and the next moment he was trying to guard his own from the furious onslaught of the foe.

"Deen! Deen! Fateh Mahomed! A Bârha to the rescue!" shouted the Syyeds, and with them the whole hundred or so of loyalists whom Fedai had brought with him. Then came battle indeed!

For no matter what Abdullah's treachery, these men of Shahjahân's, under the generalship of Darâb, had no news of it, so they fought what they deemed the foe right fiercely. At first, at any rate, for that small knot of loyalists firmly planted the foot of courage and gave no countenance to half-heartedness. Yet disaster was close at hand. One by one the combatants fraternized, turned, and made for the nearest real fighter. But the horses were not as the men; they could not, would not, change their colours in the thick of the fight. No, not even though, breathless with hot haste, Rajah Bikramajeet himself rode upon the scene bellowing, "Hold, enough!" So for a few more minutes the uproar, the confusion lasted, and one and yet one more loyalist went down by sheer weight of numbers. Then for one second all seemed lost. Fedai, who, with the courage of real loyalty, had risked even his reputation by swift return to hurry up reinforcements, would have been too late. Then it was that a chance shot from a matchlock caught Bikramajeet between the eyes, and he fell dead without a cry. It was a signal for retreat. His followers hesitated; the pillars of their courage shook.

Ere they could regain their dash, ere they could steady themselves, Mohabat's troops were on them.

The battle was brief. Discomfited, disorganized, scarcely able to discern friend from foe, the rebels broke and fled.

And as Lánat-ullah, the "Curse of God," otherwise Abdullah Khân, rode in hot haste—with a slash from Fedai's sword on his right shoulder—to join Shahjahân he cursed his luck. Why had Darâb's division been opposite the new guards? Why had Darâb not received his message of treachery? Why had not Bikramajeet given him warning?

But there was one good thing—the hell-doomed dog of a Hindu was dead. Now he, Abdullah, Lánat-ullah, call him what you will, would have a fair field with the heir apparent.

Shahjahân, however, did not view the death of his right-hand servant in the same light. Whether from regret or remorse, he refused further fight at the time, and retired westwards.

Yet even in the Emperor's camp the times were critical. The defection of Abdullah Khân had raised many questions of loyalty. Some made excuse to leave, and some returned also with excuses. And both the one apology, and the other had, as the Emperor put it, "to be bought as if genuine."

For the whole country was in a flame. So, after a while negotiations for peace were started in both camps, and finally Mohabat Khân, as Generalissimo, entered into a treaty with the discomfited yet still strong Shahjahân to the effect that no further steps should be taken against him, if he would consent to retire to Mandu and disband his army. In which case his provinces and estates would be restored to him.

To this Shahjahân consented, and for the time peace was restored; so the Emperor and the Empress, nothing loath, retired to Ajmere, there to await the coming of the child, which for the time being absorbed all Nurjahân's thought and cares; Mohabat meanwhile, with Prince Parviz, and a large army, going southward on pretence of watching the disloyal one keep his promises. But Fedai Khân, who was now almost the only reliable friend the Empress had, shook his head and augured ill of the expedition.

"May it please Majesty," he said urbanely, with his most perfect salutation, "the cunning of Mohabat Khân would instruct the devil!"

CHAPTER XII

"The wakeful, ode-rehearsing nightingale
Sang to the fading roses, wan and pale;
But like strung beads on the Beloved's arm
The rosebuds showed above the leafy veil."

NURJAHÂN and Jahângir sat once again on the terrace overlooking the great lake-reservoir at Ajmere.

And once again a little child filled their eyes, their thoughts; but it was a babe, almost new-born. It lay in the sunshine upon a satin quilt on Nurjahân's lap, naked save for a wee muslin shift, delicate as gossamer, with fine stitching, and a quaint, peaked cap of golden tissue fringed, as with hair, by brown silk and little clusters of seed-pearls. A fat morsel of a babe, not purple-red, as are Western infants, but cream-coloured, with ochre shadows, and heavy black brows and eyes; all the heavier for the antimony painted round them to keep off evil, envious glances. Jahângir, bent and broken, his hair tinged with grey, his breath at all times coming somewhat laboured, leant over the two. His face was radiant.

"We will call her Arzâni, wife," he said, "since she hath come in answer to our prayers. And she is ours—ours only! My son and thy daughter! The Gifted Lady! Yea, we will call her so, seeing that it telleth both ways—that she is God-given, and that Fate hath gifted her with all; for, see you, she is the very spit and image of her grandmother. Lo! so must thou have looked when thou layest in thy mother's arms at first."

Nurjahân's face—it was still extraordinarily beautiful despite her five and fifty years—hardened a little.

"Yet did she and my father leave me to the desert for being female," she replied. "And my lord too, he would rather it had been male." She looked up to see his face, but it smiled back at her.

"Not I!" he laughed. "At first, mayhap, the old idea came to me; but now—dear heart, when we are dead she will live to keep alive thine image." Then his smile faded. "Besides . . . it is little Chamni over again! 'Tis being here, where she found the Garden of Paradise, that hath made me think of her so much, lately; but her small grave drew me till this one came. So 'tis thou only who art disappointed."

Suddenly, with an almost passionate denial of his words, Nurjahân strained the sleeping infant to her breast, and her face grew almost exultant.

"I—nay, my lord, there, thou art mistaken! True, I wished a boy; but now the girl hath come, I see what Fate decrees. Yea, she will be like me—but more fortunate—more beloved——"

"More beloved?" echoed the Emperor in a hurt tone. "That thou canst not be. Truly, O Meru, I have loved thee——"

She turned to him tolerantly. "Yea, yea, my lord! Thou hast given me more than I deserve." How could she tell him that his best was not hers? "I meant but that she should not have so many enemies as I——"

"Enemies!" he echoed again, this time angrily. "Thou hast none that are not mine also. But have comfort, dear heart! This very morn have I received a missive from Mohabat. The disloyal one, being now worsted, hath finally fled. So there is no more need for anxiety, he writes, from the rebels: 'willingly or unwillingly the rulers of the Deccan are performing their due of obedience and submission, therefore Majesty may make his mind at ease about that quarter, and enjoy himself in hunting and travelling in whatever place in the royal dominions of which he may approve, and which is good for his health.' So what say you, dearest, to Kashmir? Do! My heart leaps at the very thought of it."

But Nurjahân's eyes had narrowed; something in the Generalissimo's report had struck her.

"What means he by 'now'?" she asked quickly. "Hath there been more fighting? I wist not——" She interrupted herself quickly. "This last month or more I have been bound up in other things. Lo! Gladness was so ill—the child's life was in danger, and so—and so——" She passed her hand over her forehead as if to sweep away such trivialities, and asked again: "Surely there hath been no more fighting—all was arranged——"

Jahângir coughed somewhat uneasily.

"Ay, but Mohabat thought it best to strike while the iron was hot——" he began.

Nurjahân was in a flame in a second. "Mohabat!" she echoed. "Who is he? What right hath he——? Besides, he made the treaty——"

Jahângir looked relieved. "Ay, dearest, that is so; and therefore he had the right to act. Beside—no harm was done. The disloyal one escaped the net that was laid for him—ay, and Lånat-ullah also, and the only one that hath paid the penalty is the dog of a Hindu that was ever shaking the chain of enmity and perversion! So fret not thyself over a broken treaty! Lo! Mohabat is wise in his measure, and he hath managed the thing well—he and my son Parviz. Lo! he is nigh as fortunate as Khurram was in the old days——"

The Empress's eyes were keenly on the Emperor's sallow, kindly face, and she turned the subject abruptly.

"Ay, truly fortunate," she said briefly. "Wast successful in the chase this morning?"

Jahângir succumbed in a second. "Did I not tell thee?" he replied delightedly. "As thou knowest, the huntsmen brought word of a tiger, but after entering the forest three others became visible. Having killed all four, I returned hitherwards. 'Tis strange the liking I have for tiger-shooting; when I can get it I go not after other sport. So it was also with Mahmud of Ghazni. Many stories are told of his deeds. Once a very large tiger, enraged with pain, got on the elephant's back; but the Amir knelt down and struck him such a blow with his sword as cut off both his forefeet, so that he fell backwards. Yet when I was Prince I did better. The same thing happened, but I had no time to seize my sword. So I clubbed the matchlock and dealt him such a shrewd blow on the head with it—but there! 'Tis not manners to talk about oneself, so I will restrain my tongue and go. God be with you both, dearest."

She looked after him pitifully as he walked away, bent and

worn and old; yet still full of memories of olden strength; yet still happy when he was with her—still happy—so must he be ever!

After he had gone she sat cuddling the child, looking out with almost vacant eyes over the shining levels of the lake to the blue Aravelli hills.

Yes, for the present, till the child grew up in her likeness, the first object of her—Nurjahân's—life must be the Emperor's health. To that all else must bow. Shahjahân's rebellion was scotched for the moment; by what unfair means she could not stop to consider, though the thought of them made her burn with anger against Mohabat. What Fedai had said of him was true. He could instruct the devil in cunning. Still, for the time he was rounding up rebellion, and making matters smooth.

So her thoughts passed to the immediate future. A holiday in Kashmir! A holiday with the child!

How true was the saying: "No woman is a mother till she is a grandmother." She sat basking in the sunshine, dreaming as any woman might do, forgetful even of her power, until the infant began to cry; then she laughed aloud at its effort to suck her finger, and clapping her hands, summoned the servants, who sat discreetly behind screens, but within call.

Then leisurely, her long white garment trailing on the white marble path, she passed by the fountain-set aqueducts to the palace, followed by a tribe of attendants carrying fans and essence-boxes, and Heaven knows what luxuries of all sorts and kinds. But she had forgotten them in the child.

So had not the child's mother, who lay, still languid, in the darkest corner of a stuffy little side room. She was a tall, thin woman, no longer quite young, and not in the least like her mother. But she had an honest, good, truthful face.

She scarce took notice of the babe, which, after it had been duly suckled by its wet nurse, was brought to her pillow. There it lay content, as its grandmother had lain content after her first draught of camel's milk. But its mother's eyes were on the sunshine beyond the narrow strip of room.

"Ah, *amma-jân*," she said suddenly, impulsively, to Nurjahân, whose eyes were on the child. "Have I not done my part? The babe is there for thee, now let me go! As thou knowest,

I had foresworn the married life. I was canoness. Did I not say, even as a child, that I cared not to have a husband? Yet did I obey thee. Thou didst not think of me, mother, it was the child that I should bear. Well! I have borne it. 'Tis pity 'tis not a son; but it is clean and healthy, and that is much—considering——" She paused, and her plain face hardened into lines of positive beauty as she went on resolutely: "But I have done my task. Shahriyâr hath other women—let them bear him sons!"

Her bitterness was concentrated into calm, and Nurjahân as she listened felt herself condemned. It was true what her daughter said. In making this marriage she had thought mostly of her own plans; yet her daughter had raised small objections—she had not protested——

"Thou hast not been unhappy, child?" she said with sudden unwonted tears in her eyes.

Gladness smiled gently. "None could be unhappy with thee, mother, and he hath not troubled me—much. But, see you, my task is done. Thou art content with the child; I see it in thine eyes. Therefore I will return to my father's people, where I have lived all these years——"

"There was no choice, daughter," began Nurjahân. Before this simple woman she felt herself defenceless.

"None, mother," assented her daughter, "after thou hadst made thy choice."

And Nurjahân made no answer. What was the use of trying to explain her action? Both women and men were against her. So she took the sleeping infant from the pillow and said gently:

"I take it as thy gift, daughter, clean and wholesome and healthy, as becomes the descendant of Ali Kul, honourable gentleman. Never child shall be loved more than this child. Thou hast done thy task well, and thou shalt have freedom."

In a way, she told herself, it was as well. Shahriyâr—what was Shahriyâr? Something to keep the throne warm for the child, that was all. Something to keep her—Nurjahân—in power for the time should unkind Fate decree that Jahângir should not survive. But he must. The defection of his favourite son had tried him much; this must be minimized to the uttermost. For the time being Mohabat and Prince Parviz must be allowed a free hand despite the opposition of her brother, Asof Khân. Curious; but she never felt she could trust the latter, despite her affection for him as the only surviving member of her family. Still, he was able, and the ordinary government of the Empire went smoothly and well.

A month or so later saw the Imperial camp starting for Kashmir. It marched leisurely, as usual, but the winter snows had hardly melted from the Pirpanjâl Pass when they arrived at it. Still, it was their favourite entrance to the Enchanted Valley, so they braved the difficulties with an advance guard from the main body. And so it came to pass that on a brilliant April morning Jahângir and Nurjahân, well wrapped up in furs, sat looking once more down the long valley that leads from the pass to the lovely levels of their Pleasant Land. Despite their ages, they were both young in heart, so it is small wonder that the atmosphere of their content, clouded with the faint mist of coming tragedy, still lingers, for those who know their story, in every stone, every turn of the rocky path they trod so often hand in hand. They had come to the first vantage-ground whence the Kashmir Plain is visible, and there, descending from their *dhoolis*, they rested for the midday halt. A small *shamianah* tent had been erected, but it was warmer in the sunshine, so cushions had been spread, backed by a rock, and there they reclined with the Gifted Lady, now a fine strapping babe of eight months old, the very joy of their hearts, fast asleep between them, showing as a mere bundle of white Astrachan fur.

For a long time they did not speak. The scene was too enthralling. Below them in the shallow rocky ravine a stream, that overnight had been a roaring torrent through the melting of the snows during the hot day, now gurgled as gently as any sucking-dove amid its boulders. On either side of it lay snow-streaks leaving the browned grass in deep toothed recessions to the on-coming hosts of spring flowers, advancing so boldly that their foremost leaders cropped up amidst the snow itself. Such gay, reckless leaders! A rose-pink primula without a petal astray, a blue gentian looking as if it had grown in a glass case, and, velvety in purple and gold a mountain heartsease, lifting up its face fearlessly to the heavens. Beyond this, inundated, lapped, almost overwhelmed, by blue morning mist, spur after spur of rock, of pine-clad slopes, seeming almost to rise out of the one wide blue cloud that lay further and further towards the blue sky, until, sharp and clear, glistening in the sunlight like diamonds, showed the eternal snows.

Jahângir's hand sought and found Nurjahân's, and his haggard face looked wistfully into hers.

"Thou hast been happy yonder with me full oft, dearest," he said. "Is't not so?"

And her whole heart went out to him in protecting affection as she smiled back her answer.

"Full oft, my lord—and never more so than now!"

His sudden laugh of gladness rang out among the rocks and amid the flowers that nestled at their feet.

"Ay, that is good to hear; and true likewise. And, see you, I have a strange tale to unfold, that I kept for thy hearing till we were in this very place. Last night, as I returned from hunting, the stream yonder over the pass was mighty swollen with the melted snows. The bed was rocky, the water running tumultuously. One of the servants was carrying my huntsman's relish—thou knowest—the gold tray with three gold cups of wine with covers—all held on a wadded coverlet. Well, his foot slipped in the pool, and the salver fell from his hands into the water, but though they searched and better searched no trace of it could be found. Being unwilling to lose my old companions, I commanded another search this morn, and by good chance, in the very place where it had fallen, it was found; and, more strange still, it had not been upset, neither had a drop of water got into the cups. They were still full of good Shirâz. 'Tis little short of miraculous! So I commanded that they be brought here for thee, for me, and for the child to drink prosperity—nay, happiness—during our stay in this Pleasant Land!"

He clapped his hands as he spoke, and a servant, duly prepared, brought forth on the instant the little golden salver and the three covered golden cups of the huntsman's relish. They were marvels of delicate workmanship, each showing adventures of the Emperor in the chase.

"The child will not relish her portion, my lord," said Nurjahân gaily. "Mayhap my lord had better drink the two."

"Fie upon thee!" retorted the Emperor as gaily. "Dost tempt me to exceed? Nay, we will pour the child's portion on the ground. Sure, there must be some life in it to give life to so many flowers, and good wine holds all things—yea, life and death—in it. Does not the poet say:

'"Lo! 'tis God's earth that nourisheth the vine,
His sun ripens the grape, His years the wine.
Drink then, O Pilgrim! 'Tis no poison-cup;
It holds a sacrament of care divine'?"

So with light heart and hand he poured the wine out upon the ground, then drank his own portion to Happiness.

"And Health!" put in Nurjahân fondly.

CHAPTER XIII

> "The tulips, love, showed red when spring was nigh,
> Yet red and gold the leaves that withered lie.
> Naught can surpass the glory of decay;
> Heaven send it may be autumn when we die."

A WHOLE year and a half had passed since the golden goblets of the hunter's relish had toasted health and happiness on the Pirpanjâl road; and both these gifts had come. After a summer in Kashmir, the Court had moved only as far as Lahore; then, as the hot weather approached once more, had flitted back to the Pleasant Land. The enforced rest—for after all, Kashmir is too small a province for much marching—and the cool bracing climate of both it and Lahore during the winter, had wrought wonders in the Emperor's health; and though he still fretted and fumed over his eldest son's rebellion, he had, with Mohabat and Prince Parviz's help, got so much the better of the disloyal one that he could afford, for the present, to disregard him as an actual enemy; and being of a forgiving nature, he was not anxious for revenge. During these eighteen months the affairs of the Empire had gone on with fair smoothness; and as Jahângir had given orders that no defective people—that is to say, those who were blind, or who had lost arms, or legs, or noses, or ears, and no sick folk of any kind—should be permitted to come near his camp, he had nothing to vex his soul. All was beauty and pleasure. The little "Gifted Lady," now two years old, was a delight, and Nurjahân, as ever, the one human being to whom he had given his unreserved confidence.

And, in truth, despite her years, she was in a way more lovable than she had been as a younger woman; for she was softer. The child had taught her much. To a great extent she had become absorbed in it and her dreams for its future. Then the doings of Mohabat Khân and Prince Parviz, far away in the south, were too remote to rouse her interest greatly, despite the fact that Asof Khân did his best to inflame her against the former. Here he was backed by Fedai Khân, who, nevertheless, more than once came to her with tales of perfidy closer at hand. These she hesitated to credit, for Asof was her only brother, and she could not believe him absolutely false to her. That he would fain have Shahjahân forgiven she knew, and condoned. He could, in his position, scarce think otherwise.

So the months had passed, bringing few excitements. The whole country northwards was gradually settling down, and one by one the recalcitrant Amirs and noblemen were coming in to seek forgiveness. And, as Jahângir writes, in the majority of cases, "in order to please and satisfy Nurjahân, the pen of pardon was drawn through the record of their faults."

Thus matters stood in the early autumn, when, on the usual slow return over the Pirpanjâl Pass to a Panjâb winter at Lahore, the Imperial camp halted amid the saffron-fields at Pampur. A quaint spot this, built on the curious plain which lies above the level of the Kashmir valley proper, below the southern slopes of the outermost range of the encircling hills. A plain that is cut through into long fingers every few miles by such abrupt ravines that it seems as if the hand of man must have excavated them as a defence to the flat fields above, so perpendicular, so absolutely unclimable, are they. And right up to the very edge of this cliff grows the flowering saffron.

Viewed from the hills above, the *karewa*-land, as it is called, shows like a purple-gloved hand stretched out over the green fields below.

And it was autumn. The plane-trees were aflame, their white branches showing skeleton-wise amongst the dense rich russet. So were the cherry-trees, and in lines along the water-courses in the valley the willows began to gleam golden.

A marvellous bit of colour truly, with the blood-red stamens of the saffron standing clear above the tangled mass of lilac petals and silvery stems.

The beauty of it was sufficient to go to Jahângir's head, without the aromatic flowers "that scented the brain," or the cups of good Shirâz that he drank as he lay among the blossoms on a coverlet of gold and silver tissue. Every atom of him was simply steeped in delight, and he watched the little "Gifted Lady" as she buried her fat hands in the basket full of the dried stigmas the contractor had brought for his inspection, with a keen appreciation of the perfect picture she made; for the child was—at least outwardly—the very image of her beautiful grandmother, saving for the dimple. Jahângir would often remark on this, and assert his pleasure that he had kept something for himself alone. He was fond of such sentimental ideas, and, when in the mood, would embody them in somewhat halting rhymes.

He made one that morning, and repeated it to Nurjahân, who, as ever, listened with smiles.

> "From head to foot, where'er I look,
> A glance plucks at the heart's skirt, saying,
> 'This is the spot for pleasant lot,
> For wine and roses, love and playing.'"

"Nay, my lord!" criticized Nurjahân archly. "It should be 'saffron,' not 'roses'; it scans as well."

Jahângir looked doubtful. "Ay, but who ever heard of saffron in a couplet? though, to be sure, being aphrodaisiac, it hath to do with love——"

"Say not so, my lord!" she interrupted quickly. "Sure, love is different—it hath so many faces. There is a father's love——"

She had not meant to touch the sore, but he shrank in a second. "Ay, and what reward hath it?"

"Hark!" put in the Empress to change his thought. "There is the jingle of a *hurkâru*—and yonder he comes, the sun slight upon his hoopoe's plume! What news bringeth he? I trust pleasant ones, to suit the place."

"More like unpleasant," grumbled the Emperor.

And half an hour afterwards he sat looking at the letter he had received by special messenger with a half smile, half frown; for it brought both bad and good news. It told of Shahjahân's serious illness, of his compunction for having rebelled against his father, and his earnest desire to be reconciled to him on any terms. It was written after partial recovery, and was couched in most repentant words.

The quick tears came into Jahângir's eyes. There could be no question as to his love for his son. Yet, as ever, he was irresolute, and looked to the Empress for support.

"He deserves it not!" he said almost apologetically. "And yet, dearest, thou knowest how I have grieved for him. And I grow old. 'Tis the duty of the old to forgive the young, and he had evil counsellors: the dog of a Hindu who hath gone to hell, and Lànet-ullah who yet awaits damnation—God's curse on them both! But Khurram! When he was a little lad—I mind——"

The Empress had been sitting looking out over the purple crocus-fields idly. She was of those whose minds are quickly made up. In a flash she saw what this would mean to the man whose life was her chief care—and she had begged forgiveness for others, possibly as guilty; besides, with care, it might mean nothing in the future. So she spoke conclusively, calmly:

"My lord, seeing that he is penitent, should forgive his offences. Nay, more! If my lord were to write the letter with his own hand, 'twould be best. Yet"—her mind always travelled fast —"seeing also that his fault is grave, 'twere better should we impose sureties. He should send his sons to my lord as hostages —they would be well received and maintained"—she paused and hesitated—"for the rest, let my lord consult my brother. He is devoted, as my lord knows, to the Prince, and will suggest nothing amiss."

It was all done on the spur of the moment, but Jahângir's relieved, almost grateful look was sufficient to prevent any regrets or second thoughts.

"Of a truth, dearest," he replied, "thou art right. We will enforce penalties, but forgive freely. Ay, and he shall have all the Deccan as his own province. So that is settled. Cup-bearer, another goblet of wine. I will drink to his entire recovery."

That same evening Nurjahân, holding a long rambling letter in her hand, was wondering whether, had she perused it first, she would have been so ready in her decision. It was a much delayed letter, written to the dictation of one Dilarâm, deceased. The news of her death down in Bundelkhand had already reached the Empress through those appointed to pay her pension; but this apparently was a farewell which had been committed to a friend's care, and been delayed.

Beyond high-sounding phrases and pathetically plain allusions to her own imminent decease, there was not much in it save these words: "This dust-like one, already treading the path of annihilation, hath naught but gratitude to send save this: it hath been great solace at last to find relatives of Phusla deceased—may God pity him!—whose real name, they say, was the 'Fat One.' (Mayhap he was, as a babe, though mothers' eyes are blind to truth.) They helped weep on proper occasions, and ate much, since the uninvited guest cometh ever with a big platter. Yet thanks to generosity there was ever enough. It seemeth that Phusla—may many tears water his ashes!—lodged with them, and they lament always that he left. But he would take none with him, neither would he remain, saying ever that he must keep his promise to his mistress ere he died. Truly a snake goeth ever crooked to his hole, and a righteous man straight to his duty."

She sat and looked at the words which supplied information she had hitherto sought in vain, with a dull wonder as to whether, after all, it made much difference. In her heart of hearts she—and many others—had always believed that Shahjahân had been responsible for his brother's death, though she had never openly declared her opinion. And she would not do so now, though she would plot harder than ever to keep the offender out of his heritage.

That was to be Shahriyâr's—and after him, the child's—her child, who was to be like her, but more fortunate—yes, more beloved!

Asof Khân, after consultation with the Emperor, came on to see her, his relief and delight showing visibly in his fat face. He was now nigh sixty years of age, but the years had given him little dignity. He was still oleaginous and somewhat pompous.

Nurjahân listened to his lengthy periods, showing how he had safe-guarded her interests by demanding the surrender of certain fortresses.

"And in exchange?" she asked briefly.

Asof became more pompous. "The promise of the whole Deccan as his fief," he replied somewhat defiantly. "Since it was ever Majesty's plan to keep him at a distance."

"Ay!" she replied curtly. "The further the better for my plans." Then suddenly she laughed. "Lo! brother," she continued, " wherefore should I seek to bring a murderer to Court? Shrink not! Thou knowest as well as I that Khushrau died by poison. I say not that 'twas Shahjahân's act, but he was his brother's keeper—ay, and by his own urgent wish. Therefore he comes not to wheedle his father while I am here—mark that! For the rest—art satisfied that the Emperor acts of his own free-will in this?"

Asof Khân had stood helplessly dumbfounded at the suddenness of her attack, to which he had indeed no counter save bold protestation. Therefore he mumbled something, to confuse the issues, about Mohabat and the breaking of the last treaty.

Nurjahân's brows met in instant anger. "True!" she broke in. "Such must not occur again. And methinks both Parviz and Mohabat have had too free a hand for safety, the latter specially. He also is best at a distance. Therefore send him to the Governorship of Bengal, and bid Parviz to Court. The Emperor is in full train to love him as much as he loved Khurram."

She flung the remark at her brother almost as if it had been a gibe, and anger showed on his face also.

"And if he comes not?" he said.

"Then we shall have two disloyal ones," she replied recklessly, "and yet another chance for Shahriyâr! Oh, brother, brother!" she added bitterly; "if thou couldst but trust a woman—but thou and thy like canst not. Still, in this have I played a man's part—ay, better than most men! But see that those orders be carried out, and at once."

So she dismissed him; but she sent for writers, and far on into the night sat at work, looking into things which for eighteen months she had allowed to slide more or less. And as the reports were read to her a cloud grew to her face. Ay, truly, Fedai, and even Asof had been right. Mohabat Khân and Prince Parviz had been having too much of their own way; but now that another temporary peace had been patched up between Shahjahân and his father, it was time to bring them to book: more especially Mohabat, who appeared not to have accounted properly for large sums which had been forfeited by rebels.

It did not do, she told herself, to let loose the reins; she would hold them more firmly in future.

CHAPTER XIV

"The millions sleep; but, with hushed, weary sound
The Wheel of Life spins ever round and round,
So when the Dawn comes THAT which was is not;
Kings are but slaves, and slaves that were are crowned."

THE winter had passed at Lahore without bringing much of importance save that Prince Parviz had remonstrated against his father's order to send the Generalissimo Mohabat Khân to Bengal; he could not, said the Prince, be spared. Whereupon, instead of instant anger, as after Shahjahân's similar disobedience, the Emperor and his advisers had contented themselves with a sharp reprimand and a more stringent order that Mohabat be immediately told to repair to Court, unattended, in order to explain certain deficiencies in his accounts. So far Asof Khân had succeeded against his old and bitter enemy. The rest he left to chance, to Nurjahân's implacable sense of discipline, and Jahângir's still uncontrollable temper.

Thus matters stood when the question of a move to a cooler climate came with the approaching hot weather. And here Jahângir, rather to the Empress's surprise, plumped for pastures new; not that he was tired of the Pleasant Land, but Nurjahân had never seen Kâbul, and he would like to show her its beauties, and once more visit the graves of his ancestors. Besides, the country had been newly settled, and he thought it right to overlook the arrangements.

So, instead of branching hillwards after the Chenab river was crossed, the Imperial camp went on, in stately march, up the Great Trunk road, which even then led from Patna to Peshawur. It was along this road that Jahângir had ordered the building, every ten miles or so, of caravanserai to afford safe resting to travellers. In many places they exist to this day; wide squares of cloisters with bastion quarters for the better folk beside the high arched gateway. But the Imperial camp was pitched right away on the hard level white plain dotted with grey caper-bushes; for it covered many acres of ground.

It moved on in very lordly, very deliberate fashion, for the country round was full of antelope and partridge, nilghai, and bustard.

So the Emperor was happy; but one evening he burst in upon Nurjahân's afternoon hour in a towering temper.

It was on a piece, he said, with the universal lack of propriety, the universal slackness of manners, and it gave weight to his suspicions that Mohabat Khân was, at heart, a rebel; an idea ever fostered by Asof Khân.

He was so breathless with his anger that the Empress feared an attack of his enemy, asthma, and ordered a goblet of good wine at once; for experience had shown her that a certain measure of excess often warded off trouble. And in this case it succeeded, though it seemed to increase his irritation. Mohabat Khân, it appeared, without asking permission to do so—which was tantamount to an insult—had actually married his daughter to a young nobleman of the Court! Unheard of impudence, intolerable lack of common decency! If that was his notion of loyalty and proper behaviour, he, Jahângir, would refuse to allow him an interview (in other words, would put upon him the greatest disgrace possible to inflict on a man of his rank and status). And as for the young man, he had had his punishment already! He had been well bastinadoed in the audience-tent!

"Yet if he be true lover!" put in Nurjahân indifferently.

The Emperor was within his rights, and her sole desire was to soothe his wrath.

"True lover!" echoed Jahângir, almost turning his anger on her. "If he be true lover, could he not wait? Did not I wait long years? Was I guilty of vulgar breach of manners? Did I cast etiquette to the winds? But 'tis not a question of etiquette only. Mohabat hath forgotten himself. They report he cometh with over two thousand Rajputs to his bodyguard—and I bid him come alone. Yea, verily, I will do as Asof Khân counsels—I will refuse to see the wretch——"

So he went on until the opium which he took regularly had effect, and he slept. Nurjahân, vexed as she ever was at anything which disturbed the Emperor's calm, told herself that the incident had but precipitated matters, since Mohabat would have had, anyhow, to learn a lesson.

The next day saw the camp on the banks of the River Jhelum, close to the bridge of boats by which on the morrow the long procession of baggage animals, and troops, and camp-followers would file across to take up their position on the opposite bank. At least, this would have been the ordinary procedure, but that day, owing to the narrowness of the bridge, which would make crossing almost a single file, Asof Khân ordered that the major part of the army and the spare tents should cross by daylight. So all day long the bridge creaked and groaned under a slow procession of camels and carts, and little bodies of horsemen, the pennons on whose lances showed clustered against the sky-line. And all day long cries and unavailing shouts and the resounding thwacks on unwilling oxen told the depth of the sand on the river-road. They cut down the tufts of river-bed grass and strawed them on the way, but the result was poor; the bullocks strained and the blows fell as ever.

About sunset-time, however, the turmoil died down. Practically the whole camp had crossed, leaving nothing but the royal tents behind, and these but scantily guarded. Yet as dusk came on the spiked tops of the tiger-grass that grew in tufts on that sandy river-land showed like the spear-points of watching pickets. A sand haze, still golden with a reflection of sunset, lay over the wide plain, and out of it the purple and red and gold tents rose like some dream vision from a cloud. Above, the sky was darkening to purple, and in the west hung the evening star. Then slowly out of the dust haze rose another star, as the Lamp of Justice swung to its place, marking where the Emperor's tent stood.

It was a still calm night. You could hear over the wastes of sand and water the distant noise of many voices, the hum of a great camp hushed to a murmur that blent with the rushing swish of the deep stream that lay close at hand.

A gong chimed midnight from the royal enclosure, and one of the sleeping four who watched at the bridge-head rose and echoed it on his gong.

A crescent moon showed now, and by its faint light vague shadows could be seen flitting among the tufts of grass; and suddenly, with one long wail, the jackals' cry rose, clamoured to wild chorus, and fell again to silence.

"God send there be no more than jackals this night!" murmured one of the four with a yawn. "What ailed them all to cross in such a hurry? 'Twas not by Quarter-master-General Fedai Khân's order, that I know, for I heard him, ere he left to mark out the new camp, telling the Deputy all was to be as usual."

"*Ballah!*" responded a still sleepier sentry. "All is well. They say Mohabat is but ten miles off, and he hath two thousand Rajputs with him—so they say. Guard enough, in conscience!"

He was asleep almost ere he finished, and silence reigned once more. Within the royal enclosure, which screened off the common outside world, Jahângir and his women-folk slept secure, ignorant even of the fact that they were unguarded.

Twelve—one—two—three struck on the gong, struck sleepily, and were echoed sleepily from the bridge-head. It was nigh time for the last jackal call; near time for dawn. Was it the pack gathering that swayed the tiger-grass tops? Or were those real spears which showed higher than the rest?

A faint jingle as of a bridle broke the sleepful silence. It was followed by a low—

"Hist, brother! No more till we have the bridge!"

The warning was reiterated adown a file of horsemen.

A minute later there was a faint scuffle, but not a cry, not a moan. The feeble bodyguard was overpowered, and men, flinging themselves from their horses, began to cut the ropes that bound the boats together with their swords.

"Four or five is enough for now," came the low voice. "So!—pitch the roadway planks to the river and let the boats drift."

It did not take long; a few minutes and the oily, sliding stream flowed uninterrupted for fifty yards or more. No one would recross the bridge that night.

"Pass the word back that all is secure," said the commandant of the advance guard; and then he laughed low and long. "We have him neatly trapped. Now may Mohabat make good the rest—as he will."

And Mohabat was already on the way to make it good. Followed by fifty or sixty of his picked men, he was at the door of the Emperor's tent, guided thereto by the Lamp of Justice. Once within it in the warm, scented, luxurious air that contrasted so strongly with the crisp, fresh night air outside, even he paused. The Emperor lay asleep—in a drugged sleep—on a low divan guarded by but two drowsy courtiers. They were awake in a second, protesting.

But Mohabat was firm; he meant, he said, to see the Emperor —he would take no denial—he intended no harm to the royal person; but he had trapped him and he meant to keep him as hostage for fair treatment.

A bold step indeed, and one that could scarce be parried. By this time orders for the rest of the bridge to be burnt had been given, and a dejected little group of camp-followers were watching its destruction. How the dry boats and the bamboo stanchions and railings crackled and flamed till they touched the water, all aflame with the reflection from above, so that the sudden hiss and splutter as fire met water seemed inexplicable, mysterious.

And then as the lashings gave way, and boat after boat, charred to the water-line, broke away to float, still glowing, down stream, converging towards each other in the perspective till they lay massed, sending out sparks against the western horizon, the spectators held their breath at the novelty, the beauty of the sight.

Meanwhile in the tent Mohabat Khân had roused the Emperor. At first, still drowsy with opium, the latter had sat up confused. Then perception dawned upon him, and he was on his feet in an instant, his hand on the drawn sword that ever lay beside him.

"Mohabat! Traitor! What means this?" he cried furiously.

Mohabat drew back. There was never any questioning Jahângir's courage or his fiery temper. So, in an instant, the Generalissimo was on his knees kissing the ground; but behind him stood his bodyguard, nonchalant yet ready.

"Highness!" whispered one of the two courtiers, who, seeing nothing for it but restraint, were standing by, sword-hand on sword-hilt, ready if need be to defend their liege lord with their lives, "your slave entreats you to be patient—the sword is the last resource of true majesty."

The appeal was crafty; it roused Jahângir's remembrance that he was the Shadow of God upon earth, and restored his dignity.

"How darest thou!" he began sternly.

"This slave dares all to make his sovereign see the truth," put in Mohabat. "Let him listen but for once, then strike his servant dead. Lo! I seek protection at the hands of the Emperor! Protection from the machinations of Asof Khân—and others."

"And others?" queried the Emperor sharply. "Speak plain! Whose?"

Mohabat gave one sharp glance round at his Rajputs.

"Asof Khân and his sister——"

"Dog of an infidel!" shouted Jahângir. "Dost dare—die! Wretch!"

And once again the sword rose and flashed.

"For the sake of God, sire!" whispered the other courtier in Turkish, "leave punishment to Him. This is a time for wisdom."

And once again the sword-arm dropped.

"Thou shalt have protection—ay, though thou beest the most hell-doomed rascal in existence," said Jahângir; "but what wantest thou now?"

"The Emperor's *palki* stands at the door," replied Mohabat hardily. "I ask that he come with me and show the world that I am forgiven. 'Tis dawn-time, and the populace expect him. Or if the Emperor prefer, there is my horse."

"Thy horse!" flamed out Jahângir. "Wherefore thy horse? Order mine own, slave; and——" He paused and looked down on his attire. "I cannot show myself in these. I go first to change my garments." And he made a move towards the tent corridor which led to the women's apartments, to Nurjahân, who stood ever betwixt him and the world.

But Mohabat was before him, barring the entrance. "Not so, my lord. The Emperor needs no more than the dignity of kingship to cover him—or, if he feel the cold, there are coats here and to spare."

He pulled off his own warm *posteen* as he spoke, but the Emperor dashed it from his hand.

"I bide my time, hell-doomed!" he cried passionately. "Heaven will repay the kidnapper of Kings."

Mohabat bowed low. Whether he had meant to go so far is uncertain; but now that circumstances shaped themselves to absolute abduction, he accepted the situation cynically.

"Majesty speaks truth as ever," he replied calmly. "I take my sovereign from unworthy influence. If Majesty is ready, I am."

The brisk fresh morning air outside brought, for the time, added confusion to Jahângir's still befogged brain. He mounted his horse without a word; but once he was on its back passionate anger at coercion took possession of him once more. He dug his bare heels into the animal's sides, and with one bound it was off like the wind.

But once again Mohabat was too strong for him. Armed Rajputs barred the way on every side, and the Emperor was nigh thrown by the sudden check.

"Majesty will find an elephant safer," said Mohabat caustically. "Mine awaits him."

With mingled curses and tears, Jahângir did as he was bid, and mounted the elephant, which moved off, a Rajput as mahout and two armed Rajputs behind the *howdah*.

"Stay!" said Mohabat suddenly. "Where is the Emperor's cup-bearer? Let him go also. Majesty will be the better of wine this cold morning—a full beaker, slave, dost hear? and as many of them as Majesty desires. There be no limits set to Majesty's wishes so long as he be in Mohabat Khân's keeping."

By this time news of the abduction had spread abroad in the camp, or what remained of it. For the most part helpless in the presence of two thousand armed Rajputs, the majority knew not what to do. But the keeper of the elephants made a bold attempt to rescue his master. Hastily mounting a huge female elephant, his son ready behind the *howdah* to give aid, he forced his way through the gathering crowd mercilessly.

"Back! Back!" he cried as the great beast ambled forward. "Back! Back! Majesty rides his own elephant, not that of disloyal rebels!"

The ruse was almost successful. The small male animal on which Jahângir was riding gave a trumpet and made instantly for the female, despite its mahout's efforts to restrain it, while the leviathan, perfectly under control, allowed it to approach. Another instant, and Jahângir, who had grasped his faithful servant's intention, would have been able to scramble over to his own beast, when Mohabat, seeing the danger, called on his lancers to charge. The huge beast swerved, and in a second the armed Rajputs from behind Jahângir's *howdah* had swarmed over to its back. There was a brief scuffle, a few murderous stabs, and both the keeper of the elephants and his son were thrown down before the feet of the infuriated animal. But the attackers had reckoned without the blind loyalty of the beast to its master; they had calculated on the flimsy faith of humanity. With a scream of terror the maddened creature started aside so violently to avoid those beloved bodies that one of the two Rajputs who had crept forward to regain control was thrown to the ground. To trample on him viciously, and then, with a wild trumpet, to gallop off, heedless of all, was the work of an instant. None but those who have seen an elephant at the gallop can have any idea of the hideous power of its action. Clinging desperately to the crupper rope, the second Rajput strove to avoid being dashed to the ground—vain precaution against death! With another fierce trumpet of defiance the animal plunged into the sliding river and made for the opposite shore, its tumultuous action changing to slow rhythm as it swam. Vain relief! The man clinging behind gave one yell of dismay, strove to lift himself higher, failed, choked, rolled over into the water, and disappeared for ever.

Meanwhile Jahângir, overcome with the excitement, the grief at seeing his servants killed before his very eyes, had helplessly held out his hand for another goblet of wine, and when he had swallowed it for another and another.

"Give him what he desires," muttered Mohabat under his breath; "he will be more easily managed drunk than sober."

The thought made him remember Nurjahân.

Fool that he had been not to send and have her kidnapped also! That was an error which must be remedied at once.

Turning his horse, after brief directions to take the Emperor to his, Mohabat's, tent and give him in charge to his, Mohabat's, two sons, he called a body of Rajputs and rode straight for the women's tents.

He found them full of excited ladies screaming and sobbing and crying.

"The Empress!" he shouted—"the Empress! where is she?"

But she was not to be found. The bird had flown. So, cursing his own short-sightedness, he returned to his captive to ply him with drink and pleasures and fulsome flatteries; for therein, he saw, lay his best chance of success.

CHAPTER XV

"In the Great Mart where Life's best goods are bought
Prudence is worthless, Caution is as naught;
He wins who counts no cost of what he buys,
But pays his money down without a thought."

When Nurjahân was awakened about dawn by noises in the innermost enclosure, she started up, threw on a quilted robe, and, going to the outer room, gave instant order for the guards to be doubled. Enclosed as she had been within the purple and gold screens, she had no idea that the royal tents stood alone that side the stream.

The answer given her opened her eyes, and with a rush it came home to her that here was treachery. But whose?

Then came with overmastering force the question: "What was to be done?"

The other women seemed to have answered it their own fashion —they had rushed in on her, begging her to save them—from what? That was the question. Of her own personal safety she did not think. There was the child, of course; but even Mohabat would not injure the child!

Nor, surely, would he dare to harm Jahângir. There was no reason why he should, since, once he got the Emperor into his grip, it would be all too easy to turn him at his will. She, of all people, knew how plastic the latter was in strong hands. Still, she must know for certain now ere she could decide on what had best be done.

So she stood, not trembling outwardly, but within all aquiver with excitement, her ear glued to a crevice in the tent, listening—listening——

With her quick wits it did not take her long to grasp the situation. The Emperor was being kidnapped, for what purpose remained to be seen. On this side the river she was powerless to prevent it. On the other side, were they all traitors? Surely not all—there was Fedai, at any rate. And Asof might be shamed into action; he was Mohabat's bitterest enemy——

Her resolve came in a second. She must somehow cross the river, and that at once, and as secretly as might be. The bridge, so they had told her, was gone; but there must be boats; if not close at hand, yet still a little way down the river-bank.

Calming the other ladies with a few words of reassurance that no harm was meant, she passed rapidly into the inner tent again, where she found a group of lower-class women servants huddled together in alarm. Their aid would be better than that of the eunuchs and such like; they would be less likely to prate. Taking off her bracelets, with them and a few swift words she bribed them without difficulty, the ignorant woman's love of mystery and deception working in her favour. So, ere a few minutes had passed, she found herself, suitably dressed and closely muffled in a coarse outdoor veil, being carried along the river-bank in one of the common square *dhoolis* in which such women usually travel, and which had been waiting outside the tent for the expected move that day. On her lap, still asleep and carefully wrapped up in another common veil, lay the Gifted Lady, whom she had not had the heart to leave behind.

One of the women, a tall strapping Panjabi, walked beside her and gave instructions to the two bearers, bidding them hasten all they knew, on promise of reward.

So far, good. Nurjahân, still vital to her finger-tips, felt her heart beat high, her spirits rise at the thought of adventures to come; adventures which must, which would, be surmounted. Their way lay for the most part along a narrow beaten path that led through dense tamarisk thickets, across sparse fields of pulse sown as a catch crop on soil new upturned from the river, and then out again on the sliding yellow stream which sapped with a tinkling sound on the crumbling edge of the sandbanks. On and on they went, the pinky-purple plumes of the tamarisk scattering pollen as they swept them back, the grey geese rising from the green crops, the fresh light of dawn falling on stretches beyond of curving water and curving sand. Nurjahân was just beginning to wonder if she had been right to trust to the chance of finding a boat below, or whether it might not have been better to brave the possibility of detection above, and make straight for the recognized ferry, when, turning a sharp corner, they came upon an encampment of those strange river-folk who haunt the banks of the Jhelum and the Indus, and who live by hunting the crocodiles, drying their flesh, and, when the summer floods come down, making further fishing impossible, by selling it round the country-side.

Big, black, long-armed, fuzzy-haired men and women are they, dressed for the most part in nakedness and blue beads, speaking a strange, uncouth language of their own, and sheltering themselves in beehive-like wigwams round a central fire. But there were a couple of dug-out boats floating in the shallows, and without a second's hesitation Nurjahân stopped the bearers and got out of the *dhooli*, the child still in her arms.

Then ensued a sharp altercation, first between the high-pitched voice of the Panjabi woman and the headman, a big fellow on whose almost black limbs the rising sun sent blue lights. It went on and on, it seemed to Nurjahân's impatience, interminably; at length, with one backward sweep of her disengaged arm, she loosened the folds of her outer veil, let it drop, and so stood before the semi-savages revealed in all her singular beauty, a vision such as they had never seen before.

"Lo!" she said clearly, majesty in speech, manner, figure, "I am your Empress, and I command you to obey. I would cross the river now, this instant. Bring yonder boat, and this shall be your reward." As she spoke, she took off the string of pearls from her neck and held it aloft. There was an instant's murmur of amazed greed, for these fishers of the big streams knew well the value of the pearls they sometimes found in the river-mussels. In an instant half a dozen long-legged lads were ankle-deep in the water, bringing the biggest of the two boats to shore. It looked surprisingly small, and the Empress's liquid eyes travelled for one instant over the wide stretch of water, a mile or more, that had to be traversed. Then, without a word, she stepped into the frail craft, still holding the pearls aloft, since not till she had really started did she mean to pay the price. Her unaccustomed feet and weight caused the boat almost to overset, but the headman, paddle in hand, readjusted the balance, and as willing arms shoved the boat up the stream she flung the string of pearls backwards. As she did so the silk on which they were threaded broke, and they fell upon the sand in little heaps and runnels, one poised on the very outermost edge of the little sand cliff that the water was eroding. A burst of laughter followed as men, women, and children scrambled for the prize. The poised pearl slipped, but a lank boy was after it like an otter, and ere the boat was in midstream rose with it in his teeth, salaaming and shaking the water from his woolly mat.

It was a good beginning, thought Nurjahân, as she began to realize that she was alone on the yellow flood with a man who any instant could overpower her, fling her body to the stream, and make off with her jewels. And in her hurry she had forgotten once more to shroud herself in her borrowed veil. Few women, even the most courageous, like to feel themselves at the mercy of a strong man, and Nurjahân was no exception to the rule. And she had no weapon save only her own beauty, her own charm. So she sat still in the bottom of the dug-out, the child still asleep at her feet, the early sunrays flashing on her jewelled hair, her liquid eyes fixed on the coarse animal face of the man in front of her, who plyed his paddle with such singular dexterity. For an instant she thought of bribing him with necklace or bracelet. But an instant's reflection showed her the uselessness of this, when all was at his bidding. There was but one thing to do—to show no fear—no fear of anything.

Ah!—there was a sandbank right ahead, a lashing current by it, a sharp curve—the little boat, caught in a whirlpool, shot round. Brave as she was, she could have cried aloud for the very tenseness of her dread of what might come; but she only clenched her hands on the gunwale tighter and tighter. Then came a swift stroke of the paddle, the dug-out righted itself and they were in slack water once more.

"Shâhbâsh!" she cried impetuously, her whole heart in the praise. "Shâhbâsh!" And the dimple showing in her delicate face brought broad smiles to that other sensual one, as the man nodded his head approvingly; this was a brave one!

After that the long voyage across the waste of waters was one series of hair-breadth escapes, for the boatman went out of his way to show his prowess, and win that swift approval.

They swept round sandbanks, they slanted across swirling rapids, they skimmed so close to a crumbling cliff or sandbank that Nurjahân instinctively clutched at the child so that at any rate they might drown together. But ever and always she was ready with her "Well done!" even from pallid lips, and he was ready with grins of pleasure. A queer couple these, out on the yellow flood, that only ended on the level horizon. Luxury and poverty, civilization and savagery, held together by a woman's charm.

The sun crept up and up, but on the water it was cool. The child woke and laughed with joy to find herself in such novel, delightful surroundings.

Despite her first fears Nurjahân felt strangely rested when at long last the dug-out shot in shore, and, stepping out, she found herself within a hundred yards or so of a sentry's tent. She gave her pioneer her brightest smile and a farewell "Shâhbâsh!" then, the child running in front of her, made her way to the tent.

A group of men lounging and smoking stared at her in blank amaze.

"I am the Empress," she said calmly. "Conduct me to the tent of Fedai Khân—and carry the child; she will tire!"

Speechless with astonishment, they obeyed. So through the camp she walked firmly, while some folk stared and others fell down, kissing the dust at her feet.

For this woman of fifty-five, walking as she had not walked for years, among crowding spectators, was Empress without doubt. What but Majesty could so sustain a woman before the public eye?

"Bid the master attend me without delay," she said right royally to the servants in Fedai's tent, and they hurried to do her bidding at once. None gainsaid her, none doubted she spoke truth.

She had not long to wait. Fedai Khân was at her feet, kissing the very dust at them in delight at her escape. But she met him with a frown.

"How comes it, slave," she cried, "that the Emperor was so

deserted? and how comes it, traitor, that thou art not at this moment rescuing him from the hands of his enemy and mine?"

Fedai drew himself up to his full height. "I am no traitor, Highness; my duty it was to go forward to the new camp. I was out-wearied with the work. I slept late, and then—lo! I have spent these two hours urging men to act, but not one will plant the foot of courage in the pathway of honour. So, Majesty permitting, I go alone!"

He turned as he spoke and would have left, but she called to him in a softer voice.

"No traitor thou, Fedai; but I am outworn and need help. The others—Asof and the rest—where are they?"

Fedai stood gloomy, his hand on his sword. "Of Asof I know naught! Lo, I have sought for him without avail. The others are dumbfoundered—petrified—such as are loyal—and the others——" He flung his sword out. "They count not, Highness. I and my followers——"

"Peace, Fedai," said the Empress, regaining the composure she had almost lost. "There must be no bloodshed this side the river till we have held council. Are the royal tents prepared?"

"As ever, Highness."

"Then bid a royal *dhooli* here to take me thither. And summon all—ay, every Amir, every courtier, every noble—to a council of war. Dost hear? A council on the instant—not a moment to be lost."

Less than half an hour afterwards Nurjahân, unattended, alone, the only woman in the vast tent, faced her audience of men. She stood, a tall slight figure, unscreened, almost unveiled, for the gauzy head-covering with which she had started on her perilous adventure was all torn and frayed by rough usage. But she looked every inch an Empress as her woman's voice, full of scorn, full of reproach, rang out.

"O resplendent noblemen of the Court! O strong bodies and brave hearts! what do ye here obeying a woman's behest when your master, your King, your God, captive in the hands of his enemy, cries aloud to you for deliverance? Is not shame yours? Lo! I, a lone woman, have crossed the river to seek aid. Could not ye, strong men, hundreds of you—nay, thousands

—have crossed it likewise? Shame on ye! Shame on ye! Lo! I say not, wherefore did ye leave the Emperor unguarded? That is past and over. Your honour is in the dust; but there remains redress. Why stand ye idle? Be up and doing! Call together the army, else I, a woman, do so, and shame ye all. Oh, had I but been born a man, I would not have stood gazing as ye do while my honour, my renown, was being trailed in the dust by a low-born scoundrel. And as for thou, Asof," she continued, turning swiftly on her brother, "I ask not even why thou didst forsake him—thou knowest best. But if thou art ever to claim Nurjahân Padshâh Begum as sister again—ay, if thou art ever to claim dead Ghiyâss-ud-din as father, and not brand thyself bastard, thou wilt, as the highest in the land—since that thou art, since my lord—the lord whom thou leavest in captivity—made thee Vizier—call on these others to action as I call on them as woman. Oh, men, up and be doing; be not cowards. Lo! I will lead the van—let the dawn see our emprise."

She was trembling like an aspen ere she finished, but her lips were firm, her hands hard clenched.

Then someone spoke. "I am no coward, Highness," he said simply; "but I was told the Emperor himself had sent a letter to bid us withhold action, nor bring about unnecessary bloodshed."

She turned like lightning on Asof Khân. "Is this true?" she asked.

"Ay," replied Asof unwillingly; "but 'twas no letter. 'Twas a verbal message, yet the bearer held the Emperor's signet as warranty."

Nurjahân laughed aloud. "That could be slipped from his finger while he slept, since——" she paused. They knew as well as she the ease with which such theft could be made from a drugged man. Ay, made perhaps not as theft, but willingly. Then she turned to them in final appeal.

"Gentlemen, high-born and honourable, if that message be true, think you the Emperor sent it of his own free will? Nay; ill, weak, unhinged as he must be by this violence, he is at the mercy of Mohabat. Will ye also be slaves—as ye will be—to one low-born, who could outmatch Satan himself in guile?"

She had touched the right chord that time, and a low grow

of dissent ran round the tent, during which Nurjahân leant forward and whispered to Asof fiercely.

"Fool!" she said. "Canst not see that if Mohabat hath the Emperor in thrall, Parviz will take the place of Shahjahân? Up, man, and tell them the message is a lie—bid them be ready at dawn, and all will go well."

He looked at her, and acquiesced. Mohabat was his bitterest enemy, it was true. So bitter that, finding he was at the head of two thousand gallant Rajputs, with reinforcements said to be behind him, Asof had meant to find discretion the best part of valour (as he did indeed the next day). But his sister's arrival and upbraidings had made retreat without dishonour impossible, so, to all appearance, he fell in with her views. A general muster was called for dawn, and each went his way, some determined to fight truly, others to look on.

But the soldiery took it in good sooth, and round the camp-fires sharpened their lances and swords and looked to the flash-pans of their matchlocks; since a fight is ever a fight to the professional.

And one man who, by profession, was Court favourite also, took it seriously. Fedai Khân had no liking for the term "coward"; and though his mistress had rescinded the accusation, it still rankled. Besides, he had no intention of leaving his master unstriven for, to spend a night alone and in captivity.

So when darkness fell, a small body of horsemen, headed by Fedai, their horses' hoofs deadened with felt pads, stole down the river-bank, and making their way from sandbank to sandbank, stood at length on the shores of the big stream which the bridge of boats had spanned. It was not so long a journey as Nurjahân's had been, for she had had to skirt round the sandbanks and gain the further side of the whole wide river-bed, whereas they had cut straight across, fording the shallow streams and swimming the deeper ones; but there were treacherous quicksands to be negotiated, and time had passed more than once in extracting an incautious trooper or two from a quagmire.

But now, with the rising of the crescent moon, they gathered in a knot on the furthest point of the big stream shore, and tightened their girths for the struggle that lay before them. As fine a body of tall, sinewy, black-bearded Rângars as ever was seen, each hardy in thought and deed, and eager for the adventure.

"Art ready?" asked Fedai. "Then follow me!" At the word he and his horse plunged into the tide, and the next instant were being swept down by the force of the current, but swimming, swimming gallantly. And behind him, in twos and threes, in groups or alone, the troopers showed like floating shadows on the water, which, dark though the night was, gleamed light.

A hard swim and a long swim; but heavy accoutrements had been left behind, and the game little Indian horses had been well fed up three hours syne with a wonderful mess of raw sugar and eggs and roasted gram-flour.

Still, it was a perilous adventure, and more than one pair of bold eyes watched the twinkling lights on the opposite shore and wished he was there with unsheathed sword ready to thrust into an enemy's wame.

"There goes Gulab Khân!" said one to his neighbour. "I warned him against the big Kâbuli mare, but he would hold it better than the little Arab. God rest him!"

"Mayhap he may find a sandbank somewhere," said his companion indifferently, as he threw himself off his mount for a spell of swimming in order to aid the beast.

But it was not only Gulab Khân who went; others followed, and it was a reduced party which, gaining the bank at last, noiselessly reformed itself some mile and a half below the enemy's tents and took stock of its number and arms.

Fedai counted them anxiously. A bare dozen; the rest had disappeared, and though some of them had doubtless found safety further down, there was no time to wait for them to rejoin. There were enough, mayhap, for his purpose of surprise; if not, it was God's will. So, spick and span still, despite the fact that he had not a dry stitch on him, Fedai Khân rode carefully on at the head of his little party of rescue; and as he rode he was carefully balancing the pros and cons for stealth all through, and defiance only at the last.

Fate, however, was against both. They had almost reached the tents when a challenge rang out from the darkness, and they found themselves surrounded by Rajputs. Thank God! By

Rajputs, for if there be one thing a Mahomedan Rângar loathes, it is a Hindu Rajput; possibly because deep down in the soul of every Rângar lurks the knowledge that before Mahomed of Ghazni converted his tribe wholesale to Mahomedanism by the sword, it had belonged to the great martial race of India.

So, with one guttural cry of "Din Din! Fatteh Mahomed!" they were at the throats of their alien brothers, and it was cut and thrust fiercely, as inch by inch they were driven back riverwards by overwhelming numbers. Fedai, a fine swordsman, engaged one after another till his horse's hoofs sank in mingled water and sand; then with a supreme effort he clove his last assailant to the very chine, and turning his game little beast by sheer pressure of his knees leapt clear into the current, his hands still clasped on his sword-hilt. "Till dawn!" he shouted, as the stream carried him down. "Till dawn, hell-doomed infidels!"

He had not succeeded, but he and his party had at least accounted for twice their number of the enemy.

So it was not a discomfited but a radiant Fedai who, just as the sun was rising, reported himself and his adventure to the Empress.

She looked grave and preoccupied in her leather hunting-dress, to which she had added a coat of mail, while a steel chain cap covered her jewel-braided hair. For she was to keep her promise of leading the men.

"'Tis well," she said. "It shows that it is fordable. And that is all we need!"

CHAPTER XVI

> "Give largesse with both hands; an empty Purse
> Is a light burden. Fate will reimburse
> The costs of those who with unbending will
> Play out the part She gives them to rehearse."

NURJAHÂN did not sleep that night. She sat waiting for the dawn—such a slow dawn! Easterly of those distant tents on the far side of the river there was just a faint lightening below the heavy bank of cloud that lay on the horizon. So by degrees the shadows on earth and sky paled, the bank of cloud curdled to little flecks, then flushed rosy like the cheek of an expectant maiden at her lover's step.

And he was here, the Great Earth-lover! the Bringer of Life!

In an instant all was bustle. Ere the sun had really risen, large bodies of horsemen stood grouped along the northern bank of the River Jhelum, waiting for the sign to advance; waiting indeterminately, since Asof Khân had issued no definite orders, and each leader was left to choose his own objective, to select his own fancied point for fording the swift stream.

It might be that this lack of disposition had its merits by allowing freedom of action, but it certainly showed a lack of unanimity, a wavering of purpose.

There was neither, however, in the armoured cohort of elephants which swept down from the royal tents, led by the Empress herself, on the celebrated Alum Gajrâj, the first and favourite male of the whole stud; a huge beast close on fifteen feet in height, which had ever been the Emperor Akbar's favourite mount. Renowned alike for courage and strength, he lilted along as if proud of his burden. And well he might be; for never in her life had Nurjahân looked more a "Queen of Women." She was dressed in her leathern hunting-suit, and over it she wore a coat of mail, while a cap of linked steel chain hid her still gem-decked hair. At her feet, in the armoured war-*howdah*, sat the little

Gifted Lady, why, it is hard to say. Possibly her grandmother expected small difficulty in her task of rejoining and rescuing the Emperor. Possibly, again, she may have anticipated evil, and been unwilling to leave the child, the Mecca of all her hopes, to the scant mercies of those who knew and detested her plans for the future. Certain it is the child was there; a well-grown, healthy little lass of two and a half, forward in every physical way, but backward mentally. Outwardly the image of her grandmother, inwardly, showing but small promise of her commanding intellect.

"Is all ready?" asked Nurjahân of Fedai, who, ever since he returned from his night's raid, had been riding up and down, seeing to this contingent, urging that one to plant the foot of honour on the path of courage, to remember that 'twas by their neglect the Emperor's freedom was endangered, that never again need they call themselves men did they not avenge the insult put upon him, and upon every loyal man, by the mean-spirited hound Mohabat—brave words, which served their purpose to a certain extent. Those behind the Empress, at least, were eager for the fray. And to the left, above the burnt bridge, Asof Khân made fine show of determination—at the start, at any rate.

"They are as ready as they can be made," replied Fedai gloomily.

"Then bid the kettledrums sound!"

With a curious crackling boom, high-pitched, insistent, the advance rang out, and on the throbbing roll of the drums rose the blare of conches from the Hindu contingent.

So in stately march the elephants, in single file, slid down the high bank, and traversed the sandbank below, their great pads leaving circular pools of water behind them.

There was a pause on the water's edge to allow the next elephant to step up and take its place to the right of the leader, its head level with the first one's girth. Thus alongside, yet in slight echelon, a veritable dam of brute force, each beast gaining a certain support from the breakwater of its fellow, the elephants struck out, slightly up stream.

"Shâhbâsh, Gajrâj!" said Nurjahân to her huge beast, as the wise creature, putting his forefoot suddenly into deep water, trumpeted the news to those behind him, to set them on guard. And now, still in rigorously kept formation, the great dam of body and mind, swimming, breasted the swift current.

Meanwhile, the news of coming assault had reached the opposite bank, and it was lined by dense bodies of Rajput horsemen ready to dispute a passage. Further down-stream, indeed, where a party of loyalists had taken advantage of the elephants' breakwater to push their horses rapidly across, the clashing of sword on sword was already to be heard. The same thing might have occurred above where Asof Khân led, for there the passage, if deeper, was narrower, had the attack been pressed home; but it was not. And that below failing in its object, the main body of the enemy was free to deal with the central force, which, led by Nurjahân, came on steadily if slowly; for the elephant is not a fast swimmer.

But in the end Gajrâj found footing, trumpeted the news, and stood like a rock despite the arrows that were already flighting round him, till his companions had formed up in battle array. Then ensued a bitter combat. The enemy had the advantage of higher ground; also they had larger targets than their foes. Still the former diminished every step taken shorewards, till, save for activity and numbers, the combatants stood equal. But both these were on the side of the rebels, joined to the daredevil rashness in which Rajput soldiers have no rival. They were in the water, swimming round the wading elephants, maddening them with their spears, regardless of the lashing trunks, the sharp tusks of the infuriated leviathans, regardless of the steady fire of matchlocks from the howdahs, the ceaseless flights of arrows. Reddened by fast-flowing blood, churned to foam by the frantic struggles of men and beasts, the waves of water lashed over the combatants and sent an ominously tinted spray into the sun-bright, crisp morning air.

And ever the fiercest of the fray raged round Gajrâj. The arrows, the javelins, flew about him in showers; but his hide was thick, his armour strong, his courage indomitable. And sterner still was the mettle of the woman whom he carried. Unmoved, though the missiles were falling round her like autumn leaves in a gale, she pressed on, dauntless.

"Well done, Gajrâj !" shouted the mahout—one who had been in the Emperor's service since he was a baby, who had been rocked to sleep in the huge beast's curled trunk, who had lived with him, and asked nothing better than to die with him. "Shâh-bâsh ! Shâhbâsh !"

And the game beast, fighting furiously, responded with a trumpet, that was answered by the others; so sound, terrific, ear-splitting, came to add to the horrors of the scene; but even as he reared his trunk a wandering arrow struck him on the tongue, and his shrieking bellow changed to a roar of pain. Mad with rage, he made a supreme effort. With the downward sweep of the trunk he tore the leader of the attack from his horse and flung him skywards, to fall and sink like a stone, while with his forefeet he beat the foe in front of him down, down, trampling them out of all shape into the soft sand.

"Shâhbâsh, Gajrâj !" cried the Empress triumphantly; but at that moment the mahout fell sideways, slipped—Gajrâj's little twinkling eyes saw the fall, his quick prehensile trunk was at his friend's disposal in a second to help him to his place again.

Too late ! The man's heart had been pierced with an arrow—too late, for with lightning swiftness a sword came down on the offered support. One shriek of pain and the animal turned to face its assailant, but confused by the double duty, it missed its footing in the soft, slimy bottom of sand and flesh and blood, slithered, and its sudden falter was the signal for wild assault.

"Down with the woman ! Down with her ! Down with the witch who beguiles men !"

So rose the cry from a hundred mouths. Nurjahân answered them with her matchlock, shooting down her assailants with the same deadly aim with which she had shot many a tiger! And her few staunch adherents fought desperately, while Gajrâj alone, unaided by guidance, continued to press on.

But there were too many against him. Inch by inch, though his courage never failed, he had to give way. Inch by inch, covered by a hundred wounds, mere pin-pricks to his stout hide, yet still draining his strength, until a crafty foe, swimming alongside, cut him twice over the proboscis with a two-edged sword, and with a mighty roar of sheer wrath he fell back into deep water; so floundering, half swimming, half unconscious, drifted down stream.

The few remaining elephants—for many of them had already given up the fight—seeing his discomfiture, turned tail and fled.

The great assault had failed.

But a few minutes afterwards the beaten giant grounded on a sandbank, happily beyond reach of arrows or javelins, and, struggling to his feet, lifted up his maimed trunk in one roar of defiance. And his challenge was unanswered.

It brought to Nurjahân's aid, however, those of her staunch adherents who remained.

They were not many, and they flocked round in terror of what they might find. What they did see was very simple—a woman on her knees busily engaged in binding up a child's wound; for an arrow had glanced on the little Gifted Lady's wrist, and her grandmother was bent on consoling her.

"Hast anyone, by chance, some sweetstuff to stop her crying?" she asked hurriedly, as she tore another strip from her own white drapery to finish her bandaging; whereupon a young trooper somewhat shamefacedly pulled a handful of sugar-drops from within his shirt of mail, and peace was restored.

But the day was lost, and there was nothing for it but to return and see if it were possible to make another attempt.

So, haltingly, the wounded veteran carried his mistress back to the other side; and during the journey she sat calm, pale, silent, the hurt baby in her arms.

Yes, the attack had failed, saving for Fedai Khân's contingent. Profiting by his last night's experience, and with a large party of the finest fighters in the camp, he had gone up stream a good bit; so, letting the current carry him down, had landed above the encampment on the further shore, meeting with but slack opposition on the bank, as most of the Rajputs were heavily engaged on the bend below.

So far, so good, and they made their way swiftly across level fields to the tent where Fedai knew the Emperor was lodged; but this they found overwhelmingly guarded at all points. Nevertheless, there was nothing for it but to attack, and Fedai, nothing daunted, went at his task with a will. For two long hours the unequal fight went on; would have gone on doubtless until the ast man had been disabled, but for the sudden appearance between the combatants of the Emperor's personal attendant, who, at the risk of his life, implored a moment's respite in which to deliver a message; whereupon Fedai withdrew a space.

The message was briefly this: that some of the arrows had actually fallen on the couch where the Emperor lay asleep, and, if he did not intend to kill the Shadow of God, Fedai Khân should desist from a violence which was quite contrary to Jahângir's wishes.

Fedai laughed scornfully. He had been badly wounded himself, his horse almost cut to pieces, and his lieutenants were seizing the lull to staunch the bleeding as best they could. "I return not without him," he said. "I will not face my mistress if I bring him not." Then suddenly he burst into angry imprecation: "Asleep, saidst thou? Nay, flatterer! Time-server! Sycophant! He is drunk—and thou and thy like are traitors! Do I not know Mohabat? Is he not false as the fiend himself? Can I not see his trick? Lo! he will give the Emperor freedom—he will tempt him—he will pander to him. Go back, fool! Tell those who sent thee that so soon as this bleeding stops Fedai will have at them again."

But the bleeding did not stop, not at any rate till he was almost unconscious. Then his friends held a hurried consultation, followed by a parley with the enemy, from which it appeared that no violence was being done to the Emperor, that none was intended. Furthermore, that Jahângir had with his own hand written an order to his troops over the water, commanding instant cessation of hostilities.

The men looked at each other and sheathed their swords.

"Since rescue by force is not to be," quoth one, "I am for home. 'Tis the safest place these times."

"Ay," said Fedai's most faithful servant, "and for wounded men most of all. My master needs rest!"

And he got it. When he came to himself he was miles away from the scene of the conflict; nor was he fit to return to it.

Meanwhile, over the water worse confusion than ever prevailed.

The Sirdars, who, owing to Asof Khân's hesitation, had scarcely known the plan of attack, were loud in blame of the faulty dispositions. Everything was at sixes and sevens, and though Motamid Khân, the Emperor's secretary, went about trying to mend matters, not one soul did he find to plant the foot of honour firmly. Asof Khân himself, after lengthy complaints about the uncertainties of this changing world, disappeared, and was no more seen; desiring, as he wrote afterwards, to be safe from the oppressive soul of Mohabat, he had fled to Attock. And, one by one, the Amirs and nobles either followed his example of retreat, or went over boldly to the opposite side of the river, leaving the Empress alone with a few faithful servants.

And she?

She sat in the royal tents and clenched her hands, not in despair, but in sheer anger.

She was no fool; she knew as well as Fedai what was happening over yonder, where Mohabat, the prince of deceivers, was virtually King. She could imagine it, long before the Emperor's secretary returned from paying his respects, with a succinct account of what he had seen.

Motamid was a tall, lank man with a pale face and piercing dark eyes. He squatted on the ground in front of the divan where Nurjahân sat in her favourite attitude, her elbow on her knee, her chin in her hand, her mouth firm and set.

"Of a truth," said Motamid mournfully, "Majesty may believe that when Mohabat introduced me to the presence, his conversation was so frivolous and trifling that, in my opinion, death would have more become him."

"But the Emperor," put in Nurjahân in a tone of irritation. "Lo! what care I for what the rebel says or does—the Emperor, my good man, the Emperor!"

Motamid shook his head. "He was not there, Majesty. My master was not there. One lay upon the couch half wake with wine, half in dreams with drugs. A slave-girl fanned him and another, with flagon and glass, knelt ready to fill a cup—not when desired, Majesty; he was past that—but when the sign was given."

There was a long pause of silence. Nurjahân did not stir,

her face set firmer; the hand upon her chin gripped it tighter. Finally she spoke—spoke more lightly.

"And Mohabat—what said he of this unheard of, this almost unconceivable plot to kidnap the Shadow of God?"

Motamid looked even more mournful. "What matters it, Majesty?" he asked. "Lo! is he not even as the man of whom 'twas said, 'He spoke and I believed him; he insisted, I doubted him; he swore, and I knew it was a lie'?"

Despite her anxiety Nurjahân smiled.

"And the Amirs, the nobles? Are they there?" she asked.

"They are on their knees, Highness. And what the Emperor says is law, what he wishes is done; but they put the words into his mouth, the thoughts into his brain."

"Thou hast dismissal," said the Empress sharply; she had heard what she wanted. After he had gone she sat alone thinking. The tent grew dark, yet still she sat thinking, thinking.

Had she been bested, or had she not been bested?

So long as she was separated from Jahângir her influence was gone; but if she were to return to him? What then?

So, as she thought, the very hardihood of the idea appealed to her. If she were voluntarily to put herself into Mohabat's power; if she were to risk her liberty—perhaps her life—on the throw of the die—what then?

And she need not do even this. Motamid could carry instructions to the Emperor, carefully worded, that, seeing no hope of rescuing the Shadow of God from the sacrilegious hands that had been laid upon him, she, as a dutiful and obedient wife, was coming back to share his captivity. What then?

The urgent desire in times of great stress to be alone, away from the rest of humanity; to be out in the open, with nothing above one save infinite space, which comes to most of us, especially to those of vivid individuality, drove her out under the stars, to stand and wonder at this little life. So, after a time, her eyes wandered from the shadow of the world which we call night to the twinkling lights that showed across the river.

No, she could not admit defeat so easily. She would go back and resume her sway, let them say what they liked! She would checkmate them with one swift move.

She passed rapidly into the tent again, and sitting down, wrote with her own hand the following letter:

" Mihr-un-nissa, whom the Light of the World hath honoured with many titles and more kindness, lays herself and her life before the Emperor, and craves an interview, that she may tell the Lord of Light that she hath forgotten as well as forgiven."

This she gave to Motamid, with instructions that he was to take it across the river, and not to return until he had succeeded in getting permission for the interview.

" If it comes not at all," she said, " then will I risk all. Meanwhile I will try wisdom."

It was two days ere the secretary returned, and she was just preparing for the final risk when the lank figure and mournful face appeared, and he brought back with him a permit signed in Jahângir's own handwriting, desiring that the bearer should have access to him on presentation.

" Lo !" said the secretary, " I was long in getting it, since they scarce left me with him alone for a moment. There is a Rajput guard of two that stays with him day and night. Praise be to God ! they eat opium comfits, and I had a friend in the buttery who used what I gave him—but not without payment; it cost ten gold *âskrafis.*"

" Ay !" interrupted Nurjahân impatiently; " but the Emperor ? How did he receive my letter ?"

Motamid Khân's eyes blinked.

" He wept, Majesty; but he was far gone in wine."

" It matters not," cried Nurjahân joyfully. " Where tears are, feeling is not dead !"

" True," assented the secretary wisely. " Yet, were I Majesty, I would be swift in action. Each day brings danger, and—I know not—but methinks some plot is afoot."

" Mayhap," replied Nurjahân nonchalantly; " but they shall not worst me. Yet go I at once—even now."

" Now ?" echoed the secretary, almost alarmed at her swiftness.

" Ay, now is ever the best time !"

CHAPTER XVII

"My heart's sweet aloe wood, my love is fire,
My body is the censer of desire.
Yet thou, like summer moth, flitt'st round my flame
While I consume my Love and so expire."

NURJAHÂN and Mohabat Khân stood looking at each other. She was dressed all in white, her thick white veil drawn tight round her oval face as widows wear their shrouds. She had chosen this attire for her interview with Jahângir because it was what she had worn on that long past day on which she had covenanted to forgive, if she could not forget.

And now that she had promised to do both, she strove to awaken a memory of vanished manhood in the man she strove once more to redeem.

"Wherefore am I not to see my lord?" she asked, and her tone was haughty.

Mohabat's strong intolerant face showed pitiless. But one short half hour since, the Keeper of the Gates had brought him word that Nurjahân Pâdshah Begum demanded admittance, and he had sworn a big oath of grudging admiration for her temerity.

Then he had shrugged his shoulders and said to the sycophant courtiers who, seeing the trend of his policy, had given it their whole-hearted approval. "'Twill save a mounted escort, anyhow. Ay! and mayhap innocent blood too, since the woman hath still followers." Then he turned to the Chamberlain. "See that she be shown to a fitting place. I will attend her ere long."

He had delayed a while. Perhaps even he, with his light estimate of womanhood, did not quite relish the task he had to perform. But it had been decided in full council; the Emperor —drugged it is true almost beyond consciousness—but what matter since Government would in future be carried on by male wisdom instead of accursed female wisdom acting through a beguiled Shadow of God ?—had set his seal to it, and the warrant for the execution of one Mihr-un-nissa, called Nurmâhal or Nurjahân, was ready in Mohabat's hand.

He gave it to her without a word. Brave as she was, the blood curdled at her heart as she read—and for a noticeable space she caught in her breath hard and the colour forsook her face, leaving it of creamy pallor.

" It will be painless," said the man of iron and relentless will, misreading her emotion, " a lethal draught and sleep——"

The ludicrous ineptitude of his words woke her ready sense of humour, and she laughed aloud; but his words also roused her contempt and with it her vitality.

" Fool !" she said, and the scorn of her tone cut even his tough hide. " Judge not of others by thine own fear of death. What matters it when the Call comes, to-day or next, since come it must ? So that for thy warrant !"

And with swift hands she tore the paper across and flung the pieces at his feet.

His face grew darker as he bent to recover them. " That avails thee not, lady," he began, when she interrupted him with another mocking laugh—

" Say not so ! O Mohabat Khân ! Prince of Deceivers ! Thou hast had to stoop to pick them up !"

He desisted from his task abruptly and glared at her as she went on. " And it avails *thee* not either. Bethink thee ! Does not the law of the land—Jahângir's own law—mind you—ordain that no warrant for death be carried out for twenty-four hours after it be received by the one who is to die, so that there may be due time for appeal ? And is not four and twenty hours sufficient, even for the disloyal, to carry out the Sovereign's wishes ? Wishes not sealed only like yonder waste paper that could be stamped by a seal slipped from a drunken finger, but written in Majesty's own hand ?"

And in her turn she handed Mohabat the Emperor's passport to his presence. Passion positively distorted his face as he seized it, tore it to fragments and scattered the pieces broadcast. " That for thy paper, woman !" he almost shouted. " Thou diest, and by the Emperor's orders !"

She looked at him with cool disdain. "That may or may not be!" she said quietly, "meanwhile it avails thee not, since I stoop not to undo thy actions. Yet do I claim the law's delay. Go! ask the judges if I be not right."

To a certain extent he felt she had mastered him in detail, and he shrugged his shoulders impatiently. "What matters it to-day or to-morrow?" he replied. "So take thy respite. Till then thou wilt be honourably dealt with."

And with the words he turned on his heel and left her.

To what reflections? First, doubtless to thought-distracting dread—since say what the bravest may, death to vivid life must ever be unwelcome. But ere long that vivid vitality was at work striving to escape. They brought her food and drink and she took both, feeling she would need all the support she could get in her battle against these men. So by degrees her mind settled on this. They desired she should not see the Emperor, therefore all her efforts must be to secure an interview. But how? If she could get at Motamid Khân the secretary—she must try! Finally, begging a slip of paper and a pen, she wrote a short petition to the Chief Judge, a man whom she knew to be one of her bitterest enemies, begging him to allow her under the law, as a convicted criminal, the services of the royal secretary in order that, ere execution, she might have her last wishes duly set down concerning her granddaughter, who, by previous arrangement with the Emperor and his son Shâhriyâr, was to be returned to her mother's keeping, there to be brought up in strictest seclusion as canoness, in the event of her grandmother's death.

It was a deft bait. The problem of Shâhriyâr's daughter, who had a strong hold on the Emperor's affection, would thus be settled without further action. Permission for Motamid to attend under surveillance was therefore given.

So much then was gained, but Nurjahân, when she faced a friend, felt the hopelessness of her position more keenly than when she had been defying an enemy. Yet, ere he came, she had her plan ready. Watched as they would be, almost every word they uttered overheard, her quick brain had had to devise means for conveying her wishes without exciting suspicion. Mercifully in order to please the Emperor she had learnt the

Turkhi language, with which Motamid as secretary had also to be acquainted. Unknown, as it was, to most of the courtiers and to all the servants, she was able when giving the address of her daughter to say rapidly a word or two which were sufficient to put the secretary on the watch for more. So with infinite ingenuity she gave her directions. Under her veil she still wore some valuable jewels; these she removed, and giving into her chief janitor's keeping those which she said belonged of rights to the Emperor, she handed the remainder to Motamid; taking the opportunity afforded by the swift greed of the former to pass unobserved under the latter's flowing coatee something small and hard, which with the quick comprehension of the Eastern, to whom such contrivings are the salt of life, he ignored for the time, his ears attuned to every word she uttered.

"See that they be given correctly and at once," she said, slowly emphasizing some words rather unduly, "to those to whom of right they belong as my last gifts; with much grief and many regrets I may not see them again, though of a truth I know how earnestly they will desire it, as do I, Mihr-un-nissa whom in childhood they called Meru. And bid them, if they give way to grief and anger at this deprivation, as likely they will, to lay the blame where blame is due, since I have prayed and my prayer has not been answered. Therefore is it God's will."

Her rich clear voice did not falter. She waited till the flourishing hand paused, poised over the ink-pot, then said shortly: "That is all—stay!" she added with a faint smile. "I have given thee no reward for thy labours, and I have nought left save this." She passed over a small, silver-filagree vinaigrette such as most women of high rank wear attached to their wrist bangle. "It is at least something. Lo! writers such as thou have oft tired confused brains, and there is a powder in it that is efficacious to bring clearness. I have oft used it for"—she paused; then went on, "but that is over. See you, so much as will be upon a thumb nail in a cupful of wine—wine is ever pleasant—will clear the brain marvellous. And thou canst take more in half an hour's time, without harm, if the first suffice not. 'Tis all I have to offer. Lo! I brought it to use myself, but I shall need it no more. Farewell, and may the blessing of the Most High attend all!"

She stood, tall, slender, still beautiful, and Motamid as he left her, the tears rolling down his sallow face, felt mingled sorrow and awe at her dignity, her supreme wit, her unshrinking courage.

The latter nerved him to effort, as safe in his own small tent he undid the little parcel she had conveyed to him so deftly and which, with the Eastern instinct of conspiracy, he had as deftly concealed.

It contained the ruby cup.

A thousand times he had seen it used; and now with this clue, her words became plain. He was to put some of the powder into wine, and filling the cup, give it to the Emperor as the last gift from Nurjahân—nay ! from one whom in childhood had been called Meru——

Nay ! further——

It was to be given twice. It had no taste—it was to be given after half an hour——

Bit by bit the meaning of Nurjahân's carefully guarded words came home to him. So much for the powder—it was to be given twice; but the cup ? The cup was to be given with regret that the giver was prevented from giving it in person. The blame for this, the anger for this, was to be poured out where anger was due !

As he sat there, looking at the ruby cup, he understood. Nurjahân, in whose keeping it was ever, had brought it with her, as she had brought the tasteless powder which cleared the brain, especially to be able to administer the dose to the Emperor herself. Now he was commissioned to do so. And he was commissioned also to arouse anger—if he could.

Since he had returned from over the river to his normal duties, Motamid had been careful to curry favour with Mohabat and his party—in no other way could he have secured access to the Emperor. And he had been still more careful to avoid the discovery of his visit over the river to Nurjahân. Thus far he was not suspect; and his friend in the buttery might help.

So, on the pretence that he had urgent papers which required the royal seal, he sat down in the anteroom tent where dozens of other claimants on the royal leisure waited.

"Majesty can transact no business," said a eunuch, his tongue in his cheek. "It sleeps."

There was a faint murmur, half chuckle, from those who waited; but Motamid spoke up.

"Lo! sleep or no sleep, my business is but with the royal seal, and sleep or no sleep, it can stamp a paper. Let me in, I pray thee, for I need no speech of Majesty."

The eunuch laughed. "If thou didst, thou wouldst get none. He is most blind drunk, and but now hath called for more wine."

Motamid accelerated his steps. "Then let me at him ere he drinks," he said. "Else may I be here all night."

As he entered the inner alcove tent, where a brazier full of perfumes was sending out a faint blue smoke that, added to the heat of the enclosed air, seemed to bring slumber with it, he saw the Emperor lying prone on a richly embroidered divan, while beside him stood a wine-bearer in the act of pouring out another goblet of wine.

"A moment, friend!" whispered the secretary. "I need but three impressions of the royal seal and methinks the Emperor, even as he is, hath enough for the task." And hastily he prostrated himself and told his errand.

Jahângir looked at him stupidly.

"What wantest thou? My signet ring? Then take it, fool, and be damned to thee!" he said. "So be it is not for death. Nay! Nay! Jahângir seals the death warrants of himself—but quick, slave! I need my wine."

Motamid hurriedly drew forth his papers and fumbled for his ink, his flurry gaining on him.

"Lo! idiot! slave! fool—what is it? Why this delay?" roared Jahângir, growing more and more indistinct.

"The ink, Highness!" faltered Motamid, "I have forgot the ink!"

"Ink! Ink!" echoed Majesty in half-drunken anger. "Go to—is there no ink in the royal tents? Bring it, slaves! Quick! Ink! Ink! Ink!"

A second afterwards Motamid breathed again. In the bustle he had contrived to slip so much as would lie on a thumb nail of the powder into the goblet which the wine-bearer had hastily set down in order to do his irate master's bidding.

So far, so good!

But for the rest? There was nothing for it save boldness.

"I stay here," he whispered to the eunuch when with great difficulty he had got Jahângir to affix his seal to several quite innocuous papers. "I have other business to transact. Mayhap when Majesty awakes he may be more fit. Meanwhile I write——"

He sat himself down by the couch as he spoke and began on work.

"As thou pleaseth," replied the eunuch grudgingly; "but Majesty will not wake these two hours. 'Tis easier work watching now than when that she-cat was ever after us." And with a yawn he passed from the alcove and sat down to dice with his companions beyond the curtain.

Majesty would not wake for two hours, thought Motamid with a sinking heart. Fortune had favoured him so far; but what if the powder failed of effect?

So, as he sat, he remembered that if he were to give a second dose, he had better make sure of having wine wherein to give it.

The ewer-bearer had left the flagon on the salver beside the royal couch; but had taken the goblet away to rinse it.

There was, however, always the ruby cup.

And with the thought came supreme satisfaction at the idea to which it gave birth; an idea he had failed to grip from Nur-jahân's necessarily halting instructions, but which, he felt sure now, she had intended. Yes, he would give the next dose in the ruby cup, and that would naturally bring about explanations; at any rate, if the drug worked.

So after filling the little cup and placing it ready, he sat down again to watch and wait.

Supposing the drug had no effect? Yet that was not likely. For years the Empress had been, as it were, Jahângir's physician in chief. She had great experience. She had brought this drug with her, evidently intending to use it, as she had doubtless used it before. Besides, there was nothing for it but to wait and hope.

So, in the semi-darkness of the alcove, he sat silent, watching the heavy face that lay so stupidly among the gorgeous cushions.

And outside in the wide tent, servants laughed in low tones, while the click of dice and the chink of money could be heard above the human voices, dominating them with the curious power these two inanimate sounds have ever.

Time was passing, and Motamid's hopes were waning, when suddenly Jahângir sat up.

"Slave!" he called in a loud, fairly clear voice. "Wine! Dost hear? Wine!"

In a second the cup-bearer was at his post; but Motamid was before him; the little ruby cup was in the Emperor's hand. Mechanically, as from a habit borne of long usage, he carried it to his mouth and drank the contents.

But then memory stepped in, and he paused, half raised among the cushions, looking at what he held.

"How came it here?" he asked thickly. "Where is the Empress? I—I forget——"

Motamid was in the dust at his feet.

"Sire!" he began, "this slave has a message." Here the eunuchs interposed, but Jahângir with one wave of his despotic hand, one swift frown of anger, stopped their interference.

"Deliver it," he said dreamily, turning his eyes again to the familiar object. Then he added in a sharper tone: "Why comes she not herself? Will she not obey? Hath she also rebelled against me?—as they said when they bade me—but I forget——" And his voice tailed off again to drowsiness.

For one instant Motamid thought of repeating exactly what Nurjahân had told him; then he realized that something sharper, more primitive, than sentiment concerning childhood might be needed to pierce that sodden, drugged brain, and with a sudden flash of inspiration he told the truth.

"Nay, my lord!" he said boldly. "Nurjahân Pâdshah Begum is as ever faithful to the Emperor. 'Tis the rebels will not let her come. 'Tis Mohabat who hath denied her entrance, even though she bears with her the sign-manual of Jahângir."

He had hit the mark. In an instant, still befogged though he was, all the former's arrogance, his intolerance of control, had been aroused. He started to his feet, swaying a little it is true, yet with distinct purpose, and stood there, still a fine figure of a man, though bent and broken.

"What!" he cried furiously. "Doth Mohabat dare? Hath

he refused? Before God, am I not the judge? Shall I not do what seemeth me right?" Then he turned on the officials of the bodyguard, who, hearing voices, had crowded in. "Is this true, slaves? Hath Mohabat dared——?"

He swayed and almost fell; but Motamid, at his right hand, saw with a thrill of hope that he steadied himself with an effort. Ere long that second dose would begin to work—he must have as much time as possible.

"Yea! O Most Mighty," began the secretary with a commendable boldness, since if he failed death was his sure portion. "I, Motamid Khân, secretary to the Lord of Light, proclaim it. Lo! did not the Shadow of God with his own hand write a permit? and did I not see the fragments of it lying torn on the ground where Mohabat's sacrilegious hand had dared to scatter them?"

He had almost gone beyond the mark. Jahângir looked at him sillily. "Thou liest, slave," he said; "he would not dare!"

"Let the Lord of Light ask him if it be not true," cried Motamid, feeling that every instant of delay was precious.

"Ay!" replied the Emperor with the sageness of half-sobriety. "There thou speakest sense. Send for Mohabat, slaves! Bid him to the Presence at once!"

And with the words, as if they absorbed all his powers mentally and bodily, he sank back among his cushions and so remained, his eyes fixed on the ruby cup, which he still held.

God send! prayed Motamid in his heart, it might bring remembrance; at any rate the pause gave time for the second dose of the drug to work.

And it did work. When Mohabat Khân after some delay entered the alcove, Jahângir sat up ready with instant, autocratic blame. "Didst dare, slave, to deny entrance to one who carried my permit?" he asked. "Wherefore?"

But Mohabat was ready with his answer. "Because after Majesty had given the permit he had condemned the bearer to deserved death."

Jahângir, startled, stood for an instant utterly befogged.

"Condemned to death!" he muttered. "Nay—we did talk of it—but—I——" He passed his hand over his brow as if to clear his brain. "I meant not surely—I—I cannot remember."

But Mohabat was inexorable. "The royal seal was affixed; so the one order counteracted the other, and I acted as was fit."

Something there was in the arrogance of his tone that roused Jahângir's instant resentment. "Who made thee judge, slave?" he burst out. "Am I not the Shadow of God? Send for the woman—be she what she may—forthwith. Dost hear?"

Mohabat took a step nearer to the Emperor. "Majesty!" he protested in a low voice, "this is not wise! Did we not discuss this?—hath it not been settled? Doth not Majesty desire untrammelled freedom?"

"God's curse upon thee, fool!" cried the monarch, his brain rising to the sarcasm. "Then give it me. Lo! I desire to see this woman—to tell her of her faults—to upbraid her—to say what thou hast said—to"—his eyes were on the ruby cup again—"to explain." Then sheer anger returned. "Send for her, or by my kingship thou diest!"

And once again he sank back among his cushions, his face working with the mingled passions of regret and resentment; so for a space there was silence in the tent. For even with a criminal condemned to death the Court proprieties must be preserved in the Emperor's presence; and this one was a lady of high rank. Even Motamid had slunk away, and Mohabat's voice came discreetly from beyond the curtain, when after five minutes' delay he said:

"Highness, the woman is here."

Jahângir rose on the instant. He was now almost sober—in truth, the sudden realization of what lay before him was enough to sober any man. What had he done? Was it true? He stood drawn up to his full height, kinglike, dignified; but he still held the ruby cup in his right hand, and his eyes were fixed on it. Then he raised them and looked at the white figure that stood quietly among the shadows waiting; so had she stood—oh God, how often! So had she looked——

There was a long, long silence.

Then one word and one word only broke it.

"Meru!"

It was enough. The drugged dream had vanished. Jahângir was once more in the Gold Scattering Garden where Love had flitted from the listless hand of Fate.

* * * * *

" 'Tis not for the Emperor of all the Indies to ask in vain," said the discomfited Mohabat ten minutes later, "but the lady must promise not to interfere again in the business of the State."

"Ay, ay," returned the Emperor joyously, "that will she do gladly, her only care being for me and my health. Lo! friend, I should have died without it."

And Mohabat, as he went off to discuss the position with his friends, while he admitted the truth of what Jahângir had said, was by no means sure how to regard the fact. The Emperor's speedy death in one way might be a consummation greatly to be desired; but it certainly would have put an end to his, Mohabat's, power; for Shahjahân would tolerate no interference. So perhaps, after all, if only the woman would keep her finger out of the pie of public affairs, the present arrangement might be better.

CHAPTER XVIII

> My bird is weary with imprisonment,
> My soul is sad with disillusionment.
> Oh, Hafiz! leave the Wherefore and the How.
> God knows! So drink Thy Wine and be content."

THE record of the next days could never be adequately written. It is hardly possible even for the imagination to grip the agony they must have brought to one of Nurjahân's nature. The weakness of the man who loved her was, it is true, no new knowledge; none the less, it must have been hard to bear. That he was remorseful goes without saying; but that, even when bedrugged and befogged, he should have consented to the undoing of the princess to whom he had given his unreserved confidence must have been to him almost pathetically incredible. So it must have bred resentment. Doubtless in those days, with nerves racked by debauchery, maudlin by turns over his wrongs and his self-reproach, Jahângir must have been difficult to guide. But Nurjahân's firm hand never wavered. It is almost appalling to think what it must have meant to her. To begin with she had to resign all outward show of power and take a place simply as the Emperor's favourite Sultana. Yet she did not flinch; she bided her time.

In all her varied life no greater sign of power shows than this, that the journey to Kâbul was resumed as if nothing had occurred to interfere with its smooth, ordinary course.

And every day must have lessened the strain, as Jahângir regained control over his nerves and his spirits. After a while, indeed, he began to discredit Mohabat's tale of a death warrant altogether. Whether he had signed one or not, however, it was quite clear that he had never meant to carry it into execution. The very thought was preposterous. And with this Nurjahân agreed. She had had no fear, she said; and this indeed was true in a way, for fear seems to have been unknown to her.

Besides, as Jahângir, with the easy palliation of his easy nature, would say, no matter what had happened there was no question that life was more pleasant now that both he and she had forsworn public affairs, and, leaving all to Mohabat, could devote themselves to each other.

To which Nurjahân, reverting to her rôle of Nurmahâl, the Light of the Home, would smile bewilderingly; but when she was alone her lip would set—she was biding her time.

So the slow months of the Imperial march crept on, and when they ended the peach-trees were abloom round Kâbul city, the tulips were ablaze on the green lawns, and in the Shahâra gardens the leafless Judas-trees flushed rosy purple to the tiniest twig.

"Truly, dear heart," said Jahângir almost rapturously, as from his great-grandfather's tomb he looked out over the fair prospect at his feet. "'Tis not the Pleasant Land, yet do I nowhere feel so virtuous as at Kâbul. 'Tis the air, methinks!"

"Mayhap," replied Nurjahân absently. She was watching the Gifted Lady playing with her dolls, and there was a troubled look on her beautiful face; but it seemed younger than ever, for the last few months of comparative rest had been physically good for her.

"Nay!" put in a thin old voice, "'tis heredity. 'Tis not possible to escape it. What doth Firdus say?" And the speaker, with much show of elocution, recited the well-known lines:

> "A tree that is bitter by nature,
> If planted on Paradise soil,
> Will never, I swear, compensate your
> Long labour, your care and your toil.
> If you pour on its rootlets pure honey
> And give it the Water of Life,
> It's fruit at the best will be funny,
> And not worth the cut of a knife!"

And old Khanzâda Râcquiya Begum lay back in her little carrying chair somewhat breathless. She was inconceivably old for an Indian woman, but she had begged so hard to be allowed another sight of her ancestors' graves that Jahângir had consented to bring her along with the camp; and she was wonderfully spry, wonderfully alive for her years.

Jahângir laughed. "'Tis not complimentary, *amma-jân*," he said cheerfully.

"And 'tis not even true," interposed Nurjahân, her eyes still upon the little girl and her dolls. It was a pretty picture, for the child was beautiful as an angel; yet when her grandmother called to ask her if she were content, the face which looked up from the play was sweet, placid beyond compare, but it lacked much expression.

"Yea," replied the little lass. "I play with my dolls. Goolu is getting married."

"Why dost not play with thy cousins yonder?" continued Nurjahân, pointing to two boys, the youngest about nine, who were amusing themselves with a ball a little way off. They were Shahjahân's sons, who had been sent as sureties for their father's good behaviour, and who were treated by the kindly Emperor as his own children. The elder, Dara Shukoh, was a fine, tall lad, the younger, Aurungzebe, small, somewhat wizen, with a sharp cunning face.

The Gifted Lady gave them a glance, then drew her tiny veil together with great decorum. "I do not play with boys," she said demurely. "I am a girl, and girls are different."

"Shâhbâsh, little one!" applauded Jahângir. "Ay, that they are; and 'tis best that they remain so;" he looked over almost pathetically at the woman who had done a man's work for so many years. "Dost not think, dearest, that we have been happy these last six months?"

"Yea, happy indeed," she answered; and in a way it was true. What need to tell him that almost her every thought was coloured by an insistent design to oust the traitor Mohabat from his sovereign's regard and the self-chosen position of Prime Minister, and resume it herself? "Ay, happy indeed. And would all Majesty's subjects were as content! But I hear much complaint of the Vizier's harshness——" She said these things constantly of aforethought.

"'Tis necessary at times," replied Jahângir gravely. "Yet will I warn him—on your words—to be as lenient as he can. Lo! I tell him all that I hear, to show my confidence."

And Nurjahân's averted face showed a slow smile. This was what she wanted. Such confidence must needs put a man off his guard.

Old Râcquiya, who was seated with her almost bald head bare to the soft wind—for they were a family party, even the servants withdrawn to a respectful distance—seemed to have got no further in comprehension than her stepson's profession of happiness.

"Yea, yea!" she assented. "It hath been happy. Hath it not brought to Majesty the best gift this world can give—the repentance of an erring son? Yea, yea! How my old heart rejoiced when I heard Shahjahân, on the instant of hearing of Mohabat's rebellion, set out to rescue the Emperor!"

Jahângir looked doubtful. "Wouldst call it a rebellion, mother?" he began, and Nurjahân hastened with diplomacy.

"Yea, Shahjahân hath redeemed much; and his boys are good lads."

But Râcquiya, old as she was, was still remarkable for decisive opinions.

"I offer excuse," she said with a sniff, "but in my poor opinion the elder is a fool, the younger a knave. Mark my words, he will make an evil name for himself. He hath Chagatâi blood in him, doubtless, but 'tis over-watered—but there! with due deference I am but old."

And there were ready tears in the old eyes.

"We all be old here, we three, O kind one," said Nurjahân gently, laying her hand as gently on the wrinkled one, so thin, so worn with long life.

"Old?" echoed the older woman tartly. "Lo! thou art but seven and fifty, and I close on my nineties. Out on thee! And never a grey strand in thy beautiful hair!"

"Old?" echoed the Emperor almost wonderingly. "Yea, I am old, as the mother sayeth. Ay, and ailing too—but thou?" He paused as if faced by fact, then shook his head. "To me, dearest, thou never canst be old, Light of my Life."

And his hand found hers.

Little Gifted Lady, the doll bride on her arm, came up and looked at them with her solemn dark eyes.

"Lo! I will play handy-pandy too," she said gravely. So there under the Judas-trees, beside the grave of Babar—the man with the joyous child-heart whose brief epitaph records that Heaven is his eternal home—these four—the childless old woman, the passionate man-lover, the woman who knew not what love meant, and the little child whose baby thoughts were with marriage, played the game which children love all over the world; and laughter, soft and gay, rose up among the flush of flowers.

Truly, as the Emperor said, they were very happy.

But Nurjahân was simply biding her time to strike a blow for her former position.

Up till now, the presence of the army of Rajputs had made all attempts to oust Mohabat impossible; besides, the Emperor, too lazy to take trouble himself, and curiously unwilling to revert to the old arrangement, found the clever, arrogant, intolerant man a great stand-by. Of late, however, the unbridled licentiousness of these same soldiers had brought about a fierce fight with the hot-headed Afghans, which resulted in the force being almost decimated; for the Kâbuli tolerates no meddling with his women. Following on this had come desertions from an army and a country in which the mercenary's recognized amusements were disallowed; the result being that Mohabat's bodyguard was reduced to half its original number. Yet still he kept his hold on the Amirs and the nobles, while the Court, almost to a man, was in favour of anyone who would keep it from falling again under a woman's rule.

Beneath the mask of peace and happiness, however, Nurjahân was at work.

Those long years of power had left their inevitable mark upon her; and then she was passionately resentful at the effect which even those few days of organized excess had had upon the man whose health had been her chief care. Do what she would, the evil asserted and reasserted itself in ever renewed attacks of his old enemy. She could not blind herself to the fact that in all probability those few days had taken years from his life.

And his unchanging love had made him very dear to her. She would sit and look at him sometimes, when, at his best, he was playing with the child, or instructing Shahjahân's boys in the art of venery, and wonder why she did not love him as a woman loves a man. But she did not. She never attempted to disguise the fact from herself; she accepted it.

In a way it put a keener edge to her resentment against the man who had done him an injury. She knew that she did not give Jahângir all he ought to have, and this made her the less tolerant of the loss others might inflict upon him.

And all the time the knowledge that she, a woman, was alone against all these men spurred her to an almost savage resistance.

She had so few friends whom she could trust. Asof her brother had been made, and was still held, a prisoner by Mohabat; even so, was he to be trusted? She was not sure. Fedai Khân had never returned to Court after his ineffectual attempt at rescue; perhaps as well, for the Emperor still spoke with resentment of the arrows that had fallen upon his couch! Motamid the secretary, who had done so much to save her life, was less ready to aid any return to power.

But one of the royal eunuchs, by name Hoshyar Khân, was a distant kinsman of Fedai's, and had in addition a cause of quarrel with Mohabat. That was the worst of it! Without some personal axe to grind, no one's service was secure.

Still, quite undaunted, she laid her plans carefully; the first thing to be done being to secure at least an equal force on her side. Mohabat had mercenaries; why not she? Her revenues were large; and stretching away through the Salt Range on the edge of which the fortress of Rhotas stood, to the very foot of the Kâbul hills, lay the Ghakker country. Now the Ghakkers were a wild predatory tribe which had never been reduced to real obedience. The fine old fort—supposed to be impregnable—had been built to keep them in order and between bounds.

Here, then, lay her chance. As the inheritress of her father's fief she had a right to a contingent at the periodical reviews; but she took care to have this as meagre as possible.

"Thou shouldst bid thy agent enlist more, dearest," quoth the Emperor, "if it hurts thy pride so to see thy contingent reduced. Yet of what good is it to thee, being woman? Lo! cannot the Shadow of God shelter thee sufficiently?

"Ay!" she would reply with a smile. "'Tis enough for myself truly; but there be others in the world. And I have issued orders to enlist; for see you, my lord, Mohabat is of use, doubtless, but he brooks no interference. Did he not check my lord's going forth without a Rajput guard even on a shooting expedition? 'Tis beyond the province of a Vizier whatever. In my father's time—ay, and in mine, as the Emperor knows—his freedom was secure."

So with deft hints and every means at her disposal, she strove to influence Jahângir.

And every now and again a secret messenger, disguised, would come in from Rhotâs ways, and her eyes would glisten at the thought that, mayhap, it might not be long now ere Mohabat's power was broken.

They started back to Lahore from Kâbul early in the season, and chose the lower route for their return. Among the low hills the coolth lingered, and there was better sport for the Emperor, who renewed all his youthful keenness in the due instruction of his grandsons.

"Dara Shukoh is the bolder," he would say, "but little Aurungzebe hath the better eye. He can follow a spoor like a trained huntsman."

"Or a jackal!" quoth Râcquiya Begum, who never missed an opportunity of giving her opinion of the boy. The journey homewards was sadly trying the old lady, and Nurjahân felt that ere long one of her earliest friends would be no more seen. Then of all the kindly folk she had known, only the Emperor would be left. And Asof, her brother! Yes, if she succeeded in her emprise, Asof must come back. He was no worse than the others, and the Emperor liked him. Had the latter not said over and over again that he regretted separation from him, since he was distinguished above all other servants for ability, good disposition and tact, very unequalled in all kinds of propriety, so that his society was pleasurable to a degree?

So Asof must return as titular Vizier, at any rate.

This and many another detail was settled as the Imperial camp wound its long length through the sharp defiles of the Salt Range. A strange country this, with its rugged, treeless peaks, its narrow valleys so bare in the rainless season, so lush with grazing grass when the torrent beds run swift with brackish water. But there was plenty of game, and in the still noons the sunlight baked into the rocks and made them show opalescent against the sky.

It was just as they were debouching into the more level ground out of which the Rhotâs foot rises, as rises the Rock of Gibraltar, that a halt was called to enable the Emperor to have a review of his troops, ere they began the march through the open plain that showed like a blue mist beyond the curving stream of the Jhelum river.

That night the news ran round the camp that the Begum's new-raised cavalry were to take part in the morrow's demonstration.

How many were there? Where had they been raised?

Some few in Kâbul; that folk knew. Some few more, *en route*; but that was not enough to warrant Mohabat Khân's restlessness.

What was up?

None knew; though one coming from the plain to the left of Rhotâs had tales to tell of a great company of wild-looking horsemen awaiting orders.

But Fedai Khân, when he rode over to pay his humble duty to the Emperor, said not one word about them. He was fairly well received, for he brought news of a great herd of antelope that had been driven into a neighbouring defile for Jahângir's special delectation.

"Lo! I will go after them to-morrow, when the review is over," said the Emperor in high delight.

Whereupon Fedai Khân remarked that there would be small chance of sport if the Lord of Light had to take his usual Rajput guard, to which Jahângir had replied in an ill humour that, Mohabat or no Mohabat, he would do as he liked.

And that evening he sent word to his Prime Minister that since the Begum was going to exhibit her new-raised cavalry it would be well if he, Mohabat, kept his Rajputs out of the way, to avoid the possibility of a quarrel.

Mohabat, doubtless, being of a cunning that would instruct the devil, smelt a rat; but he was powerless to avert the crisis, so, being a wise man, he kept his breath to cool his own porridge, and withdrew his guards.

Needlessly, it appeared at first; for when the dawn broke and the contingents stood ready for review, only Nurjahân's poor muster showed amongst the others.

"Where be thy new troops, dearest?" asked the Emperor half playfully of his consort, who ever sat with him in the *howdah* of the royal elephant. It was Gajrâj, recovered of his wounds.

"They are here, my lord!" replied Nurjahân meekly. "Give the word for advance, Gajrâj!" she added, and the wise beast, lifting its trunk—there were two long scars on it—bellowed forth his mightiest trumpet.

So from every ravine, every sparse bit of cover on every road and path, came an answering fanfare of wild horn and drums and conches, as over two thousand wild horsemen swept into view, their lean little ponies, unused to such slow work, prancing and neighing and fidgeting, until, with a sudden hoarse word of command, the leader of the first company relieved them from discipline, and like a tornado—one furious gust of lances and legs and tails, dominated by stern set faces, from which the long black curls swept backwards like a mane—they forged up to the royal elephant, then paused, irregular, yet like a rock.

It was enough.

Ere the last company had formed up, Mohabat was to horse and away.

That evening there were two camps once more on the banks of the Jhelum river; but this time the northern had the whip hand of the southern, and where Jahângir had lost his liberty he found his freedom.

And Nurjahân was once more mistress of all India; but ere she slept, with the almost terrible foresight she always possessed, she sent off two messengers—one to Mohabat, treating him as a mere Generalissimo, giving him orders to at once deliver up Asof Khân on pain of having sufficient force sent against him to compel compliance; after which he was to proceed against Shahjahân in Scende; the other to Shahjahân himself, bidding him beware of Mohabat, and advising his retreat to the Deccan, there to defend himself with better chance of success.

After which it is to be hoped she slept. She had at any rate by sheer force of purpose gained her object, and all the men in India had passed under a woman's rule.

CHAPTER XIX

> "Swift Death found Love a-cold, and gave her place
> Within his Shroud, then hurried on apace
> To Harvest. 'Oh, dread Death!' his victims cried.
> 'Nay, I am Love,' he said, and showed her face."

ONCE more it was the Pleasant Land, and yet, as Nurjahân sat beside the Emperor's couch in the Garden of the Breezes down by the Dhal lake she felt that its pleasure was, so far as she was concerned, a thing of the past; for every day, every hour, every minute was consumed by anxiety. A single look at Jahângir was sufficient to tell that he was ill indeed. He had never really recovered the shock of his kidnapping or the organized debauch which followed on it.

And yet his face, thin and hollow-cheeked, looked less heavy than in the years gone by, and his kindly smile when he met her eyes seemed more radiant than ever.

Still, the last year had brought him many sorrows. As Nurjahân had anticipated, old Khanzâda Râcquiya Begum had gone to her rest, and by her own desire had been carried back to Kâbul, there to lie beside her father's people. But who would have predicted the death of Prince Parviz, strong, hale, hearty? Yet he had died of a seizure brought on by excessive drinking. So would Jahângir have died, doubtless, years before, but for a woman's care. Then Shahjahân, joined by the time-serving Mohabat, had showed renewed signs of independence. Finally, Shahriyâr, the Emperor's sole remaining son, had not been satisfactory. He spent his time dissolutely amongst low company, and was beginning to suffer from the consequences; to what extent Nurjahân kept from the Emperor, as she strove to keep all disagreeables.

Thus, as she sat in that loveliest of all gardens, on the low marble dais that juts into the pellucid water, she smiled back at the Emperor's smiles, and applauded his versifications to the echo; for now that he was for the most part confined to his couch, his favourite amusement was stringing words together; and he was becoming curiously sensitive to praise or blame, as he was to his own bodily pain.

"Lo!" he said with his halting breath, which made his lines run rough, "these are the best I ever wrote, methinks." And he began:

> "The zephyr sheds a perfume from her skirts,
> For she hath kissed the roses, and the pool
> Roughens in smiling ripples as with curt
> 'Good-morrow, friend!' she hastens past to cool
> The forehead of the lover of good wine
> And sharpen his desire. Oh, Rose divine,
> When I, sad singer, be beneath the earth,
> Yon musky bud will bring thee a new birth.
> So, Hafiz, be of joyous heart; sure, God
> Sends Spring, although thou liest beneath the sod."

The words, the laboured breathing, the thin fluttering hands that strove to give appropriate action, sent sudden tears to the woman's eyes. Yea, it was true—ere long it must be true. And then——?

She would not, she could not think. But one thing seemed certain. The child on whose future she had built her own would never fill the place to gain which her grandmother was prepared to fight to the end.

Tall for her age, with every promise of surpassing beauty, little Gifted Lady, now in her fifth year, showed no promise of intellect beyond that of the ordinary girl-child of her years; perhaps less.

All this flashed through Nurjahân's brain, but she set it aside and turned a smiling face to the poet.

"Yea," she said, "that is better than most—yet why speak of sods—save as a rhyme to gods!" she added with a laugh. "Thou art better, dearest, far better than thou wast; and we will return sooner this year, since the cold here may be detrimental to thy cough."

So, clapping her hands, she ordered the servants to bring him instantly the violet sherbet and the candied rose-leaves which he loved so well; for he had become very dainty in his food, and scrupulous as any high-caste Hindu as to things clean and unclean. Briefly, he had outlived the coarseness of life, and invalidism had robbed him of his virility. None the less was he the more lovable to a woman of Nurjahân's type, and she came nearer to passion during those months in which slowly, almost idly, they wandered luxuriously about the low levels of Kashmir than she had ever done before. They did not attempt the hills as formerly, but Islamabad saw them when the pilgrims to Amarnath were passing through that quaint congeries of wooden temples and tanks, crowding fishes and crowding men, women, and children.

It was the sight of the mounds of hungry fish-mouths that rose out of the sacred water in pursuit of the veriest crumb that started the idea of a fishing excursion round the great sources of the river; the three springs which at the eastern end of the valley gush out from the living rock.

Asof Khân, who had done his work well—and more than his work, since secret messengers had been going backwards and forwards between his office and the Deccan—would have had Jahângir save himself the trouble of marching, and set to work to catch some of the mounds of sacred fish where they were; for he was a bigoted Mahomedan, to whom Hindu superstition was rank abomination. But Jahângir with much pomp admonished his Vizier on the duties of those who governed mixed races, mixed religions, and quoted at him a quatrain of which he was very proud:

"For the care of all subjects I keep
Mine eyes unacquainted with sleep;
For the care of the bodies of these
My own trouble and pain are as ease."

It was at Islamabad that the most crushing blow to her ambitions fell upon Nurjahân. Shahriyâr, without doubt, had been for some time past her nominee for the throne in the future. Even the conviction that his little daughter would never, and could never, rise to the level of the dream-child she had been when she was born, had not altered the Empress's plan of continuing to rule through Shahriyâr as figurehead. Even the connection of his unworthiness had not altered it. Up to a certain point——

But now something happened which turned her tolerance to loathing. Shahriyâr, as the result of his evil life, was stricken with a sort of leprosy, and was advised by his physicians to return without delay to Lahore, there to be efficiently treated.

"Miserable!" she said, facing the young man with scorn in voice and face, heart and mind. "Was not a throne sufficient bribe to make thee decent? Was not kingship enough to keep thee from the gutters? Now in the time when God's Providence may call thee to play thy part, thou wilt be absent! But go, and go quickly! Yet not one word of this to the Emperor. His dying ears shall not listen to thy shame, his dying days shall not be clouded by yet another unworthy son!"

She spoke bravely, but after he had slunk away, eager to seek relief as soon as possible, she sought solitude, flung herself on her couch, and cried as she had never cried before.

The meanness of it, the petty, miserable meanness of the man —of so many men—seared her soul as with a red-hot iron. Was life, which held such horrors, worth the trouble she gave to it? And in one illuminating flash she saw herself as she had been from the beginning—always at work, never giving mind or body an instant's rest; ever, rightly or wrongly, striving to impress something that she saw, and others did not seem to see, upon her world.

No, it was not worth it. A great distaste to effort forced itself upon her.

Then came remembrance that in speaking to Shahriyâr she had for the first time confessed, even to herself, that the Emperor was dying. She sat up in her favourite attitude, and for the first time also gripped what that confession meant; and a great pity, a great protecting love, welled up in her heart for the stricken man.

These last few days or weeks should give him all he had ever asked of her. So she rose, sent for her dressers, robed herself with unaccustomed care, and went over to where the Emperor was amusing himself mightily with examining a *manawal* pheasant which had just been brought to him from the snows.

"Look, dearest," he said. "Saw you ever such colours on the breast. Lo! when I was a lad I mind me trying to extract copper from a peacock's tail because folk said it was an antidote to poison! But there is copper here and to spare! And see you the real pheasant's ear coverts, but the hinder parts as a bustard. Truly a goodly bird, and it weighs heavy for its size. Yet is it not good eating, so they say, seeing that for the most part it lives on the juniper-berries. But the plumage is extraordinarily beautiful. God knows why 'twas made so, seeing that it liveth alone in the snows."

"It hath its mate," smiled Nurjahân, and Jahângir laughed.

"Yea, but she is a sober bird, they say. 'Tis the other way with us menfolk," he said; "and of a surety, dearest, thou dost prove it in that dress! Never didst thou look more beautiful." And his eyes had all the ardour of a young lover in them. Even the little Gifted Lady, a doll in each arm, came to stare admiringly at her beautiful grandmother with big, solemn, childish eyes.

"When the wedding-trays come I shall have many such dresses," she said confidently, and Jahângir, delighted, caught her up and kissed her.

"So thou shalt, apple of mine eye," he protested. "Yea, yea, 'the peacock's tail will hide its head,' for, see you, thou wilt never be her equal—never—never!"

Nurjahân gave a little shiver; that was true, deadly true.

But after that began the leisurely marching of a mile or two a day—for Jahângir felt even the rhythmed motion of a palanquin almost too much for him—from one beautiful camping-ground to another still more beautiful; and ever and always it was to the woman a march of death, since she knew that never again would they pass that way hand in hand.

So their steps lingered. Those who have imagination can march with them, even in these later days, from Machibâwan to Archibul, from Archibul to Vernag. After which, seriously, they set their faces to leave the Pleasant Land. Day by day, bit by bit, mounting higher and higher up the winding path till they paused to take breath below the pass proper.

Oh, strange, sad marching! One can still see the little cavalcade toiling up and up. The Emperor of all the Indies, fighting full oft for sheer breath, at other times beguiled, comforted, sustained, by the woman who was never far from his side. Love and Death hand in hand!

Their shadows fall still on the wealth of flowers that, at all seasons, blossom on the uplands.

But the pass and the march below and beyond must be crossed in hot haste, for these high altitudes are cold, and the travellers are fleeing to the plains in a last desperate hope that a warmer climate may bring relief.

It was almost starlight when they started on the long pass march. No time, now, to rest and say farewell to the rich levels below them. It was a race for life through the sharp cliffs and peaks where the snow already lay thick, and along the wild stretches of bents that seemed interminable. Nurjahân, with a wisdom beyond her generation, had given Jahângir an extra dose of opium, and he slept, happed up in furs.

And she?

Most wives, most mothers, can tell what her feelings must have been as, sometimes walking, sometimes riding, she kept up with her charge, but as the rest of the world can never even grip at the truth, words are useless.

So, hurrying along, with relays of fresh bearers every mile or so, they reached their destination in safety. It was, perhaps, the most beautiful spot in all the Pirpanjâl route. A valley nestling at the foot of the steep descent; a valley of green swards and mighty chestnut-trees that crept also amongst the sober pines up the surrounding hills. And the chestnuts were changing to scarlet and gold, and the great Himalaya lilies reared their heads from the green and gold ferns. Here, sheltered from all the winds that blow, in a warm moist atmosphere, the Emperor's asthma took a sudden turn for the better. The place had always had charms for him, since nowhere was better sport to be had, and he once more decided to stop for a few days and enjoy such hunting as he could compass.

This was not much, as stalking was beyond him; but Nurjahân, as ever, was to the fore in procuring him amusement. So at the foot of a mountain, where two small valleys debouched, a butt was hastily built wherein Jahângir could sit and shoot at the driven deer and wild goats as they came past.

The Emperor, in the seventh heaven at being once more able to use his matchlock, was merry as a cricket, and all went well. But as the light was failing one of the beaters on the steep cliff above the butt let the animal he was striving to drive downwards escape him upwards, and drew down on himself angry shouts from below. He turned rapidly to retrieve his mistake, his foot slipped, and with one yell of despair he fell, his body bounding from rock to rock till he lay a mangled corpse almost at the Emperor's feet. It was the work of a few seconds. Almost before the echo of his yell had ceased reverberating among the rocks, he was dead.

The Emperor, starting up, covered his face with his hands, and stood trembling in every limb.

"'Tis my fault!" he gasped. "I killed him! What right had I to kill God's creatures? What right? What right? Lo! I am punished! His blood is on my head!"

And the man who but a few years before had recklessly ordered two innocent men to be executed because all unwittingly they had disturbed his aim at a nilghai, would not, could not be comforted. Even the Princess to whom he had given his unreserved confidence was powerless before his self-reproach. Why had he ever broken the vow he had made when little Prince Bravery was ill, never again to injure any of God's creatures? Because he was angered with his son—a son who after all had repented him of the evil.

Ah! rightly was he punished! All hastily he sent for the young man's mother; and her story of how the dead son had been her only means of support but increased the Emperor's agitation. He could give money—ay, he could give money and to spare; but who could give back the love, the affection? And it was his fault! his fault! his fault!

Then the physical distaste at the sight of such a tragedy rose strong.

"I see it still—wherever I look I see it still," he cried. "Let us go on; let us no longer stop in this hateful place where I have called Death to me!"

And she, looking at his pallid breathlessness, the pained frown upon his forehead, acquiesced. Change of scene would doubtless weaken the impression. It must be tried, at any rate, and that without delay.

It was a cloudless day when at three in the afternoon they started for Rajaur, two marches away, for the intervening one was but a comfortless place. At Rajaur, however, the Emperor could rest awhile.

Ay, he might rest indeed!

Nurjahân's eyes did not fill with tears, her lip did not tremble at the thought. All of her, body and soul, was at the man's service; she had no time to think of grief. So they went swiftly on—to rest.

It was nigh sunset when they paused for a moment. The Emperor had asked for some wine, and Nurjahân was ready as ever with the ruby cup.

He put it to his lips, then held it out to her. "I cannot drink," he whispered. "Drink thou—for me!"

They had set down the palanquin on a tiny patch of greensward beside a trickling stream almost hidden by the dense growth of maidenhair fern. Around, in changing colour, were the autumn woods, and high up in the sky—so high that it seemed inconceivable, incredible, it should belong to earth and not to heaven—showed one snow-clad peak.

Nurjahân knelt down beside the dying man and kissed him on the lips.

"I drink for both," she whispered back; so, draining the cup, she hid it in her bosom. Its work was done. Then, rising, she bid the bearers make haste with their burden.

So they started once more, and the fallen leaves about their feet rustled a soft refrain to the musical cadence of their half-sobbing chorus of muffled voices.

It was dark ere they reached Rajaur, and the Emperor was unconscious. They laid him in the arched verandah of the fort which overhung the rushing river, and it sang a whispered lullaby to him, hiding the faint sobbing of his breath.

"Let him be," said Nurjahân sternly. "Let him have peace at the last!"

Outside and within men were passing to and fro, talking; planning and preparing; but there, in the moonlight, was silence.

Would he speak again? Would he recognize her at the last?

Mayhap. She must be patient and wait.

So when the sun had risen to show the exquisite beauty of the view—the rushing river, the clustered town, the terraced fields rising tier upon tier, and behind them the everlasting snows—he stirred. And the woman bent anxiously over him. Then his eyes opened; but he looked away from her, as a smile showed faintly on his face.

"Meru!" he whispered, and held both hands out to the empty air.

And as Nurjahân rose from her ended vigil she felt that he had indeed passed her by. All her long years of life and effort were as naught. It was "Meru," the child he had played with; the girl he had loved in the garden to whom he gave his last, his best.

As she stepped out of the verandah to make room for those who were to perform the last offices to the dead, Asof Khân stopped her.

"It will be better," he said deferentially, yet still authoritatively, "if Majesty will come to the apartment prepared for her."

She gave him one look, a look that seemed to shrivel him, body and soul.

"Traitor!" she said; and followed where he led without another word.

CHAPTER XX

> " Count in thy Life Love's kisses; count the prize
> Of Friendship and of Trust that never dies;
> But count no wrong, no Enemy, no Lie.
> They shall be counted at the Great Assize."

" THE woman keeps quiet as the grave," quoth a high functionary doubtfully. " God send she be not plotting against us. Lo! it were well, methinks, to put her out of harm's way."

Asof Khân squirmed. " Nay, Khân-*ji*," he replied hastily. " Men—ay, and women too—must be judged by actions; and she hath scarce opened her mouth since Jahângir—may the mercy of God receive him!—set out on the path of annihilation; save, indeed, to send me word that his wish and hers was that the corpse should find a resting-place in the garden—thou mindest it—on this side the Ravi. Dost remember? The Emperor desired it, bought it of the Herâti pigeon-fancier Mumîn, and gave it to—to—my sister. 'Tis a rare garden, and hath lofty plane-trees and handsome cypresses! 'Twill do well for a tomb—therefore I gave consent."

The high official sniffed; he liked not Asof's assumption of command. " Authority lies with Majesty," he said, " and Majesty lies with the eldest son of the eldest son—Dâwar Baksh."

He scanned his hearer's face narrowly; but everyone in the wide camp that still halted at Rajaur looked at his neighbour askance. What was to be the upshot of Jahângir's death? Would the two brothers fight for the throne—Shahriyâr gaining slight advantage by being closer to the spot than Shahjahân—or would the Legitimist party win it for the heir-at-law? All day and all night plots and counterplots were being hatched, and men were counting how long it would take the news to reach the Deccan, how long it would take Shahjahân to return and claim the Empire.

Asof Khân and his party admitted mournfully that four

months would scarce be sufficient; though all the while they knew that almost ere the late Emperor had breathed his last the swiftest messenger in India—an almost incredibly swift messenger—had started southwards with the news, and that his journey would be a record one, even for him.

Meanwhile, to keep finalities in abeyance, it was at last decided by all parties that Dâwar Baksh, dead Khushrau's son, should be proclaimed heir to Empire. It satisfied all factions—the Legitimists because it was the proper conventional course; Shahriyâr's faction and the Shahjahân faction because it gave time for their nominees to put in an appearance.

And it hurt no one, save poor Dâwar Baksh himself, who, after vainly seeking to be excused the dangerous honour, gave in to it.

Hitherto he had been more or less under surveillance, despite the fact that he was really a quite negligible, if well-meaning, nonentity.

This point settled, the camp moved Lahore-wards, carrying with it Nurjahân, to all intents and purposes, a prisoner.

But a silent one, greatly to the astonishment of her surroundings, more especially of her brother, who, despite his disloyalty to her ambitions, had a great affection and admiration for his sister.

And her resolute refusal to see him made him feel guilty; hence he had fallen in at once with her views as to the burial-place of the late Emperor which she sent him in writing. The preparations necessary for the journey did not take long, the prayers, the wailing, were soon over, but until she had watched the little cavalcade which escorted the embalmed body disappear round the last visible curve of the downward road, Nurjahân gave herself no time to think.

Yet all the while realities were coming home to her. Most of all the certainty that it was not she, as she knew herself—not the compound of Mihr-un-nissa, Nurmâhal, Nurjahân, that ardent, yet in a way cold, vital, capable personality—that Jahângir had loved; it was Meru, the child he had played with, the girl he had seen in the garden.

And her dulled eyes would follow the little Gifted Lady as she played with her dolls, realizing that she also was capable of playing that part in a man's life. Why, then, should she—poor child! —be asked to undertake a harder rôle? She should not! She should be married when the time came to some worthy bridegroom. Fedai Khân's son was a suitable age.

She caught up her vagrant thoughts then to ask herself why she had undertaken this harder rôle? She scarcely knew; but it had been played, and played well. Yet she would play it no more. Ever since that flood of womanly tears which had followed on Shahriyâr's miserable meanness, she had known that it would come to this. It was not as if she had been beaten, as if she had been worsted in the fight. She had gained her point; she had set herself a definite aim, and she had accomplished it.

Now—yes, now!—she would revert to being the Meru men had loved.

So, day by day, she journeyed in silence, making no comment on the gossip of the eunuchs and ladies-in-waiting who still surrounded her. None the less she was laying her plans, and one of them she carried into execution a few days ere they reached Lahore; for Dâwar Baksh had been a favourite with Jahângir, who had ever liked all simple-minded folk.

So one evening she sent a formal request to be allowed an interview with the Emperor of all the Indies, to which the young man, who was beginning to believe in his own good fortune, and take himself seriously, responded by appearing before her in person, very full of his power to open prison doors if suitable security were given against any future meddling with the affairs of State.

To which Nurjahân, dressed in her white widow's robes, had responded that she had no desire for freedom, but wished to speak to her late husband's grandson privately, as she had something to say which it would be to his advantage to hear.

Possibly to his advantage, but his good-natured face grew pale with fear as, bidding him sit beside her and listen, she told him plainly that his life was not worth purchase.

"See you," she said kindly enough, "thou art the stalking horse, for all that thy cause has followers. But thou hast neither money nor brains. Yet would I fain save thee, since thy grandfather loved thee, and hath oft spoken of thy fitness for heirship. But he decided against it—and rightly——"

"Yet by all the laws of my family, by Timurid customs, I am heir," broke in Dâwar Baksh hotly, "and——"

But Nurjahân's eyes held him silent. "Lo!" she replied, "thou canst try it an thou wilt. But it is death. So take advice! When the storm breaks—disappear! Lay thy plans beforehand and be ready."

"Easy to say," began the young man.

"Easier to perform," put in his step-grandmother with a charming smile. "See here, this ring." And she took from her finger the little signet the old Strangler had given her. "It means safety. Seek out the nearest colony of Thugs—there is one at Durga's temple in the Almond Bazaar at Lahore. Then at the first hint of danger, escape thither; show them the ring. Yet wilt thou require money, and money that is light to carry." As she spoke she drew out of her bosom the ruby cup. "This," she said, and her voice trembled, "hath done its part in my life. It hath not brought me luck—'twas the real one—that was *talismân*—but of that no more. I have no time to tell thee all, and if I did thou wouldst forget it. But if thou wilt take that cup to the Khân-phatta shrine, the split-eared *jogis* will give thee gold galore for it! Ay, and keep silence too." She laughed suddenly a bitter laugh, then went on: "So—first the ring to the stranglers; then, with their aid, negotiate the cup at the split-ear shrine—and thou art safe!"

Dâwar Baksh stared at her. "But wherefore? I understand not——"

"Neither will thine enemies," she replied curtly. "This much will I tell thee. The split-eared ones have been searching for that cup—or its marrow—these fifty and six years; that I know. So do as thou art bid, if the need comes—and come it will."

And, as usual, she was right.

They were close on Lahore now, and over the level fields came unwonted signs of coming war. From the north had come contingent after contingent to join the mock majesty of Dâwar

Baksh. A pitiful sight this—royalty surrounded by servants who, as they cringed and bowed, held their tongues in their cheeks. Asof Khân, their leader, full of wild boasts of what the Legitimists would do, even while in thought the whole manhood of him was with the Hindu messenger Binârsi, who day and night, night and day, was speeding southward with his verbal message for Shahjahân; since not one instant of time had been wasted in the writing of a letter. A signet-ring off the little finger as a sign of faith, the words, "Kingship awaits you," and, like an arrow from a bow, the man had started. Would he do the journey in the twenty days he had promised? That was the question. If it could be compassed they would have both the other factions on the hip. Shahjahân could march on Agra, the capital, and thus reduce the other claimants to the position of rebels against central authority.

Meanwhile, Shahriyâr was the immediate enemy. On hearing of his father's death he had seized the Treasury at Lahore, and with the money therein, added by Nurjahân's vast revenues, which with a curious disdain she contrived to place secretly at his disposal, he commenced bribing right and left, thus gathering together a large force.

The two armies met on the banks of the Râvi, not far from the spot where Nurjahân, listless, almost contemptuous, sat beside a new-made grave, chanting prayers over it, and watching the squirrels that raced from tree to tree, the pigeons that sidled on the roof of the summer-house which centred the garden.

How the dead man would have rejoiced in the peace and quiet —with her!

Well, he had the peace, the quiet; and he should have her also. He had given her much in life. In death she could give him his heart's desire.

So the noise of battle drifted past almost unheeding ears.

Let men-folk squabble as they pleased over the bauble of a crown they knew not how to wear. She, a woman, had done her part. She had ruled well. She had made one man die with dignity as Emperor of all the Indies. And as she sat there, while the little Gifted Lady, deprived of her two boy companions—for Asof Khân had at once removed Shahjahân's two little sons from their step-grandmother's care, as if fearful evil should befall them—played with her dolls, the mind of the women went back to the night when, a girl of fourteen, she had met the great Akbar's half sarcastic remark, "So thou art ambitious?" with the proud words, "Of my rightful place."

Well, as she had promised then, she had done no harm to the son of the Emperor Mahomed Jahâl-ud-din Akbar! Her delicate hands clenched in on themselves; she set her lip.

When her attendants came running with news of the tide of battle, she met them impatiently.

"So be it," she said; "I care not who wins. They be all men, and there is small choice between them—murderers, rakes, thieves, and liars!"

And she was not far wrong. It is an evil thing to try and get at the minds of the majority of these fighters. Mercenaries, traitors, pure unabashed deceivers. Asof Khân, for instance, one eye ever on the Deccan, the other bent in humble loyalty to the puppet whose very life depended on when Binârsi, the messenger, reached his goal.

Meanwhile, there was enough to fill the days, even after Shahriyâr, totally defeated, had fled to the fort at Lahore, and, being dragged from the women's apartments therein, had been thrown into prison along with Prince Danial's two sons, who might be suspected as collateral heirs. For the puppet Dâwar Baksh had to be crowned.

Nurjahân, over in the garden at Shâhdera, heard of the grand doings, and smiled to herself.

"Tell me not of the loyalty of the festivities. Tell me how Asof Khân bears himself. I would I could see him; 'twould be a lesson in the courtier's art!"

But she steadfastly refused an interview. There was no need, she said. His mind was occupied with this world, hers with the other. If he and his like chose to think otherwise, they were welcome to do as they chose. She would be content to rejoin her father and mother and give them the first version of the tale.

Whether this bitter sarcasm availed or not, it is impossible to say; certain it is that she was left alone in her garden seclusion where, calm, almost uninterested, she listened to all the gossip of the town that lay so close over the water. So the days passed, and a certain sense of safety grew even to Fedai Khân's heart as he watched night after night while his mistress slept the sleep of a child. At the first news of her semi-imprisonment he had ridden fast and far with a band of devoted servants to succour or die with her; but she had forbidden all attempts at rescue. So he had dismissed his followers, though he had remained himself. So much he refused to be forbidden.

"News hath come from the Deccan," said Nurjahân suddenly to him one day.

"So soon?' he exclaimed. "Impossible!"

The Empress laughed her bitter laugh. "Thou knowest not Asof," she replied. "Lo! he is my brother, and he is capable. Now we shall see what we shall see." She laid her hand suddenly on his. "And if all goes well, as it will, thou wilt be free to go, Fedai. I have ever told thee Shahjahân dare not touch me; this will prove it!"

Once again she was right. Whatever the letter sent in immediate answer to the verbal message contained, it held no penalty for Nurjahân Padshâh Begum. But that very night, as the historian puts it, Shahriyâr, the two collateral Princes, and Gurhasp, Dâwar Baksh's brother, "trod the path of annihilation, and the world was rid of their unnecessary bodies."

And Dâwar Baksh himself? Strange to say, he escaped the snare. How, none could guess, save a woman who smiled to herself when she heard the news as she sat by a new-made grave.

And what is more, he disappeared utterly. Long years after, a tale filtered through the bazaars from the north that he had been seen in the guise of a wandering fakir in Persia; so it is to be inferred that though he had escaped, he had not gained untold gold through the ruby cup. But by that time the glorious administration of Shahjahân was firm, and none cared if the other were alive or no.

And folk seemed even to have forgotten that by a curious coincidence all the available claimants, all the possible aspirants, to the throne had been disposed of, comfortably, the very day before Shahjahân entered Agra in triumph and took on his shoulders the responsibility of Empire.

Proof positive, of course, that he could not have connived in their murder! Yet it is strange that even to-day, when by the cool light of time truth becomes more manifest, the possibility of Shahjahân being implicated in his brother Khushrau's murder is stoutly denied, on the ground that there is no other record of such crime in his life. What, then, of the letter which brought about wholesale murder on the very day before his coronation? A strange coincidence, my masters! That is all.

But one woman in a garden never wavered in her certitude. And so it came to pass that after some years had sped the chance of facing one whom she had been too proud to seek with the truth, came to her.

Shahjahân, Emperor of all the Indies, being at Lahore, came to visit his father's grave. It was now enshrined in the magnificent building which remains to this day. On it Nurjahân had spent all the revenues which she had openly claimed for this purpose; claimed with a calm certainty which admitted of no refusal.

And Shahjahân on his State visit of ceremonial had been forced to acknowledge that the money had been well employed. Simple in design, curiously flamboyant in execution and decoration, the tomb seemed, and still seems, to shadow forth the personality of the man it covered. That Shahjahân appreciated this is certain; for he held in trust that inheritance of the artistic temperament which had come down to him through four generations of Great Moguls; an inheritance which, Heaven knows why, was lost to his sons and their sons, but which blossomed out again two hundred years after in the person of a young Prince, whom the West failed to recognize as worthy successor.

Be that as it may, Shahjahân, in the full blaze of his glory, surrounded by adulation, almost unique in power, certainly so in wealth, was, as he stood beside his father's grave some five years after his accession, a broken, despairing man.

For Ârjamand his wife was dead. After all their wanderings, their troubles, their discomforts together, she had died almost ere she had realized her queenship.

And the woman in the garden had set her lip still more firmly, had felt still more surely that punishment had best be left to God. As Ali Kul had said, "Let Him decide!"

So when Shahjahân, as in duty bound, had craved an audience of the Keeper of the Garden, she had refused.

But Fate ordained a meeting. Urged by Heaven knows what secret desire to be alone for a few moments beside his father's grave, Shahjahân rode over to it one night, and leaving his two retainers at the gate, went, a tall solitary figure, to the tomb, which in the full flood of moonlight showed almost as iridescent as by day; showed dim like mother-of-pearl seen through waves. The central chamber was dark and scented. The crimson, gold-edged pall that covered the low sarcophagus of marble tracery showed a dense blot of black shadow, but as he approached something tall, slender, lighter, rose from behind it, and a voice that thrilled him through and through said quietly:

"Confess not thy fault, O Shahjahân; he never knew it. I never told him. Let him rest in peace!"

CHAPTER XXI

"Two Lovers in the dark lay side by side.
'Where art thou, dearest?' each to each they cried;
But answer came there none; their bed the Grave,
Two corpses they, bloodless and hollow-eyed."

LONG years had passed since Mihr-un-nissa, widow of Ali Kul Istalijü, and of Nur-ed-din Mohamed Jahângir; Emperor of all the Indies, had taken up her abode in the rare garden down by the river Ravi that had once belonged to the pigeon-fancier from Herât.

The plane-trees were loftier, the cypress handsomer, and the pigeons more numerous. Roses and sweet jonquils had been planted everywhere, and centring all, rose a huge pile of brick masonry set with encaustic tiles, a medley of colours, blue and white, purple and red, all blending, like the iridescence on the breasts of the pigeons which circled and fluttered round the slender octagonal minarets that cornered the wide square of arched cloisters. Within, dark, cool, spacious, was the domed tomb where Jahângir the Emperor slept that last long sleep, the thought of which, he had oft said, should be a spur to every true man's wakefulness in this life.

Close by, yet aloof, stood another tomb infinitely less imposing and, as yet, untenanted by the dead. But the living habited it; and every morning, just as the first sun-rays were brightening the spring world, as they had brightened it that day at Rajaur, now nineteen years ago, when Nur-ed-din Mahomed Jahângir, the Light of the Faith, had passed into the Great Darkness, an old woman of seventy-six, frail, yet still upright, would go down the narrow staircase that led from the roof of the smaller tomb, walk slowly through the cloisters, and, entering the larger one, lay a packed posy of flowers on the sarcophagus which centred the building.

Then from the attendant canonesses—for there were no male

voices in that choir—would rise a *Marsiah,* or hymn of lamentation, and the long drawn-out minor intervals would wail up into the dome, mixing with each other into one sobbing keen, until the loud chanted " Ameen " would bring the music back to the major key, and the singers, having finished their morning task, would close their books softly, salaam to the dead and the living, so file out from the incense-laden air of the tomb to the fresh bright sunshine, leaving the two alone together.

Sometimes for a full hour the figure at the head of the sarcophagus would sit there, still, silent, while the flocks of pigeons which awaited their daily measure of corn on the plinth outside grew impatient, and fluttered and cooed for the giver to finish her prayers and attend to them. And sometimes, if she were over-long, one or two of the tamest would venture inside, and after circling round and round in the shadows of the dome, the rustle of their wings rousing a soft echo as of innumerable bees, settle down suddenly on her lap, as if they brought her something.

And they did; for she would smile as suddenly, and the adorable dimple would show as fascinating as it was, when, a girl on the threshold of life, she held Prince Salim's doves on her lap in the Garden of Scattering Gold

For even in her old age Mihr-un-nissa kept her charm; that is a gift to which the years make no difference.

And she was beautiful besides, partly because her beauty had become a cult with her. It had pleased men who were dead. Why not keep it, therefore, if she could ?

Did she dye her beautiful hair, that showed no touch of time in it ? Possibly she did. There were great hedges of the henna-bush in the garden, and henna had to be prepared to keep her finger-tips as rosy as a bride's. Anyhow, her hair was thick and long, and glossy as of yore, and she plaited it with jewels still, though she wore no other ornament save the string of huge pearls the Emperor had given her; and they were hidden by her plain white widow's veil.

So she would rise tall, slender, still lissome, a youthful figure till you saw her eyes; and they held in them the weary secrets of a long life that had kept its counsel to itself.

" *Kurru! Kurru kru!*" she called to the pigeons, and they

flocked round her in whirls and whorls while she scattered their grain.

How the Emperor would have rejoiced to see them! And Ali Kul also! Thank God the two men she had known best had loved the dumb beasts, even though they hunted them mercilessly. It was a strange thing, that, yet true. The keener the sportsman, the more comprehension of his prey.

So she passed on into the garden—it was walled in those days—walking slowly, a little breathlessly, adown the marble-edged paths that divided it into squares, until she came to the big mango-trees where the greeny-white flower-spikes stood upright, like candles on a Christmas-tree, sending out a faint perfume of honey. And there was a stickiness on the marble path-edge, as if honey had fallen there. The recognition of this made her smile again. Small use in calling the palm squirrels to their daily feast of almonds when Dame Nature gave them so much sweetstuff!

Still, she called, and some came, though one big, fat, bold-eyed morsel of a thing lay on a branch almost within reach and lolled out a long red tongue at her in a stupendous yawn. It was the young ones that came; pretty, barred, fluffy creatures with tails twice too big for them and a total lack of discrimination as to which, in her outstretched hand, were almonds and which filbert-shaped nails!

So the dimple showed again, this time a trifle wearily; for Mihr-un-nissa, despite her looks, was beginning to feel her years. But there was much to be done yet ere she could labour up the steep stairs once more for her usual rest.

Quite a tribe of women were awaiting the daily distribution of food, and there were several new claimants whose cases had to be considered. For during those nineteen years Mihr-un-nissa had kept her word, and every cowrie of the money granted her by the State, that was left after paying for the building of the tomb, went in charity. Not all in food, though; and to-day there was merriment among her audience over a petition for a husband. Suitable ones, said the somewhat clamorous mother of a young girl, who sat shamefaced, hiding her face in her veil, were not to be had without a dowry; no, not even though the daughter was not ill-looking, as the lady might see for herself.

"Come hither, child," said the voice, still strong, still sweet, that had once commanded all India; and the girl obeyed.

Not a bad-looking face, healthy and good-humoured—ay, and modest too.

"Wouldst like to be married, child?" came the question gravely.

The girl hung her head. "Mother says all girls are born to get married—that single women are accursed of God."

A spasm of pain crossed Mihr-un-nissa's face; it showed very weary indeed.

"I will enquire," she said briefly, "and if it be as thou sayest, the dowry shall be forthcoming."

A little murmur of approval rose amongst her audience, for one of the most virtuous forms of charity in India is the bestowing of husbands. So one by one, calling down blessings on their benefactress, the women drifted away with their daily doles.

"Thou hast tired thyself out, mother," said a voice with age in it, as one of the canonesses came out from a side room to sit beside her; "but the Gifted Lady will be here anon with her children, and that will cheer thee, will it not?"

And yet once more the smile showed the dimple.

"Ay," she said softly. "Both thy father, Gladness, and her grandfather loved the small folk; and thou sayest these ones are nice!"

"Nice!" echoed the grandmother in hot indignation. "They are *peris* from Paradise—they are heart's darlings!"

And even as she spoke, there came down the garden path from the gate a little group which, certes, deserved praise.

The Gifted Lady, beautiful exceedingly, all smiles and laughter, holding by one hand a small girl of four, her very image, with the other supporting the somewhat erratic steps of a sturdy young urchin of two.

Behind her came three or four maid-servants, one of the proudly carrying an infant in arms.

So there came an excited childish treble: "Look Nanni Look! how well Fedai walketh! Look! Look! He walketh like dada!"

And Mihr-un-nissa laughed, quite a youthful laugh, and was ready with huggings and kissings for all four.

"And so thou art happy, little one," she said at last when the children had gone off to look at the pigeons, and the three generations of women sat in the sunshine hand in hand.

"Who would not be happy with those darlings?" quoth Gladness, forgetful utterly that though a good grandmother, she had been but a poor mother. But the Gifted Lady went a step further, and pursed up her pretty mouth decorously. "Lo! grandmother, the possession of a good husband is all a woman needs to make her happy; and mine—Heaven save him!—is good indeed!"

Mihr-un-nissa's eyes twinkled maliciously. "Is he still, then, good-looking?" she asked, and a little scream of protest answered her.

"Lo! grandmother, he is the handsomest of all!"

"So was his father—God rest his soul!—before him," said Mihr-un-nissa gently. "I mind him well. Fedâi Khân, the beauty of the Court—and doth thy man still dress well, my child?"

"Never hath he a fold awry. Oh, grandmother, I am most blessed!"

"Never a fold awry," echoed Mihr-un-nissa dreamily. "Neither had his father—God grant him peace!—the dandy of the Court!" Then suddenly she rose. "Lo! I am more than ordinary tired, children; therefore I go to rest; but I shall see thee again, little one," and her warm clasp enfolded the younger hand.

"Yea, yea; but thou must not descend the stairs again, mother," fussed the canoness. "See you," she added to her daughter, "the stairs try her much, for she grows old!"

Old! The word lingered in Mihr-un-nissa's mind as, with many a halt for breath, she made her way up the same narrow stairs. But she would accept no help. She did not feel old, and her memory was as good as ever.

After her servants had put all things ready to her hand, and left her for her noontide rest, she sat for quite a long time on the edge of her string bed—for she had put away all luxuries nineteen years before, and had since lived the life of a religious recluse—

thinking over the past years, from the days of her infancy, wondering what was the first thing she really recollected in her life.

Was it the giving of a red, red rose to a tall dark man? Or had she learnt that from Dilarâm's tongue?

Dear old Dilarâm!—and quaint, faithful Strangler! Looking down the perspective of the years, she saw clearly how much of her success in gripping the reins of government had been due to the certainty that the news he brought her was true. Ay, true, always true!

So her mind passed to Shahjahân. Her prophecy that his sin would find him out was coming to pass. He had lost his dearest dear; Ârjamand was dead. And the son Aurungzebe—strange how the old Khanzâda had disliked him!—was giving trouble. Thank Heaven! they neither of them, now, ever came so far north as Lahore. She had been right in choosing this peaceful spot for the resting-place of the father who had never known the full treachery of his son. Of all the things in her long life that gave her pleasure to recollect, that gave the most: that she had kept her counsel, that she had done her best to make the man she had never loved, happy.

But then she had never loved anyone; not even Ali Kul, the husband of her youth. She would go down to the grave never having felt the self-surrender of a woman's love. Never! Never! Neither could she have given a man's love—not as she had known their love. Yet there might be something beyond. There might be!

So her thoughts took another turn.

Why had she failed?

Because of her beauty. It was that which had killed Ali Kul; it was that which had forced in on men the recollection that she was woman. Beauty and womanhood—those were her crimes.

A sudden desire to see the face which had at once been her blessing and her curse came over her. She rose suddenly to reach a tiny hand-mirror set in a bracelet which the Emperor had given her in days long gone by, because he said laughingly that so much beauty could not be held in the ordinary mirror-set thumb-ring all native women wear. It was the only mirror she had left herself, and she used it always; and though it gave but a small image it was wonderfully clear.

In taking a step forward her foot caught in the carpet, and she stumbled; then stood breathless, her hand on her heart for a second.

So standing, she looked down into what she held. What she saw was the head and shoulders of an unveiled woman—for her veil had fallen back in her stumble—a woman with jewel-braided hair seen against a background of clear blue sky.

A beautiful woman, without doubt! No wonder men had loved her and hated her. No wonder they——

She gave a sudden lurch forward, a sudden sigh.

So fell, her face buried against the glass which had held her fatal beauty.

She lay there in the sunshine, while the servants below waited for their lady's call.

The pigeons fluttered over her, and once a palm squirrel with barred, bottle-brush tail erect drew nearer, nearer to her with little starts and loud chirruping; then fled from her swiftly, startled.

The shadows were lengthening when they found her, quite dead.

"Lo!" said a weeping servant-maid as they turned her over, and the beautiful face showed unharmed, save for one long scratch where the dimple had been wont to be. "See, she hath hurt her poor nose. 'Twill spoil her beauty as a corpse!"

L'ENVOIE

> "Refuse not, pilgrim, what men ask of thee—
> Love, Labour, Life—give all, and give it free.
> When in thy wallet naught remains but Death,
> Know that thine own, and take it for thy fee."

It was in 1877, just two hundred and fifty years after Nurjahân Pâdshah Begum, renouncing Empire, had retired to the solitudes of the rare garden down by the banks of the Ravi river, that I first saw it.

The high wall which had "shut out the world, shut in the flowers" was gone; the plane-trees had disappeared, but some few of the cypresses, ragged, decaying, uncared for, still stood sentinel over what once had been beds of roses and jonquils. One or two stunted orange-bushes remained to show where vanished groves had been, and in one far-off corner a pomegranate was ablaze with fiery blossoms. A few pigeons still circled round the great tomb, to which age, by time's insensible softening, had given greater iridescence from the blendings of colour. The tomb itself was in fair condition. It had been thought worth while to preserve it as a sight for globe-trotters. Hard by it stood the tomb of Asof Khân; for, possibly by some strange belated remorse, that worthy yet unworthy gentleman had directed that he should be buried beside his sister.

Her tomb was sadly out of repair, but one huge white jasmine flung its wide-arched arms, all starred with scented blossoms, over the crumbling walls.

My man was engaged in taking up land for a new railway, which, intersecting the garden, was to pass within a stone's throw of these tombs, and already long files of coolies, men, women, children, were leisurely piling up the big embankment which was to lead to the iron bridge that was to span the river.

As I watched the slow process of these human ants, each contributing but a few spoonsful of earth from the shallow baskets they carried on their heads, I told myself that so were formed the great dams of human ignorance, human prejudice, each one in turn adding his or her finite experience by following in the steps of someone else.

A man of about sixty sat out in the open on a cane-bottomed chair, leisurely chewing betel and watching the orderly process with placid satisfaction.

Clothed in white, stout, oleaginous, with a long grey beard and an immaculate turban, it struck me at once that he might have stood model for Asof Khân in those old days, since his face showed courteous, intolerant, intelligent, yet bigoted to a degree.

That he was an official was evident from the *posse* of underlings smoking their pipes under a neighbouring tree. That he was in Government employ was clear from the alacrity with which he recognized the presence of one higher in rank than himself, and the profuseness of his salaams for the "Sahib." The "Mem," however, appeared not to enter into his calculations at all, so the following remarks must be considered as addressed to the sympathies of a man.

"Of a truth, Huzoor, the tomb of Jahângir Padshâh is a beautiful structure, but it was not built by a woman. She provided the money, having been enriched greatly by her artifices. It is true the Emperor gave her the title of Nurjahân, but in reality she was but a beautiful Persian. The Huzoor says truly. Rumour hath it that she was very beautiful, as it becomes a woman to be. But clever? God knows. She did the Emperor much harm, and brought his grey hairs with sorrow to the grave, by reason of her quarrel with his virtuous son Shahjahân. See you, she desired to rule the Empire after her husband's death, and to secure that end stooped, after the fashion of womenkind, to much artifice, being ambitious and without shame."

Here I broke in. "But," I said, "she retired from public life when Jahângir died; she lived in this garden in her widow's veil for nineteen years; she gave all her money that was left after building his tomb to the poor. That does not look like ambition. Why did she do it, if, as you say, she wanted to be Empress?"

Asof Khân passed my remark by with the utmost courtesy, and once more appealed to male sympathies.

"Being a woman," he said unctuously, "she doubtless had some nefarious purpose in coming to this garden." Then he sighed solemnly, and added:

"*Aurat sab makr wa fareb.*" (Women are all deceit and guile.)

* * * * *

Poor Nurjahân! destined to be judged by male standards throughout the years. Ere I left the garden I picked some of the starry jasmine blooms and laid them on her grave.

But Jahângir's remained undecorated. Though I judged him the most Compleat Lover the world has ever produced, I knew that his reputation could take care of itself.